CLIVE CUSSLER'S
THE
DEVIL'S SEA

CLIVE CUSSLER'S
THE DEVIL'S SEA

A DIRK PITT NOVEL®

DIRK CUSSLER

RANDOM HOUSE
LARGE PRINT

Copyright © 2021 by Sandecker, RLLLP

Published in the United States of America by Random House Large Print in association with G.P. Putnam's Sons, an imprint of Penguin Random House LLC.

Cover art by Mike Heath | Magnus Creative

Interior illustrations and endpaper by Roland Dahlquist Title page photo of Himalayan mountains by Kajohnwat Srikulthanakij / Shutterstock.com Tibetan victory banner symbol by Pises Tungittipokai / Shutterstock.com

The Library of Congress has established a Cataloging-in-Publication record for this title.

ISBN: 978-0-593-50123-8

www.penguinrandomhouse.com/large-print-format-books

FIRST LARGE PRINT EDITION

Printed in the United States of America

1st Printing

This Large Print edition published in accord with the standards of the N.A.V.H.

CAST OF CHARACTERS

NATIONAL UNDERWATER AND MARINE AGENCY (NUMA) TEAM

Dirk Pitt Director of NUMA

Al Giordino NUMA Director of Underwater Technology

Rudi Gunn NUMA Deputy Director

Summer Pitt NUMA Special Projects Director and daughter of Dirk Pitt

Dirk Pitt, Jr. NUMA Special Projects Director and son of Dirk Pitt

Hiram Yaeger NUMA Computer Resource Center Director

James Sandecker U.S. Vice President and former Director of NUMA

Loren Smith Pitt U.S. Congresswoman from Colorado and wife of Dirk Pitt

Bill Stenseth Captain of NUMA research ship **Caledonia**

Homer Giles Chief engineer of NUMA research ship **Caledonia**

MELBOURNE CREW

Alistair Thornton Owner of Thornton Mining Company

Margot Thornton Geophysicist and daughter of Alistair Thornton

Chuck Sonntag Navigator of the **Melbourne**

Dr. Yee Engineer from the Taiwan Ministry of National Defense

PEOPLE'S LIBERATION ARMY OF CHINA

General Xu Junhai Commander of Beijing Aerospace Flight Control Center

Colonel Yan Xiaoming Program director of **Dragonfly** project

Dr. Liu Zhenli Rocket engineer on **Dragonfly** project

Lieutenant Zheng Yijong People's Liberation Army Rocket Force Special Operations Command member and nephew of Yan Xiaoming

Ning PLA Army Rocket Force Special Ops member

Mao Jing PLA operative in Sikkim, India

TIBETANS IN INDIA

Ramapurah Chodron Tibetan guerrilla in Lhasa

Thupten Gungtsen Buddhist monk at the Nechung Monastery in Lhasa

Khyentse Rinpoche Elder lama of Central Tibetan Administration

Kuten The Nechung Oracle and the State Oracle of Tibet

Tenzin Norsang Security agent of the Central Tibetan Administration

OTHERS

James Worthington C-47 pilot in Tibet

Delbert Baker C-47 copilot in Tibet

Staff Sergeant Nathaniel Jenkins Air Force satellite analyst, 100th Missile Defense Brigade

Dr. Chen Yuan Director of Buddhist and Tibetan Art, National Palace Museum

Dr. Feng Zhoushan Former director of Tibetan Antiquities, National Palace Museum

Lee Hong Assistant director, National Palace Museum

Rob Greer Proprietor of the Tibet Club Museum in McLeod Ganj, India

Henry Buchanon Director of the American Institute in Taiwan

Jiang Ji Fisherman from the island of Qimei

CLIVE CUSSLER'S

THE
DEVIL'S SEA

PROLOGUE

C-47 over the Himalayas

The Pratt & Whitney radial engines rasped and hunted as they struggled to inhale the high-altitude air. A pair of the venerable Twin Wasp fourteen-cylinder aircraft motors, produced by the thousands during the war, powered the unmarked C-47 transport as it buffeted through a stormy night. Absent any cargo in the rear fuselage, the plane, known as the Skytrain, was particularly susceptible to the fickle air drafts it battled above the top of the world.

"Scraping twenty-two thousand feet in altitude," Delbert Baker drawled from the copilot's seat, a toothpick dangling from his lips. Disheveled and moon-faced, he had the droopy-eyed gaze of a man who would yawn if a space alien tapped him on the shoulder. "Engines ain't too happy."

"We're well under our ceiling, even if the motors don't seem to think so," the pilot said crisply.

The antithesis of his copilot, James Worthington sat upright in a clean, pressed flight suit, his grip tight on the plane's yoke. Yet he was equally impervious to the bumps and creaks of the empty cargo plane as it was knocked around the violent sky. Though unseen mountaintops passed just beneath the plane's belly, Worthington remained as calm as a man playing checkers.

Like Baker, Worthington had plenty of experience flying over the Himalayas in transports. Both had regularly flown the Hump during World War II, when the U.S. Army Air Force supplied arms and supplies to the Nationalist Chinese from bases in India. Now they flew for the CIA, but the dangers of crossing the towering mountain range in marginal weather had not lessened.

Worthington tapped a pair of red-knobbed handles protruding between their seats, assuring they were pulled fully back. The throttle quadrant controlled the engine fuel mixture. They were set to their leanest settings for the crossing of the world's tallest mountain range.

Their headsets crackled with the voice of their navigator, seated in a compartment behind them. "About twenty minutes to Lhasa. Maintain current heading."

The airplane suddenly bounced like a roller coaster flying off the rails. Baker glanced out his side window at a steady snowfall pelting the wings. "Hope our boys turn the lights on."

Worthington nodded. "They'll be hiking across the Himalayas on their own if they don't."

The plane soldiered on through the night, the pilots fighting sudden drafts that would send the craft hurtling upward. Less frequent, but more precarious, were the sharp downdrafts that struck without warning.

Soon they approached their target, and Worthington began descending, knowing the highest peaks were now behind them. Through the cold black night, a handful of lights appeared on the ground, glowing like distant candles.

"This must be the place," Baker said.

The navigator provided a new heading, and Worthington adjusted their flight path, turning over the scattered lights of Lhasa. Tibet's historic capital, it was a colorful but dusty city that stretched along the narrow Kyichu River Valley at an imposing elevation of twelve thousand feet. The country's one and only official airport lay eighty miles to the northeast, but Worthington had no intention of making a formal arrival in the Chinese-occupied territory. Instead, he guided the C-47 toward an ad hoc landing strip created for the mission by friendly locals, who had secretly cleared rocks from an open plain on the town's west side.

The snow diminished, then ceased altogether, as Worthington flew low over the city, both aviators scanning the ground through the broken cloud cover.

"There, ahead, to the right." Baker pointed out the windscreen. The toothpick in his mouth suddenly twirled, the first indication of tension.

Worthington saw it, too. A pair of faint blue lights, lined up perfectly east to west, with a long black patch between them.

Baker squinted at the distance and lowered the landing gear. "Not sure they gave us the two thousand feet we asked for."

Worthington shook his head. "Too late to argue now." He aligned the nose of the Skytrain with the nearest light and reduced speed. A brisk headwind seemed to bring the plane to a standstill, while rocking the wings. Worthington waited until the blue light disappeared beneath the nose, then called to Baker. "Landing lights."

Baker flicked on the plane's lights as the craft descended. With the skilled hand of a surgeon, Worthington countered the angry winds and eased the plane lower.

The landing lights showed a flat, dusty field as the tires kissed the ground a yard past the blue light. The C-47 bounded over the uneven surface as it slowed under Worthington's hard braking, its tail wheel licking the dust. The pilot guided the aircraft to a stop shy of the second blue light, then spun around and jostled it across the field to the first light. He turned the plane into the wind for takeoff and cut the engines.

Baker opened his side window and looked across

the field. To the south were lights from several houses, but otherwise all was dark. There was no one waiting for them. "Either we're early," he said, "or our passengers are late."

"Or not arriving at all," Worthington said. "At least there was no welcoming committee waiting." He cocked an ear, then slid open his own side window. He turned to Baker with a grimace and shook his head.

Over the murmur of the gusting winds came the unmistakable popping of gunfire in the distance.

RAMAPURAH CHODRON LISTENED to that same gunfire arising from the city's center and cringed. If the mission had gone as planned, there'd have been no shooting. Just a quick extraction and a quiet flight out of town before the Chinese knew what happened. But the gunfire from the vicinity of Potala Palace said otherwise.

Ram, as his CIA trainers had called him, pressed his palm tight against a silenced Colt .38 and peered around a low stone wall. The Nechung Monastery a dozen yards beyond had the look of a morgue, dark and silent. But the distant shooting meant their cover had been blown and they no longer had the luxury of a patient entry.

He squinted through the darkness, but saw no movement around the structure. One of a dozen Tibetan guerrillas parachuted into a wide valley northwest of Lhasa two days earlier, Ram had been assigned to lead the easier of their missions. He guided a four-man squad to capture the Nechung Oracle, the Dalai Lama's most important spiritual advisor, and whisk him to the airfield for a flight to safety.

The more difficult task lay in the center of town. There, the remaining eight men were to sneak into the Potala Palace and extract none other than the Dalai Lama himself.

While Chinese troops had occupied Tibet since 1950, things had heated up with the Lhasa Uprising. Emboldened insurgent attacks and rebellions around the country had culminated with demonstrations in Tibet's capital for independence. Those actions had brought swift retribution. A large contingent of Chinese armed forces had filtered into Lhasa a few days earlier, heightening tensions.

Rumors were rampant that the Chinese were about to seize the Dalai Lama, remove him from Tibet, and throw him in prison. Exiled Tibetan government leaders in India responded by consulting with their primary source of support, the CIA.

For years, the Central Intelligence Agency had been supporting exiled Tibetan leaders and providing arms to guerrillas as a means of gathering information on China's atomic bomb program. Now, with local resources hurried into action, the agency agreed that attempting to extract the Dalai Lama was worth the risk.

The Tibetans selected for the mission had a long history with the CIA. They had been flown across the globe to Colorado, where they trained in the Rocky Mountains and became paratroopers. Chodron was one of the earliest graduates, rising through the ranks due to his aptitude with field radios.

As he gripped his pistol tightly, Ram heard rumblings from an old yak wandering a field beside the monastery. It reminded him of the Hereford cattle he'd seen grazing in the mountain pastures of Colorado. He recalled with fondness his first taste of beefsteak, served at a roadside café near Vail.

He shook off that image as a fellow militant in dark camo crawled alongside and nudged his elbow.

"Looks clear in back," the man whispered.

"Okay, let's move in. Have Raj and Tagri hold position outside the entrance while we search inside."

The guerrilla nodded and relayed the message to a pair of gunmen in the shadows behind them. He followed as Ram rose to a crouch and moved to the monastery entrance.

No one knew how long the site had been deemed sacred, but the current monastery had been standing there for close to four hundred years. It was a modest structure, built at the base of the city's northern hills. Ram entered through open blood-red doors to find a large courtyard. Steps at the back led to chapels on either side, while an upper floor housed the resident monks.

A fire glowed yellow next to the left chapel, and the aroma of incense wafted through the air. Ram hugged the side wall and made his way toward the back steps. He detected a rustling from within and froze. A figure emerged onto the steps, unsteady on his feet.

It was a Chinese soldier, carrying a bolt-action rifle, which he waved in Ram's general direction. "Who's there?" he called in slurred Mandarin.

It was too dark for Ram to see the soldier's bloodshot eyes, but he was close enough to smell the alcohol on his breath. The .38 in his hand tilted upward, then spat two muffled bursts. The soldier's head snapped back, and he slumped to the ground, his rifle clattering onto the stone paving.

"Hide him," Ram whispered to his partner, who had hurried to his side.

Ram stepped toward the chapel and approached the small fire burning in a makeshift ring to keep the soldier warm. Its flames cast dancing shadows on the far end of the chapel, where an elevated altar was decorated with candles. The room appeared empty. Then a sliver of light appeared from a side stall. Ram raised his pistol and slipped behind a stone pillar as a figure approached. Ram waited until the man passed him, then jumped from behind and pressed his pistol into the intruder's back.

"Is there trouble?" the captive asked. He turned and faced Ram.

The light from his small candle revealed an

elderly man with a shaved head, dressed in the red robe of a monk. Unusually broad-shouldered, he stared at Ram with calm, unblinking eyes.

Ram lowered his pistol and dropped his head in a slight bow of apology. "I seek the Nechung Oracle," he said in the monk's native Tibetan tongue.

"The Oracle is not here," the monk replied. "He went to the Potala Palace two days ago to meet with the Dalai Lama. He has not returned." The monk eyed the guerrilla's dark uniform. "You are here to help him?"

Ram nodded. "It is believed the Chinese intend to imprison the Dalai Lama and his advisors. We are here to help them escape."

The monk nodded. "The Oracle foretold of imminent danger."

A walkie-talkie on Ram's hip buzzed with a static-filled voice. "Red Deer, this is Snow Leopard. The target has departed ahead of our arrival. We are under fire. Heading to the elevator. I repeat, heading to the elevator."

"Red Deer reads affirmative," Ram replied. "We will be on our way."

Ram gritted his teeth. They were to have met up with an advance team that had parachuted in a day earlier, but they hadn't appeared at the rendezvous point.

It made sense now. Something had gone wrong. Maybe the Chinese were tipped off. The advance team had either been captured or had already shuttled the Dalai Lama out of Lhasa on foot. Ram glanced at the smoldering fire and prayed it was the latter. Either way, their own mission was now for naught.

Ram replaced the walkie-talkie and looked at the monk. "Have the Dalai Lama and the Oracle already fled Lhasa?"

The monk nodded. "I believe that to be a possibility."

"Who are you?"

"My name is Thupten Gungtsen. I am the **khenpo** for the monastery and assistant to the Oracle."

As the monastery's abbot and chief administrator, Gungtsen was a man at risk.

"You will not be safe once the Chinese discover the Dalai Lama has fled. You must come with us."

The monk gave him a contemplative gaze. "I am not important, but the Nechung Idol is."

He motioned over his shoulder to the altar. Positioned in a niche above it was a dark statue. Ram recognized it as Pehar, a Tibetan deity known also as Nechung and the namesake of the monastery. "The Oracle cannot properly perform his duties without it. The statue must be taken to him."

Ram gazed across the temple and nodded. "Quickly."

"I will need your help." Gungtsen turned on his heels. He crossed the chapel at a measured pace and halted in front of the niche. Inside, the thick stone carving stood, surrounded by an assortment of smaller statues of the same color.

Ram had visited the temple as a boy, but had never been so close to the ancient artifact. Two feet high, it was hewn from a glistening black stone. The monk knelt before the statue and started to mumble a prayer, but Ram stepped over and pulled him up. "There is no time."

The monk nodded and gathered the smaller deities together. He wrapped them in a gold cloth from the altar and passed the bundle to Ram. The guerrilla stuffed the bundle in his jacket, surprised at its heavy weight, and urged the monk to hurry.

Gungtsen wound another cloth around the Nechung Idol, then hoisted it onto his shoulder. "I am ready."

They exited the chapel, joining the second guerrilla in the courtyard. As they exited the monastery's front entrance, a single gunshot sounded from a few feet away. Across the wide dirt street, an armed man in green staggered from the shadows and slumped to the ground.

The guerrilla named Tagri poked his head from behind a shrub, clutching an M1 carbine. "He was a point man for a patrol coming this way."

His words were confirmed when a deep yell echoed down the street, followed by the crunching of boots on gravel.

"The Oracle is not here," Ram said. "We must evacuate to the airfield."

"What about the enemy patrol?" Tagri asked.

"We take care of them here."

Ram grabbed the monk by the arm and pulled him behind a pillar. He thrust his pistol around the curved stonework and aimed the Colt at the far end of the street. Behind him, the monk crouched low and began whispering a chant.

The Chinese patrol was small, just three young men clutching Russian-made rifles. Their lack of training showed when they all rushed to their fallen comrade, encircling him with their guns aimed high.

Ram didn't pause for their foolishness. He aimed his .38 at the soldier nearest him and squeezed off three rounds. The first struck the man in the shoulder, while the second two missed.

But it didn't matter. The other Tibetans opened up with their carbines, cutting down all three Chinese soldiers in a flurry.

Ram tugged on the sleeve of the monk. "Come this way."

He waited for the monk to retrieve the Idol. Stepping from the monastery, Ram led them past the bodies as the other guerrillas took up a loose perimeter around them.

Nechung Monastery stood on a low rise in the northwest edge of Lhasa. The improvised airfield was just about due east, beyond a range of open hills. While a direct line would have been shorter,

Ram didn't want to get caught by a superior force out in the open. Intelligence had told them that in the past few days, a full battalion of Chinese People's Liberation Army soldiers had been transported to Lhasa.

Following the dirt road, he led the group down the hillside to the cover of the city landscape on the lower flats. To the southeast, where the large Potala Palace stood on a rocky rise, heavy gunfire sounded. Ram hoped the battle there would draw any Chinese away from their path.

Reaching a side street lined with shops and dwellings, they turned and followed it east. At that late hour, the street was dark and empty. The group moved at a fast clip, ever on the lookout for enemy soldiers. The monk, ignoring the heavy burden on his shoulder, moved with quiet urgency.

At the sound of an approaching vehicle, the group ducked for cover in the closest doorways. A Chinese military truck approached at high speed with a half dozen soldiers clinging to the fenced sides of its bed.

Ram felt the monk squeeze next to him in the doorway of a fabric shop and noted the man's rugged frame beneath his robe. "You are not from Lhasa," Ram whispered.

"No, a small village in Amdo."

"You are Golok?"

The monk nodded.

Ram knew the area and the tribal inhabitants who lived there. The Golok were known as the toughest people in Tibet, and Ram could see why.

The truck rumbled past them in a hurry elsewhere. Ram glanced at his watch as the dust raised by the vehicle's thick tires settled to the ground. The guerrilla team was late for their rendezvous.

"Let's go," he said. "We need to pick up the pace."

The team moved at a run, crossing several blocks. The buildings fell away on their left, exposing open fields that extended to the foot of the neighboring mountains. Gunfire still sounded from the distance, but it had moved from the southwest to directly ahead of them.

Ram turned to exit the streets and make for the open hills to his left. He led his team up a rocky rise, each man breathing hard. Gungtsen struggled at the rear with his cargo, but managed to keep apace. Clearing the crest of a rocky rise, they reached a flat plain. Ahead, Ram spotted a blue light.

They heard the grinding of an aircraft motor turning over and whirring to life, followed by a second one. Several muzzle flashes and accompanying pops from beyond the light told him it would be a race for their lives.

A second blue light came into sight as they hustled over the barren mound, then a faint light appeared in the aircraft's interior. The gunfire grew louder as they approached the C-47.

"Can you make it?" Ram asked the monk.

The statue weighed heavily on the old man, but the quiet monk replied in a strong voice. "Yes."

As the group reached the long plain used as an airfield, the wind blew light sleet that needled their backs. Near the distant blue light, they could both see and hear the C-47. Wisps of smoke streamed from the engines' nacelles as Worthington and Baker readied the plane for takeoff. A small group of men crowded around the open fuselage door and climbed in as the plane began to move.

Ram's walkie-talkie crackled. "Red Deer. We're at the departure point. We must leave now. Where are you?"

"Approaching now," Ram shouted. "Hold the plane." He turned to his team. "Run for it."

The guerrillas broke formation and sprinted for the plane. Ram held back to accompany the monk a few yards behind. Despite his burden, Gungtsen showed surprising fleetness, just about holding his own with the other men.

As they drew closer to the plane, muzzle flashes burst through the darkness from the far end of the field. A half dozen Chinese soldiers had crested the end of the field and begun firing at the plane. No one had to tell Ram's men to run faster, as bullets peppered the ground around them.

The last guerrilla from the other team, waiting his turn to climb aboard, dropped beneath the wing and provided covering fire, silencing several of the Chinese guns. It was enough to allow the three men from Ram's team to approach the doorway and scamper aboard.

Ram and Gungtsen were almost to the plane's tail when the monk tripped and fell, the Nechung Idol bounding off his shoulder ahead of him.

"Are you hit?" Ram yelled over the roar of the engines. He stopped and pulled Gungtsen up by his arm.

"No, I fell."

"Get on the plane. I'll get the statue."

He pushed the monk ahead, then reached to retrieve the temple artifact. The C-47's Twin Wasps howled as Worthington throttled up for takeoff. A blaze of dust and snow blew onto Ram as he shouldered the Idol. As he rose to his feet, the plane began pulling away. The monk had just reached the doorway and was yanked inside as the plane accelerated.

Ram ran after the aircraft, struggling with the Idol's weight. He couldn't believe the old monk had carried it all the way from the monastery without complaint. It was heavy, much heavier than it appeared. Its weight crushed the movement of Ram's legs as if he were mired in a pool of molasses.

But he had to move, and fast, as the C-47 was accelerating away from him. He squinted through the blowing dust, but could still see the flicker of muzzle flashes from the end of the airfield. The plane's engines roared in his ears as Ram summoned all his strength to run. With a labored effort, he sprinted alongside the fuselage. As he approached the open door, he flung the statue through the opening.

He nearly tripped at the effort, but regained his footing as the plane outpaced him.

Tagri appeared in the doorway. "Come on, Ramapurah, you can do it," he yelled.

Ram felt like collapsing, yet summoned a last burst of energy and flung himself at the door as the plane's tail bounded from the ground. His fingers grasped the sill and he started to slip, but Tagri and another guerrilla grabbed his sleeves and pulled him inside.

"Stay down," a man yelled.

Sprawled on his belly, trying to catch his breath, Ram was in no position to argue.

The plane roared down the strip and lumbered into the air. But as it rose, the pursuing Chinese soldiers blasted the craft. Two of the Tibetan guerrillas were wounded as small holes peppered the C-47's aluminum skin.

In the cockpit, Baker flinched as a round pierced the windscreen, whistling an inch over his scalp. As the lights of Lhasa vanished beneath them, he retracted the landing gear, then glanced out the side window. He squinted at the spinning propeller and turned to a cluster of gauges in front of him. "Possible oil leak on the number two engine. Pressure steady at the moment."

Worthington kept his hands tight on the yoke, his body tense and focused. "Right flap's a little shaky, too. But we're up. I actually expected worse."

Worse came twenty minutes later when the pilots heard a racket from the starboard engine. Baker tapped one of the oil pressure gauges. "Pressure's in the red, along with the temperature." He looked out the side window back at the engine. Streams of black smoke flowed from the nacelle. "Doesn't look good," he said, a hint of tension in his calm voice.

"All right," Worthington said. "Shut her down. We'll see if we can limp over the hills on one engine."

Baker worked through the engine shutdown procedure, feathering the propeller to reduce drag. Worthington inched upright in his seat, tapped the port engine throttle ahead a hair, and gripped the yoke tight.

Keeping a C-47 aloft on one engine was trouble for a fully loaded plane even in good flying conditions. Fortunately, they were carrying only a few passengers and no extra cargo. But their conditions were anything but good. They had turbulent weather and high altitude to contend with, and the barrier of the Himalayas still lay ahead.

They were retracing their route southwest to Darjeeling on the Indian side of the Himalayas. From Lhasa, it was a half hour over the relatively tame landscape of the Central Tibetan Plateau before the heights of the Himalayas rose in their path.

The towering mountain range went unseen in the night, obscured by darkness and an increasing snowfall. The winds over the Himalayas were always treacherous, but the spring blizzard magnified the effects. Icy nodules pelted the windscreen as crosswinds buffeted the aircraft. The C-47's navigator relayed heading adjustments, retracing their path along a zigzag route that kept them clear of the peaks.

As the plane approached the first mountain range, a heavy uplift pushed the plane to a welcome altitude. Worthington had tried to climb earlier, but he'd reached a ceiling at nineteen thousand feet, and the single engine refused to push them any higher. He was only too happy to see the altimeter now approach twenty-two thousand.

"Clean living?" Baker asked, watching Worthington eye the gauge.

"Hopefully that—and not a tease." The veteran pilot knew the winds could be fickle. What they gave, they took away a few minutes later.

With a stomach-dropping rush, the plane plunged several hundred feet, then flew into a seeming vortex. The winds came from multiple directions, hammering the aircraft like a prizefighter. A lateral updraft was the worst, just about flipping the plane on account of its unbalanced propulsion.

But Worthington never wavered. His steady hand on the controls instantly countered any adverse blows, leveling the plane until the winds struck again. He only hoped the guerrillas in back had secured themselves to the bulkheads.

"Position?" Worthington called out on his headset, staring into the blackness before them.

"Should be eighteen miles south of Kangmar," the navigator said. "Approaching initial high-elevation range."

For several minutes they flew without trouble. Then, without warning, a severe downdraft grabbed the plane like a giant hand and shoved it toward the earth. Worthington's eyes widened as the altimeter spun like a top until it registered eighteen thousand five hundred feet. It was an altitude well below some of the surrounding mountains.

The pilot pushed the throttle to its stops and pulled back on the controls for more lift. It came too late.

With a loud thump, the tail wheel struck the ground. By some miracle, it was only a grazing blow, and the rear assembly held together as the plane bounded forward and bounced back into the air.

In the rear compartment, Ram sat on the floor, watching Gungtsen across from him clutch the Nechung Idol, until the blow knocked the monk across the floor. The impact also unlatched the cargo door, which flung open directly behind him. As the plane lurched to the right, Ram was thrown toward the opening. He spread his arms in front of him and clawed at the sill, but his momentum was too great. He flew out the door and into space.

The cold wind and snow buffeted his body as he dropped from the plane into a blinding maelstrom. Icy particles peppered his eyes. His heart pounded and his arms flailed in a feeble attempt at flight.

The roar of the one-engine plane receded to a low rumble, then a loud grinding sound fractured the night. He had little time to consider it when the unseen earth welcomed him with a violent impact. As he tumbled across snow and ice, the sights and sounds, and then even the pain, vanished as he fell into a black abyss.

PART I

The Stingray in the Luzon Strait

1

WENCHANG SPACECRAFT LAUNCH SITE
HAINAN, CHINA
OCTOBER 2022

The missile rose in a graceful arc, the thunderous burn of its solid-fuel booster engine rippling through the predawn sky. It wasn't a large missile, barely twenty feet tall, and it was fired from an auxiliary launchpad at the sprawling coastal base, which was more accustomed to massive satellite-carrying rockets. Yet to those watching the flight, it was considerably more important than the latest spy satellite.

The missile's fiery exhaust disappeared from sight in a matter of seconds. But the cameras from a reconnaissance plane tracked its progress far out to sea, supplemented by satellites that targeted the launch. The distant lenses viewed the missile as the exhaust suddenly fell dark and it briefly sailed on in silence. If an observer had been present as it passed, they might have heard a sonic boom, followed by a motorized whooshing, now accompanied by the burning exhaust of liquid propellant. But those senses would have to be acute, as the missile was traveling more than a mile per second.

In an operations bay twelve hundred miles away at the Beijing Aerospace Flight Control Center, General Xu Junhai watched the missile on a large video screen. Long-range cameras on Hainan and on ships in the South China Sea showed only a speck as the missile sped from view. Xu turned to one of several engineers seated at a console, monitoring telemetry data. "Has the motor engaged?"

The engineer, a slight man with thick, square glasses, nodded without looking up. "Yes, sir. The **Dragonfly** has successfully transitioned from solid-fuel propulsion to scramjet flight."

"Speed?"

"Just over twenty-eight thousand kilometers per hour and accelerating."

The General turned back to the video screen, where he saw a small puff of smoke where the missile had been tracking. "What was that?"

His query was met by a long pause. "The data feeds have ceased. There . . . there seems to be a malfunction." The engineer kept his face down, fearful to make eye contact with the General. "The flight appears to have terminated."

The General, a humorless man of sixty who wore

his thinning hair slicked back, couldn't hide his displeasure. "Terminated?" he boomed. "Again?"

It was the third failure in a row for the sleek prototype missile.

The engineer nodded.

The General called across the room to a bulbous man in uniform who was conversing with the flight director. "Colonel Yan."

Colonel Yan Xiaoming turned and approached with the trepidation of a man headed to the gallows.

The General stared at him. "Tell me what has happened."

"We are still assessing the data," Yan said, "but it was a flight failure during midphase acceleration."

"I can see that. What is the cause?"

The Colonel glanced at the clipboard he gripped tightly. "Preliminary readings indicate a possible thermal failure in the lead fairing. But the vehicle did produce a new speed mark prior to failure."

"A thermal failure? That was the cause of the last launch's demise? I had been led to believe that problem had been solved."

"It is proving a difficult challenge."

The General waved at the video screen that now showed an empty sky. "The President was expecting success today." He let the words sink in. "This is your third failure. It will also be your last. When can I tell the President that the issues will be resolved?"

"I . . . I cannot provide a current time estimate.

Dr. Liu is examining potential solutions. We will not rest until we have an answer, sir."

"I want a full report of the failure on my desk in the morning," Xu said, "and a solution by the end of the week." He turned on his heel and stomped from the control center, his face flush with anger.

An uncomfortable silence hung over the room for a moment, then the technicians resumed examining the flight data.

Colonel Yan made a phone call, then turned again to the flight director. "Have Dr. Liu meet me in my office." He departed the room slowly, taking a last look at the blank video screen.

Yan made his way to a third-floor office in the headquarters building for the People's Liberation Army Rocket Force. As program manager for the **Dragonfly** missile project, Yan's office was a large but plain space that overlooked a bare dirt field. He glanced out the window at a column of fresh recruits in the People's Liberation Army marching back and forth, their khaki uniforms blending with the mud underfoot.

Yan slumped into his desk chair and rifled through a drawer for a bottle of Japanese whisky called Hakushu he had acquired on a visit to Hong Kong. He poured himself a full shot and knocked it back. As the fiery liquid trickled down his throat, he contemplated his fall from grace.

It had started with his mistress, a woman he'd been introduced to in Hong Kong two years earlier, along with the whisky. She was a patent attorney for a Chinese electronics firm who happened to be relocating to Beijing. At least that's what she'd told him. She was, in fact, an operative for the Taiwan military. He found this out only after he discovered she had copied classified files from his computer on multiple occasions. And only after his wife had decided to divorce him.

Did Communist Party officials or General Xu know? When the woman turned up missing, not a word was said. But his rising career had come to a sudden halt. Superiors dismissed him, and old friends ignored him. With the failures so far in this lone project he had been allowed to manage, he now seemed on the brink of losing everything. His commission, his membership in the Party. Maybe even his life.

As he tucked the bottle away, there was a knock at the door. Two men, at the opposite end of the age spectrum, entered the office. The first, white-haired and in a lab coat, walked with a shuffle. Dr. Liu Zhenli was a respected rocket engineer who had worked on China's first intercontinental ballistic missiles in the 1970s.

The other man, a soldier dressed in fatigues, was tall and muscular and carried himself with a forceful confidence. His name was Lieutenant Zheng Yijong, and he was a member of the Army Rocket Force Special Operations Command. He was also Colonel Yan's nephew.

Yan waved them both to sit down. "As you know, the **Dragonfly** has had another launch failure. It appears to be a thermal issue again." He gazed out the window at the marching recruits. "We are under great pressure to succeed. There can be no more failures."

"We are pushing the boundaries of physics," Liu replied. "We have already attained atmospheric speeds unheard of in a suborbital craft. It represents a great technological success, for we have solved the issue of propulsion. It is now a problem of materials management."

"The missile is melting?" Yan said.

"In a manner of speaking. As you know, the problem is that a compact missile flying within the atmosphere at hypersonic speeds encounters extreme thermal stress, particularly with the leading edge. The missiles are succumbing to heat failure from atmospheric friction on account of high velocity."

"Yes, but our ICBM rockets endure similar temperatures upon reentry, do they not? And they don't melt in flight."

"This is true. But those are large vehicles, buffered by thick shields that dissipate heat over a wide area. We don't have that luxury with tactical devices such as the **Dragonfly**. A bulky heat shield would prevent the speeds we have already attained—and hope to surpass."

"Can't the same type of materials," Yan said, "be modified for use on the **Dragonfly**?"

"We've tested all kinds of ceramic, carbon, and composite materials, but none has held up under the speeds we are dealing with."

"The flight director indicated you have discovered a potential solution."

"A bit of a fluke," Liu said, "but the lab was testing some natural amalgams and found a sample that showed remarkable thermal resistance. But sourcing the input material is a bit problematic."

Zheng cleared his throat, and Liu turned and looked at the man.

Yan caught the gesture. "Dr. Liu, this is Lieutenant Zheng, with the Special Operations Command. He is a very resourceful man. I am assigning him to the **Dragonfly** project to assist in whatever means are necessary to make the missile a success."

Zheng looked at his uncle with empty black eyes and an eager expression.

Yan knew Zheng was competent, but also something of a brutish hothead. He had knifed a man in a bar and would have been tossed out of the service if not for Yan's intervention. The Colonel doubted his nephew's mental stability, but was no longer in a position to dally. He needed results.

"Lieutenant, I need you to secure the crash site. Ensure there are no interlopers, and to protect the site until the Navy salvage team can recover the remains, whenever they decide to show up. At the same time," he said, motioning toward the engineer, "perhaps you can assign another team to assist Dr. Liu with sourcing the thermal-resistant materials he wishes to acquire."

Zheng nodded. "I will personally secure the crash site, sir. I also have personnel who can assist in the other matter." He turned to Liu. "Tell me, Doctor," he asked in a guttural voice that reminded Liu of a hyena, "where do we acquire the thermal material you desire?"

Liu gave a paternal smile. "It's not that simple."

"Why is that?" Yan asked.

Liu didn't answer right away. He looked past the Colonel and stared out the window at the brown field beyond.

"Because it is something," he finally said, "that is out of this world."

2

Staff Sergeant Nathaniel Jenkins was absentmindedly tapping a pencil against the top of his desk when his computer monitor began to beep. The sensors on a reconnaissance satellite hundreds of miles over the South China Sea had detected a small rocket launch from the Wenchang space facility. Earlier satellite data had not shown any preparation at the Chinese base's launchpads, which prompted Jenkins to sit up in his chair.

While tracking the new launch, the Air Force specialist quickly retrieved recent satellite photos of the base and magnified the images. A member of the 100th Missile Defense Brigade at Schriever Air Force Base on the eastern edge of Colorado Springs, Jenkins was one of dozens of analysts assigned to track missile launches around the world.

His supervisor, an auburn-haired lieutenant named Harrington, heard the computer's warning and stepped up behind him. "What do you have?" she asked.

"The Chinese lit off something small at Wenchang sixty seconds ago. Barely registered on infrared, nor does it appear to be headed atmospheric. Our last pad photos show empty, so there was little prep time."

"Probably a cruise missile," Harrington said. "See if Kyogamisaki or LRDR picked it up."

Jenkins typed on his keyboard, cycling through an integrated system of radars and sensors positioned around the globe to detect foreign missile threats. He accessed the surveillance feed from an AN/TPY-2 radar system at a communications station near Kyoto, Japan. "Kyogamisaki's got only limited telemetry," Jenkins said. "LRDR should have something."

LRDR, pronounced "larder," was the acronym for Long Range Discrimination Radar, a recently deployed tracking system located in the middle of Alaska. Jenkins nodded as the system consolidated the two data streams and created a visual animation of the missile's flight path across the backdrop of the sea.

"Flight has terminated," he said as the tracking data ceased. "Flight range approximately seven hundred and twenty-five miles."

Harrington nodded. "Must be a tactical vehicle. Probably an HN-3."

"Something's not right, though." Jenkins pointed

at the monitor. "Flight duration shows under three minutes."

Harrington considered the relative speed and shook her head. "No cruise missile can fly that fast."

Jenkins went back to work on the keyboard, consolidating additional metrics from each radar system. On-screen, he created a pair of columns marking the relative speed of the missile at various intervals of its brief flight. He ran a finger across the computer screen, assessing the numbers.

"Ma'am, I've confirmed the data from both radar systems. The figures are off the charts."

Harrington squinted at the screen. "Mach 25. That can't be. Are you certain?" She ran a hand through her short hair. "It just can't be."

Jenkins verified the calculations, then looked up at her and nodded.

"Double-check the data feed once more, Jenkins, then print out a full analysis. When you are finished, have Corporal Winters take over your duty station."

"Yes, ma'am. What do I do then?"

"You'll bring the data and come with me. To see the General."

3

The sunken Japanese warship appeared out of the gloom like an aged warrior. Its gray skin was dark and discolored, its decks buried under a thick layer of silt. While it was not massive, its lean, graceful lines lent an air of speed and danger. A pair of twin turrets on the bow thrust their hundred-millimeter guns upward with menacing readiness. Yet streaks of rust, algae, and layers of concretion confirmed the vessel would never again see the light of day.

"Looks to be a warship, all right." Summer Pitt leaned toward the viewport in front of her. "It's sitting nice and upright at the bottom of the canyon. I can see some damage near the stern," she added, focusing on the sunken vessel. Summer was tall and striking, with vibrant red hair that flowed past her shoulders, and her willowy figure was apparent even in the drab blue jumpsuit she wore.

Beside her, equally tall and lean, a man with dark

hair sat in the submersible's pilot's seat, his hands manipulating a pair of thrusters. "A destroyer, by the size of it," Summer's twin brother, Dirk, replied. Dirk eyed the wreck with joyful fascination. "Let's grab some video for the gang up top and maybe we can peg an identification."

Under his guidance, the submersible traversed the length of the wreck. The sunken ship was wedged in a steep, narrow subsea canyon, and Dirk had to maneuver the submersible carefully to avoid striking the sheer walls. The close proximity of the rear thrusters sent clouds of silt billowing through the water. He patiently held the submersible still until things cleared, then moved closer to capture detailed images of a jagged hole in the warship's port side.

"Looks like she swallowed a torpedo," Summer said, "and maybe a bit more."

Dirk surveyed the extensive damage. "Perhaps it set off their munitions. She must have gone down fast."

While Dirk completed the video mapping, Summer accessed a computer on the **Caledonia**, the oceanographic research ship that supported them on the surface. Though there was a notable time lag, underwater transponders allowed for the transfer of video, data, and communications between the submersible and its mother ship. Summer linked into the ship's computer and used it to search the NUMA database for shipwrecks in the region. The twins worked for NUMA, the National Underwater and Marine Agency, a federal organization responsible for studying the world's oceans. The agency was tasked with monitoring everything from weather patterns and coastal erosion to pollution and health of the marine ecosystems. With Summer an oceanographer and Dirk a marine engineer, they often worked together on projects that took them all over the globe.

"It could be the **Akizuki**," Summer said. "She was a thirty-seven-hundred-ton destroyer sunk off Cape Engaño during the Battle of Leyte Gulf."

"We're not too far from there," Dirk said. "How did she sink?"

"It's not certain. She was subject to air attacks, but may have taken a torpedo from the USS **Halibut**."

"I'd bet on the latter."

Summer grinned. "A nice discovery, despite the fact we weren't even looking for a shipwreck."

Instead, they were in the western Pacific to study the effect of deepwater currents on ocean acidification and carbon storage levels. The sunken destroyer had appeared during a sonar survey of the submerged Cagayan Canyon that extends off the northern coast of Luzon in the Philippines.

Three thousand feet above them, their father sat in a darkened operations bay at the back of the **Caledonia**, watching the submersible's video feed on a large projection screen. As the Director of NUMA, the senior Dirk Pitt should have been holding sway at the agency's headquarters in Washington. But Pitt wasn't one to just sail a desk. At every available opportunity, he escaped the polluted political climate in the nation's capital to engage in one of the agency's research projects. An upcoming oceanographic conference in Singapore had given him the opportunity to join his children for a segment of their current survey project.

"Sweet-looking wreck," came a gnarled voice. Pitt turned to a short but powerfully built man with dark curly hair seated beside him. Al Giordino, who oversaw NUMA's underwater technology department, had joined Pitt on the trip. With the remnants of an unlit cigar clamped between his teeth, he was monitoring the submersible's power and life-support systems while viewing the video feed.

"In a very unsweet location," Pitt said. A cloud of silt filled the screen as the submersible edged against the canyon walls. "I don't want to see them getting stuck down there."

Giordino grinned. "Your boy knows what he's doing. After all, he was taught by the best."

Pitt had no doubts about that. Giordino knew more about submersibles than any man alive, and had worked with his son, Dirk, on dozens of deepwater dive projects. "Just tell him not to scrape off any paint. That's a new submersible."

Giordino relayed the message over a headset

and smiled. "He claims it's insured. By the way, Summer says the wreck's a Japanese destroyer called the **Akizuki**."

"They've captured some pretty nice footage. Tell them to wrap things up and get topside. We've got a good deal more real estate to survey before I need to jet out of here."

Behind them, a shipboard alarm rang over an overhead speaker. After twenty seconds, the shrill note was replaced by the voice of the ship's captain.

"Attention, all hands. A large wave is approaching the ship. Prepare for impact. I repeat. All hands, prepare for impact."

Giordino relayed the message to the submersible, then cleared some work binders from the desktop to the floor. Pitt glanced out an open hatch door facing the starboard rail, but saw only calm seas lit by morning sunshine. Then the ship bucked like an angry bronco.

Both men were thrown airborne as the deck rose and dropped beneath them. The ship creaked, and crashes resounded throughout the vessel as loose objects took flight. Then it was over. As quickly as it struck, the wave passed by, and the ship settled back onto an even keel.

Pitt climbed to his feet and stepped out the hatch. Behind the ship, a smooth wave, about twelve feet high, traveled across the ocean's surface like a giant rolling pin. It soon vanished from sight, heading toward the tropical green shoreline of Luzon. Pitt gazed a moment at the distant coastline of the Philippines's northernmost province, then ducked his head back into the operations bay. "Is the **Stingray** okay?"

"Dirk reports only a minor disturbance downstairs."

Pitt nodded. "I'll be up on the bridge."

He turned and strode across the ship. The **Caledonia** was a large, modern oceanographic research ship, one of several in the NUMA fleet. Pitt climbed a companionway to the bridge and entered through an open door on one side of the wing. A trio of crewmen was manning the bridge, dressed in white short-sleeved tropical uniforms. Pitt approached a broad-shouldered man with sandy hair who was hanging up a ship's phone. "Any damage to the ship?"

Captain Bill Stenseth shook his head. "None reported. Looks worse than it is, rolling across a flat sea out of the blue. Rogue wave, apparently. Wasn't too much of a bump, as we were able to take it on the bow."

Pitt scanned the now smooth waters in front of them. "Likely initiated by an undersea landslide."

"A good bet. Perhaps the scientists aboard can determine if an earthquake struck nearby. Or it could be the sea currents."

Pitt gave him a quizzical look.

"The northern part of the Luzon Strait is known for its strange environment. Unusual surface currents and very strong underwater currents. Could be a mix of these conditions that set off our freak wave."

"We should see if NUMA has any wave-monitoring buoys in the area."

Stenseth nodded. "I'll look into it once the submersible is back on board. Everything okay with Summer and Dirk?"

"They reported no issues from the **Stingray**," Pitt said. He stepped to the forward windscreen and scanned the seas around them. The expanse of deep blue water was broken by a handful of islands, part of the Philippine archipelago called the Babuyan. The closest, Calayan Island, appeared less than a half mile off their port bow. Pitt turned his gaze to the west, where a small white boat was visible, towing a cable off its stern. "Somebody else probing the depths around here?"

Stenseth nodded again. "I spoke earlier with them over the radio. They're with an Australian mining company and are performing a survey in the area."

Giordino entered the bridge and approached the two men. "The **Stingray** is preparing to head topsides. Should be up in about forty minutes."

"Let's get back to work once she's aboard," Pitt said. He stepped to a map table and examined a bathymetric chart of the area. "Captain, please resume our survey grid where we last stopped, just off the southwest tip of Calayan Island."

"Will do."

Stenseth gazed at the verdant green island to the northwest of the ship, mentally computing a course heading, when suddenly the helmsman beside him shouted, "Captain. There's another wave. It's . . . it's a big one." Pitt looked ahead at a ripple on the horizon. It rolled toward them from the north, just like the prior wave. The height was difficult to determine, but the helmsman had seen both coming and knew this one was double the height of the first one.

"Engine full ahead. Come right, steer course zero-one-five," Stenseth ordered, attempting to better align the ship's bow with the incoming wave.

Pitt's first thoughts were of his children. But Giordino was already ahead of him, racing for the bridge wing exit. "I'll alert Dirk and Summer to maintain depth," he yelled before disappearing down the companionway.

Pitt turned toward the approaching wave, then eyed Calayan Island.

"We might be able to duck behind that point." He motioned toward a rocky finger of land that stretched from the southeast end of the island.

Stenseth took a quick glance and nodded. "Left full rudder, full ahead. Steer three-three-zero."

He turned to Pitt with a raised brow. "It's going to be close."

Alarms sounded throughout the ship as the **Caledonia**'s twin props dug into the sea and drove the ship toward the northwest. Stenseth radioed the Philippine Coast Guard to alert the villages along the northern coast of Luzon to the impending wall of water.

Pitt stood alongside the helm, watching the wave while silently willing the ship ahead.

The race to escape was painfully slow. The NUMA research ship wasn't built for speed, but Stenseth coaxed all he could from the vessel's power plants in short order. A mile ahead, the leading edge of the wave began to rip into the shoreline of Calayan. The high water didn't inundate the island's eastern shore, but instead kicked up a mountain of foam and spray as it collided with a rocky shoreline.

As the wave approached, Pitt watched it grow in height as it crossed shallower depths. It was breaking at its peak, a dangerous indicator that it was steep enough to inflict heavy damage.

Stenseth stood at the windscreen, calculating the wave's approach and the finger of land off their port bow. A former captain of a Navy destroyer, Stenseth had years of experience at sea and had seen all sorts of marine conditions. He also knew the **Caledonia** inside and out, its capabilities and tendencies, its very soul. As he watched the approaching wall of water, he relied on his senses and the feel of the ship as he stood there with rock-solid patience. At a precise moment, he turned to the helmsman and in a calm voice said, "All right, Mr. Hopkins, hard right rudder, engines slow to course zero-one-five degrees." He then reached for the ship's intercom. "All hands, brace for impact." The helmsman spun the ship's wheel hard over, taking his eyes off the wave to study the gyroscope mounted in front of him. As the ship eased to the new compass heading, he ventured a peek ahead.

He had only an instant to view the island's rocky extension in front of them as the water wall crashed into it. The men on the bridge heard a deep bellow from the impact as a blizzard of white foam shot into the sky. Then the massive wave emerged from the spray as if it had bounced over a speed bump.

The bow of the ship rose, then the whole ship seemed to launch skyward. Pitt felt the sudden lift in his stomach as if they were riding down a speeding elevator. The ship's steel hull shrieked under the strain as the stern rose high and the bow suddenly dipped. The men on the bridge staggered forward under the shifting momentum, falling backward when the stern followed suit as the wave passed.

Almost immediately, damage reports flowed to the bridge from all parts of the ship, yet the **Caledonia** had survived mostly unscathed. A combination of Stenseth's timing and Pitt's guidance had saved the ship from worse damage. The **Caledonia** had crept far enough behind the rocky peninsula to mitigate the wave's full force.

"A good call, to duck for cover," Stenseth said.

"I hope that's the last of them." Pitt scanned the

ocean to the north and found it flat and calm as before. He turned to the bridge wing. "I'll be down in the ops center if you need me."

He rushed off the bridge to the operations bay, where he found Giordino seated in front of a blank video screen. Books and manuals from a shelf at the back of the room littered the floor as if a tornado had blown through.

Pitt took a seat next to Giordino. "What's the word from the **Stingray**?"

"We've lost communications for the moment." His steady voice masked any concern. He tapped a transmit button and called to the submersible, but got no reply.

Pitt gazed at the monitor that tracked the submersible's relative location. A flashing yellow dot indicated a signal was still being received. Pitt noted the location with a quizzical gaze. "Al, look at this. If the beacon is correct, it looks like they've moved some four miles off the wreck site."

Giordino furrowed his bushy eyebrows. "It would take them an hour to move that distance."

Summer's voice suddenly materialized in his headset. **"Stingray** to **Caledonia**, do you read?"

"Loud and clear," Giordino said. "What's your status?"

"All good. We went on something of a sleigh ride, but we're in calm waters now. We should surface momentarily."

"What depth are you?"

"Just under fifty feet. We caught quite an uplift."

"Roger. We're heading your way for recovery. **Caledonia** out."

Pitt phoned the bridge. "Are we able to proceed to rendezvous with the **Stingray**?"

"Certainly," Stenseth said. "We've got some damaged equipment in a few of the labs and a scientist with a broken arm, but we're otherwise sound. Are Dirk and Summer okay?"

"Yes, just not where we dropped them."

"We best scoop them up quick and head to the mainland," Stenseth said. "A few coastal areas surely took a hard hit from the wave, and we might be able to lend a hand."

Pitt returned to the bridge with the submersible's new coordinates, and the **Caledonia** turned around and steamed south. As Pitt scanned the waters for the yellow submersible, he detected a low-lying object alongside their path.

"Captain, there's someone in the water off the starboard bow."

Stenseth grabbed a pair of binoculars and looked to the sea. "It's two men, clinging to an empty gas can."

"Take us alongside. Al and I will drop the Zodiac over the side."

Pitt streaked out of the bridge and grabbed Giordino on the way to the stern deck. There, they prepped a stowed rigid inflatable boat for deployment. When the **Caledonia** slowed near a pair of bobbing heads in the water a few minutes later, the Zodiac was lowered over the side. Giordino started the outboard motor the second it hit the sea, while Pitt released the lift line. The black inflatable boat raced toward the floating target.

Pitt could see two young men in the water, both with light hair, clinging to the red gas can. They were too frightened to let go of it until Giordino maneuvered the inflatable alongside and Pitt reached out to them.

"We've got you. Come aboard." Pitt grabbed the closer man by the collar and yanked him onto the Zodiac. He rolled into the boat and sat on the floor in a daze, shivering. The second man was more accommodating. He gave up his death grip on the can and reached a hand to Pitt, who promptly pulled him aboard.

"Thanks," the soggy man muttered.

"Where did you boys come from?" Giordino asked.

"Survey boat. Got flipped by the wave."

Both men appeared battered and bruised, and the talkative one had a bloody gash on his arm. The man rubbed his arm, then his eyes grew wide. "Miss Thornton. She was in the boat." He sat up and pointed frantically to the southwest.

Giordino gunned the motor, guiding the inflatable in the indicated direction. Pitt rose to his feet and quickly pointed it out to Giordino. "There it is, low in the water."

Giordino glimpsed a white rounded shape between the swells and aimed the Zodiac for it. The boat was a quarter mile away, but even as they drew in close, little was visible.

The survey boat had capsized from the encounter with the rogue wave and was ninety percent submerged. Pitt took one look and knew the boat would soon vanish into the depths. As the inflatable drew alongside, the capsized boat promptly obliged, wallowing to the side and slipping beneath the surface. The clear tropical water allowed Pitt to see the boat's cabin. For an instant, he glimpsed movement through a side porthole.

It was a woman, her face pressed against the glass, with a look of desperation in her blue eyes. She made brief eye contact with Pitt, then receded from view as the survey boat began its journey to the seabed a thousand feet below.

4

Pitt dived over the side without hesitation. The sea was warm, the visibility clear, and as he opened his eyes, he saw the survey boat descending just beneath him. He kicked toward it, but he didn't seem to move any closer. Stroking with his arms, he kicked harder in pursuit.

The boat had angled nose down and was accelerating as it sank. Pitt reached out and clutched a trailing survey cable that was covered in small disks, then pulled himself to the transom. Grasping hand over hand, he pulled himself forward along the side rail, sliding past a small winch, until he reached the cabin.

The visibility had dimmed, and Pitt shivered as the water temperature dropped. As an expert diver, he worked his jaw back and forth to clear his ears of increasing pressure. He was in a losing battle with the depths, and he moved furiously, not wasting a second.

A stream of tiny bubbles seeped from around the closed cabin door, and Pitt could hear muffled thumps from inside. He stretched and grabbed the handle with both hands and twisted. It turned easily, but the door moved only a fraction of an inch, releasing more bubbles. A sliver of light emerged through the crack. The boat's battery power had yet to short out. Now he felt the thumping, the woman on the other side frantically kicking at the door. He also detected warbled cursing, which told him there was an air pocket in the cabin.

In the fading visibility, Pitt saw why the door refused to open. The roof above it had been partially crushed when the boat had capsized, blocking the top of the doorframe. Pitt shoved a palm against the dented section, but it wouldn't budge. There would be no quick fix to force it back.

His lungs began to ache as the boat fell deeper. But with only seconds to find a solution, he acted without deliberation. He pressed himself down to the deck and let go of the door's handle. As the water flow pushed him astern, he stretched out his left arm. It collided with the winch, and he grabbed it fast with both hands. Working mostly by touch, he felt the looped cable with its trailing hook, which was attached to a crossbar.

He groped for the controls, punched the release button, and crossed his fingers. The battery-powered winch began to turn, and the cable fell loose in his hand. He reeled out a dozen feet, then pressed his feet against the side of the winch and stretched toward the cabin. With a precarious grip on the door's frame, he pulled himself up and looped the cable around the handle. He let go of the frame, slid down the cable to the winch, and hit the take-up button.

The spool spun quickly, drawing up the loose cable. The winch strained for a moment, then the door burst off its jamb.

Pitt saw a beam of light, and a large air bubble emerged from the opening, along with the figure of a woman. Then all turned dark. Pitt pushed off from the deck, and as the boat fell away beneath him, he kicked and stroked for the surface.

No longer preoccupied by the rescue attempt, he now felt the dire need to breathe. He exhaled slowly to relieve the tension, while his muscles strained as hard as possible. As he ascended toward the light, he spotted the woman above him. She moved in a lethargic manner, barely kicking her legs. Pitt angled toward her, hooked a hand under her arm, and continued to kick hard.

Pitt felt the water turn warmer and saw the silver ripple of the surface above as his body screamed for air. With a final lunge, he broke through to bright sunshine, hoisting up the woman alongside him.

The NUMA inflatable bobbed a short distance away. Giordino swooped over and grasped the woman, pulling her into the boat, as Pitt treaded water and caught his breath.

"A tad under three minutes, by my count," Giordino said, turning to Pitt and extending a hand.

Pitt drew in a few more deep breaths, then grabbed his friend's hand. "I used to be good for five, but I think those days are long gone." He gasped as he heaved himself into the boat.

Across the forward bench, the two young men propped up the woman between them. Pale and listless, she looked up as Pitt took a seat across from her. He saw she was a fit woman of about thirty-five, her damp brunette hair framing an attractive face highlighted by soft blue eyes. She sat up at Pitt's approach and tried to speak, but her attempt at a thank-you resulted in a protracted spasm of coughing.

Pitt patted her knee. "That was a long free dive. You take it easy for now. We'll have the ship's doctor take care of you shortly."

She nodded as the Zodiac pulled alongside the **Caledonia** and it was hoisted aboard. A pair of waiting crewmen hustled the woman and her companions to the infirmary for examination as Captain Stenseth approached Pitt and Giordino.

"Were there any others aboard the boat?" Stenseth asked.

"No," Giordino replied. "Just the three of them. The men said they were conducting a bottom survey when the wave struck and capsized the boat."

"They're lucky to be alive," Stenseth said.

The deck rumbled beneath their feet as the research ship began accelerating from a dead stop.

"Dirk and Summer have surfaced and are waiting for recovery." The captain pointed over the rail to the south. "I suggest we then head to Luzon and assist where we can. That wave looks to have struck a portion of the coast pretty hard."

"Al and I can scout ahead in the helicopter," Pitt said, "once I find some dry clothes."

"We've been monitoring coastal communications. The town of Aparri had some calls for help, so we'll head in that direction, unless you see the need to direct us elsewhere."

Pitt nodded, then raced to his cabin and changed into dry clothes. He made his way to the ship's helipad, which jutted over the starboard quarter. Giordino was already in the pilot's seat, warming the engines.

"Thought I'd give you a breather." Giordino tapped the yoke as Pitt climbed into the co-pilot's seat.

"Much obliged."

Giordino radioed the **Caledonia**'s bridge, then lifted the Bell 505 Jet Ranger into the clear blue sky.

"Mainland's about twelve miles off," Giordino said through his headset.

The northern coast of Luzon stretched across the edge of the horizon in a line of bright green. Pitt pulled up a digital map of the region on the Bell's flight display. "If you take a left upon hitting the beach, the town of Aparri will be about three miles down," he said. "It looks to be the largest town in the primary area of impact. There's a smaller town to the west that may be worth a flyby. Fortunately, civilization is fairly sparse in this coastal region."

After Giordino circled away from the research ship and headed south, he deviated course a moment to circle the **Stingray**. The yellow submersible was floating on the surface with no apparent damage.

Giordino continued on until the lush green coast filled the windscreen. The damage from the rogue wave was readily apparent. Uprooted palm trees littered the beach and drifted in the surf, surrounded by other foliage and debris. An inland waterline showed that the wave had inundated the shore a hundred yards from the beach.

Giordino banked the helicopter west, skimming low over the shore. The visible damage abated as they flew, then disappeared entirely. At the fifteen-mile mark, they reached the next town, called Abulug. Kids played in the dirt streets and along the beach, showing no signs of worry.

"Looks high and dry here," Giordino said. "The wave must have dispersed by this point."

"Thankfully, that made for a pretty narrow swath of damage," Pitt said. "Seems a bit odd, though. Either the wave originated close by, or perhaps the offshore islands helped break it up."

Giordino banked the helicopter in the opposite

direction, retracing their path east and continuing past their original landfall. The power of the wave became evident over a two-mile section of heavy damage, which lessened again as they traveled east. They crossed a raging river, the Cagayan, which was the longest in the Philippines. Its waters ran fast, its banks overflowed from the inland wash of the wave.

Just beyond the riverbank, a town appeared beneath them. Unlike Abulug, Aparri had not escaped harm. Mud and debris littered the streets, which were still covered with receding floodwaters. Several collapsed houses and piles of debris dotted the beachfront. Yet beyond, most of the town appeared minimally damaged.

Giordino circled overhead. "Looks like the wave had settled down by the time it struck here."

"Mostly minor flooding, aside from a few lost houses." Pitt returned the friendly wave from an old man on the ground. Then he pointed left, toward the surf. "Take a look at that."

Giordino craned his neck. Within the surf he could see the reflection of an airplane, a portion of its tail assembly protruding from the water.

"A big bird. I count four prop engines," Giordino said. "Interesting place to land."

"Must have tried for the beach and didn't make it. Looks like she's been there awhile."

They continued their flyover of the town, garnering more arm waves from the locals. The helicopter then circled back to the Cagayan River. When they were over the torrent, Pitt yelled out, "Hold up."

Giordino hovered the Jet Ranger as Pitt pointed at something in the water. Giordino squinted at the broken trunk of a palm tree whisking down the river. It was one of many dotting the surface, but this one was different.

The half-submerged trunk had the addition of a long-haired woman and two children clinging to its wet sides for dear life.

5

B ring us in low and downriver from them," Pitt said, ripping off his headset and releasing his seatbelt.

Giordino accelerated down the river, then swooped the Bell helicopter low over the water. "You going to jump?" he yelled at Pitt. "Already got wet once today." Pitt turned and slid open the side door.

Giordino eyed the approaching tree trunk and edged the helicopter sideways to align with it. He hovered just a few feet above the torrent, then turned to Pitt, but he was already gone. Pitt had stepped onto the side skid and leaped into the water.

Giordino instantly ascended and circled upriver, radioing the **Caledonia** as he tracked Pitt's rescue attempt from afar.

The instant he plunged in, Pitt felt the powerful surge of the river. Unlike his last dive, the water was dark, cold, and fast-moving. As he clawed his way to the surface, he felt unseen branches and debris colliding with his body.

He turned upriver and spotted the foundering palm tree a dozen yards away. Only two heads now showed alongside it. Over the thumping of the helicopter and the roar of the river, Pitt heard loud shrieks. They came from one of the figures, the woman with long hair. Pitt stroked against the current, angling for the approaching palm. He made no headway against the current, but held his ground enough to allow the tree to approach him.

Pitt saw that the woman's daughter clung to the trunk with her. The woman was extending an arm behind her toward a mop of black hair that poked from the river's surface. But the powerful current separated her from her son. As the boy drifted from reach, the woman let out another desperate scream.

Pitt paused to allow the palm to slip past, then dug his arms hard into the dirty water, stroking across the river. The woman's screams fell away as she drifted past with the girl. As Pitt stroked hard for his target, the boy vanished beneath a wave. For a moment, Pitt feared he had lost him. Then the small dark head appeared a few yards away. Pitt cut through the water and grasped the boy with one arm and raised his head and neck above the surface. Barely five years old, he coughed as Pitt held him tight.

"You're okay, my friend," Pitt said in a comforting voice. He looked to the riverbank for an exit point, but saw they were moving too fast to gain purchase on the rocky shore. The river had returned to its original channel, but the flooding was accelerating through a now deeper and narrower cut. Soon it would drain into the ocean, where the raging force would dissipate. Safer to ride it out, he calculated.

A few yards to the side, a thick tree floated downriver. Pitt sidestroked to its trunk, grasped it with his free hand, and pulled the boy alongside. The youth climbed aboard and straddled the log with wide-eyed terror. He had stopped coughing, and the color had returned to his face, as he grasped Pitt's hand for support.

"Hang on and enjoy the ride," Pitt said. Though the boy only spoke Tagalog, he nodded at Pitt now with a look of gratitude.

As they raced toward the mouth of the river, Pitt's attention was diverted by the Bell 505 helicopter. Giordino had been monitoring events upriver, but now swooped low and hovered a short distance away. Pitt looked up to see him pointing down the river to the woman.

The palm trunk to which she had been clinging was now submerging completely. The woman and her daughter were struggling to keep their heads above water as it did.

Pitt nodded at Giordino and patted the boy on the shoulder. "Stay put," he said as he pointed at the log. Then he shoved off and kicked downriver.

They crossed a side gully that ran into the Cagayan, which dumped more debris from the town into the river. Pitt fought his way past cardboard boxes and plastic bags of trash to approach the woman and girl.

Just as he came within reach, they both dropped beneath the surface, still clinging to the sinking palm. A few seconds later, they reappeared, splashing and sputtering.

Pitt first made for the girl, a young teen with terror in her eyes. He grabbed her by the arm and held her afloat as he tracked the woman. Neither the girl nor the woman knew how to swim, and Pitt knew it would be a challenge to keep them both afloat.

He noticed an overturned wooden bench drifting by and he towed the girl to it. She grabbed it without prompting, releasing her grip on Pitt so he could help her mother.

A short distance away, the woman flailed in the water. Barely keeping her head up, she would soon tire from her efforts. Pitt swam toward her, but hesitated as he drew near to avoid her desperate, clawing hands and kicking feet. He felt himself moving faster as the river accelerated through its last tight channel before meeting the sea. As the woman weakened and began to slip below the surface, Pitt stroked over and grabbed her.

He needn't have worried about her thrashing. She proved to be a tiny woman, no taller than her daughter. She relaxed in his grip, gulping in deep breaths of air as he grasped her under his arm.

"My kids. My kids," she shouted in Tagalog.

Pitt rotated her in the water so she could see her son and daughter behind them. It grew turbulent, then the awful current, and the riverbank, fell away. They found themselves being carried out to sea. As the Jet Ranger thumped overhead, Pitt paddled the woman over to her son on the large log. The girl kicked her way over with the wooden bench for a soggy reunion.

Pitt clung to the tree trunk as well, resting from the exhausting swim. The adrenaline was long gone and in its place he had four tired limbs. He leaned his head back and watched a cormorant swoop low over the debris looking for a meal. A distant shout disrupted his rest as the helicopter pulled away, its thumping rotor replaced by the high-pitched whine of an outboard motor. A black inflatable boat with three occupants bore down on them at high speed.

He lit up at the sight of his daughter, Summer, in the bow and his son, Dirk, manning the tiller. The third person, he noted with surprise, was the woman he had rescued from the survey boat.

The inflatable roared close, then Dirk cut the motor and let the boat drift to the people in the water.

"Who's first?" Summer brushed back a strand of her thick hair and reached toward the water.

"The ladies, of course." Pitt took the young girl

by the arm and swam her to the side of the inflatable, where Summer pulled her aboard. He repeated the drill with the girl's mother, then helped the boy scamper aboard. He shoved the log aside and bellied up onto the side of the boat, where Dirk grabbed his arm and helped him aboard.

"You all right?" the younger Pitt asked.

"Getting too old for these Olympic swims." Feeling the exhaustion of both his rescue dives, Pitt settled onto the floor of the inflatable with his back to the side and gulped down the bottled water that Summer had handed him. "I didn't expect you two on the scene."

"Summer and I just got aboard the **Caledonia** when Al radioed the ship," Dirk said. He turned and waved at the hovering Bell helicopter and watched as Giordino dipped the rotor, then turned and flew north toward the approaching research ship. "The inflatable was standing by, so we jumped in and sped over."

"Glad for it. Guess you can take our guests to shore now."

Pitt turned and faced the front of the boat. Summer sat on one side, holding the hand of the frightened girl, while the woman from the survey boat examined the young boy.

"Margot said she trained as an EMT," Dirk said, reading his father's thoughts. "Insisted on coming along in case anyone was injured."

After checking the mother, the brunette woman

inched over and took a seat on the floor next to Pitt. Wearing a borrowed NUMA jumpsuit, and her long hair pulled back in a ponytail, she looked at Pitt with quiet intensity. "How was your swim?" she asked with the hint of an Australian accent.

Pitt gave a tired grin. "Less of a swim and more of a log ride."

"Margot Thornton," she said, extending a hand. "I'm afraid I forgot to thank you earlier for saving my life."

"You were a little waterlogged at the time. Glad to see you are all right."

"Thanks to you."

"Are your friends okay?"

"Seth and Alec? Yes, they're fine. But a little embarrassed that a stranger saved their boss when they failed to. But neither one is a good swimmer."

"Right place at the right time." Pitt nodded toward the river. "I didn't expect to see you on your feet so soon."

"I was taking some fresh air on the rail when your son told me you were in the river trying to help some people. I've had some basic emergency medical training and thought I might be of some help." She glanced at the Filipino mother, who nodded in return, her arms draped around her children.

Dirk gunned the motor and raced the boat toward shore. A man in shorts and a tank top stood on the beach, waving at them frantically. Dirk guided the boat through the surf toward the man, running the inflatable ashore near the sunken aircraft that Pitt and Giordino had seen earlier. Pitt studied the wreckage as Dirk drove the boat through a light surf and ran it aground on the beach. The man sprinted over, scooped his kids out of the boat, then hugged his wife.

He turned and shook Pitt's hand until his arm almost came off. "I saw you in the water. Thank you for saving my family."

Pitt nodded. "Are there any injured people in town?"

"A few people were hurt when the wave struck, but I don't know how serious."

"We better go see if we can help," Margot said, climbing out of the boat. Dirk and Summer followed as she strode toward the town.

"We can transport any seriously injured to the ship, if need be," Dirk said.

As they moved up the beach, Summer stopped and turned toward her father, who remained standing by the inflatable, staring at the wrecked plane. "Are you going to stay here with the boat?"

"I'll be along in a minute. I just want to see what's in the water here."

Summer gazed at her father. Soaked and exhausted, he still stood tall, a wistful look on his face. As he stared at the wreckage in the surf with inquisitive eyes, Summer could only smile. Then she turned and left him to his devices. He couldn't help it, she knew. The mystery of the submerged aircraft called to him, like a Siren from the deep.

6

The airplane was inverted. Only the bottom of its twin tail rose above water, the incoming waves burying it in white foam every few seconds. Pitt waded into the surf and approached the large craft from the side. He saw that it appeared fully intact and was very old.

He reached down and placed a hand on the fuselage. The skin was aluminum, its once polished surface corroded and covered with algae. Pitt dived into an incoming wave and swam along the bottom, circling the plane's nose, which pointed offshore. He now saw that one of the wings was missing, but the other supported two large engines. Pitt swam close to the wing and examined the closest engine, which was missing a portion of its cowling.

The nacelle contained a large V12 engine. He brushed some silt from the inverted valve covers and saw the name **Rolls-Royce** painted in red.

Pitt made his way to the tail and ducked under

the waves to study its H shape. Standing in the shallows to catch his breath, he surmised the plane was an Avro Lancastrian, the commercial derivative of the British World War II Lancaster bomber, which he knew was powered by the famed Rolls-Royce Merlin engines. He moved along the fuselage, took another breath, and dived to a side door positioned just ahead of the tail boom. He reached through a broken window, twisted the door latch, and nudged a shoulder against the door. The hatch slowly opened against the flooded interior.

Pitt squeezed inside, but the gloomy interior was dark. Silt and concretion caked the windows, casting a green hue to a black interior that seemed empty. He groped along the bulkhead to the cockpit, but it was equally black, its windows embedded in the sand.

His breath nearly expended, Pitt retraced his path to the door and kicked for the surface. His tired body told him he was through, and he waded through the surf onto the beach.

From the town above, Summer saw him emerge from the water and ran down to join him. "What did you find?"

"An old British airplane, built in the forties, I suspect." Pitt pointed to the inverted tail section. "An Avro Lancastrian, I think. Missing a wing, but the interior seems intact."

"You were able to go inside?"

Pitt nodded. "Too dark to see anything."

"Then it must have crashed recently."

"No, I don't think so. The wave action here would break it up in pretty quick order. Yet the corrosion looks as if the plane had been sitting for years in deep water. I think it was just whisked up onto this beach."

"That's strange," Summer said. "The tsunami wave?"

"Has to be."

A deep bellow came from across the sea, and they looked up to see the **Caledonia** approaching offshore. Summer stood and waved in reply to the ship's horn. "Sounds like they may want us back aboard. Dirk has the radio with him."

"Then we best go find the others." With Summer at her father's side, they walked up the beach and into the town.

They found the city streets a muddy mess, yet the inhabitants appeared unfazed. Men, women, and children were already working with shovels and brooms to clean up the mess.

The damage was limited to the first block or two of houses and businesses near the beach. As the elder Pitt and Summer waded through the muddy street, Dirk stood a block ahead, in front of an open-air produce market. An old woman sat on a stone step clutching her arms as Margot wrapped one of the woman's ankles in a heavy bandage.

Dirk looked up when his father and sister approached, then tapped a handheld radio at his belt.

"The **Caledonia** called," he said to his father. "They need you back on the ship as soon as possible."

"I gathered as much. Did they say why?"

"Rudi's calling from D.C."

Pitt nodded. "How are things here?"

"Just a small section of the town took the brunt of the wave. Despite the mess, there seem to be few injuries. Margot helped a man with a lacerated arm, and this woman seems to have sprained her ankle. We spoke to a city official, and their main concern is the possibility their freshwater supply is contaminated. Disease could spread in quick order."

"The ship has a portable desalinization unit. If we can get that to shore and powered up, it will provide temporary drinking water until the locals can ensure their water is safe."

Dirk nodded. "I'll oversee that as soon as we get back aboard."

Margot stood and helped the old woman into her house, then returned to the others. "There doesn't seem to be anything more we can do on the medical front," she said, "so long as there is no outbreak of illness."

"We'll stand by with the **Caledonia** and help where we can." Pitt saw the fatigue in Margot's eyes matched his own. "You've done more than necessary. We should probably get you and your comrades back to your ship. Your friends said it was a mining vessel. Does it happen to have a helipad?"

"It does. Our helicopter is being repaired, so the pad is empty. You could fly us to our ship?"

Pitt looked up as the old woman stuck her head out a window and waved. "I think you've earned as much," Pitt said.

As they made their way back to their inflatable, Pitt filled in his son about the sunken airplane. Dirk waded closer to see for himself, then stepped to the inflatable and helped drag it into the water. "I'd say that plane is worth another look."

"You and Summer should grab some air tanks from the ship," Pitt said, "and see what else you can find out about it."

Dirk gave an appreciative smile. "And here I thought you were going to monopolize all the fun."

7

Rudi Gunn paced the room with the nervous energy of a caffeinated hummingbird. The Deputy Director of NUMA removed a thick pair of horn-rimmed glasses and wiped the lenses on his shirt for the third time. A wiry former Navy commander, Gunn was usually patient and studious. But waiting in a cramped, dark conference room in the bowels of NUMA's Washington, D.C., headquarters stoked his anxiety.

It wasn't technically a secure room, as NUMA didn't have a need for one. But the converted storage closet in the deep recesses of the building was less prone to eavesdropping than any room in the White House.

The color returned to Gunn's face when Pitt and Giordino appeared on the video screen mounted on the wall. The two men took seats in a similarly cramped room aboard the **Caledonia**.

"Sorry to keep you waiting," Pitt said. "We've had some unexpected wave activity that caused a bit of damage."

"Captain Stenseth filled me in on that," Gunn said. "I checked the global tsunami alert system, but didn't find any warnings issued in the region."

"If there were any," Giordino said, "nobody told us."

"The system still has lots of gaps, so it is far from perfect."

"Though it didn't trigger any warnings, it still packed a punch," Pitt said. "We suspect it originated nearby."

"I'll have our seismic folks look into it," Gunn said.

Giordino waved an unlit cigar toward the laptop video camera, noting the blank concrete wall behind Gunn. "Say, Rudi, are you hiding out in your parents' basement?"

"No, I'm beneath the underground test pool in the NUMA building. Are you two secure?"

"As much as possible," Pitt said. "We're on a satellite link, and we're sitting in an interior bay next to the engine room."

Giordino wiped his brow. "And there's no air-conditioning."

"I'll get right to the point. The Pentagon needs your immediate help in a recovery project."

"We're on an oceanographic survey ship," Pitt

said, "not a salvage vessel. We're not equipped to recover a sunken ship."

"It's not a ship they're interested in, but a missile. As is, you're the closest resources in the area."

"What's so urgent about a lost missile?" Giordino asked.

"It's not one of ours." Gunn wiped his glasses again. "It's a medium-range cruise missile launched by the Chinese from a base in Hainan Province. They call it the **Dragonfly**. I just came from an urgent meeting with Vice President Sandecker and the NSA director. They're asking for our help, at the President's urging."

The Vice President, Admiral James Sandecker, had led the National Underwater and Marine Agency years earlier, but had passed the reins to Pitt and Gunn when he was tapped to serve in the executive branch. A shrewd but respected leader, Sandecker kept close ties with the agency and his old friends there.

"Where do you think it is?" Pitt asked.

"It was tracked into the Luzon Strait, about eighty miles north of you. It crashed less than three hours ago. I need you on-site as soon as possible."

"What's so special about this missile?" Giordino asked.

"Its speed," Gunn said. "It's a hypersonic missile that uses scramjet technology. The Air Force believes it was approaching speeds of Mach 25 when it aborted at low altitude. That's twice as fast as any missile in our defense arsenal, faster than anything even on the drawing board. It is deemed critical that we find and recover it before the Chinese do."

"So the Pentagon is a little nervous?" Giordino said.

"Freaked out, would be a better way to put it. A few years ago, the Russians claimed they had a Mach 25 missile, but it was all bluster. This one seems to be the real deal, and a game changer for national security."

"So," Pitt said, "someone is needed to sweep up the pieces off the seafloor?"

"Yes. And, unfortunately, the appropriate naval resources are at least twelve hours away. Plus, their presence would be obvious to the Chinese. You'll be less suspicious and can be there in short order."

"If this thing hit the water at Mach 25," Giordino said, "are there going to be any pieces left larger than a penny?"

"The available telemetry and imagery suggest the missile broke apart midflight. Air Force officials believe there's a good chance the scramjet motor could have survived intact. That may be wishful thinking," Gunn said, "but it's all we have to go on."

"At that speed," Pitt said, "it could be spread over a hundred-mile swath."

Gunn shook his head. "The flight's low altitude would prevent that. I had Hiram Yaeger in the NUMA computer center run the satellite and ground-tracking data through his system, and he came up with a primary search grid. It's a fairly narrow strip, just a half mile wide by ten miles long. Better than ninety-five percent of the debris should have fallen within the zone, if our assumptions are correct."

"We're still talking pretty small pieces of debris," Pitt said.

"You'll have to adjust your search parameters accordingly. I've already sent Stenseth the coordinates. Get up there pronto and get your AUVs in the water."

"And what happens," Giordino asked, "if the Chinese show up?"

Gunn took off his glasses. "At last look, no Chinese naval vessels were anywhere near the area. They are dealing with an accidental collision between two of their warships in the Gulf of Thailand that has their salvage resources positioned far south. You should have a day or two's advantage to find it and move out. You'll still be in international waters, so just pretend you are fishing."

"Fishing," Giordino muttered, "for sharks."

"All right, Rudi," Pitt said. "Tell the Vice President we're on it."

"He bet the NSA director a bottle of scotch that you'd find it, so don't let him down. Good luck."

"Thanks," Pitt muttered. When the satellite call ended, and Gunn vanished from the screen, he turned to Giordino. "A straw-colored needle in a mountain-sized haystack might be easier to find."

"I'll do as the man says and dial down the sensors on the AUVs and configure them to run tight lanes." Giordino gave a confident nod. "If there's anything still there, we'll find it."

Pitt watched his old friend leave the room and smiled to himself. The never-say-die attitude was a permanent feature of Giordino's gruff makeup. Maybe he was right. They couldn't control what was left of the missile, but they could control the search for it.

While Giordino headed to the underwater technology shack at the stern, Pitt stepped out onto the side deck. Summer and Dirk were loading a large crate into the inflatable, along with several cases of bottled water.

"Change of plans," Pitt said. "We've been ordered to hightail it north to conduct a new survey."

Dirk and Summer looked at each other.

"Ordered by who?" Summer asked.

"Washington," Pitt said.

"I thought Rudi seemed unusually antsy," Dirk said.

"What about the people in Aparri?" Summer asked. "We need to get this water and equipment to shore to prevent an outbreak of disease."

Dirk interrupted before Pitt could answer. "Why don't you just leave us behind? We'll take the desalinization equipment ashore and get it set up. You can pick us up when you complete the survey."

"I'm not sure how long it's going to take."

"That's all right," Dirk said. "It will give us time to examine the aircraft."

Pitt noticed a pair of dive tanks were already loaded in the inflatable.

Summer nodded. "We're due in the Maldives in a few days anyway. We can just fly out of Manila."

"All right, you win. Get your things together and be on your way."

Summer gave her father a quick hug. "Don't worry about us."

"Let me know what you find out about that airplane."

Dirk and Summer quickly packed some bags and returned to the inflatable. As Giordino helped winch the boat over the side, Pitt stood at the rail and gave his kids a wave. Once the inflatable was clear of the ship, the **Caledonia**'s twin props dug into the sea, and the research ship moved north at top speed.

"One other issue," Giordino said to Pitt. "Our uninvited guests."

"Yes, we better take them home before any questions are raised. Margot said their mother ship has an empty helipad. We can fly them over in the Bell."

"I'll get her warmed up."

A half hour later, the NUMA helicopter lifted off the **Caledonia** with Pitt at the controls, Giordino by his side, and Margot and her companions crammed into some rear fold-down seats. As they cleared the ship and headed northwest, Pitt spoke to Margot over their headphones.

"We located the **Melbourne** and will have you there in twenty minutes. I never asked, but what sort of minerals are you looking for?"

"Diamonds," she replied.

"Is it economical to recover them from the seabed?"

"Technology is making it worthwhile. The bigger issue is that the conventional mines around the world are mostly played out. Even De Beers has closed many of their South African mines and is moving offshore."

"How do you know," Pitt said, "where to start searching for them at sea?"

"The whole Ring of Fire region in the Pacific is a basic starting point. Diamonds are formed deep in the earth's mantle and pushed to the surface through volcanic activity. What we are really searching for are fountainheads."

"Is that a vertical lava tube?"

"Essentially. Kimberlite pipes, as they are technically called, transfer igneous rock from the mantle during a volcanic eruption. Not all these pipes contain diamonds, and those that do may have sparse concentrations. But the right ones are the motherlode of mining. They are difficult to find under the sea, and even more difficult to access, as they are typically sealed with lava or some other geological cap."

"Any luck in this area?"

"We've hit upon a couple of target sites that show potential and are preparing for further investigation."

A large black-hulled vessel appeared on the horizon, and Pitt reduced speed as they approached.

"That's the **Melbourne**," Margot said.

It was a massive work ship, teeming with cranes, winches, and cables. An expansive stern deck held a large storage bay, its open doors revealing an assortment of underwater equipment. On either side of the ship, a row of cables dangled into the depths, suspended on a series of floating booms and buoys that extended from the hull.

"Nice-looking," Giordino said. "Looks like she means business."

"Only one like it," Margot said. "My father put his life savings into it."

Pitt radioed the ship, requesting to land on the helipad that sprouted off the starboard bow.

"Fully identify yourself," said a voice after a lengthy pause.

"Bell 505 from NUMA research ship **Caledonia**," Pitt said, "carrying Margot Thornton and two companions."

"Cleared for temporary landing to off-load

passengers only. You cannot remain, due to ongoing operations."

"Roger." Pitt glanced back at Margot. "Guess we can't stay for tea."

As he circled the ship to approach, he noticed a smaller vessel stationed nearby, a crew boat painted a military gray. Pitt eased the 505 into a slight headwind and gently touched down on the platform. Giordino jumped out and opened the rear door. The two male passengers waved in thanks, then bounded across to the helipad's stairwell. Margot lingered in the crew compartment, unfastening her seatbelt, but keeping her headset on to speak to Pitt.

"I can't thank you enough for what you did." As she reached over and shook Pitt's hand, she saw for the first time how deep green his eyes were. She couldn't help feeling attracted to him. Yet she felt something other than romantic interest. It was a sense of trust. She barely knew the man, but felt she could trust him with her life.

He gave her a wink. "You can find me a fat diamond in return."

She climbed out of the helicopter, gave Giordino a hug, then stepped to the edge of the helipad. Margot watched as Pitt lifted the Bell 505 Jet Ranger into the sky. He tossed her a quick wave, then banked around the side of the ship and accelerated toward the southern horizon.

She sensed someone behind her and turned to

find an unknown man approaching from the stairwell. He was bald, Asian, and dressed in black camouflage fatigues. Margot took a step back, but there was nowhere for her to go on the elevated pad. She turned to signal the helicopter, but it was too far gone.

The man approached calmly, staring at her with cold eyes. Margot waited for him to speak, but he said nothing. Instead, he swung his fist at her, striking her on her cheek. She would have fallen to the deck, but he grabbed her arm and held her upright, then jammed a pistol against her ribs. He gave her a depraved grin.

"Now you will come with me."

8

The Filipino Army pickup truck screeched to a halt at the sight of Summer waving to the driver. It wasn't every day that an attractive, six-foot-tall redhead was seen wandering the streets of Aparri.

"Can you help set up an emergency water filtration system for the town?" she asked. "It's down by the beach. We just off-loaded it from our ship."

She led the three soldiers from the truck to the waterside, where Dirk had beached the inflatable and was off-loading the equipment. Summer directed the men in carrying a portable generator and the filtration system, while Dirk followed with a coil of hose and a toolbox.

"Is there a public well in the city we can tap into?" Dirk asked. "Preferably in the center of town."

"Yes, just a block over there is a public spigot that is fed from a well," one of the soldiers replied.

Dirk and Summer climbed into the bed of the truck with the equipment, and the soldiers drove to a cobblestoned square. The truck pulled to a stop next to an aged stone wall. Several small children scattered from the area, revealing a leaky faucet that poked from the wall, splattering the ground beneath it.

It took less than twenty minutes for Dirk and Summer to assemble and activate the portable reverse osmosis system, using the faucet as a water source. By the time it was operational, a line of women with empty plastic jugs had assembled. A man identifying himself as the mayor appeared with an astonished look on his face.

"Where did this come from?" he asked. "I made a request to the provincial authority and was told it would take a week to obtain any assistance."

"Courtesy of the NUMA ship **Caledonia**," Summer replied. "We happened to be in the area when the wave struck."

It wasn't flooding ocean water that was the source of contamination, but the local debris, landfills, and animal waste carried by the surging waters. The bacteria-tainted water, especially if left standing, could leach into local wells and pass on a myriad of diseases. Until those wells could be checked, and treated if necessary, the NUMA filtration would provide a safe source for drinking water.

"This is a godsend." The mayor walked around the portable unit. "Thank you."

"Can you ensure the generator stays gassed up and running for as long as it is needed?" Dirk asked.

"Yes, I will take care of it." He took command of the outlet hose and established order among the people in line.

Summer looked proudly at her brother as he stepped away from the equipment. "Guess we've done our good deed for the day."

"I think he's put us out of business." Dirk grinned toward the official. "Not much else to be done here. What do you say we go dive that airplane?"

She glanced at the western skyline. "We've got another hour or two of daylight. Let's do it."

They made their way back to the beach and assembled their dive kits in the inflatable. The tide had risen, concealing the plane's tail, but upon entering the clear water they easily found it. Dirk led the way, submerging into the surf and diving alongside the inverted aircraft. He just about duplicated his father's dive, circling the exterior, then approaching the open side door. Slipping inside, with Summer close behind, he swam across the cargo compartment to the wide cockpit. He flicked on an underwater flashlight and played its beam about. The flight controls and metal seat frames dangled over his head. He turned the light down and found only a small amount of sediment beneath the pilots' seats.

Dirk turned back to the cargo bay and swam alongside Summer, who was investigating it with her own light. A glitter caught her eye, and she squeezed past Dirk to a shiny object beneath her. It was a belt buckle, beside the soles of a pair of boots. A thick leather handle lay nearby, the only remains of the pilots' luggage, she surmised.

She turned to her brother, who was shining his flashlight toward the tail assembly. The interior seemed empty. While a row of inverted seats lined one side of the fuselage, there otherwise was nothing to see but a thin layer of sediment. But as Dirk moved his light back and forth, Summer did see something.

She swam toward the narrowing tail, then turned her light up. Mounted to the inverted floor was a small wooden crate. Several of the slats had disintegrated, leaving a large opening in one side. Summer eased her way to the crate, trying not to stir up the bottom sediment, and turned her light inside the opening.

A faint metallic shine reflected back. She poked closer to see it was a thick carrying case. She reached between the slats and grabbed it. Years of concretions had secured it to the crate, but it broke free with some minor jiggling. She gently pulled it out, catching it in her arm as it came free.

Even underwater, the luggage felt heavy. The size of a large attaché, its aluminum skin was severely weathered. Dirk moved in for a closer look, then pointed toward the fuselage door. Summer nodded and waited for her brother to exit the plane, then followed him out with the case clutched under her arm. They swam to shore, stepped up the beach to their inflatable boat, and stripped off their dive gear.

"Looks like you found the one and only thing left inside," Dirk said.

"The plane, overall, is in pretty good condition, just like Dad described." Summer picked up a towel and began drying her hair. "Pretty odd for being, what, eighty years old?"

"Judging by the photos we saw on the ship, I think he's right. It does look like an Avro Lancastrian. The last one was built in the 1940s."

Summer slipped a T-shirt and shorts over her bathing suit, then picked up the carrying case. "Not light." She set it on the side of the boat and wiped it off with her towel. She shook it, anticipating the sound of sloshing water, but there was none. "It feels like it stayed watertight."

"Well, open it up, already." Dirk knelt beside her.

She pried up a pair of corroded latches and tried to lift the lid, but it didn't budge. She worked her fingers against the seam and pulled with more force. The lid protested, then opened an inch. She renewed her grip and lifted it the rest of the way.

The interior had indeed remained watertight. A red felt cloth decorated with an abstract image of the sun concealed the contents.

"There's a tag." Summer touched a square leather label affixed inside the lid. Its wording was stamped in a curvilinear script that was not familiar to either of them.

"Nothing I can decipher," Dirk said. "Let's see what's inside."

Summer carefully pulled the fabric aside, revealing eight small compartments. Though varied in shape, each contained a satin-wrapped object the size of an orange. She slipped her fingers around one of them and pulled it from the case.

"It sure is heavy for its size." She carefully studied the wrapping.

"Go ahead," Dirk said. "Unwrap it."

She slowly unwrapped the satin cover like it was a mummy. Pulling aside the last drape, she revealed an ornate carving of black stone. The intricate detail was done in a stylized fashion.

"Is that what I think it is?" she asked.

"It looks like a conch shell to me."

Summer nodded and held the carving up to the fading sunlight. The black stone was embedded with metallic flakes and lighter brushes of color that gave it an unusual look. "Interesting stone, too."

She unwrapped the other seven objects, all of the same material. One was a carved wheel, one a flower, another a pair of fish. They struggled to identify the remaining pieces. As Summer started to replace the last piece, she noticed a yellow strip along the edge of the case. She worked a fingernail into the seam and pushed out a faded business card.

"I think it's printed in Mandarin." She held it up for Dirk to see.

"At least that we can translate," he said.

She turned the card over. "We won't have to." She passed him the card, which was written in English.

"'Dr. Feng Zhoushan, Director of Tibetan Antiquities, National Palace Museum, Republic of China,'" he read.

"How's that for a lead?" Summer said. She immediately dug out her cell phone. She found a number for the museum in Taipei and called it. She shook her head when she hung up a few minutes later.

"I got routed around several times. Nobody seemed to know the name, but they promised someone would call me back."

"That will probably be tomorrow. Let's get cleaned up and see if there is a place in town to eat dinner."

Before they had the chance, Summer's phone rang. She spoke for several minutes while Dirk organized their gear and secured the boat for the night to a concrete block. Summer ended the call with a rise in her voice.

"That was the National Palace Museum in Taipei, a Dr. Chen. He knows all about the lost airplane and was shocked at our discovery. He said it went missing on a flight from Taipei to Hong Kong and was presumed lost in the waters south of Taiwan."

"They must have taken a bit of a wrong turn

somewhere to end up here," Dirk said. "Did he say when it went down?"

"In March of 1963. He said it was a great tragedy to lose Feng, who was a respected authority on Tibetan artifacts."

"Tibet?"

"Yes." She rubbed a hand over the metallic case. "Perhaps he was taking these from the museum to Tibet."

"I guess they belong to the museum."

"Dr. Chen wasn't aware of what was aboard, but seemed anxious to see it."

"I'm sure he is."

Summer gave him a guilty grin. "I told him we would bring the case to him." She paused. "Dad likely won't be back for a few days, by which time we're scheduled to leave anyway. Might as well get a head start in Taiwan and accomplish something constructive."

Dirk gazed toward the submerged aircraft and nodded his approval. "I guess it's the least we can do for the late Dr. Feng."

9

Pitt watched from the bridge wing as the bright orange autonomous underwater vehicle dangled in the air like a rocket in flight. Shaped like a torpedo, it was hoisted out of the glare of the ship's deck lights and over the side of the **Caledonia**, where it was lowered into the sea. Released from its lift cable, the battery-powered AUV motored away from the ship. Pitt watched its small wake for a moment, under the night sky, until the vehicle slipped out of view beneath the surface.

The **Caledonia** had made good time to the missile crash site, and Giordino had the two AUVs ready to launch the minute they arrived. It was now up to the electronic devices to locate any remains of the Chinese weapon.

Designed for deepwater surveying, the AUVs would dive almost a thousand feet to the ocean's floor, then initiate a preprogrammed scan of the bottom. Packed with sonar, navigation, and an

assortment of water sensors, they would methodically run in lines across an imaginary grid, oblivious to the cold dark waters and the creatures that
lived there.

Pitt looked from the empty sea to the lights of
a ship on the horizon, then climbed down and
made his way aft. In a high-tech operations bay, he
found Giordino and another man seated in front of
matching computer screens that each displayed a
rectangular survey grid. Tiny orange triangles, representing the pair of launched AUVs, crept across
the screen. The marker on Giordino's screen was
approaching a green-highlighted grid, while the
one on the other man's screen was already tracking
a line.

"**Artemis** away okay?" Pitt asked.

"All data signals were good before she went
under," Giordino said. "She'll be running about
an hour behind **Apollo**." He pointed to the AUV
marker on the other man's screen. Giordino had
nicknamed the AUVs after the twin Greek deities,
since Artemis was considered a goddess of the hunt
and Apollo a patron of seafarers.

Pitt took an empty chair and gazed at that screen
as the newly launched AUV descended to the seabed and took up its first lane. But the depictions on
the screens were only estimates. Cruising a thousand feet beneath the surface, the AUVs were not in
continuous contact with the ship. But transponders
in the water picked up sporadic position-reporting

signals. Giordino had created a tracking algorithm that included the AUVs' programmed speed and estimated current conditions to plot their antici-pated progress under the sea.

"What's their running time?" Pitt asked.

"They're good for twenty hours, but we'll call them back around lunchtime tomorrow for a data drop and a battery change."

"Working in tandem, I should think **Artemis** and **Apollo** can cover a good chunk of Rudi's sur-vey grid in their first cycle."

"Eighty-six percent, by my calculation," Giordino said.

Pitt glanced at the hands on a wall chronometer that were approaching midnight. "I guess there's only one thing to do in the meantime," he said, stifling a yawn. "Sleep."

10

The dogleg handle turned with a grinding sound and then the steel door swung open. Morning sunlight flooded into the storage locker, illuminating three bound occupants inside. Margot, Seth, and Alec lay huddled in a circle on a thick coil of towline. Margot would have shielded her eyes from the sudden brightness, but, like her companions, she had her hands bound behind her back. She could only squint as a stocky figure appeared at the door.

She guessed it had been ten or twelve hours since she'd stepped off the NUMA helicopter and promptly been bound and tossed into the ship's locker with her survey assistants. It was long enough for her stomach to grumble from lack of food, and for one of her companions to soil himself.

As her eyes adjusted to the light, she recognized the figure in the doorway as the bald man who had met her on the helipad. The same man who had knocked her to the ground with a roundhouse punch when she had hesitated and tried to wave to the departing NUMA helicopter. Her cheekbone still throbbed from the blow.

"You . . . up." He pointed a finger at her.

Margot rolled to her knees, stood up. The man glared at the other two captives, then grabbed Margot by the elbow and yanked her out of the locker. His sidearm was holstered, she noticed, but it didn't matter. Another man, also clad in black camos, stood at the ready with an automatic rifle pointed at her chest.

The bald man slammed the steel door and locked it, then turned and stepped forward. The gunman motioned for Margot to follow him. They strode slowly across the large ship, allowing Margot to regain her senses. She noted several things.

First, her Asian captors wore uniforms with no markings or insignias. Both men were on the high side of thirty and carried themselves with a cold, fearless aggression. Margot guessed they were Chinese Special Operations commandos. The bald man, in particular, had a muscular brutality. He was missing a portion of his scarred left ear, evidence, no doubt, of a knife fight.

The second thing she noticed was the **Melbourne**'s unusual tranquility. At sea, the big ship was usually a beehive of activity, with workers everywhere and the constant background noise of pumps, compressors, and generators. Now the ship was silent, like a ghost town. A glance over the side rail told her the vessel was also under way.

A gray crew boat trailed behind on a towline. That should have tipped her off when she arrived on the NUMA helicopter, but she assumed it was a Philippine or Taiwan government vessel.

The trio climbed a companionway and entered the ship's expansive bridge. Margot turned to a built-in desk at the rear of the bay, where her father usually managed the daily operations. She felt a pang of horror at the bloodied body of a dead man lying on the far side of the bridge. It was the ship's first officer, not her father. She breathed out faintly in relief.

Only two people manned the **Melbourne**'s bridge, a slight man at the helm control and a taller man in the captain's chair. Both were Asian, with close-cropped hair and the same black fatigues. It was the seated man that caught her attention. Lean, but powerfully built, Zheng Yijong had a dark aura that made the bald commando seem like a Girl Scout.

He turned to Margot and gazed at her with eyes that shimmered like black ice. "You are the one who arrived in the helicopter," he said in studied English.

Margot gave a slight nod and looked down at the deck. Those eyes. They were almost too frightening to face.

Zheng looked at the bald man. "Is that correct, Ning?"

The commando nodded.

"Where is my father?" Margot asked.

Zheng looked her up and down, then nodded. "Yes, I see the family resemblance. Your father is belowdecks. You may join him shortly . . . if you are cooperative."

He gazed at the empty helipad off the starboard bow. "Where did you come from?"

Margot could feel his potential violence and made no effort to resist his queries. "We were surveying in the Balintang Channel. Our boat was capsized by a large wave. We were rescued by a NUMA research ship that had a helicopter. They flew us here."

"Tell me about this NUMA ship."

Margot shrugged. "The **Caledonia**? A modern oceanographic research ship, carrying the typical ROVs, AUVs, and a submersible, I believe."

"What are they doing in these waters?"

"I was told they were studying acidification levels in deep water."

"I see." Zheng folded his hands and examined his knuckles. "And what, exactly, were you surveying?"

"We were searching for geological features that would warrant further examination by the **Melbourne**."

"Features that contain diamonds?"

"Yes, or those that indicate their potential presence."

Zheng nodded, and Margot let out a breath she didn't realize she'd been holding. Her description must have matched what the crew had told him. Time to change the subject.

"Where is the ship's crew?" she asked.

"Secured below." Zheng offered a humorless expression. "They have not been harmed. We may need their expertise, in due course. Yours as well. Are you a geologist?"

"I am a geophysicist." She grew tired of the questioning. "Why are you here? What do you want?"

Zheng didn't answer. Instead, he gave a barely perceptible nod to the bald man. Ning clamped a thick hand around Margot's upper arm and squeezed.

Margot thought the bone was going to snap in two, but she ground her teeth to avoid crying out. The commando eased his grip and yanked her toward the door. "Move."

Guiding her off the bridge, he led her to the ship's general housing bay two levels below. They stopped at a cabin at the end of a hall, where an armed commando sat on a folding chair. The gunman popped to his feet as the pair approached, and he unlocked and opened the door. When they reached the threshold, Ning shoved Margot inside. Unable to put out her hands, she bounced against a pair of bunk beds and fell to the floor as the door slammed shut behind her.

She rolled to her knees and staggered to her feet with a look of shock on her face. It wasn't the rough treatment, it was seeing the man lying on the lower bunk. His clothes were torn and his hair caked with dried blood. The bruised and battered face was practically unidentifiable. But not to a father's daughter.

Alistair Thornton slowly swung his legs off the side of the bed and stood. He was a hulking man, with a body hardened by years of labor. It also showed in his craggy face and jutting jaw, offset by a strong nose and piercing blue eyes. Pain and anger flared through those blue eyes, but he forced a smile.

"My girl." He draped his arms around her. "You came back."

He spoke with utter disappointment. He saw her bound hands and untied them.

She reached up and touched his battered face. "What have they done?" she said through her tears.

"It's my own fault. I didn't take too well to someone seizing my ship. I caught a rifle stock in the chops for my troubles."

Margot knew her father was as tough as nails. He'd spent years trampling the Outback of Australia and the jungles of New Guinea in search of mining deposits. He had battled everything from highway robbers to headhunters and single-handedly built a successful mining company. Alistair Thornton was not a man easily denied.

"Who are they and what do they want?"

"I'm really not sure." Thornton shook his head. "They came alongside under the guise of the Philippines Department of Environment and Natural Resources. Of course, they're not Filipino."

"Chinese paramilitary?"

"Most likely. They seem very interested in our survey capability. They initially said they only wanted to borrow the ship, and claimed nobody would get hurt." A bitter look filled his eyes as he clenched his fists. "They then proceeded to kill Murphy and White. Tossed White over the side rail like a bag of cement."

Murphy was the **Melbourne**'s first officer, and White the chief engineer. Again, Margot felt a wave of fear roll over her. "Are they after diamonds?"

"That was my first reaction, but I don't think so. They've appropriated the ship to search for something, I just don't know what." He rubbed a hand across his thick jaw. "They made a mess of things when they arrived. We were running a test over the side when they came aboard and pulled their guns."

"What about—"

Thornton pressed a finger to her lips. He glanced around the room, indicating the possibility of eavesdropping.

Margot's face turned pale. "I'm glad you're here. We were hit by a series of waves from the north, the last one quite large." She described her escape from the sinking survey boat and the visit to Aparri.

"Were there any fatalities?"

"I don't believe so. It was a powerful wave, but the damage appeared localized."

"Thank God for that."

"Where are they taking the ship?"

Thornton didn't have a chance to answer. Without warning, the cabin door burst open. The two guards who had escorted Margot earlier stood in the doorway. Ning pointed a finger at Thornton. "You. To the bridge."

Margot gave her father a peck on the cheek. He brushed his fingers through her hair, then exited the cabin.

On the bridge, the mining engineer found Zheng seated at the rear desk reading a technical operations manual with the Thornton Mining logo on the cover. The commando finished studying an equipment schematic before looking up at the ship's owner. "You designed and built the **Melbourne**?"

"She was built to my specifications," Thornton replied.

"Its abilities are quite impressive. Both a survey and excavation vessel. And perhaps more."

Thornton said nothing, barely concealing his contempt for the man.

"While you were below, some of the crew gave us a review of the ship's subsea equipment. But I'm afraid no one was able to provide us operational guidance on its survey capabilities."

"That's because you killed Reginald White. He served as my chief survey engineer." The words came out slow and angry.

"Yes, well, he ceased being cooperative about your mining results," Zheng said. "A pity for him, as that is of no real interest to us at the moment." He rose to his feet and stepped to a console marked **Sonar Station**.

"This vessel has a hull-mounted, multibeam sonar system, does it not? We'd like to use it to conduct a search for something on the seafloor. I require your assistance in calibrating for the depths and desired sensitivity."

"And if I don't care to help?"

Zheng offered a tight smile. "Then your daughter will suffer greatly at the hands of Ning." He nodded toward the bald commando.

Thornton gritted his teeth.

The helmsman, peering out the windscreen through a pair of binoculars, interrupted with a shout to his commander. "Sir, there is an American vessel with a blue hull dead ahead. It appears to be operating in the search zone."

11

The orange NUMA AUV rose to the surface like a breaching whale. Its electronic thrusters fell silent, and the large cylinder bobbed freely in a growing ocean chop. It wasn't alone on the sea for long. The turquoise hull of the **Caledonia** soon inched alongside, and a deck crew, working under the watchful eye of Al Giordino, hoisted the vehicle aboard.

The underwater vehicle was placed onto a set of wooden supports alongside the other AUV, the **Apollo**, which had been retrieved a short time earlier. As a crewman opened a sealed compartment to remove the batteries, Giordino withdrew a plug-in hard drive. He carried it to an adjacent lab, attached it to a computer workstation, and began downloading its contents.

Pitt stepped into the lab a short time later and found Giordino at the computer, typing in a series of commands.

"How soon can you turn the AUVs around?" Pitt asked.

Giordino glanced at his watch. "Swapping out the batteries should be completed soon, but there's no rush to drop them back in the drink until we see what we have."

Pitt pulled up a chair and sat down. "You're talking several hours to review the records, aren't you?"

"Only if we examined them manually, but Hiram Yaeger created a nifty software program that eliminates the grunt work." Giordino tapped the screen. "We input some parameters related to the target we're seeking, and the program will filter through the data and present us with the hot spots."

"Can it differentiate between natural and man-made objects?"

"With about ninety-eight percent accuracy. Any marginal items fall into the review bucket."

"Sounds impressive. Fire away."

Giordino typed on the keyboard, producing a grainy, gold-tinted image representing the initial sonar impression of the seafloor as collected by the two AUVs. The screen scrolled by at a high speed for several minutes, then stopped at a dark, shadowy image.

"The computer has identified forty-two targets." Giordino examined a data table on the side of the screen. "I think we can eliminate the first one."

He enlarged the screen, highlighting the target that the program had marked with a red dot. Under magnification, a cylindrical black figure filled the screen.

Pitt studied the image and nodded. "Your basic fifty-five-gallon drum. Next?"

Giordino retrieved the next target, which showed three rounded objects clumped together.

"Most likely, some rocks the computer was unsure about," Giordino said. There was nothing either man deemed suspicious in the enlarged view.

They scanned several more unremarkable targets before Pitt tapped the screen. "Now that could be something."

The object cast a rectangular shadow across the seafloor, indicating a length of about four feet. Under magnification, it showed a jagged edge on one side and an even, linear edge on the other.

"It could certainly pass for a section of rocket fairing," Giordino said. "I'll mark it for investigation."

They examined the additional targets, Giordino marking those that had a distinctive man-made appearance. As they moved through the search grid, the objects increased in both size and proximity, culminating in a large mass that cast a triangular shadow. The target lay at the extreme edge of the AUVs' survey field, rendering the details murky.

"Could be pay dirt." Giordino manipulated the image with various filters. "Or a jumble of rocks."

"No," Pitt said. "I think it's something real."

"It's the last of the Mohicans," Giordino said. "Let's see how the targets we liked map out."

He typed in a new command, displaying the search perimeter as a rectangle from the top of the screen to the bottom. Then he added location markers for the targets of interest. Appearing as small red dots, the points neatly aligned in a linear path just off the grid's centerline.

"Well, take a look at that." Giordino beamed broadly. "A nice trail of bread crumbs that runs west to east."

"Sure looks like a debris trail." Pitt slapped his old friend on the back. "And here I thought we'd be snooping around for weeks."

"The reconnaissance boys would seem to have put us right on it."

"I guess a trip downstairs is in order to see if we're right."

Giordino nodded. "Let me transfer the datapoints to the **Stingray**, and we can make it happen."

An hour later, both men climbed into a yellow submersible on the stern deck. Before sealing the hatch, Pitt gazed across the ship's railing at a dot on the horizon. A black vessel of indeterminate size appeared to be sailing in their direction. Pitt glanced at it warily, though he knew it was likely a container ship.

Released off the **Caledonia**'s stern, the submersible began a slow, gravity-induced descent to the seafloor. Constructed of carbon fiber composites, the **Stingray** was rated to a depth of more than twelve thousand feet. To Pitt and Giordino's benefit, they were deployed in a region of the West Philippine Sea that was less than a thousand feet deep.

The submersible had been dropped over the western end of Giordino's marked targets. When the **Stingray**'s fathometer indicated they were approaching a steep, rugged seafloor, Giordino adjusted the buoyancy. Pitt activated the electric thrusters and guided the vessel forward. He felt a surprisingly strong lateral current at the depth, which challenged the submersible's track.

"The computer indicates we've drifted quite a bit during our descent." Giordino compared the submersible's inertial navigation system against the target coordinates. "The first target should be about two hundred meters off, on a heading of zero-two-three degrees."

Pitt turned the **Stingray** onto the designated course toward the first target. The submersible's bright external lights displayed a drab, rocky seamount beneath them, populated with an occasional deepwater fish. As the **Stingray** approached the first target, its lights reflected off a metallic object. Pitt adjusted course, approached, and hovered over the thin fragment of metal. The jagged piece was barely a foot long and streaked with black. It was angling upright from the floor, accounting for its discovery by the AUV's sonar.

Giordino glanced from the object to the image he'd posted on the screen. "Matches the sonar hit."

"No telling what it is," Pitt said, "but there's no sediment on it."

"Looks to be worth a grab."

As Pitt nudged the submersible closer, Giordino activated a manipulator mounted on the prow. With an experienced touch, he reached out with the articulated arm and plucked the jagged metal with an aluminum claw. He drew it back to the **Stingray**, held it in front of the viewport for a closer look, then dropped it into a large mesh basket mounted to the front skids.

Pitt guided them to the next target, where they discovered similar shredded metal on the slope of a steep ridge. The underside of the piece held an assemblage of frayed wires. Nearby, Pitt detected a trail of more wires, which led to a green circuit board secured to an aluminum bracket. Giordino scooped up the items, and they proceeded to the next target.

They moved efficiently from target to target, each focused on his own task. They didn't speculate, but both knew the parts could only have come from the Chinese rocket. They worked their way through half the targets, collecting additional bits of debris missed by the sonar, until the basket was full and the **Stingray**'s batteries began to waver. Using an underwater transponder, Pitt radioed the **Caledonia** that they were preparing to surface.

Giordino purged the ballast tanks, and they began a slow ascent.

They were greeted on the surface at dusk by heavy seas and a threatening sky. A ship was visible out the forward viewport, but it wasn't the NUMA vessel. Large, black, and sprouting numerous cranes, the **Melbourne** sat only a half mile away.

"Are we treading on someone's diamond mine?" Giordino asked.

"Possibly. I know we could do without an audience."

Pitt engaged one of the side thrusters and pivoted the submersible until it faced east. The **Caledonia** appeared a short distance away and promptly moved alongside. The NUMA ship maneuvered between the submersible and the **Melbourne**, blocking the latter's view as the **Stingray** was retrieved from the sea. The dripping submersible had barely been set onto the deck when a trio of NUMA crewmen began hustling the contents of the collection basket into a secure lab. Captain Stenseth stood close by, overseeing the retrieval, when Pitt and Giordino climbed out the hatch.

Stenseth held the green circuit board in front of him. "Looks like you boys hit the jackpot."

"I'm not sure," Pitt replied, "that there is enough here to piece anything together."

"The Pentagon seems desperate for anything," Stenseth said. "They're already clamoring for photos of what you brought up." He nodded toward the research lab. "Did you grab all there was to be found?"

"No. We've got a few more targets to investigate."

"A few of the larger pieces, in fact," Giordino said.

Pitt turned to the rail and motioned toward the other ship, which had backed to the south and was now in view of the **Caledonia**'s stern. "That's Margot's vessel, the **Melbourne**."

"They crept up an hour or so ago," Stenseth said. "Haven't heard a peep out of them. I called them off, told them we have underwater operations in progress, but they didn't even respond. Just parked themselves off our beam. Would they have an inkling of why we're here?"

"I can't imagine. I'll give Margot a call and find out what they're up to."

"Well, that's not our real problem," Stenseth said as the ship lurched beneath them.

"What is?" Giordino asked.

"The weather. A strong storm front is developing rapidly and moving in from the southeast. Possible typhoon. Looks like it will sideline us for about forty-eight hours."

"Do we have time," Pitt said, "to slip in another dive?"

"Radar shows things will get ugly in about two hours. I'd advise against it."

Pitt nodded at Giordino, who turned and sprinted to a side bay.

"Where's he going?" Stenseth asked.

"To grab some fresh batteries for the **Stingray**. No sense in waiting around if we can finish the job now."

Stenseth nodded, not the least bit surprised. "I don't like the idea of retrieving you in rough seas at night."

Pitt smiled. "We'll leave the lights on."

While the submersible was prepped for another dive, Pitt followed Stenseth to the bridge and hailed the **Melbourne** on the ship's radio. After several calls, a hostile voice replied in a thick Asian accent.

"Melbourne."

"My name is Pitt. I'd like to speak to Margot Thornton, please."

After a brief pause, the voice replied curtly, "Not available."

"Then let me speak to Mr. Thornton."

There was another pause, followed by the same response.

"Please have Margot call me when she is available," Pitt said. When there was no acknowledgment, he asked, "What is the nature of your presence here?"

"Mining survey," came the cold response. "What are you doing here?"

"Subsea terrain mapping," Pitt said. "We have submersible operations in progress. Please stand clear."

A click from the other vessel's transceiver was the only response.

"Chatty fellow," Stenseth said.

Pitt gazed at the neighboring ship, now brightly illuminated in the growing dusk. A crane moved along the starboard beam, appearing to deploy something over the side. "Keep a close eye on her, Captain, and see what you can learn from Margot if she calls back."

Giordino ducked his head in the bridge wing door. "The battery packs have been replaced on **Stingray**. We're ready to dive."

Pitt followed him back to the stern deck, where they were soon deployed in the submersible. White-caps littered the sea as a growing wind kicked spray into the air. The **Stingray** rocked through the rest-less surface as it submerged for its slow descent.

"What's up with the **Melbourne**?" Giordino asked.

"I don't know. I tried to speak to Margot and her father, but they weren't available."

Giordino could see the concerned look on Pitt's face. "Something amiss?"

"Without a doubt. Their radio operator was un-usually rude and uncooperative. Aside from the blunt fact that they suddenly appeared right here."

"Do you think they're after the same thing we are?"

"It would seem so. Or waiting to see what we find."

Giordino nodded. "I'll coordinate with the **Caledonia** to position us on her far side when we surface. Maybe we can even get aboard in the dark without being seen."

"A good thought, if we retrieve anything else."

The question was affirmed when they reached the next target, which proved to be a piece of a crushed fuel tank. Giordino plucked it from the sand and placed it in the basket. Pitt guided the submersible forward, scanning and locating the next several targets, each a bit of mechanical debris that Giordino scooped up. As he secured the last piece, he gazed at the sonar records.

"Down to the last batch. There's a cluster of two or three targets about fifty yards away."

Pitt elevated the **Stingray** and engaged the thrusters. The steep slope of the surrounding seamount eased, allowing Pitt to skim over the surface at a quicker pace. The bottom turned sandy, and, at the designated distance, they spotted a pair of small objects protruding from the bottom. Pitt turned toward the items, which reflected silver in the submersible's lights, and hovered above them.

On closer inspection, the men could see it was not a pair, but a single large mass resting in a low burrow that had deceived the sonar. The metallic assembly contained pumps, valves, and injectors that surrounded an elongated air intake chamber. All of it was remarkably intact.

The two men looked at each other without saying a word.

They had found the missile's scramjet motor.

12

To minimize chances of detection, the small inflatable approached the NUMA ship from the stern. The **Caledonia** was aligned with the current, holding its location, thanks to a dynamic positioning system, with its bow to the waves.

It was the perfect placement for Zheng's insertion operation. Once over the side, his team of covert divers would swim against the current while still fresh. When their mission was complete, they could ride it clear of the research ship, for the extraction.

Zheng guided the boat in darkness, fighting a strong crosswind under low power. He ran the motor just above idle, seeking to minimize its rumbling and its exhaust. The seas were building quickly, but to their benefit, he thought. Higher waves would disguise the small boat on a ship's radar and reduce the chance of a crewman making visual contact. It would also offer better cover for the divers in the water, even if they bore the brunt of the angry sea.

Dressed in black to match the fresh coat of deck paint just applied to one of the **Melbourne**'s inflatables, Zheng glanced at the two men in front of him. Also in black, they were wearing matching lightweight wetsuits and buoyancy compensators. They carried single air tanks and a pair of large mesh satchels.

With the **Caledonia** several hundred yards in front of them, Zheng cut the motor. "Ready?" he asked as waves slapped against the hull.

Both divers nodded. A second later, they slipped backward over the gunnel and into the water.

Zheng tracked their bubbles as they descended to twenty feet. Guided by luminescent compasses, they swam toward the NUMA ship, tracking their time from entry. The current was forceful even at depth, and the divers kicked fully with their fins to propel themselves forward.

In the dark water, the men swam shoulder to shoulder. Only the silvery wash of the rolling waves overhead gave them a clear sense of orientation. After ten minutes, the divers stopped. One clicked on a waterproof penlight. Barely thirty feet ahead, the curved form of one of the **Caledonia**'s propellers gleamed through the murk.

Killing the light, the divers swam forward, arms outstretched, until they touched the large bronze blade. The **Caledonia**'s hull cast a shadow over them as they rested a moment. Rising to meet its hard, flat surface, the divers followed the line of the ship's transom to the port flank, where they ascended several feet and retrieved their mesh bags.

Closer to the surface, the wave action was more forceful. They struggled to maintain position as one man took a ball-shaped mass of plastic explosives with a suction device attached and mounted it on the hull. Around the area, he applied a number of smaller charges. The second diver produced a detonator and timer and wired them to the charges. With the press of a rubberized button, he activated the device, a glowing LED display indicating a two-hour countdown.

The divers descended beneath the **Caledonia**. Adjusting their compass bearings one hundred and eighty degrees from their original heading, they moved away from the ship. They swam easily this time, running with the current, until rising to the surface a few minutes later. They drifted a moment until they spotted the dark rubber boat fifty yards down current.

Zheng motored to the divers and helped them aboard through the breaking waves. "Is it set?" he asked as they removed their dive equipment.

"Yes, on the port quarter," one of the divers said. "Sufficient to damage but not sink the ship. As you directed."

Zheng nodded. He took a seat at the transom, started the outboard, and swung the craft in a wide arc toward the leeward side of the **Melbourne**. As the small boat bucked through the growing seas, he stole a glance at the twinkling lights of the NUMA ship, knowing they would soon be forced to depart.

But his satisfaction was incomplete. He had one more task to perform before the night was through.

13

Summer clutched the armrest of her window seat as the jetliner took a sudden dip on its approach to Taiwan Taoyuan International Airport. It was at least the third time the craft had sustained a heavy lurch, leaving her stomach somewhere near her throat. She swallowed hard, wishing the plane would hurry up and land. Sitting beside her, Dirk kept his nose in a car magazine, seemingly oblivious to the bumps and rolls of the Airbus A330.

She turned to the window and looked past the streaks of raindrops to dark clouds beyond. The mass of gray parted just seconds before a concrete runway appeared beneath them, and the plane thudded down.

"Guess we brought the damp with us," Dirk said, eyeing the soggy tarmac.

The rains had started on their jeepney ride from Aparri to Tuguegarao and intensified during their commuter flight to Manila. The fast-moving, off-shore storm had caused a two-hour delay in their departure from the Philippines. Summer checked her watch, then sent a text from her phone as the plane approached the gate. Before the jet's doors were opened, she received a response.

"Dr. Chen says he is working late tonight and can still meet with us at the museum if we'd rather not reschedule for tomorrow."

"Let's give it a try." Dirk removed the Tibetan case from the overhead compartment. "Weather won't be any better tomorrow."

"He's left word with the guards to let us in," she said, "if we don't make it before closing."

They retrieved their bags and cleared customs, then hopped in a taxi to Taipei. The capital city at the northern tip of Taiwan was a half hour ride through steady traffic. As their driver weaved through the congestion with a heavy foot on the accelerator, Summer marveled that despite much nicer vehicles on the road, the lack of regard for traffic rules was little different than in Manila.

They crossed the Tamsui River into the western portion of the city, then drove north to an affluent suburb named Shilin. The driver pulled to a stop in front of a grand complex tucked against a luxuriant green hillside.

The National Palace Museum was one of the world's premier art institutions, hosting a stellar collection of Chinese artifacts. Built upon the ancient collections of the Forbidden City in Beijing, the bulk of the collection's artifacts had been shuttled to Formosa by Chiang Kai-shek in 1949, ahead of the Communist takeover of the mainland.

Dirk and Summer made their way past some departing busloads of tourists and strode up a set of central entry steps. They passed beneath an ornamental arch and walked across a long, open courtyard and up an additional staircase to the Main Exhibition Hall. The imposing structure resembled a Buddhist temple, with a high, arched roof and graceful, skyward-pointing eaves. The last few tourists were trickling out the doors, as closing time had passed. Summer approached a ticket window that was still occupied and was directed to one of the side buildings that flanked the courtyard on an elevated rise.

"The Tibetan artifacts are housed in a side annex, the East Wing," she told her brother. They walked to the building's entrance, where a stream of employees was leaving for the day. A guard stopped them as they approached the glass door entry.

"The museum closed twenty minutes ago," he said, raising a hand.

"We have an appointment with Dr. Chen." She passed him a note with his name and contact information.

"Follow me," he said. They entered the foyer of an expansive exhibit hall, empty of tourists with the lights already dimmed. The guard led them through several large rooms filled with paintings, tapestries, and sculptures, many depicting the Buddha. They proceeded into a smaller side hall that featured musical instruments, prayer wheels, and bronze and stone artifacts housed in glass cases. The guard approached a door on the back wall and knocked twice.

Dr. Chen Yuan pulled it open and stepped into the hall. The museum's director of Buddhist and Tibetan art was a spry, elderly man, dressed in a houndstooth jacket, khakis, and running shoes. He waved off the guard, looked up at the two tall guests, and smiled. "Welcome to the museum. I am so glad you arrived safely."

"Thank you for seeing us after hours," Summer said, shaking hands. "I apologize for our late arrival."

"It is no inconvenience, as I have been working late every night this week. We have been preparing a new exhibit for display. Come, I'll show you."

He took a few steps past a display case full of black stone tools and amulets to a narrow glass cabinet. Inside were a dozen strips of wood that resembled a collection of thick rulers. Each was carved from a different wood and varied in dimension, with unique symbols and images engraved on the sides.

"We just acquired a large collection of **zanpar**s from Nepal and Tibet." Chen beamed. "These are the first pieces that have been conserved and placed on display."

"What is a **zanpar**?" Summer asked.

"They are molds. One presses dough, typically made of barley and yak butter, into the engraving to produce a tiny effigy. The effigies were placed on special altars, for good fortune." He pointed to a dark walnut **zanpar**. "Hard to see since they just dimmed the lights, but that one was used at Jokhang Temple in Lhasa."

"They are very beautiful," Summer said.

Chen smiled again, at their polite interest, then shook his head. "I'm sorry. You must be tired from your travels. Please, come to my office and sit."

They returned to his office, which was overflowing with small crates. "More samples from the museum's repository." He guided them to a small table. A large pane of one-way glass allowed them a view of the exhibit hall.

The curator boiled water in an electric kettle and brewed a pot of green tea in an ancient ceramic urn. He carefully poured a cup for each of them and took a seat with Dirk and Summer at the table.

"So, you have discovered some Tibetan artifacts in the Philippines that belong to the museum?" He tried not to stare at the corroded aluminum case Dirk had been lugging.

Summer handed Chen the business card they had found with the artifacts as Dirk set the case on the table and unhooked the latches. Chen held the card and read it with reverence.

"Dr. Feng Zhoushan was a well-known expert in Tibetan art when the historic collection first went on display in Taiwan. I've read some of his journals and conservation notes. He expanded the museum's holdings of Tibetan artifacts some tenfold, through many trips to the region. Our records indicate he disappeared on a trip to India, when his flight vanished in bad weather somewhere between Taipei and Hong Kong."

"We believe we have found the plane he was in, an Avro Lancastrian," Dirk said. "It's in the surf off the northern coast of Luzon."

"The plane is in surprisingly good shape," Summer said. "We found this case inside."

Dirk opened the lid and removed the silk coverings, revealing the stone carvings. Chen's eyes instantly lit up. He reached into the case and removed one of the pieces, which was in the shape of a flower blossom. Chen studied it closely, weighing it in his hands, then replacing it in the case. He examined each sculpture in turn, carefully returning it to the case when he was finished.

"Quite remarkable," he said. "And yet, I've seen them before."

He stepped to a tall file cabinet and rifled through one of the drawers. He retrieved a file and spread the contents on the table. They were black and white photos of all eight of the small black carvings.

"What are they?" Summer asked.

"The carvings exemplify the **Tashi Tag Gye**, or eight auspicious symbols of Tibetan Buddhism. They represent gifts received when the Buddha first obtained enlightenment and are believed to bring good luck and secure protection. Each has its own significance. The lotus flower blossom, for example, represents original purity. They are rather common symbols in Tibet."

"So these are not especially unique?" Summer asked.

"On the contrary, these are quite rare, both for their material, called **thokcha**, and their provenance." He pointed to a typed sheet of notes included with the photos. "These particular carvings are very old. They were known to have come from the Nechung Monastery in Lhasa. Somehow, they ended up in private hands shortly after the Communist Chinese overran the country. Dr. Feng's notes indicate he had negotiated a temporary exhibit of the carvings here in Taipei. That is when the photos were taken, before they were put on display. The carvings were then lost with Dr. Feng in the plane crash. But now you have rescued them from oblivion."

"So they don't belong to the National Palace Museum?" Summer asked.

"I'm afraid not. Feng was returning them to India when he perished."

"There may be identification in the case." Summer tapped the stamped leather label under the lid.

"Yes, indeed." Chen read the label. "They apparently belong to a Tibetan in India, at least as of 1963. It indicates a name in care of the Tibetan Museum, in McLeod Ganj, India." He looked at Dirk and Summer with a wistful expression. "As much as I would like to keep them for display here, I'm afraid they rightfully belong to someone else."

Dirk picked up the carving of the lotus and bounced it in his hand. "These are very heavy. You mentioned a name for the type of stone they were carved from?"

"Thokcha," Chen said. "Only it's not just stone." He sat back in his chair and gazed at the ceiling. "There are conflicting stories, but the most common legend states that a meteor shower struck Tibet during the ascension of the first bestowed Dalai Lama in the year 1578. Several meteorite fragments were recovered and carved as altar offerings for the leading monasteries. The meteorite pieces are called **thokcha**, or sky iron. As you can see, they are incredibly dense. While the material is very difficult to work with, the Tibetans discovered that by heating the **thokcha** at a high temperature and then quickly cooling it in snow, the material could be fractured, and sculpted, in the hands of a skilled artisan. Some were carved into weapons and tools, but the larger pieces were reserved for religious artifacts. The most famous was a large statue known as the Nechung Idol." He shook his head. "Though it, too, disappeared. It was from the same monastery in Lhasa as the relics you have recovered."

Chen pointed toward the hallway. "We possess a nice collection of smaller **thokcha** items, which were also used to make amulets and other sacred objects. Only a handful of museums are known to have any."

"So these carvings were made from meteorites?" Summer said.

Chen nodded as Dirk passed her the lotus carving.

"Feel the material," Chen said. "It is most unique."

Summer rubbed a finger across the smooth relic, marveling at its significance, both culturally and geologically. She turned it over in her hand and noticed a gold streak across the side. "Scorch marks from entry through the atmosphere?"

Chen shrugged. "It is possible."

"These would seem to have great importance," Dirk said. "Can you help us return them to their rightful owner?"

"Of course. But first I would love to take some updated color photographs."

Chen retrieved a Nikon D6 camera from a side

cabinet. He positioned the carvings on a white cloth and carefully snapped several pictures of each piece. He was nearly finished when the crash of shattering glass sounded in the adjacent room.

Through the one-way window, they saw a shadowy figure ransacking one of the museum display cases.

14

"What's going on here?" Chen Yuan challenged, springing from his office.

The intruder gave Chen a blank look and turned back to his task. Wearing black jeans and a black shirt, he hunched over an artifacts case with a knapsack in one hand and a metal baton in the other. Shards of broken glass littered the floor around his feet.

It was the display case that held the **thokcha** artifacts. The thief pulled out the carved black objects and dropped them in the backpack.

Chen moved toward the man, calling for him to stop. As Chen stepped closer, the intruder dropped the backpack and turned toward him. He raised the metal baton high and lunged at the curator, swinging it like a samurai sword. Chen tried to jump back, but was a step slow. The baton struck him in the upper arm, breaking the bone with a muffled crunch.

Dirk and Summer spilled out of the office as Chen sunk to the ground. The assailant tossed the remaining **thokcha** artifacts into his knapsack and sprinted toward the exit.

"See if he's okay," Dirk said to Summer, then took off after the thief.

He had to thread his way through a maze of display cases to cross the room. By the time he reached the first exhibit room, the thief was in the foyer and rushing out the exit.

Dirk sprinted after him, his shoes pounding on the polished marble floor. Near the entrance, a figure lay supine next to the base of a Nepalese dragon statue. It was the guard who had escorted them to Chen's office. Dirk stopped to check on the man. A nasty bruise marked his temple, but no other signs of injury were evident. The guard's moaning and his heaving chest showed he was quite alive. Dirk pulled a silk drape from the base of the statue, fashioned it into a pillow, and slid it under the guard's head. Having done all he could do for him, Dirk continued the chase.

Bursting out the doors, he found a different environment than when they had arrived. The tourists and museum employees had departed, and the rain-dampened grounds were now empty. Night had fallen, but landscape lighting cast a rich yellow glow. Dirk glanced to his right at the Main Exhibition Hall. The imposing building was bathed in spotlights that made it appear luminescent against the dark mountainous backdrop.

Well ahead of him, he spotted the thief descending a steep hill that separated the East Wing from the museum's long entry courtyard. The man lost his footing and fell face-first, allowing Dirk to gain some steps.

Dirk hopped a railing and followed after him, skidding and sliding down the steep, wet embankment. At the bottom of the hill, he followed the man's trail through a row of trees and onto a manicured lawn that abutted the central walkway they had crossed to enter the museum.

The thief angled in the opposite direction, toward the street entrance, where a driveway looping off Zhishan Road served as a drop-off for taxis and buses. He glanced over his shoulder repeatedly, tracking Dirk's pursuit.

Across the flat terrain, Dirk capitalized on his longer stride and began to close the gap. He kept a steady pace, aided by a high level of stamina acquired by swimming on a regular basis. The man in front of him was fit, but not fast, and continued to lose ground.

At the far edge of the grass, the thief jumped onto the stone entryway and turned toward the street. Gasping, he sprinted past an elderly couple exiting the grounds, then ran beneath the ornamental archway. From there, a small plaza funneled into a wide stairway that descended to the street.

Dirk's chest burned with pain as he passed under the arch a few yards behind. He glanced about for police or security, but there were only a few straggling tourists. He willed himself to run faster. Ahead of him, the other man seemed to falter.

Racing across the plaza, Dirk closed to within a few steps as the thief reached the top of the stairs. The assailant bounded down the stairs two at a time, and Dirk followed suit.

Glancing ahead, Dirk saw the driveway was mostly empty. A taxi was picking up a couple at the foot of the stairs, and a city bus was pulling out from a stand a short distance behind that. A dark sedan had parked on the inside loop of the drive. Its lights flicked on as the driver started the engine.

The thief saw it, too, and angled toward the car as he reached the last step. Six feet above, Dirk realized the height gave him his last, best chance to catch the man. Sizing up his trajectory, he sprang off the stairs and lunged for the man.

He nearly fell short, but he stretched out his arms and grasped the man's backpack as he landed. The action pulled the assailant to a stop and dropped him to his knees, breaking Dirk's fall. The man popped up and tried to step into the street, but was jerked to a halt.

Dirk still had a grip on the backpack and refused to let go. Realizing he hadn't broken free, the thief whipped around his baton. Anticipating the blow,

Dirk let go of the pack and gave it a hard push. He then fell back, just avoiding the baton's arc.

The man staggered into the street in front of the idling taxi, but stayed on his feet. Facing the sidewalk, he looked at Dirk on the ground, then spun and ran toward the waiting car.

He stepped right in front of the oncoming city bus.

Before its driver could react, the coach knocked the thief flat and rolled over him. The driver stopped and swung open the passenger's door, then rushed out to check on the victim.

The thief's legs protruded from beneath the vehicle. Dirk helped the driver pull the man out by his legs, but his mangled torso gave no hope that he was still alive. Dirk noted he had a military haircut and carried a pistol in a shoulder holster beneath his jacket.

The bus driver began flailing his arms and proclaiming his innocence as the cabbie and some tourists gathered around. Summer had already summoned the police, and a siren sounded in the distance.

"This doesn't belong to him," Dirk said. He reached down and slipped the backpack off the man's shoulders and stepped to the curb.

Across the road, an engine revved. The dark sedan had crept forward so its occupant could see what had happened. The car then screeched forward, speeding away before the police arrived.

The driver of the taxi succeeded in calming the bus driver, then walked over to Dirk. "I saw the struggle. That man stole your backpack?"

"No. He took some artifacts from the museum."

The cabbie eyed the pack curiously. "It must be something valuable. Jewelry? Gemstones? Gold?"

"No." Dirk shook his head and casually gazed skyward. "Just some very old rocks."

15

The missile's propulsion assembly was longer than the **Stingray**'s width. Pitt and Giordino examined it from several angles, deciding how best to acquire it. Pitt ultimately approached the motor from a slope on one side, fighting a heavy current as he maneuvered the submersible at a low angle to the motor. Once centered on the object, he dropped the **Stingray** to the seafloor for better stability.

Giordino went to work, deploying the mechanical arm and picking his way across the assembly, searching for a place to grab hold. He spotted a small welded plate and tightened the articulated claw over it.

"Fingers crossed," he muttered, then raised the arm. It trembled a moment, then lifted the engine assembly off the sand, releasing a cloud of sediment that soon vanished in the current.

"We have liftoff," Pitt said. "If only we have enough room to carry it home."

"Too big for the basket, but I think I can retract the arm enough to carry it on the front skids."

Giordino guided the manipulator toward its receptacle, bringing the rocket motor with it until it brushed the submersible's nose. He lowered the arm until the assembly rested on the two forward skids.

He maintained a firm grip with the mechanical claw and twisted it forward slightly to lock the artifact in place. "If you don't do any barrel rolls on the way up, I think it'll stay in place."

"I'll keep the flaps down," Pitt replied. As he reached for the thruster controls, he noted a light off to the side. He elevated the submersible off the bottom and pivoted for a better look, fighting the current to keep the vessel steady.

In the far reaches of darkness shimmered a dozen tiny white bulbs. They glowed in distinct vertical rows, like strings of Christmas lights dangling from the surface.

"Electric, neon squid?" Giordino asked.

"The long arm of the **Melbourne**, more likely." Pitt felt a faint, buzzing pain in his ears. He propelled the submersible forward to take a better look.

They hadn't traveled far when they detected a deep hum, each unsure whether it was from internal vibration. The submersible began to buck as it fought to make headway.

"Mining ops?" Giordino said.

"I don't know, but the current's picked up." Pitt increased thrust as the submersible pitched and buffeted.

Then a high-pitched whine, like a jet turbine on overdrive, resounded through the submersible. Both men reached for their ears to block the sharply painful sound. Pitt felt like his entire skull was ringing. He forced a hand down to the yoke and tried to turn the submersible around. Then a second force hit.

An unseen wall of water struck the **Stingray** with the impact of an avalanche. The seafloor zoomed past beneath them as the submersible was shoved backward. For a moment, the vessel kept its orientation, then the front end began to rise. The rocket motor on the skids deflected the current, forcing up the prow. Pitt applied the thrusters to counterbalance the force, but the pressure was too much. The nose spun up and over, inverting the submersible. It continued to rotate in an uncontrolled spin.

"Purging ballast." Giordino reached for the control that would empty seawater from the main tank and send the **Stingray** into ascent.

He didn't make it. Bounding above the seabed, the submersible slammed into a seamount. The blow threw the men into their seatbacks and knocked the air from their lungs. The exterior floodlights went out, pitching the waters around them into blackness. The interior fell almost as dark as well, save for a console full of flashing warning lights.

The two men had little time to react, as the submersible continued rolling like a tumbleweed in a hurricane. The force was so great, the ten-ton submersible barreled up the slope of the seamount as if gravity failed to exist in the ocean depths.

Both men managed to tuck their legs beneath their chairs and remained seated as the **Stingray** rolled. But there was little free space around them, so they were slammed and knocked against the surrounding equipment. Loose manuals, water bottles, and laptops took to the air like mini missiles, striking them repeatedly during the endless revolutions.

The tumbling began to slow, but only because the submersible's increased speed bounced it across the sea bottom like a skipping stone. Pitt tried manipulating the thruster, but to no avail. The force was too powerful and too relentless. In the chaotic darkness, time and distance vanished in the mere effort to survive.

Eventually, the wicked force expended itself. The **Stingray** struck bottom, and its mangled skids dug into the sand for the final time. Gradually, the sea returned to its former state. The cold depths fell black and silent, enveloping the battered submersible that lay dead on the seafloor.

16

The sudden lurch almost tossed Stenseth from this bunk. The **Caledonia**'s captain shook off a short rest and sat upright, thinking the storm must have arrived early. He waited for a deep roll from the high seas to toss him in the opposite direction, but it never came. Another rogue wave? The ship still rocked from side to side, but not as severely as that lone deep wallow.

The chronometer over his desk read two-ten a.m. He splashed cold water on his face, dressed quickly in a crisp white uniform that would have passed a Naval Academy inspection, then left his cabin.

He made his way to the bridge, noting the winds had grown strong and the seas rough. The ship seemed to be holding relatively stable. The vessel's second officer, a man named Blake, was huddled over the radar screen. He looked up as Stenseth entered.

"Sir, I was just about to call you."

"Did we take a broadside wave, Mr. Blake?"

"Yes, sir. Quite out of the blue. We've had our nose to the weather." He motioned toward the ship's bow. "But we got tagged on our flank. Likely another rogue wave."

Stenseth gazed at their location on an overhead monitor. "The source would be different than the ones that struck earlier."

"Seismic activity," Blake said. "At least that's what one of the scientists aboard thinks. He says we're right in the heart of the Ring of Fire. Plenty of tectonic activity in these parts that can generate subsurface landslides."

"True," Stenseth said. "What's the status of the **Stingray**?"

Blake glanced at an open logbook. "They're past the one-hundred-and-twenty-minute mark on the bottom. They should have another hour or so before ascending."

"Are we in communication?"

Blake picked up a ship's phone and dialed the submersible's operations center. He spoke briefly, then hung up.

"Ops reports a disturbance with the communications link. Both acoustic telephone and USBL data transponder are nonresponsive. They're trying to update the link. The last transmission was about twenty minutes ago, when all systems were operational."

"Let me know as soon as we hear anything."

"Yes, sir."

Stenseth stepped to the bridge wing and peered out the portside window. "Something to do with our neighbors?" he asked aloud. The lights of the **Melbourne** twinkled a half mile away.

"They deployed some equipment into the ocean earlier." Blake passed a pair of binoculars to the captain. "It looked like they were dropping some cabled equipment over the side. But we didn't actually see any ROVs."

Stenseth focused the lenses on the nearby ship. "I see the booms and cable alongside the rail, but nothing appears to be deployed now. They must have reeled in whatever they had out. Odd that they deployed it over the side, rather than from the stern."

As he lowered the binoculars, a deep, muffled boom sounded across the water. The deck rocked beneath his feet, and the stern rose noticeably a moment before settling.

"What the heck was that?" the second officer asked.

Stenseth reached for a buzzing bridge phone.

"Engine room, Reese here," a gruff voice shouted.

"I hear you fine, Reese."

"Sorry, sir. My ears are ringing after the bang."

"What's going on down there?"

"Not sure, sir. Explosion of some sort. At the stern, maybe external to the ship."

"Any damage?"

"We're taking on water at the aft bulkhead. It's not good. We could use some extra help down here."

"I'll get some men there right away. Everyone all right?"

"Aye, sir. But I think we're going to have a battle on our hands."

Stenseth hung up the phone and turned to Blake. "Sound the general alarm. I need a damage control team to the engine room right away. Then get yourself down there and give me a full assessment."

"Yes, sir. Any idea of the cause?"

Stenseth shook his head. "May be external. Wake the third officer and have him examine the stern."

It didn't take long for Stenseth to discover that the **Caledonia** was severely damaged. A gaping hole was found below the port waterline, and hull plates were buckled along nearby sections. Damage control teams attacked the breach, while supporting crewmen deployed emergency pumps.

Stenseth weighed his options. If the engine room flooded, they would find themselves without power. That was dangerous enough in normal weather, but potentially fatal in the throes of an approaching typhoon. He shook his head and radioed the **Melbourne** to request assistance.

Unbelievably, the mining ship failed to answer his pleas. It confirmed his worst fears. Someone on the **Melbourne** wanted them sunk.

Yet the explosion had not been meant to sink

the **Caledonia**, just damage her. As Zheng had expected, the NUMA ship's well-trained crew was able to slow the flooding, yet there was too much damage to fully overcome. Slowly and steadily, the leaking seawater was overwhelming the emergency pumps. Blake relayed the assessment to Stenseth by phone a short time later.

"We've slowed the major leak, and will continue to shore up the smaller ones. But I'm afraid it's not enough. All emergency pumps are operating, but the water level is still rising."

"How long before it impacts our propulsion?"

Blake paused. "Four, maybe five hours, if we're lucky."

"Understood. Have the chief engineer give us as much power as he can muster for as long as he can. Bridge out."

Stenseth stepped to a navigation station and pulled up a map of the region. Four hours in heavy seas meant a range of fifty to sixty miles. He scanned a rough circle around them. There was only one option for a safe port, Kaohsiung, on the southeast coast of Taiwan. He dragged a line across the screen with a computer mouse to calculate the distance. Eighty-five miles.

"Taiwan or bust," he muttered. He relayed the heading to the helmsman as the third officer rushed onto the bridge.

"Mr. Blake, have the number two tender stocked with emergency provisions and a three-man crew, then prepare to deploy," Stenseth ordered. "Get us under way the second she's in the water. You have the conn."

Stenseth climbed down the side companionway and sprinted to the submersible operations center near the stern. The wind howled across the deck, and a light rain pelted his uniform before he ducked into the bay. Two women and a man in blue jumpsuits sat at workstations in front of a wall with several large video screens. Each was busy examining data at his or her station. But all the wall-mounted monitors showed a snowy, blank picture.

"What's the status of the **Stingray**?" he asked the collective group.

The woman seated closest to him shook her head. "I'm sorry, Captain, but we've lost all contact with them. Communications became impaired about thirty minutes ago, and have since gone completely dark."

"No diagnostics or tracking?"

"I'm afraid not. All shipboard systems were reporting as normal. There was a sudden acoustic disturbance that lasted several minutes, then all went silent." She looked at Stenseth with concern. "It's very unusual, sir. Voice and data, on redundant systems, were all lost within a five-minute span."

"When were they scheduled to surface?"

She glanced at her screen. "Approximately fifty minutes from now. We've posted a lookout, just in case."

Stenseth grimaced. Waiting on station that long would eliminate any chance of the ship making it to port under its own power.

"Maybe they can hear us," he said. "Signal them that the **Caledonia** has to move off-site, but that a support craft will remain on station."

The woman turned pale. "Leave them, sir, in this weather? Mr. Pitt is down there."

Stenseth looked down at the deck, well aware of his decision. "The ship's survival is at stake. I'm afraid we have no choice. Keep trying to reach them . . . And let me know if you hear anything. Anything at all."

He stepped onto the deck as a large, enclosed tender was hoisted over the rail. Stenseth spoke to the three men aboard.

"We don't know the status of the **Stingray**. She's scheduled to surface in an hour, but could be up sooner. Stay on-site as long as you are able. You can evacuate south to the leeward side of one of the Philippine Islands if the weather dictates. I'm sorry, it's liable to get rough."

"We've seen worse, sir," replied a burly crewman with a flattop. "We've got plenty of provisions and medical equipment aboard, and this bucket can handle anything the seas throw at us. We'll wait it out as long as we have to. Take care of the ship, Captain, and don't worry about us."

"Thanks. I'll get a vessel back to you as soon as I can."

As the boat was lowered into the sea, he gave the men a wave and headed to the bridge. The **Caledonia** swayed beneath his feet, with a noticeable list to the stern. He burst onto the bridge, looked to the second officer, and gave the hardest order of his life. "All ahead full, Mr. Blake. Get us to Kaohsiung yesterday."

As the order was relayed to the helm, Stenseth stepped to the side window and gazed at the sea with anguish. He hoped to heaven that beneath the frenzied black waters, Pitt and Giordino were still alive.

17

The wiry man wearing a long robe exited the Dalai Lama's private living quarters and closed the door quietly behind him. He padded down a hallway and entered a large office several doors down. Like the rest of the residence, it had been tastefully constructed, featuring a parquet floor, cedar paneling, and wide picture windows that captured the snowcapped Indian Himalayas to the north. Modern furniture, blended with antique rugs and tapestries, reflected the Dalai Lama's forward-thinking nature while honoring the traditions of a fourteen-hundred-year-old religion.

A man in a red robe sat on a tribal carpet, his legs crossed and his eyes closed in meditation. Though in his early sixties, Khyentse Rinpoche still carried a boyish face behind thick eyeglasses. An elder lama, Rinpoche was deemed a reincarnated teacher of dharma and held a position of high respect in the Tibetan religion. His eyes opened at the arrival of the visitor, a man almost his own age, and he looked up with an anxious gaze. "How is the state of His Holiness?"

"Not well." The thin man took a seat on a couch as Rinpoche rose and moved to an adjacent chair. "His spirit is as high as the mountains, but his body trembles like the poppies in the wind. He has a high fever to accompany his other discomforts, and I fear for his safety if it does not break soon."

"We must consider the potential outcome," Rinpoche said.

"It is a moment I have feared for a long while."

"Kuten, are you not prepared for what follows?"

Kuten was not the man's name, but a term for his duties as a channel to the spiritual realm. His official title was the medium for the State Oracle of Tibet. But he was better known as the Nechung Oracle, a position that originated at the monastery of the same name in Lhasa. When he transcended into a trance-like state, the Kuten was capable of channeling Pehar, the divine protector of both the Dalai Lama and the exiled Tibetan government, to obtain prophecy and advice.

The Kuten shook his head with a forlorn look in his eyes, clearly ill at ease. "Should His Holiness elect to reincarnate, I know what will come next. But I will be unable to fulfill my duties without the consultation of Pehar."

Rinpoche stared at the Kuten with an arched brow. "I do not understand. You are the Oracle.

You have the ability to channel Pehar, and have done so on many occasions. If the Dalai Lama should depart us, you can call on the wisdom of Pehar to identify the path to the next reincarnate."

The Kuten shook his head. "It is true I can act as medium for Pehar. But the question of a reincarnate requires his physical presence, only not through me. It is with the Nechung Idol that the path to all Dalai Lamas is illuminated. The Nechung Idol must be present for both the physical and spiritual deliverance from Pehar to lead us on our journey to the next reincarnate. It is the way it has always been."

"But the selection cannot be left to chance," Rinpoche said. "We know what the Chinese have in store. They will deliberately select the next Dalai Lama from within their confines and keep him under their tight control. We must have Pehar guide us to the true successor." He stood and paced about the room. "Where is the Nechung Idol?"

"It was lost at the time of the Dalai Lama's escape from Tibet in 1959."

"Has there been an attempt to locate it?"

"I asked Norsang in security to initiate an investigation a few weeks ago."

"Tenzin Norsang, of the Dalai Lama's security detail?"

The Kuten nodded. "Yes. He has contact with many of the old warriors involved in the Dalai Lama's escape from Tibet. His father was a Chushi

Gangdruk." It was the name of the Tibetan guerrilla resistance force organized after the Chinese
invasion.

"Of course. Why don't we see what he's found?"
Rinpoche stepped to a desk phone and dialed a
number. He spoke briefly, then hung up. "He's
here, and will be sent up at once."

Barely two minutes later, a young man appeared
in the doorway.

"Come in, Norsang, and please sit down."
Rinpoche closed the door behind him.

Muscular and tall for a Tibetan, the security man
took a seat opposite the Kuten. He moved with a
wraith-like grace, while carrying an air of relaxed
confidence. He wore Western attire—khaki pants,
a button-down shirt, and colored socks, having left
his shoes outside the residence.

"Thank you for responding so promptly,"
Rinpoche said.

"I serve at the wish of the monastery."

Like many who surrounded the Dalai Lama,
Norsang was a second-generation servant of the
spiritual leader. His late father had also served on
the Dalai Lama's security detail, dating back to
his time in Lhasa. Unlike most of those who assisted
the Dalai Lama, Norsang was college-educated and
had also served briefly in the Indian Army.

An uncomfortable silence stifled the room.

"We wish to know the status of your investigation into the Nechung Idol," Rinpoche finally said,

realizing the Kuten feared the answer too much to ask himself.

"It is not an easy task to resurrect the events of the past," Norsang said. "I have spoken to several families who lived in Lhasa during the 1950s and had sons who studied at the Nechung Monastery, or visited it in the subsequent decade. I have also visited the local museums for historical information. Regrettably," he said, "there are too few now living who survive from that era. I have learned that when the Chinese moved additional forces into Lhasa in March of 1959, prompting the departure of His Holiness, things became quite chaotic. As you know, there was much bloodshed, and life for those in Tibet became quite oppressive."

"As it remains to this day," Rinpoche said.

"Many monasteries were destroyed during that era. Hundreds of monks disappeared," Norsang said. "But several lamas from Nechung did escape with the Dalai Lama."

"Yes, the previous Oracle and three lamas, who helped establish the monastery here," the Kuten said.

Norsang nodded. "Unfortunately, those men have all passed away. I have spoken to some who knew them and their families. Very brave men, all of them."

"And what of the Nechung Idol?"

"There was a hurried exit from Lhasa," Norsang said. "The Oracle and the Nechung lamas were with the Dalai Lama at Potala Palace at the time of their escape. They did not have time to return to Nechung to safeguard anything."

"So the Chinese came in," the Kuten said, "and destroyed everything at the monastery?"

"Yes, but much of the destruction came later, in the 1960s, during Mao's Cultural Revolution. Still, I can find no evidence that the Nechung Idol remained at the monastery after the events of March 1959. Sadly, there is no clue to its whereabouts. It may have been destroyed by the Chinese or taken to Beijing."

"Or sold in the black market to a private collector," the Kuten said.

"Also a possibility."

"Could it have been hidden?" the Kuten asked.

"Perhaps," Norsang said. "There was an elder lama known to have been left at the monastery when the others fled with the Dalai Lama. His name was Thupten Gungtsen. Regrettably, he seems to have disappeared from the historical record at the same time and is presumed to be a casualty of events."

"So there is no hope." The Kuten's eyes turned glassy as he stared at the carpet.

Norsang looked at the Kuten and took a deep breath. "At the moment, I fear that hope is our best ally. But I do have one more lead to pursue, a friend of my great-uncle. He resides in the hills close by and has reportedly spoken of Thupten

Gungtsen. With your permission, I would like to speak with him."

"Is it even worth the effort?" Rinpoche asked.

The Kuten countered with a laser beam glare at Norsang and a slight nod.

"I will meet with the old man. Perhaps he knows something." Norsang tried to sound optimistic. "He was a Chushi Gangdruk guerrilla who trained with the CIA. His name is Ramapurah Chodron."

THE SECLUDED HILLSIDE shack, across a steep gully from the Tsuglagkhang complex that housed the Dalai Lama's residence, appeared unfit for a squatter. Its mud brick walls were crumbling, while its battered roof appeared ready to collapse with the next drop of rain. One corner remained charred black from a long-ago fire. Surrounding the perimeter were a handful of rusty barrels and some scattered trash, which added to the decrepit appearance. Only a careful observer would note that several antennas rose along the face of the aged chimney, painted flat black to match the soot.

With a direct line of sight to the Dalai Lama's residence, it served as the perfect eavesdropping station for the two Chinese operatives stationed inside.

As the meeting in the conference room with the Kuten broke up, one of the Chinese listeners tapped the keys of a laptop computer. The private conversation, detected by a concealed transmitter on the residence grounds and relayed across the valley, was digitally recorded and sent by encrypted packet to a People's Liberation Army satellite.

"Anything worthwhile?" asked the second agent, removing a set of earphones.

The man gave a wishful nod. "Something, in fact, that might just get us rotated out of this stinking hovel before winter sets in."

18

Is there any sign of the submersible?"

Zheng fumbled to light a cigarette as he asked the question. He stood in the center of the **Melbourne**'s operations control room, which now resembled the combat information center on a modern warship. The dimly lit bay was filled with a dozen computer workstations, each equipped with large graphic displays. The consoles formed an arc facing a massive video screen on the bulkhead.

The screen displayed a half dozen video feeds showing blurry images from the seafloor. A vertical band on one side displayed three additional inputs—a three-hundred-and-sixty-degree surface radar display, a subsurface sonar feed, and a three-dimensional animation of the seafloor beneath the ship. In addition, the animation showed the equipment deployed from the **Melbourne**—numerous illuminated cables, tiny sensors at their ends, dangling from the ship, as well as a small remotely operated vehicle.

One of Zheng's commandos looked up from a workstation. "Nothing has been detected from the ROV's sonar unit."

"What is its range?"

"Approximately a hundred meters."

"And what does our host have to say about it?" Zheng turned to Alistair Thornton.

The mining magnate was sitting in a chair, his wrists bound behind his back. Beside him, an Asian man in a white lab coat was similarly bound, but hunched over, unconscious. Thornton remained awake, though dried blood caked his hair and shirt. His face was swollen, a black, puffy eyelid blocking half his vision. Despite the physical abuse, he looked up at Zheng with a defiant stare.

"Mr. Thornton?" Zheng said. "Do I need to ask Ning to entice some further conversation?"

The bald commando stood nearby, clutching a bloodstained bludgeon as he rocked on his heels.

Thornton forced a smile. "The submersible bloody well blew across the bottom of the ocean, you damn fool. What do you think?"

"Your diamond mining equipment," Zheng said with a smirk, "would seem to have very impressive power."

Another commando entered the bay and approached Zheng. "A call for you, sir, on the satellite phone. It's Colonel Yan."

Zheng nodded and turned to one of his subordinates. "Retrieve the acoustic lines, but keep the ROV scanning the bottom. Determine if there is any debris in this area."

He made his way forward to the bridge. Before taking the call, he peered out the windscreen. To the northwest, the lights of the **Caledonia** were shrinking in the distance. Closer off the starboard flank, he studied the lights from a small tender that bobbed in the growing seas. Zheng frowned and turned to the commando manning the helm. "Notify me when the NUMA ship is over the horizon."

He stepped to a corner table at the rear of the bridge where a military satellite phone had been wired to an external antenna. "Zheng reporting," he said.

"You have a status update for me?" Yan's voice was loud and clear, though the encrypted satellite link carried a slight time lag.

"Yes, Colonel. My apologies for not reporting earlier. We have disabled the American research ship, and it is now departing the area. They have deployed a small boat to wait for a submersible deployed on the seafloor. We have taken care of the submersible, however, and will dispose of the boat shortly."

"Do not create an international incident, nephew."

"No, sir. There is no reason to worry. A strong storm approaches, which provides the perfect cover.

Any remaining suspicions would only accrue to the Australian ship."

"You were rash in boarding her, which makes for a new problem."

"They were operating close to the presumed debris zone. We feared they had already recovered something, but that now appears unfounded. Since it is a private vessel, I thought it prudent to act. We can sail it into our territorial waters and sink it without attention when we have concluded operations here. By good fortune, we have stumbled upon something of great value."

"What of the Americans? Did they find or recover anything?"

"The satellite imaging you provided indicates they couldn't have made more than one dive before we arrived. We observed one recovery, which may have included some small pieces at best. It is highly doubtful they retrieved anything of value, if it even was from the rocket. As it is, the submersible will never surface again."

"I should hope that is the case. A salvage vessel has been appropriated and will be sailing in your direction shortly. What of your own recovery efforts?"

"We have just initiated a survey with the ship's ROV to check the area where the Americans were operating. There is nothing to report yet."

"Very well. You are to stay on-site and survey

what you can, while monitoring the area for any other activity."

"Yes, sir. The storm is nearly upon us, so we will be forced to suspend any search operations for a day or so. Have you heard from my other team?"

"Yes. We have some leads from Dr. Liu, and they are moving now to acquire the samples he seeks. Aquisitions that require additional operations of delicacy."

"The men of Rocket Force Special Ops will not let you down, sir."

"I am counting on it."

"We will do our best. Colonel, are you alone?"

"Yes."

"Then I must tell you something I have discovered that may be more important than the rocket. It is about this mining ship."

A half hour later, Colonel Yan hung up the secure phone in his office. He sat back in his chair and stared at the ceiling a long while, trying to absorb what his nephew had told him. He leaned forward, pulled a file from atop his desk, and rifled through the pages. Though he had seen the perquisites of his job gradually vanish, the bureaucracy had yet to cancel his receipt of the daily intelligence briefing issued for the military's top officials.

After a moment's searching, he found the page he was looking for. He scrolled down the sheet and stopped at a boldfaced heading.

**U.S. Vice President and Taiwan President
to meet during American naval fleet visit in
Kaohsiung to discuss new defense pact.**

"Perfect," Yan said to himself, feeling better than
he had in weeks. "Absolutely perfect."

19

Dr. Chen was sitting upright in his hospital bed, chatting amiably with a man in a blue suit, when Dirk and Summer entered the room. The curator looked up and smiled.

"Here are my American friends now," he said. "This is a most pleasant surprise."

Summer carried a vase of flowers she had purchased in the lobby and placed them on the nightstand. "How are you feeling?"

Chen tipped up his left arm, covered in a soft cast from his shoulder to his wrist. "A bit immobile on the left side, but otherwise quite well. Summer, Dirk, may I introduce Mr. Lee Hong, the assistant director of the National Palace Museum?" He turned to his colleague. "Hong, these are the people who recovered the **thokcha** artifacts."

The bespectacled man pushed up his glasses, bowed to Dirk and Summer, then shook their hands. "The museum is extremely grateful for your actions, and for helping Dr. Chen."

"We were happy to help," Summer said.

Chen turned to Dirk. "I was told you made a daring chase after the culprit."

"I just wanted to see the museum grounds," Dirk joked. "Is the guard all right?"

"Yes," Lee said. "He was knocked cold, but was quite fine once he came around. Apparently, the thief had hidden in a bathroom until the building was closed. The guard surprised him in the foyer after escorting you to Dr. Chen's office. The thief hit him with the same weapon that broke our friend's arm."

"A nasty baton," Dirk said. "I'm glad the artifacts were recovered, but I didn't mean for anybody to be killed. Was he a known criminal?"

"No," Chen said. "Hong was just telling me the man was not Taiwanese."

The administrator nodded. "The police told me he arrived on an indirect flight from the mainland under what they now believe to be a false passport. Hence, they don't have an actual identification."

"It sounds like he was specifically targeting the museum's **thokcha** artifacts," Summer said. "Are they that valuable?"

Chen tried to shrug. "There were considerably more valuable artifacts in some of the other cases. But private collectors are choosy about their desires, if that was the impetus for the theft."

"Which reminds me," Lee said. "Did you hear there was a similar break-in at the Asian Civilisations Museum in Singapore?"

Chen shook his head.

"I heard from the museum director," Lee said. "It was also a targeted theft of Tibetan pieces. Their collection of **thokcha** artifacts happened to be in storage, but they may have been after the same artifacts."

"That can be no coincidence," Chen said.

"Must be someone with deep pockets," Dirk said, "to assault a pair of Asia's largest museums."

"Deep pockets and a lot of nerve." Chen looked at Summer. "You best be careful while you are in possession of the Nechung carvings."

"We'll be happy to dispose of them as soon as possible," Dirk said.

"What is your intent?" Lee asked.

Dirk started to shrug, but Summer cleared her throat. "I contacted NUMA's Assistant Director, and we've been authorized to proceed to India with the case and return it to its owner."

"You didn't . . ." Dirk said, unaware of the edict.

Chen nodded. "It will be a rewarding venture, of this I am certain. Please let me know how it goes. And don't forget me," he said with a wink, "if you should run across any other Tibetan antiquities that can be shared with our museum."

Dirk and Summer bid Chen a speedy recovery and said their good-byes. As they walked out of the hospital, Dirk turned to his sister. "So what's all this about going to India?"

"I couldn't get through to the **Caledonia** last night, so I emailed Rudi Gunn. He gave us the okay to divert to India on the way to the Maldives. We've got a direct flight to New Delhi booked for this afternoon."

Dirk looked at his sister and shook his head. Even when Summer was young, she had a wanderlust that kept her on the go. He used to call her the Shark, not for ferociousness, but because she was always moving forward.

"I had thought we might explore Taiwan before we left," he said. "The mountains, the lakes, the all-night karaoke bars."

Summer stopped in her tracks and gave him a cold stare.

"Absolutely not," she said, in sober rebuttal. "I've heard you sing before."

20

Margot paced around the tiny cabin for the thousandth time. Two hours had passed since the commandos had dragged away her father at gunpoint, and she couldn't help but fear the worst. Her mind kept replaying the image of the murdered first officer. Murphy's bloodied body had been left sprawled across the bridge deck like so much forgotten roadkill. The intruders were cold-blooded killers, and the odds looked slim that her father's fate would be any different than Murphy's. She had to summon help, but couldn't do it trapped in a cabin. She had to find a way out.

The answer came when she stubbed her toe on the wooden leg of a tiny writing table wedged in the corner of the cabin. She hopped backward from the table and noticed the leg had twisted. She returned to the table, grasped the leg, and gave it a twist. It turned freely, being held in place by a single thick screw only.

Margot removed the leg, then propped the table, with its remaining three legs, against the bulkhead so it remained upright. She gripped the freed maple piece and swung it through the air like a baseball bat. Not a gun or knife, but maybe just as good for what she needed.

She stepped to the doorway with her new weapon and flicked off the light, plunging the interior into darkness. She waited several minutes, letting her eyes adjust, while moving to one side of the door. Margot took a deep breath, then reached out and rapped on the door three times with the leg.

"Can you please help me?" she called.

There was no response.

She took another breath and was preparing to call out again when she heard the door handle turn. She raised the table leg and stood poised as the door was pushed open.

The guard took a tentative step in, his assault rifle raised in his arms. The dim hallway light failed to illuminate the room, so he reached across with his left hand and groped for the light switch. Margot could see enough movement to react and swung with all her might.

As the overhead light flashed on, the leg's blunt end smashed the guard's hand against the bulkhead. The crunch of bones was followed by a scream as the guard pulled his hand back. He doubled over in pain for an instant before jerking upright to bring his weapon to bear.

Margot didn't give him the chance.

She swung again, harder than before, her target clearly visible in the light. The wooden weapon struck the guard square in the jaw, cracking the maple in two. His head snapped back, and he wilted to the floor.

Margot dropped the cracked table leg and approached the guard. He lay facedown, unconscious, but was still breathing. She grabbed his sleeve and pulled, dragging his body fully into the cabin. She closed the door and picked up the rifle that had clattered to the floor. Having seldom fired a weapon, she decided to leave it behind and stashed it under a mattress.

She stripped the sheets from one of the bunks and used them to bind the guard's ankles and wrists behind his back. A twisted pillowcase was just long enough to wrap over his mouth. She winced at his bloodied face as she tied the case tight behind his head.

Margot crept into the corridor and made her way to the nearest outside exit. At night, she'd be harder to find on the ship's crowded exterior deck, where pieces of machinery offered ready places to hide.

But what about her father? Alistair Thornton was likely being held either on the bridge or in the subsea operations bay, where he could provide instruction on using the ship's equipment. An empty spot on the deck beside a crane indicated cabling had been deployed over the port rail, so the operations bay was more likely.

She crept along the bulkhead toward the ops's main entrance, then halted. She remembered there was a utility room at the back of the bay that had an entrance on the starboard side. It would be a safer entry point, if it was unlocked.

Turning and moving aft, she was pelted by a gusting light rain. Through the gloom, the decks appeared empty. Her father had said about a dozen commandos had boarded the ship. As she snuck through the shadows, she hoped none were alert.

The ship rocked heavily in the swells as she made her way to the stern. As long as she could, she held tight against the bulkhead and its overhanging shadows. As she skulked into the open to bypass a large windlass, she froze at the sight of a tiny red glow near the rail. A guard with a cigarette puffed out a cloud of smoke, then tossed the butt over the rail. Wearing all black, with an assault rifle dangling across his chest, he almost blended in with the night.

Margot held her breath, then slowly scrunched down low, her back against the windlass, trying to make herself invisible beneath its horizontal spool. The commando moved in her direction, but his eyes were on the rain-pelted sea. He gripped the rail as the ship rolled and swayed, until he made his way past the windlass, and Margot.

She let out a silent breath once he was gone from view and resumed her journey. She continued to the starboard side of the ship, stopping every few yards to take stock of her surroundings. As she approached the utility room entrance, a murmur of voices came from the deck up ahead. She lurched forward and twisted the door handle. It was locked.

The voices grew louder, and Margot saw the dancing beam of a flashlight making its way in her direction. Had they already discovered her escape?

The side wall of the operations bay offered no cover, so she sprinted across the deck to a dark object by the rail. It was one of the ship's tenders, stationed beneath a large crane. She felt along the hull and backtracked toward its stern. The boat was mounted on a wooden deck rack, which offered a foothold. Margot climbed onto the rack, pulled herself over the transom, and dropped flat onto the stern deck. The boat had an enclosed wheelhouse, so she crawled across the deck, entered it, and crouched beneath the pilot's seat.

The men stopped, their voices rising alongside the boat. They were speaking Mandarin, so Margot couldn't understand them, but their tone didn't sound urgent. Their voices fell silent, then a whirring generator sprang to life. Margot felt the boat she was in rock slightly, then clomping as someone began climbing aboard.

The footfalls of heavy boots sounded across the

fiberglass deck as a commando stepped toward the wheelhouse. Margot cowered under the seat as he approached the doorway. But the commando didn't enter. Instead, he pulled himself onto the roof. Margot heard the sound of a cable sliding across overhead, and she felt a sickening realization. The commandos didn't know she was there—and were about to deploy the boat.

A crane was lowered to the tender, and the commando attached a lift cable. He climbed down from the roof and glanced into the darkened wheelhouse, but failed to notice Margot. He moved to the back of the boat and sat on the transom as the cables were drawn taut a minute later, and the boat lifted into the air.

Margot felt her heart pounding as she contemplated what to do. She crawled forward from the pilot's seat to a small, step-down storage area. Operating by touch, she opened the narrow doors and found the cabinets stuffed with life jackets and emergency provisions. The wheelhouse offered no place to hide.

In mere seconds, the boat would be lowered over the side and boarded. She scrambled on her knees to the open door. The commando was still sitting on the transom, speaking with someone on the ship. The deck between offered a pair of side benches, but again no cover.

The boat wallowed beneath her as it was swung over the ship's rail and began to descend. Out of time and out of options, she crawled to the seaward rail. A narrow catwalk ran along the side of the wheelhouse to the bow, and Margot climbed onto it. Pulling herself forward to hide her feet, she lay flat on the narrow ledge and closed her eyes as three armed men jumped onto the deck behind her.

21

Hiram Yaeger sat at his usual command post, the apex of a large horseshoe-shaped table in the NUMA Computer Resource Center. He faced a massive floor-to-ceiling video board peppered with live data feeds from the agency's worldwide network of ocean buoys and sensors. Yaeger was studying a weather radar image at the top of the video board when Rudi Gunn walked in and took a seat next to him.

"You've heard about the **Caledonia**?" Gunn asked.

"Yes. I was just trying to see what sort of weather conditions she is facing en route to Taiwan." He pointed to the upper portion of the screen. "She's the black dot up there."

A square displayed a billowy mass of gray clouds from edge to edge. The small dot was superimposed near the lower center, while a yellow semicircle at the top represented the southern coast of Taiwan.

"Looks like she's got a rough ride every inch of the way," Gunn said.

"She's right in the thick of the storm. The saving grace, from a navigation standpoint, is the ship and storm are both moving in the same general direction."

"What about Pitt and Giordino?"

"The **Caledonia** has relayed all their tracking and diagnostic data. I've run it through Max," he said, referring to the artificial female interface he had created to communicate with the advanced supercomputer behind the video wall. "Max thinks there was an underwater disturbance of some sort. The last readings from the submersible indicate they were moving at a high speed across the seafloor."

"What would have caused that?" Gunn asked.

"Something of a mystery. The duty officers aboard the **Caledonia** report a mining ship named **Melbourne** was positioned nearby and engaged in some sort of activity." He displayed a photo of the ship he'd found online.

"Looks to be a large commercial vessel, but nothing unusual there," Gunn said. "Could it have been an explosion?"

"It's possible. Unfortunately, the **Melbourne** is offering no assistance or even communications. With the weather situation, we're talking at least forty-eight hours before an ROV or submersible can be deployed on-site to conduct a search."

Gunn had expected bad news, but the hopelessness of the situation shook him. Even if Pitt and Giordino were still alive at the bottom of the sea, they would have a long wait until rescue. "I've informed the Vice President," he said. "We're meeting on Capitol Hill to inform Loren."

Yaeger looked down and shook his head. "I wish there was better news to offer."

"Stay on it, Hiram, and let me know if you come up with anything more."

"Will do."

Gunn started to rise, but Yaeger held him up. "Before you go, there's one unrelated thing I wanted to share. Summer emailed me photos of the Tibetan carvings they discovered in the Philippines."

Gunn nodded. "She and Dirk are on their way to India to return them."

"It turns out they are carved from a material called **thokcha**. It's a Tibetan term that means 'sky iron.'"

Gunn considered the term. "Sky iron? Do you mean meteorites?"

"Exactly. It turns out that the break-in at the Taipei museum was for artifacts of the same material. Within the past two days, there have been similar smash-and-grabs at museums in Singapore, Hong Kong, and New Delhi. Each time, they took items made of this same stuff."

"It sounds like the work of a wealthy and unscrupulous collector."

"No," Yaeger said. "There's evidence that it's a state-sponsored effort by the People's Republic of China. The thief killed in Taipei is believed to be a mainland Chinese operative. Possibly the same with all of the attempts."

"China," Gunn said. "Were the other thefts successful?"

"The Singapore museum had most of their display rotated into storage at the time, so only one small item was taken. Police responded quickly in Hong Kong and disrupted the attempt there. I have no details about the New Delhi heist."

"Why would the Chinese act so brazenly to acquire Tibetan pieces?"

"I posed that question to Max. One of her theories is intriguing."

Yaeger typed on a keyboard and retrieved the photo of a tiny yak carved from a shiny black material. The photo was part of an article from a scientific journal.

"Max ran across this study of **thokcha** artifacts conducted by the University of Adelaide. It's not the cultural factors that are interesting, but the physical makeup of the pieces they tested. Laboratory analysis revealed that a number of the samples were composed of a rare type of meteorite called mesosiderites."

"Does that make a difference?"

"It does when the material is examined at the atomic level. Besides the usual mix of iron and nickel found in most meteorites, some specimens show an unusual combination of other rare elements, including hafnium, tantalite, and reidite."

"Okay," Gunn said. "What else?"

"These elements are extremely difficult to combine uniformly in a lab setting, but are found naturally in that state in the certain samples. It's believed it has something to do with the materials being superheated as they entered the atmosphere, combined with the pressure at impact when they strike the ground. For whatever reason, the molecules are realigned and tightly packed in a dense structure. The result is an amalgam with remarkable thermal properties. The **thokcha** appears to withstand temperatures exceeding five thousand degrees Celsius, which is higher than the composite materials used in our space program."

Gunn slowly nodded. "That makes for a compelling reason to acquire samples of the stuff."

"Agreed. I spoke with an Air Force buddy who was remotely viewing the components that Pitt and Giordino had retrieved earlier. He told me the Chinese missile was flying at a record speed, but likely didn't make it due to thermal failure. Hypersonic speed creates extreme friction, and preventing the resulting meltdown is a major hurdle in developing faster missiles. It's possible the Chinese believe something in these meteorites can solve the problem."

"So if they can use or duplicate the **thokcha**

material for their missile housings," Gunn said, "they can create an arsenal of hypersonic weapons—faster than anything else on the planet."

Yaeger gave a concerned nod. "The Pentagon would have no answer . . . and would run the risk of being overwhelmed in a shooting match."

"We best pass that information along to the Air Force." Gunn glanced at his watch. "I'll also advise the Vice President, whom I am now late to meet."

The drive from the NUMA building on the Virginia side of the Potomac to the Capitol took less than ten minutes, as Gunn hit a few green lights along the way. After parking in an underground lot at the Rayburn House Office Building, he hurried to the fourth floor. He found Vice President James Sandecker pacing the hallway with a Secret Service contingent in tow.

"Sorry I'm late, sir," Gunn said.

"Just been here a minute."

James Sandecker was a small man with an outsized personality. He was well respected in Washington as a tough administrator and nobody's fool. As a retired Navy Admiral, he had headed up NUMA years earlier, tapping Rudi Gunn as one of his first hires. With a shock of red hair and a matching Van Dyke beard, Sandecker peered at Gunn with determined blue eyes. "Anything new to report on Pitt and Giordino?"

"I'm afraid not. The arrival of the typhoon is complicating search efforts."

"We owe it to Loren to tell her the truth." Sandecker turned and entered a side door.

It was the office of Congresswoman Loren Smith, a long-serving representative from Colorado and the wife of Dirk Pitt. A cheerful receptionist, though startled by the unexpected appearance of the Vice President, ushered the men without hesitation to the Congresswoman's private office.

Loren was seated at her desk reviewing the language on an environmental safety bill when the two men walked in. Dressed in a Prada business suit, her cinnamon hair grazing her shoulders, she met all definitions of a professional beauty. Her warm smile vanished when she saw the men's downturned expressions.

"We're sorry to intrude, but we wanted you to know that Dirk and Al have gone missing," Sandecker said with typical bluntness. He turned to Gunn. "Rudi can fill you in on the details."

They took a seat across from Loren and updated her on the missing submersible. Loren's eyes welled with tears, but she asked probing questions about their mission and the search efforts.

"I feel," she said in a low voice, "that I would like to be closer to the search efforts."

"That's part of the reason I'm here," Sandecker said. "As you know from your work on the Foreign Affairs Committee, the President will be signing an important defense pact with Taiwan, strengthening our support in the region. I plan to leave late tonight to conduct a formal ratification with the President of Taiwan aboard one of our Navy destroyers. I thought you might want to come along. And you as well, Rudi."

"Yes, of course," Loren said.

"Thank you, Mr. Vice President." Gunn nodded. "I would be glad to help coordinate search efforts there locally."

Loren gazed out her window at a tranquil view of the Washington Mall, trying to picture the faraway ocean. "Do you think they have a chance?"

"It's Pitt and Giordino," Sandecker said. "I'd give them odds over any two men on the planet."

22

Inside the **Stingray**, a high-pitched hiss filled the air. Pitt, head throbbing, just wanted to sleep, but the noise was too annoying. He mentally climbed from the depths of a deep black well and forced his eyes to open. It was just as dark, save for a bank of multicolored lights flashing above him.

His awareness gradually crept back, and Pitt shook his head to clear the fog. The movement worked, but also generated a searing pain in his head. He felt his skull and discovered a large knot on the side. Fighting to keep his balance, he squirmed onto the side armrest of his pilot's seat, realizing that the submersible lay on its side. His elbow bumped into the helm controls, and a lone external light flickered on, illuminating the empty, sandy bottom in front of them.

"Al." Giordino was slumped over to the side, and Pitt reached over and shook his shoulder. Giordino responded with a low grunt. Pitt slid out of his seat and crawled to the back of Giordino's seat. "You okay?"

"Yeah," Giordino said in an unconvincing tone.

Under the glow of the panel lights, Pitt saw Giordino had a nasty gash on the side of his head that had left a trail of blood across the bulkhead. Pitt opened a storage compartment and grabbed a first-aid kit. He taped a gauze bandage to Giordino's wound as the shorter man regained his senses.

"What the heck hit us?" Giordino asked. "Felt like Mr. Toad's Wild Ride on steroids."

Pitt shook his head. "I don't think it was an explosion. Seemed more like an extended blast of current, like we got tossed into the Colorado River during a spring runoff. And there was some sort of auditory assault along with it."

"My eardrums are still ringing." Giordino rubbed a sore shoulder, then noticed the hissing. "Not an external leak, I take it." At their depth, a pinprick in the submersible's skin would have resulted in a fire hose stream of water rushing in.

Pitt motioned toward the source, beneath their seats. "Emergency oxygen tank broke loose in the tumble and sprang a leak. Maybe a good thing, as we might have overslept if not for the noise."

As the hissing faded, Giordino pulled himself up and knelt on the slanted bulkhead. "Getting topside might be a good idea."

Pitt handed him a flashlight and grabbed one for himself. "Let's see what we have to work with."

The two men shook off their injuries and set about assessing the damage. They found themselves ankle-deep in damaged panel debris and electronic components. The loose oxygen tank was one of two that had bounded about the rear of the submersible, crushing circuit breaker panels and controls. Giordino examined the life-support systems while Pitt checked the ballast tank and controls to shift them upright.

"CO_2 scrubber appears damaged and is inoperable at the moment," Giordino said. "Our alpine-fresh air in here is likely to turn a bit tepid."

"It appears that almost every electrical system took a beating." Pitt held up a smashed circuit board that was part of a VHF radio. "External transponders are dead. Guess we won't be calling home soon."

Giordino picked up the handset to an acoustic underwater telephone and tried speaking. "Seems to have juice, but no response upstairs."

"I bet we're well out of range. The **Caledonia** should come looking our way eventually."

Pitt continued finessing a shattered control panel on the helm, then slammed his palm against it in frustration. "There's no response to the ballast controls." He aimed his flashlight out a tiny side porthole and peered toward the stern. "Port ballast appears punctured anyway. I can't get a look at the starboard side. Port gauge reads eighty percent flooded, if accurate."

"We've still got some battery power," Giordino said, "so all is not lost."

"Then we can rewire it." Pitt opened a tool bin and retrieved a screwdriver, which he used to pry up a section of the floor paneling. Beneath it, a small compartment housed the port ballast tank pump. Giordino crawled over with a long strand of wire he'd cannibalized from a console sensor.

Without the myriad of heat-producing computers and electrical equipment that were normally powered on, the interior temperature began to drop. And with no filtration and circulation, the cold air soon turned pungent. The effects of carbon dioxide buildup were slow to accrue, but eventually both men began to feel light-headed.

Working in limited illumination, with the submersible on its side, added to their difficulty. But at last when Giordino attached the makeshift lead to a battery, the men were rewarded with the whirring of a pump motor. Compressed air was forced into the port ballast tank, purging it of seawater. The two men felt the floor shift as the increased buoyancy took hold, turning the **Stingray** to a more upright position.

"At least we can die sitting down," Giordino said, releasing the power to the pump when a pressure gauge indicated the tank was fully purged.

"I'd prefer to go horizontal in a feather bed." Pitt took the pilot's seat. He checked the propulsion controls but got a response from only two of the submersible's five thrusters. "As much as I appreciate you turning us upright," he said, "what I'd really prefer is a breath of fresh air."

"Wrong deodorant?" Giordino asked.

"Eau de Battery Acid was never my favorite. I think we need to jettison the emergency drop weights and be on our way."

"My pleasure." Giordino knelt and opened a small floor panel, exposing a recessed T handle. He twisted it perpendicular, which released a thousand-pound lead weight affixed to the bottom. Immediately, the **Stingray** rose off the seafloor, ascending at a slight list.

Giordino retook his chair as dark, murky water slid past the viewport. "How long to surface?"

"Maybe an hour, in our lopsided state."

He rubbed his head. "I hope someone is waiting with a steak and an ice pack."

Pitt didn't answer. As he stared at the dark ocean in front of them, he doubted there would be anyone waiting at all.

23

The **Melbourne**'s tender touched the sea—
and began bucking like a rodeo bull. Six-foot
waves thundered against its sides as it motored into the stormy night.

The boat turned and accelerated away from the
ship, spray bounding over the sides. As Margot
clung to a small deck cleat on the catwalk, she felt
like she was going to be pitched into the ocean.
Whatever part of her body wasn't already wet from
the falling rain was soon doused by the sea. She
dared not move, for there was no place she wouldn't
be visible from either the cabin or the rear deck.
Hold on, she told herself, convinced she could remain undetected until the boat returned to the
Melbourne.

The boat turned into the oncoming waves and
slowly picked up speed. Margot repeatedly felt her
body take to the air, then fall hard to the deck.
She peered ahead and soon made out their target.

A small boat was keeping position a half mile away. She scanned the black sea for the NUMA ship, but it was nowhere to be seen.

As the tender drew closer, Margot could see the other vessel was a utility boat, similar in size to the one to which she was clinging. Three men stood in the illuminated enclosed cabin. Detecting the approaching tender on radar, two of them slipped on foul-weather jackets and stepped onto the open deck.

As the NUMA boat idled with its bow to the southeast, the **Melbourne**'s tender approached its starboard flank. To Margot's relief, it meant the gunmen's focus would be on the opposite side.

Approaching the NUMA boat, two commandos knelt beneath the port rail, each cradling a QCW-05 submachine gun with a silencer attached. Margot felt the tender cut power as it drew close, and she crawled forward a few inches to peer at the other vessel. The tender's spotlights revealed it was painted turquoise, and a nameplate on the wheelhouse proclaimed it **Caledonia 2**. It was a boat from the **Caledonia**, but where was the NUMA ship?

"Ahoy." One of the NUMA crewmen on deck waved cautiously at the tender.

Both commandos stood and opened fire. The submachine guns' muffled rattle sent a chill up Margot's spine. The feeling was replaced by horror

as the two NUMA crewmen, cut apart by the gunfire, fell to the deck. She looked away and wrapped
her arms around her head in shock.

Though she refused to watch, she could hear and
feel what happened next. One of the commandos
tossed an incendiary grenade onto the NUMA
boat, where it rolled against the wheelhouse door.
The detonation blasted it open, and a small fireball
engulfed the compartment. The remaining crewman was knocked off his feet, but reappeared in
the doorway to fight the inferno.

Instantly, he was cut down by gunfire.

The tender drew closer for inspection and
bumped sides with the NUMA vessel. As the
tender recoiled to starboard, a large wave struck
at that side, washing over the bow and rail, cata-
pulting Margot toward the sea. With her arms
outstretched, she grasped at the boat, but didn't
succeed. She splashed headfirst into the water.

Initially stunned, she found that the immersion
helped calm her nerves and forced her to focus on
one thing. Survival. That meant avoiding the gun-
sights of the Chinese commandos. But had they
seen her?

Rather than surface, she kicked hard, swimming
deep into the dark water while trying to formu-
late what to do. Maybe they hadn't seen her. Surely
their attention had been focused on the NUMA
boat. Perhaps she could pull herself back aboard

the tender and return unseen to the **Melbourne**. She wrestled with that quandary until the tightness in her chest told her she needed air.

She swam toward the surface, slowing her pace as she drew closer. She watched a white frothy wave roll by, surfaced behind it, and took in a full breath of air.

She nearly gagged.

The air tasted foul, and she realized she lay astern of the tender, sucking in its exhaust. Leery of its idling propellers, she started to move to its side, when suddenly the engine bellowed and the vessel began to pull away. She stroked toward it, reaching out and placing a hand on its flank, only to feel the boat slip past as it roared away.

The boat began to circle around, and she dived under the water to avoid being seen. As she held herself under, the boat passed close by. When desperate for air, she surfaced to see its lights receding toward the **Melbourne**.

Her fear of being abandoned at sea diminished when she noticed a bright glow behind her. She turned in the water to face her only hope of salvation.

It was the NUMA boat, its deck and wheelhouse glowing yellow from the rising mass of flames.

24

A hulking wave rolled over Margot, burying her in a boiling turbulence. She clawed her way back to the surface and spit out a mouthful of seawater. She found herself a dozen yards farther from the NUMA boat as the current pushed her west. Despite the fire, the inboard motor still churned at low speed, keeping the boat in place.

Margot began swimming toward the boat with a sense of dread. She was weak with hunger, having barely been fed by her captors. The adrenaline rush from escaping the **Melbourne** on the tender had since passed. As another wave crashed into her, she looked up to see she was no closer to the vessel.

For an instant, she gave up hope. It would be easier to simply let go. Then she thought of her father. Maybe he wasn't still alive. But if he was, she had no choice. She had to try to save him.

Margot lowered her head and started stroking for

the boat in earnest. Digging deep, she pulled her weary limbs through the sea, kicking and thrashing without letup. The nonstop barrage of waves made it feel like she was swimming up and down rather than forward, but she fell into a rhythm and kept going. After several minutes of steady exertion, she paused to catch her breath.

To her surprise, the NUMA boat was less than twenty yards away. Without a hand on the helm, the boat had been nudged leeway to the waves and was being pushed in Margot's direction. She resumed her efforts, pulling forward, until her hand grazed the side of the boat.

She clasped the pitching hull as best she could, nearing exhaustion. She now had a new problem—getting aboard. She avoided the stern, as the spinning propellers could dice her to pieces. Clinging to the side was almost as dangerous, as the boat's action in the turbulent waters could easily crush her.

She swam to the boat's leeward side, where she was better protected from the waves, and positioned herself along the rear quarter.

Under the light of the flames, she studied the waves' rhythm and the boat's movements. When a large wave angled into the boat's opposite side, she was ready. As the near hull dipped toward the sea, she kicked upward and reached for the side rail.

Her fingers just slipped over the top, grasping a corner cleat. She hung on desperately as the momentum reversed and the boat wallowed in the opposite direction. She used the force to throw a foot over the side and hung on as the boat rocked back in her direction.

With the next pitch, she pulled herself up over the gunnel and dropped onto the deck. An inch or two of water sloshed about the deck, but her head struck something soft. Rolling over, she recoiled at the sight of one of the dead crewmen. She grasped the side rail and pulled herself unsteadily to her feet. For a moment, she couldn't take her eyes off the man, and his companion a few feet away. Finally, she turned to the burning wheelhouse.

The incendiary grenade had blown off the door and set the compartment's interior deck ablaze. The flames had since spread up the bulkheads and to the ceiling.

Margot glanced about the rear deck, searching for something to fight the fire. She found it in the guise of an empty, tub-shaped beverage cooler. She ripped off the lid, filled the cooler with seawater, and hurled the contents through the open door. She targeted the next douse on the smoldering body of the pilot, who lay beneath the helm. Somehow, she continued her one-woman bucket brigade, flooding the wheelhouse deck, then working up the side bulkheads. Flames rose above the roof, so she flung several loads atop the cabin to supplement the rain, then returned to attacking the interior.

Feeling exhausted, she flung a final dose of water onto some fire in the corner, then realized the boat had fallen dark. She had extinguished all the flames.

Margot rested a moment, then stepped for the first time all the way into the wheelhouse. She instantly recoiled. The cabin reeked of smoke, burnt wiring, and charred flesh. She staggered back onto the deck and took a breath of fresh air. To her side, she noticed a generator she had bumped into earlier, covered with a waterproof tarp.

She released the tarp's fastenings and carried it into the wheelhouse, where she draped it over the pilot's body. Holding her breath, she tucked one end under his legs and pulled the body onto the rear deck. She barely made it outside before she had to drop the bundle, step to the rail, and retch over the side.

As Margot shivered in the rain while sucking in the sea air, she realized the inboard motor beneath her feet was still running. But the water sloshing about the rear deck seemed deeper than when she had boarded.

She staggered her way back to the cabin, opened the side windows for fresh air, and groped around the charred interior. She found the fried remains of a radio set beside a melted box that once was a radar system. A ruined pair of video monitors still stood upright on the helm console, smoldering beside other electronic devices.

To the right of the pilot's seat, she found the remains of the throttle control—a mass of plastic and aluminum melted into the side console. She had no way to reduce or increase power to the motor.

She placed a hand on the ship's wheel, thankful it was made of steel and not wood, but drew back in pain. While it hadn't melted, it still held the heat of the fire. Margot pulled a strip of charred vinyl from the seat, fastened a small grip on the wheel, and gave it a turn. The boat responded, its bow nudging to the side. She continued turning until it was headed away from the wind and current. The boat ceased its violent rocking and began to make headway.

With no compass or GPS, Margot guided her path off the lights of the **Melbourne**. When she was perpendicular to the mining ship's bow, she straightened the wheel and locked onto a heading she hoped was northerly. It seemed her best chance at finding civilization or a passing freighter.

The boat pitched and wallowed as it crept through the storm. Margot was too tired to care. She only wanted to get far away from the murderous commandos.

With a mix of sadness, anger, and exhaustion, she watched the lights of her father's ship recede into the horizon, until the sea and sky around her became an indistinguishable mass of black.

25

Stenseth felt it in his feet. With each passing hour, the stern list was increasing. Despite everyone's efforts, the **Caledonia** was slowly sinking. But hope remained a glimmer as long as the ship continued to draw closer to salvation at the coastal city of Kaohsiung, Taiwan.

It was the nearest substantial open-water port, and the ship had moved forty-five miles closer. The problem was completing the forty miles still remaining. Despite the ship's settling, they were making good headway—due in no small part to the fact that the storm was blowing directly on their tail.

Another three or four hours at speed was all they needed, but Stenseth knew that probably wasn't in the cards. His fear was realized a short time later when the ship's phone buzzed.

"Bridge," he answered.

"Captain, I'm afraid we're about wrung out,"

said the **Caledonia**'s chief engineer, a frog-voiced man named Giles. "Water is sloshing around the turbine housing and encroaching on the main control panel. Frankly, I don't know why we haven't already shorted our electrical system. I'm afraid I can't keep her running much longer."

"I understand. Go ahead and shut her down, and get all your people out of there. Then see if you can rig auxiliary power to the pumps."

"Will do. I'm sorry, sir."

"I know you've done all you could," Stenseth said. "Bridge out."

The bridge lights flickered a minute later as electrical power was sourced to a forward generator. The familiar sound and vibration from the propulsion system fell away, like a death sentence, in its silence. The waves' crashing into the ship grew thunderous. The **Caledonia** was at the mercy of the sea. For the seasoned captain, the feeling couldn't have been more unnerving.

He turned to the communications officer. "Radio the **Tianjin Queen** and tell her we've lost power."

Stenseth looked out a side window at a small, overloaded container ship. The vessel had been en route from Long Beach to Hong Kong with a shipment of farm equipment when it had picked up the **Caledonia**'s distress call and rushed to her side.

"The **Tianjin Queen** acknowledges and regrets to inform us that she is incapable of offering a tow at this time," the officer said. "Her captain says she will position herself on our windward to help break the swell." The radioman looked up with an anxious gaze. "They will be standing by to take on any crew and passengers."

Stenseth peered at the neighboring vessel, which rode low in the water. Besides the shipping containers stored in its holds, the flat deck was stacked high with them. The vessel appeared to be a recent build, meaning it was highly automated, with only a skeleton crew. Her captain likely didn't trust the few crewmen to attempt a towline transfer, at least not in the **Tianjin Queen**'s overloaded state. Running across a small boat would be even more perilous.

"Keep an open line," Stenseth finally said as his ship swayed violently and swung broadside to the weather. His options were now gone. He had radioed ahead to Kaohsiung for assistance, but was told the weather was too rough to send out any tugs for the next few hours. Soon, abandoning ship would be his only choice.

He stepped to the radarscope and took a final look, hoping for a miracle. A possibility appeared in the form of a small dot five miles away. The radar signal showed it was a small vessel, identified on the automatic identification system only as **Rover**.

He looked at the radioman. "Find out who that is."

The officer spoke over his headset for a moment,

then turned to the **Caledonia**'s captain with a broad smile.

"Sir, the **Rover** is a blue-water tug, here to assist. She came at the request of the Taiwan Ocean Research Institute."

It was Stenseth's turn to smile. While their request for a tow had been deferred by port authorities, TORI, Taiwan's version of NUMA, had acted at once. Rudi Gunn must have called in a favor.

Stenseth picked up a pair of binoculars and gazed through the charcoal dawn. He could just make out a large tug bearing down on their position. As it drew closer, he brightened at the sight as the weathered black hull rose and fell on the turbulent seas, the tire bumpers along its sides flapping in the liquid onslaught.

The **Caledonia**'s radio officer opened a broadcast channel.

"**Rover** here," came a gritty voice. "Are you adrift?"

Stenseth picked up a communications phone. "Yes, we lost power about a half hour ago. Very glad to see you arrive."

"You're looking a little low at the stern."

"We have a damaged hull and are taking on water," Stenseth said. "I won't sugarcoat it, Captain. We'll be a risk for you while under tow."

"No worries," the man on the tug replied. "How long you reckon?"

Stenseth was humored by the stranger's forth-
rightness. "Three hours, maybe four, if we're lucky.
We've got every pump deployed, doing all we can."

There was a long pause, then the radio crackled.
"We'll get you home. Stand by to collect a towline
leader."

Stenseth positioned several crewmen at the bow
as the tug pulled dangerously close to their leeward
side, then crept forward toward the bow. An older
man with a gray beard exited the wheelhouse and
shuffled to the stern rail. He wore a yellow rain
slicker, with his long white hair tucked beneath a
Greek fisherman's cap. A black dachshund had followed him out of the cabin, tracking a few steps
behind.

The man elbowed past a young Taiwanese crewman and coiled up a length of rope affixed to a
small buoy. Rather than heave the buoyed end into
the water for the **Caledonia**'s crew to retrieve, he
stepped to the rail and tossed the coiled rope up to
the NUMA ship's bow. It uncoiled in perfect sym-
metry as it flew until the buoy at its end pulled taut
and dropped perfectly onto the deck.

A waiting crewman grabbed the rope and secured it to a nearby capstan. Watching out the
bridge window, Stenseth radioed the tug. "Leader
secured."

"Roger," came the soft, accented voice of a
Taiwanese crewwoman who had taken the wheel.
"Proceeding ahead to deploy towline."

The **Rover** did as she said, pulling forward as the old man and his assistant uncoiled a thick line, its end attached to the leader. The nine-and-a-half-inch-thick braid of Kevlar could have pulled a battleship. The tug bounced violently in the white water, but the two men and the dog kept their feet as the line was spooled out over the stern.

Aboard the **Caledonia**, the crew pulled the thick line aboard with the aid of the capstan and secured it around a forward pair of bitts. The white-haired man stood on the deck, confirming the line was cleanly released as the tug pulled ahead.

"The towline is secure," Stenseth radioed. "My compliments to your captain. That was a remarkable deployment in this weather."

"I'll tell Mr. Clive," the Asian woman said. "Prepare to get under way shortly."

The tug edged forward through the swells until the line pulled taut. The tug's twin diesels, each generating better than thirty-five hundred horsepower, were put to the task. Its propellers biting into the sea, the old vessel churned ahead, dragging the stricken vessel with it.

From the **Caledonia**'s bridge, the tug would ominously disappear from view behind the high swells, then suddenly reappear, a wisp of black smoke tailing from its exhaust stack. As they eased toward the northwest, the NUMA ship's pitching and rocking began to subside as both vessels churned through the storm.

Stenseth radioed his thanks to the container ship for standing by and freed it to depart, expecting they would be close enough for Coast Guard assistance in another hour or two.

"We're up to twelve knots," the helmsman said. "She's got some bite, for an old dog."

Stenseth nodded, mentally calculating it would take four hours to reach port at that rate.

The ship's second officer entered the bridge, rainwater dripping off his clothes. He gazed out the forward window with a look of relief, then faced Stenseth. "We contained about eighty percent of the engine room leaks before pulling out," he said. "All pumps are operational. We're putting up a good fight."

"Thanks, Blake. Keep those pumps manned at all times. As is, we're going to be cutting it by the skin of our teeth."

"Will do, sir. Giles and his men are still in the engine room, but will be out shortly and have her buttoned up." He lowered his voice and leaned close to the captain. "Can we stay afloat with the engine room flooded?"

Stenseth nodded. "We can in calm water." He motioned toward some cresting waves. "No guarantee in this stuff. We'll just have to gut it out."

"I think we can do it," Blake replied. "But there's one more thing. The subsea operations crew stopped me on the way up." He looked down at his shoes. "It seems they've lost contact with the tender."

"Radio contact?"

"Both radio and satellite GPS, I'm afraid. They were on station one moment and gone the next." He shook his head. "It's like they simply disappeared."

26

Margot's eyes burst open. She found herself still on the charred pilot's seat, her hands gripping the blackened wheel. She must not have slept for long, because she still felt exhausted. Thankfully, the motor of the NUMA tender was still running. But the weather had shown no sign of improvement. The wind still gusted, the rain still beat down, and the seas still churned in a violent frenzy. The muddy gray light of dawn creeping over the horizon was new. But it was something else that had awakened her with a start.

Water. A good four inches of it sloshed across the wheelhouse deck. Margot raised her soggy feet as she watched it cascade into a small galley three steps beneath the helm. She rose, stepped to the doorway, and peered across the stern deck. Close to a foot of water washed around the transom, which had sunk dangerously low. Margot saw, with discomfort, the bodies of the three crewmen sway as the water rippled.

The boat was clearly sinking, and Margot could only guess why. Between the grenade and the submachine gun fire, there were no doubt breaches in the hull. Who knew if the bilge pump was still operating? The motor, she noticed, now intermittently skipped a beat in an ominous manner.

Margot thought back. When she was a child, she would go sailing with her parents off Sydney Harbour. The family had a thirty-four-foot coastal yawl built in Hong Kong that was put into the wind almost every weekend. It represented some of her happiest childhood memories. But when Margot was a teen, that all ended after her mother died of breast cancer. The memories were too painful for her father, and he sold the boat shortly thereafter.

A lot of years had passed, but Margot knew her family's sailboat had a manual bilge pump stored with the life jackets. The NUMA boat must have one, too. She stepped into the wheelhouse and climbed down into the small galley. It was too dark to see, so she felt her way around the space. She stopped when her hands brushed a coffee urn that was still heated. She found a cup dangling from a hook, filled it with the brew, and gulped it down, relishing its warmth.

She stuffed some apples from a hanging basket into her pockets, then located a small refrigerator filled with sandwiches. She wolfed down one piled high with roast beef and cheese, then kicked herself for not investigating earlier.

Revitalized, she moved past the galley and discovered a pair of bunk beds. Three overnight bags rested on the lower bunk. She unzipped one, pulled out a T-shirt to replace her wet top, and added a light jacket for warmth.

She groped around the rest of the compartment, poking into storage closets and drawers. She found coils of rope, life jackets, and additional provisions, but no pump. She grabbed one of the life jackets and felt her way back toward the helm. As she climbed a short stepladder, her shoulder brushed the knob of a narrow storage bin.

She opened the compartment, reached inside, and felt a thick coil of plastic hose. She yanked it out, pulling with it a stout lever pump attached to more hose. Smiling in victory, she set up the emergency pump in the shallow light of the wheelhouse. She stretched the input hose to the flooded stern deck and ran the outlet through a side window and over the side.

Standing to the left of the helm, she pulled the pump handle toward her until it reached a stop, then reversed effort. The resistance increased, and with it came gurgling as water flowed through the system and out.

"We're not going down just yet," she said aloud as she worked the lever back and forth.

She pumped for twenty minutes, then rested in the pilot's seat. The muted gray dawn began to offer some minimal visibility. Margot scanned for any sight of land, or another ship, but to no avail. While the clouds were still painted an ominous black, the rains had receded for now. Margot tapped the wheel, keeping the boat running with the wind, hoping the mass of an island in the Luzon Strait would eventually fill the window.

She worked the pump for another hour, taking longer breaks every few minutes as her arms grew weary. She glanced at the stern deck and tried to convince herself it was riding higher. But her feelings of jubilation were thwarted when the motor began to rasp. She stepped onto the stern just in time to hear the diesel stutter and die.

The dead motor gave way to an eerie quiet on the open ocean, disturbed only by the splattering of waves against the boat. Margot stood in the doorway and waited until the boat dipped into a trough and the water on the deck temporarily drained out the rear scuppers.

She crossed to the center deck and pulled open a hatch, revealing the inboard diesel. Turning away from the steam billowing up, she looked down at a crushing sight.

The compartment was half flooded, and Margot marveled at how the motor had run for as long as it had. An aluminum fuel tank tucked behind it was pockmarked with a seam of bullet holes that angled below the waterline. It wasn't the flooded compartment that had killed the motor, she realized, it was the water's contamination of the fuel. There was no fixing that.

She slid the hatch cover back in place as a wave washed over the side, and she hurried to the wheelhouse. She scanned the horizon again, searching desperately for signs of land or another vessel. An empty gray slab was all she could see, peppered with mountainous caps of white foam.

She returned to the bilge pump and began working the lever, mostly to relieve her anxiety. Without any propulsion, the boat was knocked haphazardly about, absorbing the sea's full fury. Margot felt at times like the waves were crashing into the boat from all directions. Other times, the vessel wallowed violently, and it was all she could do to keep her footing.

The stern deck became awash with more and more seawater. Margot took a rest from the pump and slipped on the life jacket. The vessel's time was running short, but at least she wasn't going to be trapped in the cabin.

Knowing the boat would have an emergency life raft, she searched for the tell-tale cylindrical container in which it would usually be housed. Not finding it on the stern, she crawled along the side rail to check the bow, getting doused by an incoming wave. Not seeing it there, she looked up to the one place she prayed it wasn't.

Sitting atop the wheelhouse was the emergency raft's fiberglass container. As she feared, the canister was charred and had split open during the fire. A mass of black and yellow goo from inside— the remains of the raft—had coagulated across the roof. With a pang of defeat, Margot staggered back inside the cabin and resumed working the bilge pump.

The slow death came twenty minutes later, when a large wave swept over the side and buried the stern for good. The bow rose skyward as the boat began to slide beneath the waves. Margot used the momentum to step out of the wheelhouse into waist-deep water. A few seconds later, the boat fell away beneath her.

Thunder cracked in a dark peal overhead as Margot found herself bobbing in an empty sea. Never in her life had she felt so alone.

27

"How did this happen?" While the tone of Zheng's voice was calm, the look in his eyes was pure fire.

"She . . . she had a weapon," the commando mumbled. The side of his jaw was red and swollen from Margot's handiwork, and he felt a spasm of pain with every word he spoke. But that couldn't compete with the throbbing in his bandaged left hand, which hung limp at his side.

"A stick?"

The guard looked away.

That was not the response Zheng desired. He stepped forward and kicked with his left leg, striking the man's hip. The blow sent the commando sprawling across the bridge deck. "You are a disgrace to the unit. Get out of my sight."

The commando scrambled to his feet and made a hasty exit out a side door. Zheng turned to his adjutant, the bald commando Ning. "You have not found her?"

"Not yet. None of the ship's boats or rafts is missing, but she'd be a fool to try to escape in these seas. She's got to be hiding somewhere. We'll find her."

It took two hours of examining every square inch of the ship to realize he was wrong.

On hearing the news, Zheng visited the operations control room, where Thornton was still tied up. "Your daughter is missing," Zheng said.

The mining engineer's eyes flickered with satisfaction. He glanced at the ropes binding him to the chair. "I'm afraid I haven't seen her."

"Where would she hide?"

"Perhaps she didn't like the company aboard ship and is on her way to Luzon. She's a good swimmer."

Zheng felt for the grip of the QX-04 pistol on his hip, then thought better of it. He exited the operations bay with Ning at his side. "The ship's crew is secure?"

"Yes, they are still locked up. Nothing seems amiss."

"Keep two guards on Thornton at all times," Zheng said. "She'll come for him if she's aboard."

Zheng and Ning made their way across the swaying ship to the bridge. Visibility was barely a mile under the soggy gray skies.

Zheng looked to the helmsman. "Has there been any sign of the NUMA boat?"

"No, sir."

"The boat surely burned and sank," Ning said.

Zheng thought a moment. "What if she got aboard?"

"The boat was heavily damaged. At best, she could have drifted a few miles before it sank."

Zheng moved to a chart table and studied a map of the strait. He dragged a finger from their position to the northwest, in the direction of the storm. Barely noticeable were two small islands, some twenty miles away. He stabbed at them with his finger.

"When the seas calm, take a team and search these islands. I want to know that she is dead."

28

Margot wasn't dead, but she was creeping closer with every passing minute. Although the ocean temperature was nearly eighty degrees, the wind and wave action still placed her at risk of hypothermia. She paddled lightly, trying to keep her back to the onslaught. Something inside told her to keep heading north, but she was too spent to make any headway. She was at the complete mercy of the sea and all its fury.

The winds had lessened and, with them, the height of the waves. But tall swells still washed over her with painful regularity. The repeated drenching dashed any hope of being able to rest. The wind whipping at her soaked hair made her teeth chatter, and she cursed herself for not having searched the NUMA boat for an immersion suit or at least a wetsuit.

Her initial fears of the stormy sea had given way to depression the longer she was battered about.

Wave after wave barreled into her, each sapping her energy and eroding her willingness to survive. Her mind began to drift into the early stages of delirium. She stared up at the gray clouds overhead, absorbed by their glowering force. After a while, she felt she could reach up and touch them. She wanted to run among the clouds. Her arms and legs flailed to take her there, but to no avail. She had to get closer, but something was holding her back.

It was the bulky life jacket.

She stripped it off, tossed it aside, and reached her arms up high for the heavens. But rather than dance among the clouds, she slid beneath the surface. As she struggled to breathe, she was jarred back to her senses and kicked to the surface. She took a deep breath and looked for her life jacket, but it was no longer in sight. Perhaps this was better. She could end it all now by just slipping silently away.

She turned her gaze skyward again, closed her eyes, and treaded water for a few minutes. When her arms and legs grew weary, she decided that it was time. She opened her eyes, took a last breath, and fell limp as a wave washed over her. But an instant before she went under, something caught her eye.

It was the torso of a man protruding from the waves.

29

Was it real? Margot couldn't be sure, but instinct made her kick to the surface. As she shook the drops from her eyes, she no longer saw the man, but instead a yellow object in the water a short distance away. She heard a splash as a large wave rolled over her.

Margot came up sputtering to find Dirk Pitt next to her. He grabbed her arm and flashed a calm smile. "Lonely place to be out for a swim."

Margot could only nod before collapsing onto his shoulder.

Pitt sidestroked toward the **Stingray**, towing the woman under one arm. The yellow submersible sat low in the water, rocked by the sea that washed around its top hatch. Giordino poked his head out, using his blunt body to block any high waves from flooding the interior.

Pitt swam alongside and thrust Margot's body toward the base of the hatch. Giordino climbed out and grasped the rim for support with one hand. He leaned over and tucked an arm beneath Margot.

With an ease built on natural strength, Giordino scooped her from the water and stood her upright next to him. "There's only room for one at a time," he said. "Can you climb down yourself?"

He didn't wait for her approval, instead picked her up and lowered her down the opening. As she collapsed onto the interior's deck, Giordino turned and thrust a hand in Pitt's direction. A battering wave struck at the same instant, nearly washing both away before Pitt emerged from the water at the end of Giordino's crane-like arm. Giordino shot down the hatch, followed by Pitt, who sealed them in and away from the raging sea.

Margot lay sprawled on the deck, and the two men lifted her onto the copilot's seat. She took in her surroundings, gradually shaking off the shock and exhaustion, but unable to stop shivering.

Pitt found a light jacket and draped it around her shoulders while Giordino offered her a sip from a water bottle. "Sorry we're fresh out of donuts and hot coffee."

She stared at them in shock. "What . . . what are you doing here?"

"We were engaged in an underwater survey when we were kicked across the seafloor by a sudden blast of current," Pitt said. "Unfortunately, it knocked out most of our electrical equipment. We managed to surface, but haven't seen any sign of the **Caledonia**." He gave her a discerning look. "A more pertinent question is, what are you doing swimming around in the middle of a typhoon?"

Margot shook her head, trying to clear her mind. She didn't know where to start.

"They boarded the **Melbourne** and killed the first officer and chief engineer. They have my father . . ." She took a sip of Giordino's water. "I escaped the cabin where I was locked."

"Who captured the **Melbourne**?" Pitt asked.

Margot shrugged. "Military commandos. Chinese, I think. They wore unmarked uniforms, but were heavily armed."

"Why would they assault your ship?" Giordino asked.

"I don't know. For diamonds, perhaps. My father thought they might have wanted the ship for its surveying capabilities."

Pitt and Giordino glanced at each other.

"Is your father all right?" Pitt asked.

"I think so . . ." Tears welled in her eyes. "They beat him, but he is a strong man." She noticed that both men also had battered faces, and Giordino wore a bloodied bandage on his scalp.

"What happened to your boat?" Pitt asked.

"After I escaped my cabin, I heard people on the deck. I hid aboard the tender, only to have it launched over the side. I clung to the side rail as it was sailed over to a small boat from your ship. I saw the boat's name. It was the **Caledonia 2**."

"Yes," Giordino said. "That's a rescue tender."

"I don't know what happened to your ship," she said. "I didn't see it. The NUMA boat had three men and seemed to be waiting in place."

"Waiting for us," Giordino said quietly. "The **Caledonia** must have been called away."

He and Pitt both knew Stenseth would never have abandoned the submersible except under extraordinary circumstances. Clearly, the Chinese commandos on the **Melbourne** knew what the NUMA vessel was up to.

"What happened next?" Pitt asked.

Margot closed her eyes tight before speaking. "The gunmen on the boat shot them. They didn't have a chance." She shook her head at the memory. "The gunmen shot up the boat—and set it on fire. About that time, a wave knocked me off the side of the tender. I was too petrified to climb back aboard, afraid they would shoot me, too. So I stayed in the water until they left, then swam to the NUMA boat. I put out the fire and was able to sail it for a while, but it eventually sank. I would have drowned . . ." Her voice weakened as she looked up at Pitt.

"Al swore he saw a mermaid swim by, so I went topside to prove him wrong. A lucky thing we crossed paths."

"Can you call for help?" she asked.

"Our radio and most of our electronics were destroyed in our tumble across the seafloor," Giordino said. "Probably lost a few brain cells as well." He rubbed the side of his head.

Margot sunk down in exhaustion. She glanced out the viewport and watched a wave crash over the submersible.

"All is not lost." Pitt climbed into the pilot's seat. "We still have a bit of propulsion and a few hours of battery power left."

"That and a bathymetric map of the Luzon Strait." Giordino pointed to a chart he had found in their supplies and taped to the wall. "If only we knew where we were."

"Margot might be able to help," Pitt said. "Do you know what time you boarded the NUMA tender and got under way?"

The exhausted woman shrugged. "It was late, maybe around midnight."

"Any idea of your speed and direction?"

"The boat was running just above idle. I steered with my back to the weather. I can't remember how long ago it died and sank. Maybe three or four hours?"

Pitt glanced at an orange-faced Doxa dive watch on his wrist. "Let's call it six hours at three knots. That's maybe twenty miles from where we splashed down."

He ran a finger across the chart, estimating their position. Blue water surrounded the spot, except for two small specks to the west.

"We're in relative luck," Pitt said. "A pair of tiny

islands show on the chart, perhaps within ten miles. Otherwise, it's a long sail to Taiwan."

"Really long," Giordino said, "if the wind or current changes."

"Island living it is." Pitt engaged the remaining thrusters and turned the submersible in a westerly heading.

The submersible rocked and swayed as it crept through the boiling sea. Margot snuggled into the seat and promptly fell asleep as Giordino tracked their power usage. Pitt kept a steady hand on the controls, fighting through the wave-battered waters. But he had little regard for their present state of danger. He could only think of one thing.

Between the violent storm and the arrival of the Chinese commandos, was the **Caledonia** still afloat?

30

The NUMA research vessel was indeed still afloat, but just barely. The stern hung low, like a cowering hound dog dragging its tail. But the **Caledonia** was now clear of the heavy seas that had threatened her survival. Still under tow by the indefatigable black tugboat, she had limped around the southern tip of Taiwan and approached the Port of Kaohsiung in the calmer shallows close to shore.

Free of the worst of the storm's waters, she now became a magnet for other tugs and rescue boats. Additional pumps and generators were transferred aboard, along with the hands to operate them, and the flooded compartments were attacked anew. In short order, the **Caledonia**'s damage was stabilized. By the time the vessel reached Kaohsiung and was hauled toward a dry dock at the northern end of the commercial wharves, she was riding four feet higher.

The towline was retrieved by the black tug, which proceeded to sail away with just a passing wave from its bearded captain. The other tugs moved in for a share of the rescue, taking up positions at the stern and nudging the ship into the flooded dry dock.

Stenseth watched from a bridge wing as the ship was positioned and secured at the center of the basin. Water-filled pontoons at the base and sides were then pumped full of compressed air.

As the ship and dock began to inch above the harbor's surface, the **Caledonia**'s chief engineer, a stocky Texan named Homer Giles, stepped onto the bridge wing. He was soaking wet, and his face was streaked with oil, yet he flashed a bright white smile at Stenseth. "We did it, sir. Got her back safely. I think we even saved most of the engine room."

"A small miracle." Stenseth looked at the engineer and cocked his head. "What do you mean, the engine room? It was reported flooded and sealed a few hours ago."

"Well, sir, it was close. We ran all the pumps we could out of there. Me and Hobbs stayed in and operated a pair of manual pumps to help out. We did our best to keep the turbine dry. I think we pulled it off."

"You're a lunatic, Giles." Stenseth patted the engineer on the back. "I guess we'll know soon enough, once the ship gets up and dry. Get yourself cleaned up and grab some rest. It will be a few hours before we can perform a full inspection."

"Aye, sir, happy to oblige." Giles staggered down an adjacent companionway in total exhaustion.

Stenseth scheduled ship repairs with the port authorities while the vessel was still being raised from the harbor. As the extra pumps began to drain the flooded compartments, the captain took a peek inside the engine room, then made his way to the video conference room.

He found Second Officer Blake engaged in a video call with Rudi Gunn in Washington. NUMA's Assistant Director wore a wrinkled oxford shirt with no tie and sat behind a scattered row of drained coffee cups. He looked like he hadn't left the building in days.

Gunn saw Stenseth enter the frame. "How are you making out, Bill?"

"It appears the ship survived without any major damage," Stenseth said. "But we're still missing a submersible and a rescue tender."

"Yes, Blake filled me in on the situation. We've already asked the Navy in Okinawa to send some P-3 Orion search planes over the area, and they have a frigate en route. We'll press the Taiwan Coast Guard again, while we start in on satellite reconnaissance. We'll find them."

Stenseth frowned. "Weather's still a mess here, Rudi. Typhoon-force winds. Nobody local is going out there. Aircraft won't be able to see much until things settle down in the next day or so."

"Maybe that's affecting the support boat's GPS signal," Gunn suggested.

Blake shook his head. "We lost the signal quite some time ago, along with radio. There have been no signals since."

"And no signals from Pitt?" Gunn asked.

"Nothing," Blake said.

Gunn turned pale. He had joined NUMA with Pitt when the agency was established. To him, Pitt was more than a boss. He was a friend and the nearest thing he had to a brother.

"Typhoon or no typhoon, I'll make sure a search happens if I have to conduct it myself." Gunn tried to shake off his anger. "What do you think happened out there, Bill?"

"Something tore up our stern," Stenseth said. "Possibly an external explosion. All I can tell you is, that mining ship, the **Melbourne**, was a half mile away at the time, and they didn't respond to our distress calls."

"You think they were responsible?"

"I do. Which makes me even more concerned about Pitt and Giordino, and the rescue tender."

"Where is the **Melbourne** now?" Gunn asked. "Did they remain on-site?"

Blake tapped on a laptop in front of him. "There's no signal from the commercial AIS tracking system. They're either missing or trying to keep quiet, wherever they are."

"Maybe they were after the same thing we were," Gunn said. "But you said it's an Australian ship, not Chinese?"

"That's correct," Stenseth said. "Privately owned by an Australian mining company called Thornton."

"A mining ship . . ." Gunn said. "Even if they found a valuable underwater claim, why would they attack an oceanographic research ship?"

"I don't know," Stenseth replied, shaking his head. "But there must be a reason, and a good one."

31

Exhaustion had long since engulfed the submersible's three occupants. Margot remained in a deep slumber in the copilot's seat, but Pitt and Giordino had no such luxury. They were in a race against time. More precisely, a race against the vessel's remaining battery charge.

Once the batteries were drained, they would be at the mercy of the sea. While shipping traffic was normally high in the neighboring South China Sea and Taiwan Strait, the storm would have diverted most vessels to the north and south. Worse, the prevailing currents in that part of Luzon Strait were generally to the northeast. As the storm passed, the **Stingray** might be carried in a new direction, to the east of Taiwan. In that sparsely traveled area, they might drift for weeks unseen.

Knowing this, Pitt and Giordino remained focused despite their fatigue. Pitt guided the submersible through the wallowing seas at a snail's pace, steering west in hopes of finding landfall, if not a passing freighter.

While Pitt fought the seas from the pilot's seat, Giordino stood on the ladder rungs of the top hatch, his torso exposed to the elements as he scanned the horizon. Massive waves continually washed over the low-riding vessel. Like a jack-in-the-box, Giordino would duck down and pull the hatch closed as the waves struck, then pop back up again when they had passed. Inevitably, he would be surprised by a follow-on wave that hit home. Dripping with salt water, he would shake off the dousing like a warm shower and continue to search for deliverance.

He ducked under from one of the waves and checked their battery usage as his stomach grumbled loudly.

Reminded of his own hunger, Pitt turned to him. "How about snaring a wayward tuna during your next frolic in the waves?"

"They're smart enough to be swimming well under the suds." Giordino tapped a voltmeter. "Batteries are down to about fifteen percent."

Pitt nodded. "They've lasted longer than I expected. What do you say we run another ten minutes, then hold the last in reserve?"

"I'd say that's as good a plan as any."

Giordino climbed back up the ladder, waiting for the submersible to cease swaying for a moment, then popped once more through the hatch.

The scene around him was entirely monochromatic. Charcoal clouds, shedding random squalls of gray, hovered above the slate-colored seas. Giordino scanned the misty horizon, searching for any deviation. Sea spray from a sudden gust whipped at his face, briefly blinding him. As he wiped away the salt water, something caught his eye in the distance. A speck of green.

He didn't have a chance to confirm it, as a pair of waves converged at the stern and washed over topside. Giordino dropped into the interior amid a flood of water, clanging the hatch closed behind him.

"Bucking for an indoor swimming pool?" Pitt asked.

Giordino shook the water from his head. "I was, in fact, just considering the merits of relocating to the desert when we get out of here."

"You'd miss surfing."

"Perhaps." He took a step back up the ladder. "Humor me and steer a course heading of three hundred degrees while keeping the juice on."

"See something?"

"Probably a hallucination."

Pitt adjusted their heading with the aid of a backup bubble compass mounted beneath their console of dead electronics.

Giordino returned to the elements, ignoring a series of small waves that struck him as he strained his vision. A squall streaked across the sky and shrouded visibility in a hazy curtain. After a few minutes, the submersible entered the downpour. Giordino remained steadfast like a statue, peering ahead, while using his arms and torso to block the rain from falling inside. The drops fell hard, pounding against the hull with metallic raps, while assaulting Giordino's unprotected head.

Gradually, the downpour eased. The skies ahead to the west lightened, and the rain receded to a firm drizzle. With it, Giordino's range of visibility extended.

A tiny patch of green emerged in their path, then vanished in the mist. Giordino slapped his hand on the top of the submersible and grinned. It was no hallucination at all.

He had seen land ahead.

32

North Island stood less than a mile wide and rose from the sea in a classic cone-shaped silhouette. A mostly forgotten speck representing the second most northerly island in the Philippine chain, the first honor went to a larger landmass called Mavulis, a few miles away. The steep eastern flank of North Island was lush green with low grasses, but a dark coastal band indicated a rugged wall of rock at the waterline.

Pitt caught glimpses of the island through the continuing rain and the waves splashing the viewport and he shook his head. "A high, rocky shoreline does not look appetizing in these conditions."

Giordino agreed. "I didn't see a welcome mat anywhere on this side of the coast."

"Let's hope things look friendlier on the leeward side, if we can get there."

Their battery juice had dropped precipitously.

Pitt had cut the thrusters, allowing the wind and current to push them toward the island. The storm continued to blow to the northwest, and as they approached the eastern shore, he applied quick bursts of power to push them. The seas did the rest, carrying them around the island's northern tip.

Giordino resumed his post in the open hatch, warning of rocky hazards and shouting course corrections to Pitt, whose view from inside was still obscured by the waves. As the submersible rounded the point, Pitt propelled them along the island's contour. The nose of the **Stingray** came around, but the vessel's forward progress halted. Pitt could sense it right away, confirmed by their movement away from shore.

"We've lost propulsion," he shouted to Giordino. "Batteries still show power."

Spun around by the waves, Pitt could glimpse the island falling away from them.

Giordino leaned out the hatch and saw a green mass near the stern. "I think we sailed into a kelp bed chewed up by the storm. Must have fouled the thrusters."

Before Pitt could respond, Giordino climbed out and dived over the side. He surfaced next to the submersible and stroked his way to the multiple thruster assemblies at the stern. Ducking underwater, he could see that two of the outer thrusters had been bent during the submersible's tumble, but three center assemblies were still intact. As he suspected, they were clogged with a mass of kelp that had been driven into the impellers by a stern wave.

He broke to the surface for a fresh breath of rain-damp air, then dived back and began methodically removing the slimy green strands from each assembly. It was a one-handed job, as the wave action demanded he brace himself against the hull with an arm around a rudder mount, lest he be ripped away.

Clearing the last of the debris, he kicked to the surface, detecting a light splash in the water as a powerful wave pulled him from the **Stingray**. A mooring line had slapped the water. He turned to find it extended up to the submersible's hatch, where Pitt clutched the other end. Giordino grabbed ahold and let Pitt pull him alongside. He scampered up the hull with the aid of a passing wave.

Pitt grinned. "Jealous you hadn't had a bath like Margot and me?"

"No, I just didn't want to be late to the beach luau." Giordino gestured toward the island.

Pitt ducked down the ladder. "I'll be happy if there is a beach."

As Giordino retook his spot in the hatch, Pitt slid into the pilot's seat and engaged the thrusters. The submersible moved forward again. Pitt angled against the swell as he sought the protected waters of the island's leeward side. After some intermittent progress, the buffeting gradually lessened. Pitt steered along the island's west coast, hugging the shoreline just beyond the breakers. The viewport remained awash with waves, forcing him to rely on Giordino for navigation. His glimpses of the coast still revealed only a rocky, blunt shoreline.

"Steady on," Giordino called. A few minutes later, he reported again. "There's a small cove coming up. I don't see anything more promising beyond."

"Let's try for it," Pitt said. "We're almost out of power." He tried to ignore the blinking red readout on a voltage meter.

Following Giordino's direction, he turned toward the island and a cut shaped like a horseshoe in the rocky coastline. High, tumbling waves pounded against the shore like a white barricade. Both men knew unseen shallows could imperil the vessel by grounding it in the middle of the breakers.

As the tumult surrounded them, Giordino picked a careful route and fed course adjustments to Pitt.

The controls became less responsive as the force of the tumbling surf took hold. Wave after wave broke around and over them, pounding into Giordino and spilling seawater into the interior.

Pitt lost all sight of the island as the viewport remained covered in froth. He held steady on the controls, tweaking the course at Giordino's urging. The submersible rocked fore and aft. Its hull scraped over soft sand at one point, then clanged against a hard bottom the next.

The action of the waves sent the vessel teetering to the side, almost throwing Giordino from the hatch. Spotting a massive wave approaching, he dropped down the ladder and sealed the hatch seconds before it washed over them.

The interior briefly fell black, then the submersible fought to regain its balance. Pitt's calm voice wafted through the gloom. "This is your idea of the easy way in?"

"Somebody left the coral reef off the guide map," Giordino replied.

He remained where he was, as the submersible lacked the power, even under the best circumstances, to battle the line of breakers.

The **Stingray** continued to rock violently back and forth. Time and again, they heard and felt the hull scrape against the bottom. At one point, the **Stingray** seemed to collide with a wall, holding fast there for several seconds, but the waves eventually freed the vessel and shoved it closer to shore.

Margot jolted awake from the turbulence and eyed the dark froth covering the viewport. "What's happening?"

"Al found us some dry land," Pitt said. "Trying to work our way there."

Giordino took advantage of a moment of stability to look out the hatch. He dropped back inside an instant later as a wave rolled over the top of them. "I think we're past the worst of the breakers," he said, "but at risk of overshooting the cove's entrance."

They were rocked and battered a few more minutes, then the fury subsided. They caught a glimpse out the viewport of the narrow entry, and Giordino retook his navigator's position. "Anything you can give us to port," he called out.

Pitt activated the thrusters. A fading battery propelled them a few yards in the designated direction. It was just enough to align them with the mouth of the cove. The waves pushed the submersible the rest of the way. The **Stingray** drifted a short distance across the sandy cove, then kissed the bottom near some moss-covered rocks.

Giordino leaped into the shallow water and tied the mooring line around one of the boulders. He climbed back aboard and helped a groggy Margot onto the beach.

Pitt followed. He closed the hatch behind him, then stood atop the hull. He peered down for a moment toward the submersible's prow. Through the calm water, he could see the **Stingray**'s front skids. Unbelievably, the section of Chinese missile still lay in the unyielding grip of the mechanical arm, having survived the tumultuous journey intact.

Pitt stepped off and waded to shore, where Margot and Giordino waited. A fierce wind whipped down the beach, swaying the trees and bushes that crowded the narrow strip. As his feet touched the sand, the skies opened up, releasing a heavy downpour upon them.

Giordino stood in the rain with his arm around Margot and smiled at Pitt. He was soaked to the bone, with the nub of a soggy cigar dangling from his lips.

"We made it to dry land," he said. "Ain't it great?"

PART II

Chase to Dharamsala

33

A pair of visas for travel to India were waiting for Dirk and Summer at Taipei Songshan Airport before they boarded their direct flight to New Delhi. After landing at the Indian capital that evening, they spent the night at an airport hotel, then caught a morning commuter to Dharamsala.

Located two hundred and fifty miles north of New Delhi, Dharamsala was a small city built on the upper hillsides of the Kangra Valley at the base of the Himalaya Mountains. With its high elevation and towering backdrop of jagged peaks, the region had been a favored vacation spot for British colonials to escape the oppressive summer heat of Delhi and Calcutta. In recent times, it had grown into a popular base for trekkers and mountaineers seeking to test their mettle in the Himalayan range. But it was mostly known as a place of pilgrimage for Buddhists from all over the world who sought a glimpse of the Dalai Lama, whose residence was just up the hill.

After landing at the Kangra Airport in the lower valley a few miles south, Dirk and Summer exited the plane to a crisp, clear day. The snow-covered mountains to the north sprouted like a row of sugar-glazed pyramids that gouged the sapphire skies.

"Look at the mountains," Summer said. "It's gorgeous."

"The abode of snow," Dirk said, citing the Sanskrit definition of **Himalaya**. "They appear to live up to the billing."

They retrieved their bags and the **thokcha** artifacts case, then hailed a cab at the front of the airport. The shy driver of the dirty, compact Nissan said little as he navigated the five-mile climb up the valley heights to the sprawling hillside town. They rode through the city on a bumpy paved road, winding past the congested town center and an assortment of shops and tea gardens.

Motoring past the town's northern end, they continued up a series of switchbacks to the smaller community of McLeod Ganj, built on a forested ridge. The taxi dropped Dirk and Summer at a small modern hotel called the Imperial, perched in a thick cedar grove. They grabbed a quick lunch of curry and tandoori chicken at the lodging's restaurant, then took to the streets, carrying the artifacts case.

Summer checked a tourist map of the town. "The hotel clerk said it was only a couple of blocks to the Tibet Museum."

"I'm glad for the walk after all the cramped airplane rides," Dirk said.

They hiked from the forested area around their hotel down a hill to the main part of town. Its odd name, McLeod Ganj, came from a mash-up of Sir Donald McLeod, a British colonial governor in India, and the Persian word for neighborhood, **ganj**.

Dirk and Summer found it unusual in another aspect. While the buildings were generally as drab as in the other Indian towns they had seen, the people on the streets were not. Tibetan monks in bright red robes mixed with Western tourists, long-haired backpackers, and pilgrims from an assortment of nations. The many lively cafés, hostels, and B&Bs catered to a throng of visitors to the remote location. As the home of the Tibetan government-in-exile, along with the Dalai Lama, McLeod Ganj had earned a second moniker, Little Lhasa.

South of the town center, they reached a fork in the road. Summer stopped a young woman wearing jeans and a Moncler vest. "Do you know where the Tibet Museum is located?"

"Yes, it's in the Dalai Lama's compound, called Tsuglagkhang," she said. "Just follow the road down the hill and to the right."

Summer thanked the woman, and they proceeded until they reached a line of people entering a gate. A large green sign proclaimed it the entrance to Tsuglagkhang. As they passed through a security check, the guards paid careful attention to Dirk's case.

"This is the Dalai Lama's residence?" Dirk looked around at the assortment of colorful structures.

Summer nodded. "There is also a monastery here. The guidebook says the grounds and two temple areas are open to the public, along with the museum."

As they started to cross the grounds, Dirk heard the whir and cough of a motor turning over but failing to start. Through a side gate, he saw an old stake-bed pickup truck with a robe-clad monk behind the wheel, grinding the starter.

Dirk's gearhead instincts kicked in, and he made a beeline for the vehicle. Stepping closer, he was surprised to see the pickup truck was American-made, an International Harvester, from 1953. Its dark green paint was scratched and faded, and the wood pickets along the bed were weather-beaten. Despite the wear, it showed a tidy appearance of being well maintained.

Dirk nodded at the man as he approached the open driver's window. "Nice truck. Trouble starting?"

"Yes," the monk said. "It is old and tired, and

does not like to run when it is cold." He smiled. "Just like me."

Dirk peered into the cab. The gas gauge read full, but the choke lever was not engaged. "Did you try the choke?"

The monk reached over and pulled the knob, which drew a metal rod sliding out of the dash. "It is of no help." The monk turned the ignition again, letting the starter whine.

Dirk held up a hand. "Let me take a look."

He set down the case, walked to the front of the truck, and opened its bulbous hood. Beneath a light layer of grime was an inline, six-cylinder engine that, when new, produced an even one hundred horsepower. The engine bay looked tidy, but when Dirk stepped to the side, he noticed the choke linkage lying loose atop the cylinder head. He reached in and removed the air filter to expose the carburetor. Dirk popped the loose link back into its lever on the side of the carburetor, replaced the air filter, and closed the hood.

"The choke's connected now." He reached past the monk and pulled the knob on the dash out. "Give it some gas and try again."

The monk did as instructed, and the truck started right up. He turned to Dirk, beaming. "May the Lord look kindly upon you."

Dirk grinned and waved as the monk pulled away from the compound. He turned to Summer, who stood watching, tapping her foot. "Really?" she said.

"Just generating some good karma."

They made their way down a lane to a brick and stucco building labeled **The Tibet Museum**. Inside they found a dramatic collection of photographs and artifacts focused on the Chinese occupation of Tibet and the resulting exile to northern India.

Summer approached an elderly woman seated at an information desk. "We have discovered some Tibetan artifacts that belong to the museum and would like to return them."

Dirk set the case on the counter, opened it up, and pointed to the label inside the lid.

"Our curator is presently at the new museum in Gangchen Kyishong," the woman said. She looked closely at the label and shook her head. "I'm afraid your items don't belong to the Tibet Museum anyway."

"We were told," Summer said, "that the tag indicates the items were in the care of the museum here in McLeod Ganj."

"Yes, this is true, but it's not our museum," the woman said. "The label says the items are on loan from Ramapurah Chodron in care of the Tibet Club Museum. That is a different entity."

"The Tibet Club Museum?" Dirk asked. "Is that still in existence?"

The woman nodded with a look of disapproval. "Yes. You can find it across town." She wrote down directions on a slip of paper and handed it to Summer. "It's now three o'clock. They should just be opening."

Dirk and Summer gave each other a quizzical look, thanked the woman, and exited the museum.

"The wrong museum?" Summer shook her head. "How many Tibetan museums do they have here?"

"Well, at least we got the right town."

They retraced their steps to the center of town, then followed the directions down a gravel side street. Summer stopped in front of an aged building sided with cedar shingles. A small sign beside the door, in both English and the curled Tibetan script, identified it as the **Tibet Club Museum**. Below it said **Open 3–2**.

"This must be the place," Summer said. "Strange hours, for a museum."

"Note **Museum** takes second billing to **Club**." Dirk opened the door and stood aside to allow his sister to enter first.

They stepped into what resembled neither a nightclub nor a museum, but rather the drawing room of an English manor. Tribal carpets covered the dark wood floor, cushioning several couches and stuffed chairs, with attendant reading lamps. Floor-to-ceiling shelves sprouted from two walls, filled with books, sculptures, pottery, and colorful weavings.

Another wall was plastered with photographs, mostly black and white, featuring scenes from

Tibet and personal portraits. The fourth wall featured several glass display cases and a long polished wood bar. Rows of liquor bottles behind the bar were guarded at either end by a pair of massive stone dragons that looked very old.

A faint but pleasing odor of incense and bourbon filled the air. The dimly lit room appeared empty as Summer and Dirk stepped inside. A young woman popped up from behind the bar, carrying a tray of empty glasses. Dressed in a yellow blouse, wool vest, and **chupa**, she turned to the visitors and smiled. With dark skin, a broad face, and deep almond eyes, she was unmistakably Tibetan.

"Can I get you a drink?" she asked in near-flawless English.

"Not just yet, thank you." Dirk set the case on the bar. "We're here to return some artifacts."

The girl nodded. "Let me get the owner." She stepped into a room behind the bar. A minute later, she returned with a man resembling a robust version of Billy Bob Thornton.

"Rob Greer," he said pleasantly. "What can I do for you?"

Startled the man was an American, Dirk proceeded to introduce themselves. "You are the owner?" he asked.

"Yes," Greer replied. "I was a photographer by trade and joined an expedition years ago to document the monasteries of Tibet. Those are my photos on the wall over there," he said with a proud wave of his arm. "I came to McLeod Ganj to photograph the Dalai Lama and members of the government-in-exile and never left." He gave a bemused look. "I acquired the establishment when I married the owner's daughter."

Dirk explained their discovery in the Philippines, and Summer opened the case on the bar.

"You came all the way here with these?" Greer said with an air of suspicion.

"The curator at the National Palace Museum in Taiwan indicated they are important cultural relics," Summer said. "We were traveling to the Maldives, so it wasn't terribly far out of the way to come here. My brother and I work for NUMA."

"I know about NUMA," the man said. "Let's see what you have."

Dirk removed the silk covering, picked up one of the carvings, and handed it to Greer. "We thought they belonged to the Tibet Museum at the Dalai Lama's compound."

"For many years, we paid better prices for the antiquities smuggled out of Tibet," he said. "As a result, we have acquired a better collection than the Tibet Museum." He pointed to one of the glass cases. "We have some seventh-century idols from Jokhang, for example. The Tibet Museum has nothing that old."

He slipped on a pair of reading glasses that

dangled from a cord around his neck and took hold of the artifact. "A **thokcha** carving." He cupped it in his hand. "Very nice."

Dirk and Summer looked at each other and nodded. "We were told," Summer said, "they were sculpted from meteorites."

"That's right," Greer said. "I've got a small example, an amulet, on the shelf behind you. Tibet, with its high, open plains, was a favorite hunting ground for meteorites. The sky iron, as the locals call it, has always been highly valued. Depending on the composition, they can be very difficult to work with. So carved specimens, particularly of this size and quality, are quite rare."

He studied each carving carefully, examining them in detail, as he made his way through the collection. "The eight auspicious symbols of Buddhism. The parasol, shell, vase, victory banner, dharma wheel, fish, knot, and lotus." He replaced the last carving in the case. "A rare and desirable collection, without doubt."

"They are believed to have come from the Nechung Monastery in Lhasa," Summer said.

Greer nodded, but said nothing.

"The label indicates they were under the care of the Tibet Club Museum, does it not?" Dirk asked.

Greer studied the label. "Yes, that's what it says. Of course, I have no direct knowledge of events or any idea who this Chodron character is. You said the Taiwan plane crashed in 1959? That was many years before my arrival, but my father-in-law was a bit of a pack rat." He turned to the young woman. "Talai, get these folks a drink while I go check the files in back."

After Greer disappeared into the back room, Summer ordered a cup of local Kangra green tea, while Dirk sampled a Simba, an Indian beer. Over the pleasant sounds of 1940s big band music, quietly piped in, Dirk could detect the bar's owner speaking softly on a phone. Greer emerged from the back ten minutes later and slapped a thick folder of handwritten invoices on the bar.

"I'm afraid no luck so far." Greer reached under the bar for a shot glass and poured himself three fingers from a dusty bottle of bourbon. "The old man kept pretty good records of the artifacts he acquired, but I can't find anything related to these items." He threw back the bourbon and set the empty glass on the bar.

"Perhaps they were only loaned to the club, not purchased," Summer said.

"Yes, but something this rare should have been noted." Greer reached into the case and removed one of the carvings, which featured swirling banners emanating from an ornate pole. "My favorite, the banner. A symbol of the victory of Buddhist thought over ignorance, negativity, and other pernicious forces."

He gave Dirk and Summer a stern gaze. "You may think I'm some callous collector exploiting the poor, ragged Tibetans who managed to flee their oppressed lands. But the fact is, I've never sold so much as a button." He peered across the room, but his eyes were looking much farther away.

"The Chinese are putting a bulldozer to Tibet," he said. "After decades of razing monasteries and looting artifacts, they're now inundating the culture with financed mass immigration from across China. That's in addition to their blatant assault on the environment. Huge Chinese dams are already drying up the Mekong and Brahmaputra Rivers. The Indus is next. This side of the Himalayas will eventually be turned into a desert."

He shook his head. "Sixty years of oppression isn't enough. Now they're quietly overrunning the place. It won't end until the last vestiges of native language, culture, and beliefs are wiped off the Tibetan Plateau."

He poured himself another bourbon and waved a hand around the room. "It's not much, but this will all go to Tsuglagkhang, and the museum there, when I'm gone. A remnant of Tibet will survive, even if it has to remain in India."

The front door banged open, and a thickset man entered the club. He carefully scrutinized the occupants, then shut the door behind him and slid the dead bolt to its locked position. All eyes were on him as he moved farther into the room.

He was short and wore a heavy coat. A dark blue cap was pulled down low over his brow, but not enough to hide his hostile black eyes. He crossed the room with a brusque confidence, stopping a few feet shy of the bar. He reached beneath his coat, pulled out an automatic pistol, and leveled it at the group.

"All of you," he said in accented English. "On the floor."

34

L isten here." Greer stepped from behind the bar. "You can't—"

His words were truncated by the bark of the pistol. The bullet struck Greer high in the shoulder, sprouting a red stain on his shirt. Talai screamed.

"On the floor," the gunman countered.

Summer slowly reached for a bar towel while maintaining eye contact with the gunman. She pressed it against Greer's shoulder and helped him to the floor as Talai and Dirk dropped down beside them.

"The money's in the register," Greer said. "Take it and leave us be."

"Shut up." The intruder trained his gun on Dirk, viewing him as the highest threat, then stepped to the bar. He went right for the open case, pulled the wrappings off the carvings and inspected each one. Replacing them, he backed away from the bar and considered the captives on the floor. He waved his gun at Summer. "You . . . stand up."

Dirk started to move, but the gunman was quick to level the pistol at his head. "Stay where you are."

Summer slowly got to her feet, and the gunman transferred his aim to her. "Close the case on the bar and pick it up."

Summer followed his instructions, closing and locking the case, then picked it up.

The gunman spoke to the trio on the floor. "You will stay here and do nothing. If you try to follow us, I will kill her. If you call the police, I will kill her."

Dirk glanced at his sister. He was several steps from the gunman, but might be able to leap at the man's knees. He knew Summer would assist in the attack. But her eyes warned him off. The sight of the bleeding proprietor told her the attempt was not worth the risk. The gunman was simply too dangerous.

Dirk lay still and watched with futility as Summer was marched to the front door. At the gunman's urging, she reached up with her free hand and unlocked the dead bolt, then grabbed the handle.

The door suddenly flew open, and she jumped back as another man entered the club. He was tall and broad-shouldered, with a brawny but pleasant face. He smiled at Summer, began to apologize— and was struck in the head from behind.

Summer gasped as he crumpled to the ground at her feet, and yet another man appeared in the doorway. He lowered the stock of the Chinese-made assault rifle he'd used to strike the Tibetan and glared at Summer. He spoke a few words to the first gunman, then slipped his weapon beneath his coat and disappeared outside.

Summer bent down to see if the Tibetan was okay, but felt a pistol poke in her spine. "Go."

She stepped over the prone man, out into the daylight.

A small white sedan idled nearby, the second gunman behind its right-side steering wheel. Summer was escorted to the rear door and climbed in, putting the artifacts case between her feet. The short gunman slid next to her and aimed the pistol across his lap at her. The driver hit the gas, and the car lurched down the road.

Summer glanced back at the club as it disappeared in the dust behind them, wondering if she would ever see her brother again.

35

Inside the Tibet Club Museum, Dirk jumped to his feet and helped Greer to a barstool. "You okay?"

"Just nicked me." The club's owner grimaced as he held the towel to his shoulder.

"Who were they? How did they know about the case?"

"I don't know," Greer said. "Artifact thieves, maybe. Or Chinese agents bent on undermining the Dalai Lama. Lord knows, there's plenty of 'em around this town. You going after them?"

"Yes," Dirk said, rushing toward the door.

"Be careful."

In the front entry, Tenzin Norsang had regained his senses and was trying to get to his feet. He glanced across the room. Greer was sitting on a stool with a bloody shoulder, but Dirk was sprinting in his direction.

Norsang reached beneath a light jacket and

produced a Glock 19 automatic pistol, which he leveled at Dirk's chest. **"Ga ka-da,"** he shouted. "Stop."

Dirk halted and raised his hands.

Greer called out to the man, in Tibetan, prompting him to lower the gun. Dirk slid past him, muttered something about guns in his face, and burst out the door.

Down the street, he could just glimpse a white sedan rounding a corner, Summer's red hair visible through the rear window. Dirk glanced around for some way to give chase, but there were no other cars on the side road, just some light foot traffic. A motor sputtered behind him, and he turned to see a faded green vehicle approach at a leisurely pace.

It was the International Harvester pickup truck Dirk had helped start earlier, with the same monk behind the wheel. Dirk ran to the center of the road, waving his arms, and it stopped. Dirk rushed to the driver's door, flung it open, and climbed inside, sliding the monk across the bench seat.

"My sister is in danger," he said as he put the manual transmission into gear. "I need to borrow your truck."

As the pickup started to move, the passenger's door flew open, and Norsang jumped in and took a seat, squeezing the monk into the middle. Dirk floored the accelerator and brought the truck up to speed, dodging a stray dog that was crossing the street.

The International Harvester was neither fast nor agile, but the narrow, winding roads of McLeod Ganj were roughly paved and would have slowed a Lamborghini. Dirk steered the truck down a steep, curving lane that ended at a cross street lined with vendors. He took a quick glance in either direction, but failed to spot the white sedan.

"Turn right," Norsang said. "It's a dead end, behind Tsuglagkhang, to the left," he added with a tinge of Queen's English.

Dirk turned right and headed up a long hill.

"There are only two roads out of McLeod Ganj," Norsang added. "This is the primary one, which will lead to Dharamsala."

Dirk had to downshift into second to keep the speed up as he crested the hill. The pickup lurched over the top, where the road wound east above the town through scattered stands of cedars. A quarter mile ahead, the sedan flashed white through gaps in the trees.

When the Harvester entered a wide, gentle curve, Dirk glanced at his Tibetan navigator. Unlike the bald monk beside him, Norsang had long hair pulled back and braided in a ponytail. Athletically built, he was dressed like he'd stepped from an L.L. Bean catalog.

"Who are you?" Dirk shifted back into third as the truck regained speed.

"My name is Tenzin Norsang. I work with the Namgyal Monastery and the Central Tibetan Administration."

"Do all employees of the monastery carry Glock 19s?"

"No," Norsang replied, without elaboration.

"So why did the Tibet Club's owner call you?"

Norsang raised an eyebrow. "He thought you may have been trafficking in stolen antiquities that are of great religious significance to our people."

The road straightened for a short distance, and ahead of them the sedan was motoring along at a normal speed. Dirk kept the accelerator to the floor until the pickup was bounding over the rough road, ready to take flight.

"Too fast. Too fast," the monk yelled, gripping the dash with white knuckles.

"Our story is no fabrication," Dirk said, ignoring the monk's pleas. "We discovered the case of carvings in an airplane that crashed in the Philippines. We have no financial interest in them and were only seeking their rightful owner."

"Mr. Greer was not so sure, but I believe you."

The road descended from the forested ridge and curved in a series of switchbacks that ended at the northern outskirts of Dharamsala. Dirk kept one eye on the sedan as it passed below them on the first switchback. The tight curves favored the smaller vehicle, and it began to outdistance the truck.

"Do you know who they are?" Dirk asked.

"Chinese operatives, most likely," Norsang said.

"Any idea where they are headed?"

"If they are Chinese, they will have a safe house in Dharamsala. It will be well protected."

Dirk wheeled the International Harvester around the first hairpin turn, its worn tires squealing in protest. The sedan was already exiting the far turn ahead. Another turn or two, and it would be entering the maze-like streets of Dharamsala. Dirk checked the car's path, and the steep, barren hillside between the switchbacks, and computed an angle of attack.

"Hang on." He spun the steering wheel hard over.

The old truck bounded over the side curb and nosed down the steep embankment. The monk gasped, and began chanting a Tibetan mantra, as they were all sprung up and down in their seats.

Dirk managed to align the Harvester straight down the hill, then stomped on the brakes. It did little to slow the vehicle, as the wheels slid across the loose soil. The truck bounced and shimmied, rumbling over rocks and low shrubs while gaining momentum down the steep grade.

Out of the corner of his eye, Dirk saw the white sedan approach from his left below. Its driver hadn't yet noticed the runaway truck, but casually followed the road as it straightened along the base of the hill.

The driver looked up to see the pickup hurtling down the slope, trailing a plume of dust. It was on a direct collision course with the sedan.

The driver hesitated a moment, then calculated he could outrun the Harvester's imminent arrival. He punched the accelerator and angled the car toward the left to try to distance himself from the green missile.

Dirk saw the car accelerate and he let off his own brakes. The pickup reached the bottom of the hill and bounded high over the curb, its ancient springs groaning. The front wheels slammed hard onto the road, blowing out both tires, as the truck skittered across the road. Inside, the occupants saw the white sedan cross their path.

The sedan almost made it unscathed, but Dirk kicked the wheel to the right. It was just enough to direct his front fender into the sedan's rear flank. The impact spun the back of the car around hard until it hit the opposite curb. The Harvester's momentum carried it farther, over the curb and into the wooden sides of an empty vendor's stall.

Silence filled the air as the road dust settled to the ground. Summer felt dazed after smacking into the headrest in front of her, but was otherwise unhurt. She fared better than the two gunmen. The driver had sliced the top of his head on the rear-view mirror and was trying to stop the bleeding.

The gunman in back had knocked his head against the side window and sat, hunched over, in a woozy state.

Summer didn't wait for them to recover. She pulled up the door handle, threw her shoulder against the side, and rolled out of the car, clutching the artifacts case.

In the adjacent truck, the occupants had absorbed a similar collection of cuts and bruises, yet nothing worse, as the wooden stall had absorbed much of the impact. Dirk tried to get out, but his door was jammed shut. Norsang had already opened the passenger's door, shoving aside some splintered boards as he staggered out.

He saw Summer kneeling near the car as the driver tried to restart the stalled vehicle. There was movement in the backseat, and the short gunman leaned out the open door. He took a look at Summer, then noticed Norsang approaching. The gunman raised his pistol at the Tibetan and started firing.

His first two shots went wide, the third struck Norsang in the arm as he reached for his Glock.

The next shot would have killed him, but Summer caused it to deflect high. Kneeling forward, she swung the aluminum case in an arc and struck the gunman in the head, connecting at the same spot where he had struck the window. He slumped down and dropped his pistol. The white sedan started a second later.

The driver stomped on the gas, and the car lurched forward. Summer rolled away as the gunman on the backseat slid onto the floor and the door banged shut against his head. The car weaved down the road, one rear wheel wobbling. But the driver didn't slow. He sped into an alley and disappeared into the back streets of Dharamsala.

Summer watched its trail of dust, then got to her feet and turned toward the bashed green truck. If she hadn't been so scared, she might have laughed at its bloody trio of passengers. The handsome Tibetan man stood there, clutching the wound on his left triceps. The monk, in his red robe, had a bloody gash across his bald head. And Dirk, with a scrape on his cheek and a cut on his chin, clutched one of his knees.

"Are you all right?" Dirk asked.

"Me? I just got my clothes dirty," she said, brushing them. "But the three of you look like death warmed over." She stepped toward Norsang and looked at his bleeding arm. "You were hit?"

"It would have been a lot worse if you hadn't acted. Thank you."

Summer watched as the monk fell to the ground by the side of the pickup and began chanting a prayer. She turned to her brother. "I don't think he likes your driving."

"Don't know why," he said with mock innocence. "I already agreed to repair the damage."

"That was a crazy move, but I'm grateful you did

it." She looked again at the International Harvester, then stared at the monk. "That . . . that's the same truck and monk from this morning?"

It was Dirk's turn to smile.

"Yes, it is. I believe that's what they call in these parts good karma."

36

A security team from the Central Tibetan Administration arrived on the scene before the local police appeared and whisked the group back to McLeod Ganj. At the Tsuglagkhang complex, they were taken to a small medical bay and treated for their injuries. Norsang's wound was the most serious, but the bullet had missed bone. His wound was cleaned and bandaged, and he was pumped full of antibiotics.

But before he was released, the elder lama, Khyentse Rinpoche, entered the room and closed the door. He noted the bandage around Norsang's upper arm. "You are injured?"

"It's minor."

"I just spoke with the head of security. He confirms his belief that the infiltrators are Chinese agents. Why would they abduct the American?"

"It was the relics they possess. They are supposedly from the Nechung Monastery."

"The Nechung Idol?" His voice rose in a rare display of emotion.

"No, smaller relics. But an interesting coincidence. They supposedly belong to Ramapurah Chodron. I will speak with him as soon as possible. But I am concerned that the Chinese may be aware of our interest in the Nechung Idol."

"How could they know?"

"They must have intercepted the phone call made from the Tibet Club Museum. I have cautioned that without further technological firewalls, our communications throughout the compound may be at risk."

"I will bring the matter to the attention of His Holiness. As for the Americans, they are who they claim. Their father is the head of a large oceanographic agency. We can always use allies in their government, so perhaps we should be cooperative with them in any way possible."

"It shall be done."

Dirk and Summer were waiting for Norsang in a small meeting room, where they had been served tea after Dirk's cuts were treated.

"Your wing is still intact," Dirk said as the Tibetan sat down beside them.

Norsang raised his arm in a supportive sling. "The injury is minor." He looked at Summer. "Only on account of your intervention."

She tapped the artifacts case at her feet. "I had a hefty weapon at hand."

"I am glad neither of you was seriously injured. Such a display of violence is very unwelcome here."

"Perhaps you can enlighten us on what exactly happened today." Summer poured a cup of tea and passed it to the security man.

"It is, of course, speculation, but one cannot help but suspect the Chinese government. The Central Tibetan Administration and His Holiness, the Dalai Lama, in exile here are a thorn in the side of China. It is no secret they wish the Dalai Lama ill, along with the people of Tibet they oppress. So there are spies and observers all about Dharamsala."

"Ones that rob tourists at gunpoint?" Dirk asked.

Norsang shook his head. "A highly unusual incident." He motioned toward the case. "They are obviously interested in the artifacts."

"It doesn't seem likely, but we could have been tracked from Taiwan," Summer said. "A similar theft was attempted in Taiwan, and also in Singapore."

"Possibly," Norsang said. "It is also possible they intercepted communications between Mr. Greer and myself."

"Are they also interested in trafficking Tibetan artifacts?" Dirk asked with a hint of sarcasm.

"I do not know why they would be especially interested in these particular **thokcha** relics, but in this region they willingly purchase or commandeer anything that might give the Dalai Lama additional attention, prestige, or power."

"Including these carvings?"

Norsang nodded. "If they are indeed from the Nechung Monastery, they would prove valuable to the Oracle here. He will wish to inspect them, but he is in consultation this afternoon. In the interim, I thought we could pay a visit to Ramapurah Chodron."

"Who's that?" Summer asked.

"According to Mr. Greer," Norsang said, "he is the owner of your artifacts."

THE TINY HOUSE lay at the end of a forested footpath northwest of McLeod Ganj, perched atop a steep precipice. A backdrop of snowcapped peaks, part of the Dhauladhar range, towered majestically behind it. The stone and wood house appeared to be immaculately maintained, with a neat vegetable garden along its side. But in October, just a scattering of plants remained, struggling against the autumn chill.

"What a beautiful spot to escape civilization," Summer remarked.

Dirk pointed to an outhouse in the woods. "But missing a few creature comforts."

They followed Norsang as he moved cautiously along the footpath. He stopped and looked back to the road, where a pair of fellow security men stood guard, having tailed them in a separate vehicle. Like Norsang, they had been trained by the Indian

Army, serving in the elite National Security Guard, where they learned counterterrorism skills to protect the Dalai Lama.

Summer noted a curl of smoke rising from the chimney as they approached the front porch and Norsang knocked on the door. The thick wooden door was pulled open, revealing an old man in a flannel shirt. He looked to be well into his eighties, but still carried a rugged frame. His dark eyes probed the three visitors, but then the stone-like face broke into a warm smile.

"Tenzin Norsang, is that you?"

Norsang bowed before his elder. "Yes, Ram-la. It is good to see you."

"You were no taller than a goat the last time I saw you. Is your great-uncle well?"

"Yes, he is fighting age with a strong heart. He bids you to come visit him sometime." Norsang turned and introduced Dirk and Summer.

"Americans? I was in America once, many years ago. It was nearly as cold as the Himalayas. Please, come in."

Ramapurah Chodron led them inside, walking with a limp as he escorted them to a small couch and chair. He set about brewing a pot of tea on a wood stove and poured them each a cup in squat mugs. Summer noticed the tea was yellow and possessed a harsh, salty taste, not realizing it had been flavored with yak butter in the traditional Tibetan manner.

"Ram and my great-uncle," Norsang said, "served together in the Chushi Gangdruk, a Tibetan guerrilla force that fought against the Chinese many years ago."

Dirk noticed a photo on the wall of some young Tibetan men in military fatigues, standing at attention, in the snow. He recognized the state flag of Colorado on a mast in the background. "You were in Colorado?"

"Yes, we trained with the CIA at a secret base in the mountains," Ram said proudly. "They taught us how to communicate in code and operate radios in the mountains." He grinned. "We also ate beef, potatoes, and chocolate every day."

"My friends here have found some important artifacts from the old days that are attributed to you," Norsang said. "I would also like to ask you about another related item."

Summer set the case on a low table and opened the lid, while Ram refilled their teacups. She explained what they had discovered as she removed one of the carvings and unwrapped it. She passed the carving of the conch shell to Ram, who held it with both hands.

The old man's eyes grew large as he studied the object, holding it like a treasured gem. "Do you have all eight pieces?" he asked without looking at the open case.

"Yes," Summer said. "Are they yours?"

Ram closed his eyes and sat back in his chair as

he gripped the carving tightly. He seemed lost in a different time and place. After a few moments, he opened his eyes and nodded. "So they were lost in transit from Taiwan," he said in a low voice.

"How did they end up there?" Norsang asked.

"It's the reason I'm in McLeod Ganj." Ram rubbed the carving. "Once I recovered from my injury enough to escape Tibet, I traveled to Nepal, where I stayed for several months. I then made my way here. It was my intention to return the relics to the Oracle. On arriving, I met an officer from the Chushi Gangdruk who saw my injuries and insisted on buying me a meal." He tapped his right leg. "We went to a place in town . . . the Tibet Club, I think it's called."

Summer nodded. "Yes, we've been there."

"I was showing the relics to my friend, but they were noticed by another man who was dining with the proprietor. He was a Nationalist Chinese from Formosa, and he wished to purchase the relics for his museum there."

"Was his name Feng?" Dirk asked.

Ram tapped the arm of his chair in thought. "It may have been," he said, nodding. "He offered me quite a lot of money, but they were not mine to sell. They belonged to the monastery." He paused to sip his tea. "He then asked if he could borrow them for a temporary exhibit in Formosa. I was very reluctant to do so, then he offered to make a sizable donation to the monastery. Both my friend and the owner of the Tibet Club Museum, Mr. Hunt, vouched for the man. He said he would come back to Dharamsala in three months and would return the relics to the monastery at that time. I agreed to let him take them and left them with Mr. Hunt to prepare for transit." He pointed at the artifacts case.

"That was the last time I saw the relics." Ram shook his head. "The man never returned, so I assumed he had stolen them. I was so ashamed that I never told the monastery. I was able to confirm later that he did make the donation. But I had no idea that he died while attempting to return the **thokcha** relics."

"If I may ask," Dirk said, "how did you acquire the carvings?"

Ram looked at Norsang, who nodded for him to answer.

"My family was killed in 1956 by the Chinese during an uprising close to my home in Tsetang. I joined a rebel group with other men from my village who fought a guerrilla campaign against the occupiers. We were later supported by your CIA and brought to America for training. In March of 1959, tensions rose in Lhasa, and there were fears that the Chinese would abduct the Dalai Lama. A group of us were parachuted in to help him escape."

Summer's jaw dropped. "You helped the Dalai Lama escape Tibet?"

"It didn't work out that way. I actually led a separate team to Nechung Monastery, where we were to evacuate the Oracle." He paused a moment, recalling the events of that night.

"We discovered the Dalai Lama and the Oracle had already left Lhasa with an advance scouting team. I found a senior monk at the monastery and convinced him to come with us. But he would leave only if we helped secure its most holy relics."

He waved a hand toward the case. "These he gave to me. I stuffed them in my jacket."

"So these really are from Nechung Monastery?" Norsang asked.

Ram nodded. "Now you know why I was ashamed to inform the monastery here of their absence."

"But didn't the elder monk know?" Summer asked.

"Yes. Thupten Gungtsen was his name. That name, I never forget. Unfortunately, he did not survive the trip out. He died along with all the others . . ." His voice fell away.

The visitors remained silent, letting the old man collect his thoughts.

"A CIA airplane flew to Lhasa, at great risk, to take us out. We barely got off the ground under the small-arms fire from the Chinese. They damaged one of the aircraft's engines, but we still flew on. The weather was bad, and we hit a snowstorm. The plane was knocked all over the sky. We struck a mountain, and I was thrown out the door. But the plane flew on, then crashed. I still had these relics under my jacket."

Dirk, Summer, and Norsang all leaned forward. "How did you possibly survive?" Summer asked.

"I was thrown onto a glacier covered with fresh snow. When I regained consciousness, I could hardly move. I had a broken pelvis and a fractured leg." He pointed at his right leg. "I crawled through the night on my elbows. The storm passed in the morning, and I was found, barely alive, by some Nepalese traders. They nursed me back to health and helped me across the mountains into Nepal."

While Dirk and Summer sat there, enraptured by the story, Norsang stared with newfound interest at the **thokcha** carvings. Ram noticed his focus.

"You may take them to the Namgyal Monastery and present them to the Nechung Oracle."

"A most gracious gift," Norsang said. "The Oracle will be very pleased."

"He should thank these discoverers." Ram deferred to Dirk and Summer.

"Of course. Ram-la, if I may ask again, you acquired these after His Holiness was evacuated from Lhasa?"

"Yes, but it was within hours or a day."

"And the Chinese had not ransacked the temple?"

"There were Chinese militiamen there, but I don't know that anything had been removed or destroyed. There was panic in the city. Chinese forces had been mobilized on the west side of town, and rumor had it they were about to seize the Dalai Lama. That's why we rushed in."

"There was, in the monastery, another holy relic." Norsang paused. "It was called the Nechung Idol. Do you know if it was still there?"

"It was, but the monk took it with him."

"Which monk?"

"Thupten Gungtsen, the one I mentioned earlier. He was a very brave man. And strong. He carried the Idol all the way to the airfield. It must have weighed twenty kilos."

"It was . . . taken with you . . . on the flight out of Lhasa?"

"Yes," Ram said. "It was lost with Gungtsen and my men when the plane crashed."

Summer saw Norsang's face turn pale. "What is the significance of the Nechung Idol?"

"Nechung is one of the most sacred monasteries in all of Tibet," he said. "It was the historical seat of the State Oracle, at least until 1959."

"What," Dirk asked, "is the State Oracle?"

"In Tibet," Norsang said, "an oracle is a re-incarnated individual who acts as a medium to a spiritual deity. They carry out an important role in deciphering events and foretelling the future. The Nechung Oracle is our most important medium. He channels Pehar, the divine protector of the Dalai Lama and the Tibetan government-in-exile.

In this role as the State Oracle, he is one of His Holiness's most trusted advisors."

"The Nechung Oracle is alive and here in McLeod Ganj?" Summer asked.

"Of course," Norsang said. "But the Nechung Idol—"

"The Nechung Idol holds great significance to the Oracle, does it not?" Ram said. "That is what Gungtsen told me."

Norsang nodded slowly. "It is a matter of grave concern with the senior lamas, particularly after the time when the current Dalai Lama draws his last breath."

Ram gave a knowing nod. "In the matter of his reincarnation."

"There are now political implications to the matter," Norsang said. "The Chinese are eager to select the next Dalai Lama in order to exert control over all Tibetans, even those outside the country. If they were to possess the Idol, it would enable a more convincing claim on their part . . . or possibly to dissuade the Dalai Lama from reincarnating at all."

"Is the Nechung Idol," Summer asked, "made of **thokcha**?"

"Yes."

"That alone would seem to make it a target for the Chinese."

Norsang peered at the old man. "Could it have survived the plane crash?"

"Yes, it is quite possible," Ram said. "To my knowledge, the wreckage was not discovered at the time of the incident. Of course, it has been many years now, but it was in a remote area of the mountains."

Norsang stood and paced the small room. He stopped and knelt in front of the old warrior. "Ram-la, do you think you could identify where the plane crashed?"

Ram put his hand on Norsang's shoulder and shook his head. "I could only tell you the general area." He limped to a bookshelf and returned with a worn map of the Himalayas. He spread it out on the table and studied it a moment. Ram dragged a finger from their location in northern India, following the range of the Himalayas east across Nepal. He hesitated at a small bulge of Indian territory that jutted into the mountains between Nepal and Bhutan.

"It was here, in this area called Sikkim." He stepped to a desk, rummaged through a drawer for a magnifying glass, then returned to the map. "I was brought down a mountain and carried through a long valley to a herdsman's house in Rakamo, then on to the village of Dambung." He searched for it on the map, but couldn't find it.

"Wait, it is near Lachung." He pointed at a small town marked on the map, then drew his finger to the northeast, following the contours of the mountains. "Dambung would be somewhere around here, maybe seven kilometers from Lachung. This may be the valley." He then pointed to a remote glen that extended north between two high ridges. "The base of the peaks at the end of the valley. I think that is where I was found."

Norsang took careful note of the old man's descriptions. "May I borrow this map?"

"Certainly." Ram took a pencil and circled the area.

Norsang sat quietly for a moment. "Thank you, Ram-la. I will pursue the Nechung Idol in the mountains there. If you should remember anything else, please contact the monastery at Tsuglagkhang."

The old man tapped the circle on the map. "You must be very careful. The Tibet border runs behind the eastern slope of the valley. You cannot dare cross into Tibet. If the Chinese capture you there, you will vanish into prison for the rest of your days."

"The mountains you indicated are in India," Norsang said. "There will be no need to enter Tibet."

"Still, that is a very rugged area for you to search on your own."

"Yes . . ." Norsang studied the map with a mix of hope and dread.

The room fell silent before Dirk glanced at his sister, then turned to Norsang. "We'll assist you."

"You?" Norsang said. "You have done enough already."

"We can do more," Dirk said. "We have access to

satellite imagery and computer modeling that can narrow the search area. If the Nechung Idol is so important, we'd like to help."

"We have lots of experience at finding lost shipwrecks," Summer added. "We've already found one aircraft in the Philippines. It might be fun to find another."

"A trek into the Himalayas as fun?" Ram looked at Norsang, and both began to laugh.

Summer didn't see the humor and turned to her brother with a sudden look of trepidation.

"What," she whispered, "have we done now?"

37

Margot was the one to spot it, a small lean-to hidden by some bushes just off the beach. She, Pitt, and Giordino staggered off the windswept cove, where the hard-driving rain pelted the skin with stinging force. They found a bit of shelter under the low tropical vegetation as they made their way to the small structure.

It had been built of cut palm trunks, fitted around the base of a large banyan tree. Rafters across the top, covered with palm fronds, kept out most of the rain. Margot found the narrow entrance on the back side, facing inland. She ducked around a firepit just inside and took shelter from the storm. Pitt and Giordino followed her in, finding the structure roomier than it first appeared from outside. A bundle of firewood had been stacked in a corner next to a cast-iron pot, while a bench carved from a tree trunk ran across the back wall.

The sand floor was littered with cigarette butts, and Pitt noticed some dusty fish bones in the firepit next to an empty liquor bottle.

"It's not the Taj Mahal," Giordino said, "but it beats drowning on the beach."

Once Pitt's eyes adjusted to the dark interior, he noticed a rusty fish knife and some old netting on the wall. "Must be a fisherman's hut, used in rough weather."

"Or maybe a party hut." Giordino picked up the liquor bottle and poured out a cupful of sand.

Pitt took the bottle from Giordino. "Why don't you get us some heat?" He pointed at the woodpile. "While I work on some drinks."

"Deal."

Giordino gathered some of the dry wood from the pile and constructed a brace in the firepit with a few thick branches. He placed tinder on top of that and built a surrounding structure with smaller branches, keeping some larger ones nearby. Using a Zippo lighter he carried for his cigars, he ignited the tinder and, as the flames grew, carefully fed larger pieces onto the fire. In a few minutes, he had a roaring blaze that warmed the hut.

Pitt took the liquor bottle, along with two other empties by the bench, and stepped to an outside corner of the hut where rainwater gushed off the roof. He used its stream to carefully rinse out each bottle. Then he filled each with the water and returned inside, placing the bottles upright in the middle of Giordino's fire.

"Those aren't going to break and ruin my fine incendiary skills, are they?" Giordino asked.

"It's possible, but they're pretty durable. I suggest you yank them out shortly after the water starts boiling."

They watched for several minutes until large bubbles appeared. Giordino then used a pair of sticks as tongs to pull the bottles aside to cool.

"Look at you two," Margot said as she crouched next to the fire. "I got shipwrecked with a couple of Boy Scouts."

Giordino stretched out on the sand. "If only I'd gotten my merit badge in hammock-making."

By the time the boiled rainwater had cooled enough to drink, the tropical storm was striking with full fury. The small island lay in the heart of an area known as Typhoon Alley. Each year, perhaps two dozen churned through the region after forming in the open Pacific near the Marianas. This storm was mild by historical standards, but still reached typhoon status when its winds were clocked at over sixty-five knots.

The wind whistled through the hut, stirring up ashes from the fire. But the structure was well built and shrugged off the tempest, allowing very little water to enter. For the occupants, there was little to do but wait out the storm, and that suited them fine. Exhausted from their ordeals, they stretched out by the fire. Once their clothes had dried, they slept through the blustery night.

Margot woke in the morning to find Giordino stoking the fire.

He saw her stir. "Sleep well?"

"Like the dead." She looked around the hut. "Where's Dirk?" she asked, noticing Pitt was absent.

"Attempting to rustle us up something to eat." He gave her a wink. "I hope you're not too hungry."

Pitt appeared a few minutes later, carrying several mangoes and a large light-green grapefruit-shaped item.

"Breakfast is served," he said. "We won't starve just yet."

He took the hut's fish knife and ran the blade through Giordino's fire, then sliced the mangoes.

"Nice and ripe," Margot said, taking a bite.

Pitt nodded toward the entrance. "There's a loaded tree just around the corner."

She eyed the green fruit. "What else do you have there?"

"Breadfruit. They were a little high up on the tree. I thought I'd try one, for taste."

"Are they safe to eat raw?"

"They are if they're ripe. We'll cook this one just to be sure."

Pitt cut the breadfruit into chunks and roasted them on a stick like marshmallows. Margot sampled the first piece and nodded. "Tastes a little like a potato."

"Wasn't breadfruit what Captain Bligh was after when they mutinied on the **Bounty**?" Giordino asked.

"Yes," Pitt said with a laugh, "but don't get any ideas."

After they polished off the fruit, Pitt peered out the hut entrance. "The rains seem to have abated for the time being. I think I'll take a hike up to the top of the island and have a look around." He turned to Margot. "Care to join me?"

"Sure. I could go for a stretch of the legs."

"While you're out nature-loving," Giordino said, "I think I'll take a look at the damage on the **Stingray**."

Pitt and Margot headed south along the beach to the end of the cove, where the sand turned to black stone. They followed the shoreline along a rocky ledge that rose until ending at a short bluff. They watched the sea crash into the rocks below for several minutes before Pitt turned his sights upward.

The island's peak was visible from the bluff, and Pitt made a bead on it before leading Margot into the thick brush that grew above them. The western half of the island was dense with tropical vegetation, and Pitt had to snake his way through the foliage, gradually working his way up the rise.

"You didn't tell me it would be all uphill." Margot paused by a stand of bamboo to catch her breath.

"It's not too far to the top," Pitt said.

They hiked for several more minutes, eventually working their way out of the thick brush. Pitt angled to the south, where the terrain was clearer, falling away to low shrubs and grasses. They climbed to within a hundred yards of the summit, where the incline turned steep, and the grass dwindled away. The exposed terrain led through a corridor of red clay that was slick and muddy from the heavy rains.

They moved cautiously up the slope, but couldn't avoid slipping on occasion, smearing their clothes with the clay. Pitt guided them to a rocky ledge with some fallen trees, where they escaped the slick ground and took a moment to rest.

"Let's find a cleaner way down," Pitt said as he wiped the mud from his pants.

Margot looked at their messy clothes and laughed. "I hope Al lets us back in the hut."

It was a short climb from there to the rocky knoll of the island's summit, where they had an unfettered view of the island. While the rain had eased, the wind gusted briskly at the top, and Margot was soon shivering as they scouted their temporary home. Ocean waves crashed hard against the eastern shoreline. Nearly all the island's eastern half was a steep, barren slope that dropped sharply to the sea. But the western half, protected from the prevailing winds, was lush with tropical growth.

Pitt surveyed the island's perimeter and concluded

there was only one possible place to come ashore, and they had found it in the small cove. Looking down at the tiny ring of protected water, Pitt could make out the submersible and Giordino working alongside it.

"Dirk, over here."

Margot faced southeast, her arm out, pointing a finger toward the sea, as her hair blew wildly in the wind.

Beyond the island, the sky and ocean were still a messy swirl of gray. Dark thunderheads rolled in an endless stream from the east, pelting the sea with scattered squalls. The high winds whipped the sea, casting long, leaden rollers that pounded into the island.

But out to sea, past the tip of Margot's finger, Pitt detected something else. A small boat was making its way to the island.

It, too, was colored gray.

38

The small commercial plane descended out of a crystal clear blue sky. Waggling its wings in alignment, it settled on the lone runway of the recently built Pakyong Airport. Dirk was the first person off the plane, stepping onto the tarmac and stretching his arms in the crisp mountain air. Summer and Norsang exited a few steps behind him, followed by a pair of Tibetan security men. Dirk and Summer couldn't pronounce their multisyllabic names, so they took to calling the taller one Tash and the other Arie.

Summer gazed at the high green mountains surrounding the airport. "I don't see any snow. Maybe we'll avoid the cold."

"Don't bank on it," Dirk said. "I've looked at the satellite photos. There's plenty of white stuff on the higher slopes where we're headed."

They had traveled some seven hundred miles

east of New Delhi to the Indian state of Sikkim. At India's northeast corner, Sikkim was a finger of territory that protruded into the Himalaya Mountains, surrounded by Nepal to the west, Bhutan to the east, and Tibet to the north and northeast. More than a third of Sikkim was designated a national park, and its mountains, which included the world's third-highest, were some of the most rugged and remote parts of the Himalayan range.

"Let's collect our gear," Norsang said. "We should have a vehicle waiting for us."

Dirk and Summer had hurriedly shopped in New Delhi for boots, jackets, and camping equipment before their flight out. After assessing the satellite photos Hiram Yaeger had sent from NUMA headquarters, Dirk had also insisted on stopping at a dive shop. As they each collected a large backpack from the baggage stand, Summer noted the three Tibetans immediately checked to see if their Glock pistols had arrived intact in the luggage.

Inside the terminal, they approached a bearded man at the car rental counter, who examined Norsang's passport and quizzed him about their travel plans.

"We hope to do some trekking in Khangchendzonga National Park," Norsang said.

"Do you have travel permits? They are required in North Sikkim, which is highly restricted."

Norsang showed their permits, which they had acquired in New Delhi with the help of the Central Tibetan Administration.

The man gave Norsang the keys to a van and pointed him to the parking lot. "There can be landslides on the roads, so be careful." Once the group exited the building, he pulled out a cell phone and made a call, eyeing the group from a small window.

The visitors piled their belongings into a battered white Tata van, and Norsang took to the wheel. They drove north, winding through several valleys, then up a rise to the city of Gangtok. Built on top of a hill, Sikkim's capital had been the hub of the nineteenth-century trade route between Lhasa and Calcutta. More recently, Gangtok had become a base for ecotourism, as well as a growing commerce center, after a neighboring mountain pass to Tibet was reopened for trade in 2006.

After stopping for lunch at a vegetarian restaurant, they located a grocery store and stocked up on a week's supply of food and water. Stuffing the van full of the goods, Summer asked, "Are there pack mules where we're going?"

"No," Norsang said. "But if you're lucky, maybe some yaks."

They left the civilized confines and temperate climate of Gangtok behind as they traveled north into the Himalayas proper. The rich, lush vegetation turned to alpine wilderness as they climbed in elevation. Soon the temperature dropped, and snow-capped mountains fringed their route. To their west, the commanding presence of Kangchenjunga, a massive peak that rose twenty-eight thousand feet high, often filled the horizon.

As they progressed through narrow valleys, the mountainsides grew steeper. The roads were rough and narrow and, true to the rental agent's caution, dotted with landslides. North Sikkim had a dangerous mix of unstable geology and frequent seismic activity. When heavy monsoon rains were added to the equation, landslides became frequent and ubiquitous. Norsang had to creep over several mounds of rubble from earlier slides. Several times, they had to stop and clear rocks off the road so the van could proceed.

As darkness approached, they stopped at the confluence of two rivers at the small town of Lachung.

"We'll stay here for the night," Norsang said. "The main road turns east, but we need to continue north. There do not appear to be food or lodging options beyond here."

"Looks good to me." Summer appraised the small but colorful mountain town. "I'll take a soft bed over a sleeping bag anytime."

"It will also be a good opportunity," Norsang said, "for us to acclimate to the elevation."

They found a small lodge and took five rooms. As

Summer hauled her backpack up a flight of stairs, she nearly collapsed against the railing as she tried to catch her breath.

"Welcome to nine-thousand-foot elevation," Dirk said as he also gasped for air.

Norsang stood at the landing, bent over in laughter at their exertion. Like many Tibetans, he found friendly humor in the everyday struggles of others.

The group reconvened for dinner in the lodge's restaurant. Tash and Arie took a seat at a table in the back, while Dirk, Summer, and Norsang sat near the entrance. Hot Sikkim tea was served, then they ordered a mix of vegetarian dishes from India and Nepal.

"No beer after the road trip?" Summer asked when Dirk ordered only tea.

"I've learned the hard way that altitude and alcohol don't mix," he said, recalling a dose of altitude sickness he endured on a ski trip to Telluride.

A shared appetizer of Nepalese dumplings called **momo**s were served, then Norsang asked about the search plans. Dirk unfolded a satellite image he'd brought from the room and spread it across the table.

"I received this just before we left McLeod Ganj," he said. "We had our computer expert at NUMA try to compute a search grid based on the information Ram told us and available CIA records."

Norsang looked at the photo. It displayed a long valley that extended up from the bottom of the page, flanked by high mountain ranges to the east and west. The valley ended at a cluster of snowy peaks that spread across the top third of the page. In several locations, bright yellow lines and boxes were superimposed over the terrain.

"Where, exactly, is this?" Norsang asked.

"Not far from here, actually. Ram told us he was first taken to a house at a place called Rakamo, then he recuperated in the village of Dambung. The name Rakamo threw us for a loop, as it no longer seems to exist. But Hiram Yaeger, our computer expert, was able to locate it on an old map, and he transposed it onto the satellite image here." Dirk pointed to a yellow circle at the bottom.

"If you look close," Summer said, "you can see what appears to be the remains of an old house or structure of some sort."

Norsang studied the photo and nodded. "Yes, I see it. There's a clearing next to it, perhaps a pasture. Ram told us the traders brought him down the valley to a herdsman's house. There were probably yaks there at one time."

"This has to be the valley." Dirk traced his finger along a dotted yellow line that ran up the center of the photo. "He couldn't have been taken to Rakamo unless he was brought down through here. It's a fair bet he was found in the mountains at the valley's northern end."

The valley extended to the north, curving slightly to the east before ending in a box canyon. A high range blocked the valley, running roughly south-west to northeast. Long glaciers sprouted from both the north and south heights of the range, while several small green lakes dotted the lower elevations. The entire terrain appeared rugged and foreboding.

"What do they call these two mountains?" Norsang pointed to a prominent pair that dominated the top of the image.

Dirk shook his head. "No local names that we could find. It's part of a nature reserve, and pretty remote. Over to the west is what they call the Yumthang Valley. To the east is the border with Tibet. There is nothing in the way of roads or other visible activity anywhere in the vicinity."

"Yes, there are more than fifty peaks in the Himalayas that are over twenty-three thousand feet high," Norsang said. "The lesser ones can't all be named. But this is an encouraging sign that our objective may still be undisturbed. Where do you think the plane may have crashed?"

"That's where things turn dicey," Dirk said. "We really don't know how far Ram traveled off the mountain . . . or which mountain, for that matter. He crawled for several hours and said it was downhill. Could he have crawled a mile or two? Or even farther?"

"Ram is a very tough man. I would not doubt his ability, in such circumstances."

"That's good to know, based on our primary search grid. The computer was fed the aircraft's presumed flight path between Lhasa and Darjeeling, as well as the approximate weather conditions."

"Hiram determined the plane's destination?" Summer asked.

"The Tibetan guerrillas were mostly operating out of this neighborhood. He found evidence that the Civil Air Transport, an airline owned by the CIA, ran regular flights from Darjeeling while supporting actions in Tibet. He also found reference to a C-47 that went missing in March of 1959, so he thinks there's a match. Hiram ran computer simulations using a combined scenario of engine failure and poor weather as the cause of the crash."

"How would the computer know that?" Norsang asked.

"An educated guess based on experience from World War Two," Dirk said. "It's hard to believe, but some six hundred transport planes were lost over the Hump, flying supplies to the Nationalist Chinese during the war. The C-46s and C-47s suffered at the mercy of turbulent winds and icing over the Himalayas, in addition to mechanical failure."

"Six hundred planes. That's terrible," Summer said. "How will we know if we have the right one?"

"The normal supply routes were much farther east, so that shouldn't be a worry here." Dirk returned to the satellite image. "The computer simulations suggest the plane struck the northern face of one of these two mountains in the center, at the end of the box canyon." He pointed to two yellow squares superimposed near the northern summit of each. "The one to the southwest is taller, so the odds favor starting the search there."

"That makes sense," Norsang said. "What are these other yellow boxes?" He pointed to a half dozen squares north of the two peaks.

"Additional search grids, I'm afraid. The reality is, that plane could have gone down anywhere in this range."

"I didn't bring my snowshoes," Summer said, noting the white patches visible on the summits.

"Another risk," Dirk said. "The wreckage could be buried under snow, in which case we'll have little hope of discovering it. But at the moment, only the upper summits are covered."

"It appears there have been no heavy snows yet this fall," Norsang said. "The ground looks clear for that altitude. Where do you advise we start the search?"

"These first two blocks represent the highest probability. But they are the highest up and will take some rugged hiking to get there. Tonight, Hiram is going to run some additional scenarios and prioritize the remaining areas. I best check in with him after dinner, while we still have an internet connection."

Dirk put away the photo as the rest of their meal was brought to the table. They started with a noodle soup, followed by a vegetable curry with rice and lentils. Dirk relented and tried a taste of **tongba**, a hot millet beer served in a bamboo mug.

When all were stuffed and the dishes cleared away, Dirk excused himself to check for an email update from Yaeger. For dessert, Norsang and Summer ordered **lassi**, a sweetened fermented yogurt drink popular in India.

"Is this your first visit to the Himalayas?" Norsang asked.

"Yes. I'm not much of a mountain person. Dirk and I grew up in Hawaii and have spent most of our lives near the ocean."

"I have longed to visit the sea," Norsang said, "but the mountains hold great purpose. I hope you appreciate their beauty and perhaps find enlightenment during our upcoming trek."

"The Himalayas are a spiritual place for Tibetans?"

"For all Buddhists," he said. "Many gods and goddesses are believed to reside there. But evil spirits and demons exist there as well. The **nyen**, for example, are evil entities that roam the mountains. Other spirits dwell in the lakes and rivers."

"Also in the water?"

"Yes. Every lake, in fact, is said to hold a dragon."

"Will they do us harm?"

"Trespassers can be cursed with injury or plague, but I am sure they would never harm a pretty girl from Hawaii." He smiled.

"But you respect the spirits."

"I believe it is never wise to offend others, in this world or the next."

Summer was intrigued by the man. Like most Buddhists, he carried a steady calmness laced with good humor. He had a strong sense of inner self that she found alluring.

"I've been wondering something," she said. "How do you reconcile your faith with the need to carry arms and potentially commit violence in your duties?"

"It is a difficult issue for some," he said. "But the Dalai Lama represents our faith. So for me, protecting our faith supersedes any other contradictions."

"Have you always lived in Dharamsala?"

"Yes, except for when I served in the Indian Army. My grandparents fled Tibet in the 1950s during the Chinese occupation. They crossed the mountains in winter with only the clothes on their backs and settled in Dharamsala. My father loved hiking, and we took many treks together in the mountains. There are four sacred peaks in Tibet we always hoped to visit, but that is impossible."

"You can never go to Tibet?"

"Not as things stand now." His normally upbeat face hardened, and Summer could see a hint of sadness in his eyes. He caught her gaze and returned it with another smile.

"I've never been to Hawaii either," he said.

"Perhaps one day you could show me around there and teach me to dance the hula."

Summer touched his hand and laughed. "If you promise to keep the spirits away from us while we are in the mountains, you've got a deal."

39

How about that," Pitt said, eyeing the distant boat. "Help is already headed our way."

Margot clasped a hand around his arm and squeezed hard. "It's the commandos' boat. They're not coming here to save us," she said with fear. "They're coming to kill me."

Pitt took another look and recognized the gray support boat that had lain alongside the **Melbourne** when he'd dropped Margot off in the helicopter.

He turned to her, knowing they were just as likely searching for the submersible. "Why would they battle rough seas to come look for you?"

"They discovered I was missing and correctly guessed I escaped the ship. Perhaps they realize I saw them murder your crewmen."

"Are there any other reasons?"

Margot stared at the ground. "It's the **Melbourne**. They must have discovered its true capability. They'd already tortured my father once, and they must have again when they found me miss-ing." She looked up at Pitt, tears streaming down her face.

"What sort of capability?" he asked.

"Subsea ultrasonic wave cavitation." She wiped away the tears. "It was an accidental discovery. My father was experimenting with acoustic waves, something called sonolysis, at various frequencies to break up lava and light sediment formations on the seabed for mining."

"To get at the fountainheads."

"Exactly. For mining diamonds. The application of sonic waves was designed to incite cavitation in the tiny pockets of subsurface lava that contain water. The cavitation creates bubbles in the water pockets that expand with great force, blowing apart the lava bit by bit. We could then get beneath the lava caps to determine if there were diamonds present.

"When my father first started testing the system, he had mixed results on the seafloor, but found a startling side effect."

"He could alter undersea currents to create tsu-nami waves."

"How did you know?"

"NUMA has been researching ways to alleviate or redirect tsunamis through the use of acoustic gravity waves. We're far from cracking the code, but it sounds like your father has figured out an-other means."

"Not entirely. Project Waterfall, as we called it, is not able to generate physical waves outright. But in the right locations, it can redirect and amplify subsea currents through the cavitation effect, potentially creating a large wave force. Especially in areas such as the Luzon Strait and surrounding waters, where there are powerful deep-sea currents."

"Mariners call that region the Devil's Sea," Pitt said. "So the system can generate surface waves?"

Margot gave a reluctant nod. "That was the latest focus of research and testing. My father received a contract from the Taiwan government to develop the technology. He didn't want to pursue it, but it was a generous offer, and he thought the goal was worthy. It paid for the construction of the **Melbourne**, and the Taiwanese opened up mining rights in their territorial waters in a sharing arrangement with my father . . . He's a miner at heart. That's all he really wants to do."

"Taiwan? What do they aim to do with the technology?"

Margot drew a semicircle in the dirt with the toe of her shoe. "They want to build a seawall, if you will. Using remote devices that are fixed underwater at key locations around the island's western perimeter. For defensive purposes."

"A tsunami defense?"

Margot nodded. "In the event mainland China ever decided to launch an amphibious assault. It would allow Taiwan to wipe out the attacking fleet before they reached the shore."

"Is it possible?"

"My father and the Taiwanese engineers involved in its development think so. The turbulent waters found in the Luzon Strait extend north into the Taiwan Strait. If the technology can be perfected and deployed in the proper areas, it is very much possible."

"So the rogue waves that struck Aparri and sank your survey boat were no flukes of nature."

"Unfortunately, no. The Chinese commandos apparently came aboard during a test procedure and interfered with the operation. The system's transducers remained activated for an extended period, generating multiple waves. I was surveying for another location to test the system when we were struck."

"I had noticed you weren't dragging a traditional sonar system," Pitt said. "Do the commandos understand it?"

Margot shrugged. "My father claims they were ignorant of the system when they boarded and seemed to have hijacked the ship to perform an underwater survey. Maybe they are just after diamonds, but I fear they have now discovered the ship's capabilities."

"I know what they are after." Pitt explained the downed hypersonic missile and motioned toward the approaching boat. "They may well be looking for Al and me, not you."

"That fits with what I saw on the bridge," she said. "They wanted to find something in the northern part of the strait. Either way, we're all in danger."

"Perhaps many more people than just us." Pitt looked at the gray boat pounding over the waves. "I need to get back to Al. It might be better if you stayed here on the high ground."

He pointed to the northwest side of the summit, where a forested bulge extended into the upper grass slope. "Head over to those trees and hide yourself in the rocks. Stay hidden until Al or I come for you."

Margot didn't like the idea of being left alone but understood the risk. "I'll be there. Be careful." She scampered down to the tree line, then hunkered down in a hollow between several boulders.

Pitt turned in the other direction and took off at a run down the slope. To avoid the slippery clay, he moved to the north before descending. A short distance into the brush, he noticed a small creek and used it as a pathway down the mountain.

The ground was still slippery, and he lost his footing several times. His path was slowed when he encountered a thick grove of bamboo. After threading his way through the tall shoots, he worked his way past a steep incline dense with undergrowth. The creek bed provided an opening in the brush and a

view to the sea. He splashed his way down the narrow waterway until it trickled into the ocean at the
edge of the cove.

Giordino was standing waist-deep in the water,
working on the submersible's thrusters, when Pitt
ran up.

Giordino commented on Pitt's soiled clothes.
"Did I miss the invite to the mud wrestling tour-
nament?"

"You certainly missed a couple of good take-
downs," Pitt said. "We've got trouble on the way.
An armed party from the **Melbourne** that won't be
happy to find us."

"How'd they track us here?"

"I don't know. They could also be looking for
Margot."

"Is she all right?"

"Yes, I left her up high." He gestured toward the
submersible. "We need to ditch the rocket motor.
Do you think there's enough juice left to raise the
hydraulic arm?"

"Hold your breath and we'll find out."

Giordino climbed into the submersible and took
a seat at the copilot's controls. Following his own
advice, he held his breath as he activated the manipulator. To his surprise, the arm moved upward
without hesitation, and the aluminum claw released its grip on the rocket motor. He was able to
turn the arm a foot or two to the side before the
controls fell dead from lack of power.

"Don't ask for any more miracles today," he said as he climbed out the hatch.

"No miracles, just some muscle." Pitt stood in the water with a hand on the motor.

He waited for his powerful friend to join him, and they tried to pull the rocket assembly off the submersible's skids. The unit weighed several hundred pounds, but they could slide it a foot or two at a time, grunting in unison.

Once they had freed it from the submersible, they found they could drag the unit across the hard-packed sand bottom. Stepping parallel to the **Stingray**, they moved it twenty feet away. Then they immersed themselves in the water and pulled it as deep as they could. They broke to the surface, swam to the submersible, and climbed atop to study their handiwork. The choppy conditions in the cove and the deeper location where they'd dropped it were just enough to obscure the rocket from view.

"What we do for the red, white, and blue," Giordino muttered, wiping salt water from his eye.

The two men waded ashore and crossed the beach to the small hut, where Pitt retrieved the fish knife.

Giordino peered through the slats of the lean-to. "Company's arriving."

The gray crew boat was visible offshore, just beyond the southern entrance to the cove. The boat lingered for a moment, then changed course and accelerated through the breakers to access the cove.

Pitt and Giordino scurried into the jungle, climbing upward a short distance before Pitt took an abrupt turn to the south.

"A shortcut?" Giordino asked.

"No, but easier going, with a view thrown in."

Pitt led them laterally until they reached the jagged ravine with the running creek. He climbed a short distance until he reached an opening in the tree canopy. A few yards farther, he ducked behind some large boulders in the middle of the gurgling water.

Giordino followed him, then gazed at the streambed that wound its way to the top of the island. "Nice little staircase up and down the mountain."

"Wish I'd found it earlier," Pitt said. "At the bottom, it's obscured by the brush."

They looked down the narrow cut, which was swallowed by a wall of trees and vegetation just short of the beach. To their right, they had a clear view of the gray boat as it pulled into the cove and ran aground beside the NUMA submersible.

40

Before the boat touched the beach, Ning was on the radio, calling to Zheng on the **Melbourne**.

"The NUMA submersible," he said, failing to suppress his surprise. "It's here, on the island."

"Are the operators alive?"

"I don't know. We will investigate."

"Take them alive, if you can," Zheng said. "I want to know what they recovered."

The boat nudged onto the sand next to the **Stingray**. A four-man commando team took a defensive position around both vessels as Ning waded to the submersible with a drawn pistol.

He studied the exterior, noting its scarred paint and damaged lights and thrusters, then climbed into the hatch. Finding it empty, he emerged and jumped into the water, carefully examining the empty mesh basket at the prow. He took a cursory look around the submersible, then joined the other men.

"Sir, there's a structure in the trees." One of the gunmen pointed to the fisherman's hut.

Ning nodded, but hesitated when he saw two sets of footprints in the sand that crossed the beach to the cove's south end. He made his way to the hut with one of the commandos, but found it empty except for a few bottles of water and some fresh fruit rinds. He stooped and placed his hands low over the firepit. "Still warm. They were here a short time ago."

He walked back to the beach and looked up toward the island's peak, then gathered his team.

"The windward side of the island is barren. There is no place to hide there, so they will likely be in the jungle above us." He pointed to the south end of the cove. "You two men, go follow those tracks to the south as far as you can, then ascend along the fringe of the jungle to the mountain."

He turned and pointed in the other direction. "The rest will move north of the hut fifty meters and climb up from there. Rendezvous at the peak, then descend above us here to the center of the cove. Try to capture them alive."

"What if they are armed?" one of the men asked.

"If they don't surrender," Ning said, "kill them."

41

Pitt and Giordino counted five armed men stepping onto the beach. After they converged out of sight near the hut, two commandos appeared and began tracking Pitt's and Margot's footprints to the south.

Giordino craned his head over the rocks. "I can't make out where the other three went."

"If they went the other direction, there's nowhere to go but up. That puts us in a good spot to make a play for their boat."

Giordino nodded. "I haven't seen signs of anyone left aboard."

"Let's go find Margot," Pitt said, "and make a run for it."

They made a spirited hike up the narrow gully, stopping only briefly to catch their breath. They exited the tree line, and Pitt led them north toward the forested bulge at the base of the summit.

Margot spotted their approach and rose from

her hiding spot in the rocks. As she waved to them, she took a step forward, but tripped and fell hard. When she didn't immediately rise, Pitt and Giordino rushed over to her.

"I'm okay," she said as they helped her up, but she collapsed when she took a step forward. "It's my ankle. I'm so sorry."

"Not to worry," Giordino said. "You've got a couple of shoulders to lean on." He helped her to her feet.

"Are they coming for us?" she asked.

"Yes, on either side," Pitt said. "But I found a faster way back down. We're going to try for their boat."

"Wouldn't it be better to hide?"

"No. They know we're here. They'd find us eventually."

Margot put an arm around each man, and they helped her across the open slope to the south. She shook off the initial pain and tried to put some weight on her left foot, but not enough for her to walk on her own.

They were nearly across the open base of the summit and approaching the head of the creek when Pitt suddenly stopped. "Down," he whispered.

They dropped into a shallow rut. To their right, the line of underbrush extended for forty or fifty yards before falling away in a steep expanse of slick red clay that descended to the south. It was the same slope Pitt and Margot had climbed earlier.

Following in their tracks, midway up the field, came two of Ning's commandos armed with assault rifles.

"They were a little quicker than I thought," Pitt said.

"You two go on without me," Margot said. "I'll be okay. They won't kill me."

Pitt ignored her plea and turned to Giordino. "Take her into the brush and work your way to the creek bed. I'll see if I can slow them down a bit. Head to the beach. I'll try to catch up."

Giordino didn't hesitate. "Sorry, my dear, no time to debate." He slid an arm beneath Margot and picked her up like a rag doll. His thick legs churned as he sped down to the brush, disappearing into the thicket before Margot had a chance to protest.

Pitt slithered forward until he came to a thin ridge that afforded some cover. From there, he could see the two commandos moving slowly up the incline. Struggling with the slick mud, they seldom looked up.

The slope above them rose to a short bluff, where Pitt and Margot had rested beside a stand of dead trees. Pitt focused on their resting spot's bench, where he could see a fallen log about twelve feet long.

Pitt set off for the tiny promontory. His best hope to avoid detection was to angle up the mountain, then descend using the dead trees as cover. He had little time to act, but waited until one of the commandos slipped and fell. Pitt rose and sprinted up the high slope, then turned south.

The wet ground was slick beneath his feet, and he sent a few loose rocks tumbling, but he proceeded down the hill until he reached the bluff.

Pitt dropped to the ground behind a large rock. Gasping for breath, he briefly wished for a younger man's lungs. The climb up the peak, combined with the short sprint, had left him winded. When his heart rate settled, he peered over the side.

The commandos showed no sign of having seen him. They still progressed up the slope and were now less than thirty yards from the rise.

Pitt crawled to the large fallen log and took cover behind it. He turned onto his back and pressed his feet against its side, testing its grip on the terrain. The log broke free of the wet ground and rocked freely, except for one section near the end. Pitt found a portion of the root was still buried. He dug at the damp soil, but the root ran too deep to free. He turned and kicked at it instead. Luckily, the damp wood had begun to rot and crumbled under force. After a few well-placed blows, the root gave way.

He crawled back to the center of the log and took a last peek over its top. The commandos were still struggling up the grade, approaching the hill's steepest part. Pitt aligned his feet on the side of the log and gave a hearty shove, sending it rolling off the bluff.

The dead tree accelerated as it bounded down the hill. One of the commandos yelled a warning as he saw it approach. He jumped to the side to escape its reach and promptly lost his footing. He fell backward and slid down the slope, caking his rifle in mud, before digging in his heels.

The second gunman hesitated at the sight of the log before he tried to jump to the right, opposite his partner. He didn't make it.

The thick log rolled over his left foot, briefly locking him in place. The ligaments in his knee snapped as if he'd been blindsided by a Baltimore Ravens lineman. He gasped as the mass of timber rolled over him and down the hill, not stopping until it crashed into a thicket far below.

Pitt didn't wait around to watch his handiwork, but bolted back across the summit. He guessed at least one of the commandos had seen him, so he altered his path. He ran straight north, sprinting well past the head of the creek before ducking into the brush. He had to stop to catch his breath, leaning against an acacia tree a moment, before backtracking through the bushes. When he reached the creek, he stopped and cocked his ear to the breeze.

He could detect the two commandos conversing in the distance. By Pitt's reckoning, they were still on the muddy incline, nowhere near him. Secure in that knowledge, he began to make his way down the bed of the creek.

He descended at a measured pace, regulating his breathing while ignoring the pain in his legs. He kept an ear open for any trackers while looking ahead for signs of Margot and Giordino. Once, at an exposed stretch, he caught a glimpse of the two of them far below. Based on their progress, Margot must have been moving better on her injured ankle.

Pitt paused midway down the hill, then picked up his pace until he reached the small overlook where he and Giordino had stopped earlier. He took a quick look at the beach and the crew boat, which both appeared vacant. Pitt continued down the meandering creek to the thicket in front of the cove.

He followed the line of the beach, remaining in the brush, until he found Margot crouched behind a tree. He crept over and knelt beside her. "Everything okay?" he whispered.

She smiled at his arrival. "Al just ran out to check the boat." She pointed through the bushes. Giordino stood in the water between the boat and submersible, then waded ashore and jogged over to them.

"Lights are on, but nobody's home," he said, showing no surprise at Pitt's timely arrival.

Pitt took a quick look up and down the beach. "Okay, let's take it."

He and Giordino aided Margot to her feet and

helped her scurry across the beach. Though still limping, she could now put weight on her left foot.

They reached the water and splashed toward the boat. Giordino was the first to get there and reached out a hand to the rail to pull himself aboard. As he did so, the heavy clatter of gunfire erupted. Just beyond them, a stream of bullets struck the water.

They turned as one toward the NUMA submersible a few feet away. Standing in the hatch, a man in combat fatigues cradled a QCW-05 submachine gun.

"Miss Thornton," Ning said with a cruel expression. "It is nice to see you again. And your friends, too."

42

Frost covered the ground in Lachung when the white van rolled out of the lodge's gravel parking lot early in the morning. Norsang drove past an apple orchard at the end of town, then took a northerly side road that followed the meandering Lachung River. Five miles later, he turned onto an even smaller road that crossed the river over a rickety bridge.

A short distance beyond, they reached the tiny village of Dambung, where Ram had been taken many years before. Norsang crept the van past a small Indian Army post, thankful nobody was manning the checkpoint, then drove by a few scattered residences. When they reached a small stream rushing down a narrow valley from the north, he pulled to the side of the road and turned to Dirk. "Is this the place?"

Dirk confirmed their position on a handheld GPS unit. "Time for some exercise."

They unloaded their backpacks, divvied up the food supplies, then bid the van good-bye. Norsang led them through some underbrush and began following the stream up the center of the valley. Summer took only a few steps before she was breathing hard. "This," she said, "is going to be . . . a long day."

"Don't worry about . . . keeping up with the Tibetan mountain goats," Dirk said. "Just take it slow."

Summer nodded, taking in the beauty around her to distract herself from the exertion. The hotel manager had told them the area was known as the Switzerland of Sikkim, and she could see why. Steep, craggy mountains rose on either side of them, while the narrow valley they hiked was lush green, even in the late fall. A few hearty rhododendrons still bloomed amid thick clusters of fir and pine trees.

The weather was clear and mild, the dry air crisp, and Summer decided there were few better places to be trekking when out of breath. She glanced at her brother, who carried a bulky duffel bag in addition to his backpack. He had it resting on top of the pack, so it protruded over his head. Seeing how heavy it looked, Summer decided she had no reason to complain.

They followed the remnants of an old trail alongside the stream, climbing steadily up the long valley. At the first sight of the tall mountains at its end, the three Tibetans fell prostrate to the ground. Dirk and Summer were only too thankful for the rest while the Buddhists prayed to the deities.

They quickly regained the trail. The two Tibetan guards, accustomed to high altitude, set a quick tempo and gradually pulled ahead of the others. Norsang hung back, staying within sight of Dirk and Summer, who followed at a measured pace.

Summer stopped her brother. "Do you hear that?"

"What?"

"I keep hearing a faint buzzing."

"Mosquitoes, maybe? I can't hear anything over the water." He pointed to the rushing stream. "Or the blood pounding in my ears."

They followed the valley north for several miles, then stopped for lunch when it curved east and ended in a horseshoe-shaped canyon. Dirk and Summer caught up to the three Tibetans, boiling tea over an open fire, and peered up at the rising slopes around them. The skyline was dominated by two snowcapped mountains, one to the northwest, the other slightly east. They were connected by a narrow brown ridge beneath their summits. A vertical band of ice reached from the northwest peak nearly to their position, feeding the valley stream that flowed below.

Summer stared at the towering mountains. "Where's my Sherpa and oxygen tank?"

"Might have been a good idea," Dirk said. "The

summits are nineteen thousand feet. Unfortunately, we're on our own."

Norsang handed each a steaming cup of tea with yak butter, which seemed to be an elixir in this part of the world. "Soup will be prepared shortly, then we will continue," he said. "We'll have a hard climb this afternoon, but then we will be situated for searching on the other side of the ridge."

"How does our route look?" Dirk asked.

"It appears there is a satisfactory path to the upper ridge that will require no technical climbing."

"Where," Summer asked, "will we camp for the night?"

"We can see a small plateau just below the ridge, which looks promising." He saw the trepidation in her eyes and laughed. "Is it the mountains you fear or the climb?"

"Most definitely the climb."

"Do not worry. The gods have blessed us with clear weather. It is a good omen."

They downed a lunch of hot lentil soup and fried bread. The sun was shining brightly when they continued their trek a short time later. A breeze wafting from the upper slopes put a chill to the sun's warmth as they proceeded up the incline. The security man Arie, an experienced trekker, led the way up the lower slope. As the terrain grew steep, he began crisscrossing the mountainside, constantly seeking the easiest path through the rocky landscape.

After an hour of climbing, the group stopped for a rest. Summer noted the Tibetans gathering sticks and bits of dry wood and piling them atop their backpacks.

"Wood for fires," Norsang said. "Before long, we will be passing above the tree line."

Summer saw that the slopes above were barren of trees and most vegetation. "But we brought gas stoves."

"Call us old-fashioned, but we prefer open fires," Norsang said.

Summer shrugged and tied a few sticks onto her pack for the cause. They resumed climbing. The route became more arduous the higher they went, their rest breaks more frequent. At times, they had to scale boulders or skirt around piles of scree that blocked their path. By late afternoon, the Tibetans had approached the ridgeline and began setting up camp on the wind-sheltered plateau that Norsang had targeted. Dirk and Summer joined them a short time later, gratefully dropping their packs as they tried to breathe the thin mountain air.

Norsang saw the exhaustion on their faces and joined them with a relaxed grin. "A tough climb today, but you did well."

"I'll sleep tonight," Dirk said. "Oxygen or no oxygen."

Summer slapped the flat rock she was sitting on. "And bed or no bed."

Norsang laughed. "It won't be that bad." He

motioned to Tash, who was setting up their tents in a semicircle.

Summer stood and gazed at the vista to the south and west, beyond the slopes they had just conquered. She had been too busy laboring up the heights and watching her footing to pay much attention to the scenery. From their elevated perspective, she marveled at the postcard view of green valleys and mountain ridges below them. "It's gorgeous. Worth the climb."

"It's even better on the other side," Norsang said. "Come, take a look." He rose and climbed to the top of the ridge. Dirk and Summer followed with less vigor. The summit measured less than a dozen feet wide, before falling away on the opposite side to the north. Norsang stopped on a slab of sun-baked slate on the narrow crest and waited for the pair to join him.

A brisk wind blew across the heights, but Summer shrugged off the cold as she took in a staggering sight of the Himalayas that extended to the west in a seemingly endless string of rugged, snow-covered mountains.

Norsang pointed to a high peak that dominated the vista. "That's Kangchenjunga, the world's third-highest mountain. Over ten thousand feet higher than we are now."

"Where's Mount Everest?" Summer asked.

"Chomolungma, as it is called in Tibet, lies about one hundred and twenty miles to the west of us."

Dirk surveyed the immediate terrain. They stood on the ridge that linked two high peaks. For lack of an established name, he had designated the mountain to their left, or west, as Whisky, and the smaller pinnacle to the northeast as November. Like its southern slope, Whisky also had a long glacier trailing from the northern side that descended almost two miles to a rugged plateau. At the base of the glacier lay the teal lake he had seen in the satellite photo.

But their first planned search area was directly in front of them, a rock- and gravel-strewn slope that dropped steeply away to the plateau and lake. Dirk stepped to the edge of the ridge and gazed down at the uneven hillside. His eyes scanned for signs of aircraft wreckage.

"I already made a quick examination, but found nothing," Norsang said. "We'll perform a thorough search tomorrow."

Summer grabbed Dirk by the elbow and pulled him toward their tents. "He's right. It's too windy to muck around here now. Let's get something to eat."

The rays of the setting sun were striking the mountaintops in an explosion of orange as they started to hike back. They reached their campsite in time to watch the last moments of a brilliant sunset. Just before the sun vanished, Summer caught a flash in the corner of her eye. She turned to her brother. "Did you see that?"

"See what?"

"A reflection of some sort, just as the sun went down."

"Whereabouts?"

Summer pointed up the ridgeline toward Whisky. "Just beneath the lip of the ridge, before it angles up to the peak. About a hundred yards from here."

Dirk called to Norsang, who was helping prepare dinner. "We'll be right back." He turned to Summer. "Take us there."

As the sky turned purple, Summer made her way up and across the ridge, staying beneath its crown to avoid the wind. The terrain was a tumble of earth-colored rocks and gravel, mixed with small patches of ice. In front of her, the snowy summit of Whisky trailed a white river of ice, which descended along the trail they had climbed from the valley.

The reflection she'd seen had come from just before the edge of the glacier, but nothing was apparent as they drew close. Had it just been off the ice?

She stopped to catch her breath, then took a step forward—and saw it. Below them, a flat piece of metal lay wedged behind a large mound of boulders. She pointed down the hillside.

"I see it," Dirk said.

Curiosity gave them both a jolt of energy, and they quickly scrambled down the rocky slope. As she drew near, Summer lost her footing on some loose gravel. She stopped herself by grasping a boulder, then jumped to an open ledge beside the object.

It was triangular in shape, measuring about eight feet long. At one end, a rounded tip had lost its faded brown paint, blasted by windblown snow and sand. The scoured finish remained bright enough to have reflected the rays of the sun. Summer stepped closer. She saw it was a buttressed wedge of aluminum, about six inches thick. One edge was rough and jagged, while the opposite side was dented, but otherwise smoothly rounded. Despite its lonely position atop the mountain, she had no doubt as to the object's design.

Summer had found the wingtip from an airplane.

43

A cursory search of the mountainside before complete darkness set in revealed no additional wreckage. Dirk and Summer, who'd been joined by Norsang, reluctantly broke off their investigation and returned to camp, using flashlights. Tash and Arie had a fire burning and a pot of hot stew prepared.

Dirk accepted a steaming bowl from Arie and took a seat on a rock. He pointed toward Whisky and shook his head. "It doesn't make sense. We're on the south-facing slope. A plane flying from Lhasa would strike on the northern side, where Hiram laid out our search grids."

"The wind and storms here can become very violent," Norsang said. "Perhaps they become disoriented in bad weather."

Summer nodded. "I read an account from the survivors of a C-47 that crashed in Tibet during

World War Two. They were flying the Hump and ended up three hundred miles off course."

"That's not the answer I wanted to hear," Dirk said, "but you are right. Still, we didn't find any other wreckage."

"We'll look again in the morning," Summer said. Finishing dinner, she set down her bowl and yawned. "Which I hope will not arrive anytime soon."

She helped the others clean up, then headed straight to bed. The Tibetans retired a short time later, but Dirk lingered by the dying fire. Though he was physically exhausted, his mind replayed the conversation with Ram, trying to picture the flight from Lhasa. He finally stood and looked up at the night sky.

There were only a few scattered clouds and a blanket of bright stars glistened above him. He stared at the heavens for some time, spotting a pair of meteors streaking by, before retiring to his tent.

Had he looked down the mountainside rather than up at the night sky, he might have noticed another illumination—three small lights moving through the woods far, far below.

PART III

Escape from Whisky Peak

44

Margot stared out the wheelhouse window at the gray horizon, trying to quell a wave of nausea. It wasn't just the turbulent seas that made her ill. A glance at the arrogant figure of Ning at the crew boat's helm was enough to incite queasiness throughout her tired body. Added to that was her father's condition, and what else she might find when they returned to the **Melbourne**. As her stomach churned, she took a look out the rear window and reminded herself that at least she didn't have it as bad as Pitt and Giordino.

The two men sat on the open stern deck, their backs secured to the transom. They were soaking wet from both the seawater that sloshed around the deck and the pummeling waves that crashed over the rail. Despite their discomfort, the two men appeared to be chatting amiably with all the worries of a pair of sightseers riding a tour bus through the streets of London.

Margot had never met anyone like them. While her father was tough, Pitt and Giordino carried an unwavering fearlessness about them. It was as if their bond had been forged through trial by fire, and they had come out the other side far stronger. Their confidence gave her a glimmer of hope, and eased her anxiety.

The boat wallowed heavily, and a large wave washed over the stern deck, inundating the two men. Giordino shook the water from his face. "Our sea anchor still there?"

Sitting a head taller, Pitt glanced over the transom at the **Stingray**, which teetered on a towline some thirty yards behind. "Our pig boat is still secure. I'm surprised they haven't popped the hatch and sunk her."

"They probably would have done so by now." Giordino noted that North Island was now a dot on the rear horizon. "Guess they mean to keep her."

Pitt gave him a wry grin. "Maybe they want to use it to fish for rocket parts."

The two had held their breath back on the island when the bald commando had ordered one of his subordinates to secure a towline to the submersible. Though the crew boat had drifted directly over the sunken rocket assembly while they rigged the line, no one had noticed it beneath the surface. As the crew boat and the **Stingray** reentered the stormy seas, the rocket was left hidden in the cove.

Pitt watched as a large wave pounded into the

boat's port side, sending a high spray of foam over them. After the water settled, he turned to Giordino. "Been meaning to ask, did you make any headway with your submersible repairs on the beach?"

"Some," Giordino said. "The communications gear is a lost cause, but I did fix two more of the thruster assemblies that had bent impeller blades. And another of the headlights may be operational again. Enough, I think, to increase the trade-in value a bit."

"They might have kept it for the data. Will they be able to glean anything from the survey records?"

"We weren't rolling any video on the last dive, so all they'll be able to resurrect is our relative tracking and positioning history. Enough to put a rope around our necks, but not to see what we pulled up."

That was something, at least. As Pitt contemplated the rocket assembly in the cove, Giordino nudged him. "Looks like we're about home."

Pitt looked ahead of the crew boat and glimpsed the **Melbourne**. The big mining ship was steaming to the northwest, but drifted to a halt when the boat drew alongside a short time later. The submersible was pulled aboard by one of the ship's massive cranes and deposited on the stern deck. A pair of commandos quickly concealed it under a large tarp.

With an assault rifle at the ready, Ning guided

Margot up an accommodation ladder to the **Melbourne**'s main deck. Pitt and Giordino, their hands freed to allow them to climb up the steps, followed under the escort of two armed commandos. Ning then led all three captives up to the ship's bridge.

Zheng was seated in the captain's chair and gave the visitors a disdainful look as they entered. He rose slowly and eased across the room like a big cat. He stopped directly in front of Margot as she looked down, avoiding his gaze.

"Miss Thornton, you departed without saying good-bye."

"Where is my father?"

"He is still alive, for the moment, down in the wardroom. Now tell me, how did you leave the ship?"

When Margot failed to reply, Zheng swung his arm at a blinding speed and struck the side of her face with an open hand. The blow knocked her sideways, and would have sent her to the deck had Pitt not grabbed her. Anger flared in Zheng's eyes after Pitt's save, but Giordino reacted first. He took a half step forward and launched a jackhammer uppercut that connected with Zheng's lower jawline. Zheng was nearly knocked out of his shoes by the punch. The commando leader fell back and collapsed against the captain's chair.

A startled Ning jammed the stock of his rifle into Giordino's lower back, driving him to his knees.

He raised the muzzle and aimed it at Pitt as the other commandos brought their weapons to bear.

Ning pivoted his rifle between Pitt and Giordino. "Another move by anyone and you will all die."

Zheng slowly climbed to his feet and approached the group. Giordino's knockdown had left the commando wobbly and his eyes glassy. He tried to smile, as if the blow had been harmless, but he swayed on his feet.

"Yes, our other guests, from the submersible," he said. "You traveled quite far. Tell me, what did you find and recover from the seafloor?"

He pointed a finger at Giordino, who had struggled to his feet. "You."

Giordino raised himself upright. "Seashells."

He saw the blow coming this time and braced himself as Ning's rifle stock laid into his side. Giordino dropped to one knee as he tried to absorb the blow. Grimacing, he quickly regained his feet.

"We were performing a subsea geological survey in the Luzon Strait," Pitt said.

Ning jabbed the muzzle of his rifle in Pitt's chest. "Shut up. We aren't speaking to you." The commando tried to shove him backward with the barrel, but Pitt held his ground. Ning stepped back to Giordino. "Answer his question. What were you doing and what did you find?"

Giordino nodded toward Pitt. "What he said. And we found some seashells."

This time, the blow was to the gut, knocking the

wind out of Giordino and sending him to the deck. The combined strikes would have laid out most men for a long sleep, but not Giordino. Ning could only stare as the tough little Italian pulled himself to his feet and glared at the commando while regaining his breath.

Ning took a step back, pointed his rifle at Giordino's head, and seemingly prepared to shoot.

"Get them out of here," Zheng shouted, regaining his composure. "I do not have time for these games."

He stepped closer and looked at the two Americans. "We have your submersible. I'm sure its video cameras will tell us exactly what you found. If not, then Ning will be paying you a most unpleasant visit later."

Ning and the other gunmen began to march the three captives off the bridge. As Margot clutched Pitt's arm, Zheng spoke again.

"Wait," he said.

Margot stared straight ahead, but could feel the commando leader's eyes on her.

"Leave Miss Thornton here," Zheng said with an icy command. "I should like her company a bit longer."

45

The mountaineers awoke at sunrise and promptly began to search around the battered wingtip for additional wreckage of the C-47. The party split up and backtracked several hundred yards down the mountainside, then worked their way up to the ridge. Then they scoured the hogback between Whisky and November.

They didn't find so much as a single bolt.

Summer pondered the ice sheet just beyond the wingtip. "Could the rest of the plane be embedded in the glacier?"

"It's possible, but not likely," Norsang said. "Glaciers in the Himalayas have been in rapid retreat over the past fifty years. If the plane became buried in ice after it crashed, it would most likely be exposed by now."

"There's little more we can do here, except work farther down the mountain," Dirk said. "I think we should proceed to the original search area on the other side of the ridge."

"I agree," Norsang said. He looked at Summer. "And you?"

"Yes," she said with a smile. "I have a feeling Shambhala is just over the hill."

They packed their tents, crossed over the ridge, and deposited their gear in a rocky nook. The mountains' north sides held more ice as glaciers that extended from the centers of both peaks. The five of them spread across a half mile of open terrain between the two ice sheets and began methodically working their way down the slope. They spent the better part of the morning combing the ridge for signs of the plane. Though Dirk and Summer still had nagging headaches from the altitude, they felt they were beginning to adapt to the thinner air.

After surveying down the ridge for several hundred yards, the group shifted west and worked their way back to the top of the ridge. Arie was searching on the fringe, hiking ahead of the others, when he stopped at an object he saw near his feet. He waved an arm. "Something's here."

The others made their way up the hill and converged on Arie a few feet just below the crown of the ridge. The Tibetan toed the ground in front of him with his worn boot. Norsang bent down and worked free a round object embedded in the soil.

It was a six-inch wheel, affixed to a forked, corroded spindle. The remnants of a tire were still attached to the rim, the rubber having cracked, dried, and faded to gray. Norsang held it up for the others to see.

"It's a tail wheel," Dirk said.

Summer dug through her jacket pocket and produced a blowup diagram of a Douglas C-47 Skytrain. She pointed to the image of the tail assembly. "It looks to be the same."

"There must be more debris around." Norsang set the wheel back on the ground.

They conducted a circular search around the spot, exploring the upper ridge and working west to the edge of the glacier. When no other debris was found, Dirk and Norsang began kicking over rocks and poking through the thin layer of soil. But like the wingtip, the tail wheel seemed an isolated part, mysteriously deposited on the mountaintop. No mangled fuselage sections or smashed radial engines were visible, nor even finger-sized pieces of debris.

The group stopped for lunch and contemplated their discoveries as the sun shone brightly overhead, sparkling off the Whisky glacier. Norsang noticed Dirk studying the surrounding terrain. "Perhaps it is not our destiny to find the plane. There were many souls aboard."

"Or perhaps we have been given the clues," Dirk said, "but are not reading them properly."

"Could it be embedded in the ground farther down the slope, obscured from view?" Norsang asked. "Perhaps the winds have blanketed it with dust over the decades."

"I don't think so," Dirk said. "It was a sizable plane, with two big radial engines. There should be more wreckage visible. No, I think its flight ended somewhere else."

Summer looked at him. "What are you saying?"

"Let's say the plane was coming in from the north . . . or better yet, the northeast, which is the direction to Lhasa." He stood and pointed in that direction, then tried to visualize the conditions the pilots had faced. "There's a snowstorm, probably high winds and no visibility. Ram said one of the engines was damaged by gunfire, so maybe it's a battle to keep the plane at a high enough altitude, or maybe they were hit with a downdraft. Either way, they approach this unseen ridge and just barely clip it. The tail wheel gets torn off. And with the bump, Ram gets thrown from the plane."

Dirk turned and pointed to the top of the ridge. "The left wingtip then grazes the side of the ridge. The impact doesn't rip off the entire wing, just the tip, which goes bounding up and over the ridge."

Summer nodded. "It is nearly even with where we found the tail wheel on this side."

"Indicating the tail may have touched down hard, shearing off the wheel," Dirk said, "but the plane caught a bounce and some lift. Just enough to carry it a bit farther."

"Ram never heard a crash before he passed out," Norsang said. "Just a loud thump."

Summer stepped to her brother's side and looked to the southwest toward Whisky's rising slope. "That means the plane might have made it as far as the glacier."

"Which would have been much larger in 1959," Norsang said, "probably encompassing where we stand now."

Summer shielded her eyes from the sun and studied the mass of ice. "There is nothing visible, and Hiram's satellite image didn't show anything."

"That's because the plane didn't stop there," Dirk said. "The slope turns quite steep below the summit. If the plane touched down on its belly, landing on the ice, it could have slid down the mountainside."

The three of them followed the ice-covered terrain from the pinnacle of Whisky down its northern slope to the basin below. Shimmering green at the bottom of the ice field was the small lake.

"You don't mean the lake?" Summer asked.

"Why not? The wreckage is not visible elsewhere."

"But it's a lake." Norsang shook his head. "There's no way we can search that."

"Actually, there is." Dirk gave him a broad grin. "You see, I wasn't imitating a Grand Canyon pack mule for nothing."

46

Mao Jing stared up at the barren mountain slopes and took a deep breath. Scaling a Himalayan peak was not something he was mentally prepared to do. While his men were well trained and in good physical shape, he had to admit that in the past few months he'd grown a bit soft. His covert work in Sikkim had involved little more than monitoring Indian troop movements along the border, which he normally carried out from the comfort of a roadside lodge.

He had never received orders of such urgency as the one that now directed him to track the Tibetan security man named Tenzin Norsang and his companions. His orders were blunt. "Follow and recover all items found . . . at any cost."

The last part of the directive had caught his attention. When operating in an opponent's country, the first rule of business was to maintain stealth. On a good day, Mao and his operatives had to tiptoe around Sikkim, masquerading as merchant traders or even yak herders. But such necessities were now out the window. "At any cost," he mumbled to himself. The meaning couldn't be more clear.

A Chinese spy for the People's Liberation Army, Mao had been notified of Norsang's arrival in Sikkim by the car rental agent, a paid informant. He had waited off the main road leading into Gangtok, intercepted the white van, and loosely tailed it to the lodge in Lachung. Three heavily armed agents in a rugged four-wheel-drive vehicle packed with food and survival gear had joined him that night.

Under the cover of darkness, they had attached a GPS tracker to the van. The next morning, they easily followed the vehicle from a distance as it made its way to Dambung. When the Tibetan group began their hike on foot, the Chinese briefly deployed a drone to track their route, observing them from high over the valley floor.

They had remained hidden among the straggly pines at the tree line for an hour after their quarry had packed their tents and crossed the ridge to the north. The rest of the morning, Mao led his men up the laborious slope toward the heights. They rested on the ledge where the Tibetans had pitched camp the night before, then Mao crawled up to the crown of the ridge and peered over the opposite side.

He was initially overcome by the mountain

views, to the east and west, and the dry, dusty high plains of Tibet far to the north. Then Mao surveyed the open slope that descended before him. At first, he saw no sign of the Tibetan group. Then he gazed farther down the mountainside. Some two thousand feet below, he spotted the figures standing near the shore of a mountain lake.

Mao pulled a pair of binoculars from his pack and focused on the figures. Two men were building a fire, while a tall man and woman stood at the edge of the glacier where it met the lake.

Four people. There should be five. He carefully checked the surrounding basin, then searched up and down the mountain. He looked up with a troubled expression as one of his agents crawled to his side.

"What is the matter?" the man asked, seeing the concern on Mao's face.

"I see only four people. One of the men is missing."

The other agent scanned the terrain and came to the same conclusion. "Do you think they could have found something already? One of them could have traveled west from the lake, toward the Yumthang Valley."

Mao gave a disgruntled nod and looked again at the four figures. They didn't appear to be going anywhere soon. Perhaps they knew they were being followed and were stalling for time while one of them departed with the artifacts? If that was the case, he had no choice but to react.

"Bring up the others," Mao said. "As quietly as possible, we'll descend to their position and find out what they are up to."

"What if they engage us?"

"Then we will do our best not to kill them all."

47

Summer gazed at the dive kit Dirk had hauled with him in his duffel bag and shook her head. There was just a drysuit, a mask and snorkel, and a short pair of lightweight fins. A regulator, with a lone second-stage mouthpiece, was attached to a small aluminum dive tank typically used as an emergency backup. Less than half the standard size, it contained just thirty cubic feet of compressed air.

"No buoyancy compensator, no dive computer, no octopus regulator." She shook her head. "Diving alone at high altitude in an unknown body of water with just a pony bottle. And the water temperature is about forty degrees. I think that breaks just about every rule in the book on safe diving."

"Perhaps if we had invested in a yak to carry our supplies, I could have brought more equipment," Dirk said. "This was more than heavy enough to haul up the mountainside."

"How much of the lake can you hope to cover with such limited air?"

"I'll swim the surface first and see if anything is visible. The lake doesn't appear to be too deep."

"What do you plan on using for weight?"

Dirk rummaged through his backpack and pulled out an extra-large fisherman's vest covered with numerous zippered pockets. "If you help me find some rocks to fill the pockets, I'll be good to go."

"Crazy," she said. "You are absolutely crazy."

Dirk grinned at his sister. "You're just jealous you won't be able to say you dived the Himalayas."

He stripped off his outer clothes and donned the drysuit, tucking his hair under the hood. Stepping off the rocky shoreline, he waded into the mountain lake and affixed his mask and fins. He gave Summer a thumbs-up, then sprawled forward and kicked toward the center of the lake while breathing through his snorkel.

The icy water stung at the exposed portions of his face, but the initial chill to his body soon vanished as the insulated air pocket between his drysuit and body warmed. Protected from the wind in its moraine-formed basin, the lake's waters were still. Fine particles of sediment called rock flour, created by glacial erosion, gave the lake its brilliant green hue, but slightly shrouded the otherwise crystalline waters. The visibility was still good, allowing Dirk to see almost thirty feet. But there was little to see, aside from some muddy brown rocks and boulders.

Though the lake was not big, large portions were too deep to see the bottom, and he feared he might miss a sunken plane. He crisscrossed the lake several times, occasionally bumping into large chunks of floating ice that had broken off the glacier.

He hesitated at one point near the northern shore, not on account of anything he saw, but something he felt. The water temperature around his face mask turned from bitter cold to unbelievably hot. He saw nothing different about the rocky bed, then recalled Norsang had pointed out some hot springs along their drive from Gangtok. There must be a geothermal vent at the bottom of the lake.

As Norsang paced along the shoreline, Dirk worked his way to the southern bank, where the glacier spilled into the lake. The bottom vanished from sight as he moved past the lake's center. But he kept on his path, facing down and kicking hard. As the brown bed returned to view, he spotted faint discoloration at the periphery of his vision. Something green contrasted with the bottom rocks, but that's all he could tell. He circled the area without deciphering more, then took his bearings using landmarks on shore. He completed his survey, then swam back to his starting point on the eastern shore.

As Dirk stepped out of the lake, Norsang rushed to the water's edge. "Did you see anything?"

"Lake's a little deeper than I thought," Dirk replied, catching his breath. "I saw something off-color in the depths, but it could be geology."

Summer looked skeptical. "Worth a dive?"

"I think so." He stepped onto the shore. "Any luck with my vest?"

Summer held up a now bulky fisherman's vest. "I secured the tank and regulator to it as best I could." She pointed to some Velcro straps. "It's weighted with about thirty pounds of rocks. If that's too much, and you sink to the bottom, then you deserve to stay there."

He laughed. "I knew I could rely on your support."

Norsang helped Summer hold the vest while Dirk slipped it over his drysuit. Summer had already attached the regulator to the tank, but Dirk took an auxiliary low-pressure inflator hose and attached it to a valve on the drysuit. He applied a short burst of air to add initial buoyancy to it, then stepped back into the water. "Be back shortly," he said, departing with a wave.

He swam to the south side of the lake and realigned himself with a pair of boulders he had used for a bearing. After a few quick circles, he spotted the green object below.

He traded out the snorkel for the regulator and purged some air from the drysuit through a dump valve on his sleeve. Summer's weighing down the vest with rocks was spot-on, and he dropped easily beneath the surface. He turned and kicked toward the bottom, taking slow, deep breaths to conserve his limited air supply.

The water clarity improved as he descended, and he guessed the bottom depth exceeded forty feet. The lake became dim as the afternoon sun dipped behind the mountains.

He leveled off just above the lake's bed and turned toward the green object. After a few kicks of his fins, he looked ahead and felt his heart skip a beat.

The silhouette of a twin-engine aircraft materialized from the shadows.

Its low-mounted wings and slightly bulbous fuselage confirmed it was a C-47. Dirk approached from the rear, noting the plane was upright. The old transport was largely intact, though a horizontal stabilizer was missing, and the left wingtip was gone. He swam forward and saw that the plane's nose had crumpled upon impact.

Dirk turned and swam over the left wing and engine, its three-bladed propeller mangled when the plane struck the glacier. For it was the glacier where the C-47 had come down. By the looks of it, the aircraft had slid intact down the mountainside and into the lake, which was likely much smaller then.

He swiftly made his way around the mashed front end and swam down the right side of the fuselage. Behind the wing, an open cargo door beckoned, the same one Ramapurah Chodron had fallen through sixty years before. Dirk slipped through the door, then cursed himself for not bringing an underwater flashlight.

While the Skytrain's fuselage was lined with numerous windows, the glass was opaque from years of immersion. Dirk didn't have the time to let his eyes adjust to the dim, murky interior. He swam forward, determined to start at the cockpit and work his way back in search of the Nechung Idol.

He made it only a few inches when his elbow bumped into something inside the doorway. A pair of boots. He recoiled after a closer look revealed the bones of its owner protruding from the tops.

The frigid, fresh water had preserved the aircraft in a near-pristine state, along with everything inside. A bench ran along each bulkhead, and Dirk swam above them, trying not to kick up sediment with his fins. Dark mounds lay on the benches, but for the moment he ignored them.

The cockpit had a faint glow from its multiple windows. Dirk reached its open door and poked his head in.

The C-47's cockpit reminded him of the controls on a school bus. A simple, flat panel displayed the flight instruments in front of a pair of no-frills pilots' seats. A heavy, side-mounted steering yoke was positioned in front of each seat, operated by a large, truncated steering wheel. Everything looked like it belonged in a museum. The gauges remained clear and readable, the altimeter pegged at eighteen thousand feet. The green paint on the steering yokes looked like it had been applied yesterday. And the skull and neat pile of bones in each seat had only lightly browned with age.

Dirk knew the dark mounds on the floor and benches behind him contained a similar collection of human remains. If the Nechung Idol was aboard—and it had to be—he would have to sort through the grisly debris. He glanced at a Doxa dive watch he wore over the sleeve of his drysuit. Fourteen minutes had already elapsed, well over half his time on the bottom with the pony bottle.

He turned and faced the gloomy cabin. There would be only one way to search it. He dropped to his knees and crawled down the aisle, his arms extended out to either side, patting down the benches and the floor. He didn't travel far before he touched a rifle and ammunition belt on one side and some boots and bones on the other.

Dirk felt like he was crawling blindfolded through a crypt. He pushed aside his revulsion— his air supply was dwindling rapidly—and kept moving forward, touching boots, uniforms, weapons, and bones. Losing count of the number of individual remains, he reached the rear door, which let in a welcome dose of light. There was just a short distance to the tail section left to examine.

He kicked forward and glided over the rear floor section, his fingers dragging along the planked surface. He had felt nothing along the right side when his head bumped into the tail's bulkhead. He turned around, felt along the opposite side, and touched something small, round, and hard. He grasped the object, took it to the doorway, and held it to the light. It was a hand grenade.

Dirk placed it gently under the starboard bench and returned to the tail. His hands ran across a skeleton, scattered across the flooring on one side. He gently began to probe the remains when it happened. A partial draw of air from the tank, then nothing.

He'd known it was coming. But he had hoped to be clear of the aircraft before his air ran out. He hadn't found what he came for, and he had inspected almost the entire interior.

As he felt the first discomfort of not breathing, he gently touched the remains beneath him while eyeing the open door a short distance ahead. He gave a light kick to propel himself forward when his right hand brushed against something protruding from the side bulkhead. He stopped and ran a palm over it.

It felt smooth, but solid, and stood almost two feet tall. Dirk reached out his other hand and grasped it with both. Tall, heavy, and rounded, it could be only one thing. The Nechung Idol.

Dirk glanced through the darkness toward the bones he knew were behind him. The outstretched arms of the monk clinging to the relic in his last moments? The thought sent a chill up his spine, but he had a more immediate concern.

His head was starting to pound, and the urge to flee to the surface grew overwhelming. But he couldn't leave with the object just yet or he'd never make it to the surface.

He set the Idol down and peeled off his rock-filled fishing vest. He spit out his mouthpiece, tossed aside the vest, tank, and regulator, and only then grabbed the heavy, carved piece of **thokcha**.

He kicked hard, making his way out the side door, where he dropped to the lake bed. The Nechung Idol weighed at least ten pounds more than his vest had. He'd have to overcome the lack of buoyancy by force.

Dirk stood, pushed off from the bottom, and kicked upward with heavy thrusts. The lack of air added to his urgency, and he kicked with powerful, even strokes while exhaling a light stream of air so as not to rupture his lungs.

He hadn't been at depth long enough to worry about a decompression stop, even at the extreme altitude, and he drove toward the surface with all his might.

His head shot through the calm surface like a missile, and he took a huge gulp of air. He managed to grab his snorkel before the weight of the Idol pulled him back under. With his arms around the statue, he had no choice but to kick across the surface toward the closest shore, breaching like a dolphin every few seconds to grab a breath of air.

He was too engaged with his struggle to look for anyone on shore. He didn't dare display his find until he reached waist-deep waters for fear of dropping it. At last, he reached the shallows and stood up, gasping for more air. He raised the Nechung Idol over his head in triumph. "I found it."

Silence.

Only then did he look to the lakeshore and see his welcoming committee. It was two Chinese men holding assault rifles aimed at his chest.

48

The Chinese operatives had moved unseen down the mountainside, their brown fatigues blending in with the rocky landscape. The four men had spread across the hillside and worked their way to within fifty yards of the lake when they were spotted by Tash.

The Tibetan reached for his sidearm, but was cut down by a burst of gunfire from the closest commando. Standing a few feet away, Arie fired a few shots in defense before he was taken down in a cross fire.

Norsang grabbed Summer and pulled her to the ground, and they slithered to some rocks for cover. He raised his Glock and put down Tash's gunman with two perfectly placed shots to the chest, then ducked as automatic fire sprayed over his head. He rose to take aim at another operative when a grenade tumbled through the air and landed near his feet. He stretched to kick it away, but it detonated before he could reach it.

A bright flash was followed by a thundering bang that shook the ground. It wasn't a deadly fragmentation grenade, it was a stun device. It temporarily blinded Summer and Norsang and disrupted their hearing. By the time Norsang could shake off the effects, it was too late. The muzzle of an assault rifle jabbed him in the back, and he had no choice but to drop his pistol.

Summer was already on her feet, her arms in the air, in front of another gunman. Norsang rose to his feet and looked at Summer apologetically. She reassured him with a strong-willed stare at their captors.

"What do you want?" she yelled. Her hearing had not yet recovered from the blast.

The third surviving member of the Chinese team, a keen-eyed man with dark, leathery skin, stood uphill, examining the bodies of Tash and Arie. Mao turned and made his way down the hill with his weapon drawn. He stopped inches in front of Summer and Norsang.

"Where . . . the other man?" he asked in broken English.

Summer gave him her best "I don't know what you're talking about" gaze, but it was for naught. A second later, Dirk surfaced at the middle of the lake and began swimming toward them. The three

Chinese crouched in the rocks until Dirk reached the shallows, where he was confronted by two of the gunmen.

Dirk dropped the Nechung Idol on the edge of the glacier, then was escorted across the rocks to Summer and Norsang.

"You found it," Norsang said under his breath.

"Yes, but wish I'd left it there," Dirk whispered. "Where did these guys come from?"

"Quiet." Mao stepped past the captives to the edge of the glacier, crouched, and studied the Idol for several minutes. He smiled, retrieved a satellite phone from a backpack, and sent a text message. Then he took an ordinary cell phone and used it to photograph several views of the Idol. He compressed the photos, plugged the cell into the sat phone, and transferred the images. Finally, Mao uploaded the photos via satellite to his handler.

While Mao waited for a response, the other two commandos used zip ties to bind their captives' hands behind their backs. Then they shoved each person to the ground and bound the ankles. Mao was still looking at his phone, so the two men attended to their dead comrade, stripping him of his weapons and burying him in a shallow trench they covered with rocks.

They offered Tash and Arie no such courtesy. Instead, the commandos dragged their bodies to the lake and filled their pockets with stones. One of the operatives pointed to a broken chunk of ice and, with a high-pitched laugh, said something to the other. The second man nodded.

They dragged the two bodies onto the chunk, shoved it into the water, and stared at it as it floated to the center of the lake. The saturated ice eventually crumbled, and the two bodies slid into the depths. The watery burial generated more laughter from both men.

Summer couldn't watch and just stared at her captors with disbelief.

Mao reviewed several text messages that appeared on his satellite phone, then put the device away. He picked up the Nechung Idol, carried it to his captives, and dropped it at Norsang's feet. "You have an artifact of great interest to my government."

"It is a religious relic that belongs in the Namgyal Monastery."

"Apparently, it has much greater value than as a relic," Mao said. "You will carry it back to Tibet for us."

He spoke to one of the operatives, who emptied the main compartment of Norsang's backpack and stuffed the Idol inside. The gunman pulled Norsang to his feet and cut his hand and ankle ties. He forced Norsang to slip the backpack onto his shoulders, then zip-tied the Tibetan's hands in front of him.

The gunman stepped close to Mao, pointed to the lake, and spoke a few words. Mao called over the other operative, and together they grabbed Summer's arms and dragged her backward onto the glacier and deposited her on a shelf of ice that overhung the lake. They collected Dirk in the same manner and dumped him alongside his sister. Forcing them to sit back-to-back, they added a third zip tie, linking their wrists behind them.

"I'm not liking the looks of this," Summer whispered.

"We'll be okay if they go on their way," Dirk said.

But the Chinese weren't through. The gunman with the high laugh stepped close to Dirk and pulled a knife from a belt sheath. He grabbed a fistful of Dirk's drysuit from behind his neck and sliced open a wide, horizontal seam. He stepped off the glacier and collected an armload of small rocks, then returned and dropped them down the back of the drysuit. When Dirk wiggled to the side to avoid some of the ballast, the gunman whacked him in the head with an elbow.

Across the shore, Mao gave an exasperated look and yelled at the gunman to hurry. The man stepped in front of Dirk and Summer, then hopped up and down on the ice. A large crack appeared on one side, and he shifted positions to complete the break.

"What are you doing?" Norsang yelled. "Stop it."

The Tibetan tried to run over to help, but Mao intercepted him. Swinging the stock of his assault rifle, he connected with Norsang's midsection, sending him lurching to the ground. A crack sounded ahead of them. They looked to see the gunman jump back from the glacier's edge as a flat chunk of ice broke away.

With yet another hearty laugh, the gunman placed a boot on the edge of the small iceberg and shoved it away from the shoreline.

Sitting aboard the ice, afraid to move a muscle, Dirk and Summer drifted silently toward the center of the lake.

49

Zheng paced the bridge of the **Melbourne**, awaiting his visitor.

"Sir, an unidentified aircraft is approaching on radar."

Zheng stepped to the radarscope and nudged the helmsman aside. The small dot on the screen was approaching rapidly from the northwest. Zheng moved to the side window to see what it was, but the gray clouds had obscured everything in the distance.

The unmarked Changhe Z-11J light utility helicopter skimmed low over the waves, maintaining radio silence since its departure from a coastal military base in Guangdong Province. Buffeting headwinds and sporadic rain made for a dangerous flight, but the pilot had little choice in the flight plan. He glanced at the Colonel, seated next to him, who had ordered the flight be taken undetected across the South China Sea regardless of the weather.

Sweat was streaming off the pilot's brow when the **Melbourne** came into view. He circled twice after requesting to land, waiting for the ship to turn about to accommodate a safer landing. As the ship's helipad heaved beneath him, he knew he had no business flying in these conditions, let alone trying to land at sea.

Without a choice, he slowly descended over the pad, watching it rise and fall beneath him. Timing a swell that carried the ship high, he cut power and let the craft drop, striking the helipad hard before the next uplift.

Colonel Yan didn't bother to acknowledge the pilot's landing or even wait for the rotors to die, flipping open the side door and hopping out. He almost fell to the deck due to the motion of the rocking ship, but found his balance and made his way to a side stairwell where Zheng stood waiting.

The younger man saluted his uncle. "Welcome, Colonel. We had not been expecting you to fly in this weather," he said with an uneasy tone.

"It was an unauthorized flight taken at an opportune time." Yan motioned toward the helicopter as a light rain began to fall. "Secrecy is best at this moment. Where can we go to discuss our change of plans?"

"The wardroom, sir. This way, please."

The **Melbourne**'s wardroom resembled a five-star restaurant, with plush burgundy carpeting and rich, abstract oil paintings on the walls. To one side of the dining area, a lounge featured leather chairs and sofas, and a large-screen television. Zheng directed Yan to a pair of chairs in the corner. An array of charts and documents lay stacked on a low table between them.

"So, Yijong," the Colonel said, "is what you have told me about this ship proven to be true?"

"More so than I imagined," Zheng replied. "We found a scientist aboard—an engineer, actually—by the name of Yee. He is a Taiwan national who admitted to working for the Ministry of National Defense." He pointed to the table. "We found these in his stateroom."

Yan examined the documents. They were navigational charts displaying sections of the Taiwan Strait along the island's western coast. Groupings of red triangles appeared on the charts at various locales, running north to south, about twenty miles from shore.

"What do these red marks represent?" Yan asked.

"They are the proposed fixed subsurface ultrasonic stations for Project Waterfall."

Yan gave a blank look. "Project Waterfall?"

"A proposed defensive measure against amphibious assault. The acoustic stations, in concert with one another, would create a wall of water that could destroy an invading fleet."

"Why was our intelligence not aware of this?"

"Yee indicated it was a tightly controlled program, brought about by the relationship with Mr.

Thornton. Plus, it is still in the early experimental stages."

"A wall of water? You can't be serious."

"We discovered the effect ourselves when we boarded the ship. They were conducting a test of some sort and were about to abort it when we interrupted them. The ship produced a large wave. I saw it for myself."

"Yes, that's what you told me. And this can be repeated?"

"Yee confirmed as much."

"How soon will this system become operational?"

Zheng shrugged. "Yee fell unconscious while we were last questioning him."

Yan's eyes narrowed. "I would like to know how the system works."

"I will have the inventor tell you. The man who built the ship." He pulled out a handheld radio and called one of his subordinates.

A few minutes later, a haggard-looking Alistair Thornton was escorted into the room and given a seat near the two officers. He glanced at Yan's military uniform, then looked at Zheng with repulsion.

"The Colonel," Zheng said, "wishes to have a full overview on Project Waterfall."

"I told you," Thornton said in a dry voice, "I'm bloody well through talking to you."

"I think you may wish to reconsider." Zheng made a brief transmission into his handheld radio.

The main door opened, and Margot stepped into

the wardroom, followed by Ning, who held a pistol against the back of her neck. Thornton jerked upright at the sudden appearance of his daughter. They looked at each other in relief, and despair, as Margot knelt beside her father and held his hand.

"You are well?" Thornton asked.

Margot nodded and forced a smile.

"A happy reunion," Zheng said. "If you wish to keep it that way, you will tell the Colonel all about Project Waterfall."

"Project Waterfall is . . . a phantom." Thornton stared at the floor. "It's all still on the drawing board. I have no idea if it will ever work."

"But," Yan said, "you have already created massive waves, have you not?"

"He has." Thornton pointed at Zheng with a scowl.

"So it can be done," Yan said.

Thornton gave a reluctant nod. "Yes, but you must be in the right place, with the right conditions. Here in the Luzon Strait, if that's where we still are, certain areas of unusually powerful subsea currents are susceptible to manipulation via multiple acoustic signals."

"Manipulation that can redirect a subsea current to the surface in the form of a devastating wave." Zheng tapped the file on the table. "I read it right here, in Yee's papers."

"And this surface wave, or tsunami," Yan asked, "it can be sent in a particular direction?"

Thornton remained silent until Ning stepped behind Margot and stroked her hair.

"Yes, that is the proposed theory," Thornton said. "A line of sensors detects the water movements. Once a pattern is detected, the transponders transmit acoustic waves at an amplitude that interacts with the physical flow. Given a powerful enough transmission, the water current can be redirected."

Yan retrieved a chart that displayed the waters off the Port of Kaohsiung on Taiwan's southwest coast. He pointed to a row of red triangles twenty miles off the coast. "This location here . . . This is a spot where the system would operate?"

"I . . . I don't know," Thornton said.

Ning grabbed a fistful of Margot's hair and yanked her off the floor, eliciting a sharp cry. Thornton tried to spring from the chair, but Zheng grabbed his shirt and held him in place. One of the other commandos moved closer and raised his weapon to Thornton.

"Answer the question," Zheng said.

Tears of pain rolled down Margot's cheeks as she fought to hold still.

"Let her go," Thornton yelled, "you bloody animals."

Zheng nodded. Ning lowered his arm, but kept his grip on Margot's hair.

"Yes," Thornton said through gritted teeth. "That is one of Taiwan's proposed defensive sites."

"So the conditions there must be ripe to utilize the Waterfall system," Yan said.

Thornton simply stared at him.

Yan pointed at the chart and turned to Zheng. "Take the vessel to this position. At the appropriate time, we will activate the system. But the wave should be directed in the opposite direction. I wish to send a large 'waterfall' to Taiwan."

"Are you mad?" Thornton leaped from his chair. "You'd wipe out a third of the country. Millions could die. On top of that, you'd likely start World War Three."

Yan looked at Thornton with an amused gaze and just smiled.

50

Summer and Dirk watched from their icy perch as one of the Chinese gunmen threw their backpacks into the lake, then joined his comrades in leading Norsang up the mountainside. The Tibetan looked back at his friends with anguish until a gun muzzle prodded him along.

"Leaving us at the bottom of the lake with no trace of our existence," Summer said.

"Trust me," Dirk said as he fought his wrist ties, "there would be more than a trace of us on the lake bottom for quite a while."

"How about we try sinking somewhere other than the middle of the lake."

"Been waiting for them to get out of easy range." Dirk was facing the eastern shoreline and had a clear view of the gunmen, who had worked their way a few hundred yards up the mountainside. "I think it's safe to try now."

"It'll be too dark to see us pretty soon." Summer

noted the darkening sky of approaching dusk. "If our iceberg should last so long."

Their floating platform was roomy, but chunks of ice on its fringes had already fallen away. Dirk stretched out his feet, falling short of the edge of the slab. He looked back toward his sister. "Try scooting my way. On three."

Summer dug her heels into the ice and slid toward her brother as he moved forward. Summer gasped as her slight movement caused the platform to rock. One edge dipped below the lake surface and rebounded, sending a layer of chilly water across the top.

Dirk cleared his throat. "This thing's a bit unstable."

"Just get us to shore," Summer whispered as a large chunk of ice on her side broke away.

The pair had moved enough to allow Dirk to dangle his feet in the water. With his ankles bound, he began a light, but awkward, kick. The ice floe started moving slowly toward the northern shore.

"Not to criticize," Summer said, "but the eastern bank looks a bit closer."

"True." Dirk looked over his shoulder to gauge their heading. "But the northern lake bottom has less of a gradient."

"In case we don't make it?"

"In case we don't make it."

Large pieces continued to break off the edges, gradually shrinking their raft. Summer felt the ice shift beneath her, accompanied by subtle cracking. "I don't think we're going to get there."

The slab submerged as they moved, until they were sitting in three inches of water. Summer cursed the frigid water, not yet being endured by Dirk in his ripped drysuit. Another chunk broke free, and Dirk began kicking as hard as his bound feet would allow. The submerged ice proved more stable than before, and its reduced size helped it move faster through the water. But not for long.

When they were within thirty feet of shore, the platform split in two beneath them. Dirk and Summer plunged into the glacial lake and disappeared beneath the surface.

A HALF MILE up the eastern slope, the gunman who had set them on the ice let out a whoop and another high-pitched laugh.

Norsang stopped and turned, gazing at the lake through the growing darkness. Two empty chunks of ice bobbed in the center of a circular, widening wake.

"May the dragon have mercy on their souls," he muttered, then resumed his forced climb up the hill.

51

The icy waters pricked Summer's skin like a thousand needles. She gasped, then fought an involuntary reflex to inhale underwater. She kicked against her bindings as her mind raged. She was experiencing a shock response to the cold and knew she could drown inside of a minute if she gave in to the impulse. Though her heart was pounding, she forced herself to relax, aided by years of diving in similar conditions.

Behind her, Dirk experienced a similar, if less jarring, agony. The cold lake water poured down the slit in the back of his drysuit, adding weight to the rocks that had settled at his rear. But the insulated drysuit held the water that entered and soon started to warm against his skin. His bigger fear was that he had drawn Summer with him toward the lake's bottom. Otherwise, she might have been able to stay afloat and kick her way to shore.

He did his best to ignore the discomfort and

focused on the approaching rocky floor. The depth was about fifteen feet and the visibility clear. He eyed a couple of protruding rocks, and as he and Summer descended, he tried to maneuver above the nearest one. He had only one shot. With his sister in tow, he tugged and wriggled to align himself.

As they dropped to the lake bed, he extended his legs and splayed his feet toward the rock. When the inside edges of his feet grazed its top, he bent his knees and brought his full weight to bear. Straining to split his bound feet and legs, he struck the rock with all the force he could muster.

The momentum was enough to split the zip tie at its connector. Dirk stumbled to remain upright as his feet spread apart and his legs straddled the rock. At least they now had a chance. As Summer's body bounced against his back, he stood, and his legs began to churn forward. Hunched over, so Summer could ride him back-to-back, he began striding across the bottom of the lake.

They had maybe twenty feet to go until they reached shallow water, a distance he could cover in seconds on land. But underwater, with no air, and climbing a rocky incline with his sister on his back, along with rocks in his drysuit, it was a different story.

He had to stagger forward, fighting the water's resistance, while the cold and physical effort magnified his need for air. But with his hands bound behind him, maintaining his balance was the most challenging aspect. He thought about stopping at a rock and trying to break their wrist ties, as he had done with his feet, but he couldn't afford the time or risk the failure.

He knew Summer was a strong swimmer and, like him, in great physical shape. On a good day, two or three minutes underwater without air wouldn't be a stretch for either of them. But Dirk was already weary from his dive, and the effect of the high, thin air was crushing. And then there was the freezing-cold water.

On his back, Summer felt like deadweight. He knew she had to have suffered from thermal shock. Was she still conscious? Had she drowned?

Those questions ignited his adrenaline, and he bulled forward with robotic determination. He stumbled past a wide rock, reached a clear slope, and kept charging. His head felt like it was being squeezed in a vise, and his heart was about to pound out of his chest. He saw the surface just above him, then felt a disturbance as Summer broke through first. He staggered a few more steps, then lifted his head above water, gasping to inhale. He could hardly speak for a moment as the cold mountain air slowly replenished his body's oxygen.

"Are . . . you . . . okay?" he finally managed as he moved again toward shore.

Summer was alive, for she was rasping for air in even louder desperation. She muttered something in response, but all Dirk could hear was the chattering of her teeth.

Still hunched over, he carried her from the lake and fell onto a shoreline boulder to rest. The sky had turned an inky blue as dusk crept over the landscape. He scanned the mountainside, barely spotting the four climbers a mile or so up the slope, looking like ants on the landscape.

He turned and gazed at some rocks at his feet. "Summer, we've got to get the zip ties off our wrists. I'm going to try to slam the loop connecting us against a rock. Can you help?"

Something close to an affirmation came from her quivering lips.

Dirk angled himself upright to support his sister's weight and shuffled to a pointed rock nearby. He backed over the center of it, then said, "Let's drop down on it. On three. One . . . two . . . three."

He squatted quickly, and Summer followed suit by her mere deadweight alone. While each one's wrists had been bound tightly with a zip tie, only a loose tie secured them together. The tip of the rock caught it as they dropped, their combined weight forcing it down until it snapped.

Summer tumbled to the ground as Dirk fell forward on his knees. He backed up to the rock and rubbed his remaining zip tie across the jagged edge, trying to wear it down. After a minute or two, he centered his wrists over the rock and again dropped down hard while pulling at his wrists. With this second try, the zip tie finally snapped. He pulled his arms in front of him and rubbed his wrists, thankful the Chinese hadn't used a stronger cuff.

He spun around and helped his sister to sit upright. Her appearance startled him. Her lips were blue, she was shivering uncontrollably, and her normally bright gray eyes had a glazed, thousand-yard stare. She was on the path to lethal hypothermia.

"Hang on, sis, we'll get you warmed up." He stripped off his drysuit and dumped out the rocks. With her arms and legs still bound, he could only drape it around her. She didn't have the strength to help break the other ties, so he tied the loose sleeves of the suit in a knot around her chest and pulled the hood over her head to try to capture additional body heat.

He knew he had to get her into dry clothes and warmed up fast. Both matches and dry clothes were in their backpacks, in sealed pouches that may have kept them dry even underwater. But recovering the packs from the lake and building a fire would take precious time that Summer might not have.

Still, he had no other options. He got up to run to the east end of the lake and find the backpacks. But as he rose, something caught his eye on the water to the west. A light mist appeared over a small section of the lake. Dirk stared at it a moment, then smiled. It wasn't mist. It was steam. From the submerged hot spring.

"C'mon, Summer, we're going for another swim." He lifted her to her feet. She uttered a vague protest as Dirk hoisted her over his shoulder, then carried her toward the lake.

A dozen yards to the west, he stepped into the water. Instead of an icy bite, he encountered a tropical warmth. He strode about, seeking the hottest spot he could find along the shoreline, then set his sister in the water. He removed her shoes and jacket, tossed them ashore, then balled up the drysuit and tucked it under her as a backrest. He left her for a moment, stepping to shore and scouring the ground until he located a shard of granite with a sharp edge. Returning, he used it to saw through her wrist and ankle zip ties.

With her hands and legs free, Summer could lie down in the hot water more fully, allowing it to lap just beneath her chin. Right away, her color improved and her eyes brightened.

"Enjoy the warm bath," he said. "I'll be back in a few minutes."

She gave him a thankful gaze. "The dragon's breath," she uttered.

Dirk hiked in the growing darkness to the eastern end of the shoreline. He'd worn sweatpants and a thermal shirt under the drysuit, but they were now soaked, and he shivered as a cold breeze wafted across the lake. But it was his feet that were most uncomfortable. The drysuit had built-in booties, so he'd worn only socks. His toes were numb, while the soles of his feet had been rubbed raw from crossing the rocky lakefront.

Thankfully, he spotted his hiking boots where he'd left them, tucked between two rocks. He stripped off his socks and clothes and waded into the lake, feeling the full icy bitterness without the protection of the drysuit.

He spotted Summer's backpack in the shallows and pulled it to shore, grateful to escape the water for a moment. His feet and legs were already numb as he waded back in. He found his own pack and pulled it to shore, quelling the urge to curse aloud at his discomfort. He rummaged through his pack and found the interior compartments had remained mostly dry. He slipped on dry clothes, a damp down jacket, and a wool knit cap.

He reached for his dry boots and then hopped around to warm himself. Feeling that his blood was once again circulating, he hiked up the hill to where Tash and Arie had been killed. They had been preparing to brew tea when they were ambushed. Dirk grabbed a bundle of the dry firewood the Tibetans had packed in and carried it to the backpacks. He emptied his, stuffed it with the wood, and shouldered it on one arm while hoisting Summer's pack on the other. He made his way back around the lake in the darkness, tripping only once, but making much better time with boots on his feet.

He found Summer groggy, but responsive, complaining that her ears were cold. Dirk explored the shore until he found a low gully surrounded by boulders. It was well protected from the wind and had the added benefit of seclusion from the eastern slope.

Dirk looked up and spotted several lights fixed near the summit. The Chinese were camping as well, confident in their planned escape to Tibet the next day.

Dirk jumped into the gully, built a rock pit, then set the wood alight with matches from his backpack. When he had coaxed the flame into a blaze, he returned to the lake and helped Summer out of the water. Steam wafted off her clothes as she took a few uneasy steps, then began moving freely.

"The hot water was nice. I didn't want to leave." Her teeth chattered as her wet clothes turned cold.

Dirk led her to the fire, where she changed into dry clothes, then sat next to the fire. Dirk already had her boots and jacket drying next to it and a pot of tea brewing.

He dug through their food supplies and cooked some rice and onions, with a tin of Spam as a side. Summer regained her strength quickly and stopped shivering once her long hair had dried.

"Do you think they've taken Norsang to Tibet?" she asked.

"No." Dirk stood and pointed up the eastern mountainside. "At least, not yet. They're camped up by the ridgeline."

Summer stood up and followed him to the edge

of the gully. She looked up and spotted a small light high up the mountain. "Is that them?"

Dirk nodded.

"They have Norsang and the Nechung Idol," she said. "He'll rot in a Tibetan jail for the rest of his life. We have to go get him."

Dirk looked at his sister. "You about died from hypothermia."

She grabbed him by the arm and squeezed. "I'm fine now. We've got to try. You know we do."

Dirk saw the determination in her eyes, then gazed at the flickering light on the mountain.

"All right. That seems all we can do," he said. "Try."

52

The last of the campfire's embers died at three in the morning. Dirk nudged his sister awake before the cold did. "Are you still up to climbing?"

"Yes," she said. "I feel much better."

Dirk brewed them each a cup of tea on a camp burner, which they used to wash down a few trail bars. Duly fortified, they slipped on their backpacks, and proceeded along the quiet lake's shoreline. High up the slope, the yellow lights no longer shone near the ridge.

"Do you think they are still there?" Summer asked.

"Yes. The light was fixed for some time."

From the lake's eastern shore, they began the arduous climb up the mountainside. They were blessed with clear skies overhead, which provided silvery illumination from the stars and the rising quarter moon. Less welcome was the frigid temperature that came with the cloudless night. Summer rubbed her hands together as they started up the steep incline that led to the ridge. It took only a few minutes of exerted climbing for her body to warm and her heart to pound.

They climbed in silence, whispering only when they stopped every few minutes to catch their breath. Their ordeal on the lake had sapped more of their strength than they cared to admit, and the battle for oxygen at this altitude never ceased. But Norsang's life, and the recovery of the Nechung Idol, were more than enough to make them overlook their pain.

Their track detoured to the south, hiking along the side of the glacier. They were tempted to ascend on the glacier itself, which would have been easier trekking, but they feared that their two dark figures on the white ice would be easier to detect. While they hoped the Chinese would feel no need to post a sentry, they didn't want to bank on it.

Their pace slowed the higher they climbed, both from fatigue and the need to approach in silence. A hundred yards from the top, they rested behind a car-sized boulder. Dirk peeked around its side. The Chinese camp was just below the top of the ridge. A pair of tents were pitched on a narrow rise, but little else was visible amid the rocky terrain.

"Are . . . they there?" Summer asked between heavy breaths.

"Yes. I can see two tents."

"Anyone standing guard?"

"Not that I could tell, but we best assume some-one is awake." He slipped off his backpack and took another look. "The terrain is rockier to the left, which will provide more cover. Let's maneuver to that side and work our way up, then approach from above. We can leave our packs here."

He opened his backpack and pulled out a small folding knife and a thick stick with a rock tied to one end.

Summer stared at the item. "What is that?"

"A tomahawk. I made it after you fell asleep." He'd taken another trip around the lake in the middle of the night, searching for Tash's and Arie's handguns. They'd apparently been taken by the Chinese, so he made his own weapon. He'd found a stout stick, carefully split the end, and inserted a wedge-shaped rock, which he bound to it using drawstrings from the backpack tied top and bot-tom. If it held together, it would make for a nice close-fighting weapon.

Summer admired the homemade ax, but shook her head. "Nice, but we're bringing sticks and stones to a gunfight."

"I'd bring a howitzer, if I had one." He passed the tomahawk to Summer and palmed the knife. "Let's go."

It took a half hour to work their way up to the ridge, moving laterally, before scaling the rocky route to the left of the tents. They crept along the crown of the ridge, then dropped into a small hollow that overlooked the camp. Dirk and Summer crawled to the edge and looked down in silence.

The camp was quiet, save for the wind rippling the sides of the tents. Besides the tents, the only sign of life was several backpacks braced against a boulder. The twins studied the camp for a solid ten minutes, but saw no evidence of anyone standing watch, no signs of movement at all.

Dirk and Summer hunkered down in the hollow.

"I didn't see anyone," Summer whispered.

"Me neither. Hopefully, everyone's asleep." It crossed his mind that the group may have abandoned camp and been airlifted off the mountain, but they hadn't heard a helicopter.

"How should we get him out?" Summer asked.

"I'll check the backpacks for a weapon. If I don't find anything, I'll slice open the side of one of the tents and hope for a gun—or take one of them hostage." Dirk squeezed the knife in his hand. "Maybe you can cover the back side of the tents."

Summer nodded. It wasn't much of a plan, but they had few options. The Chinese could easily march Tenzin Norsang across the Tibetan border at daybreak, where additional security forces could be summoned. They had to try now.

She followed Dirk cat-like down the slope and stopped a few feet from the two tents, which were nestled together.

Dirk tiptoed past them to the row of backpacks

leaning against the boulder. He found Norsang's first. Its weight confirmed it still held the Nechung Idol. As he set it back down, he heard a scuffle at his feet and saw a sudden movement. In the shadows of the boulder, tucked behind the packs, someone was sleeping on the ground, a blanket pulled over him.

Dirk dropped to one knee and grabbed its hem. He ripped the blanket away with one hand and thrust the knife forward with the other. He froze. It was Norsang. He was lying on his side, his arms and legs hog-tied behind him and staked to the ground.

Through sleep-deprived eyes, Norsang looked up with shock at the sight of Dirk with a raised knife.

Dirk silently shook his head in return, brought the knife down, and sliced through the zip ties and rope. Norsang rolled over and climbed gingerly to his feet, trying to restore circulation to his legs and arms.

Though no one had said a word, their light scuffling had not gone undetected. Dirk and Norsang turned as a rustling came from the closer tent. A Chinese agent poked his head out the flap, gripping a pistol. He squinted at the two men, then grunted as he raised the weapon to fire.

From the opposite side of the tent, Summer leaped forward and swung the tomahawk in an arc toward the man. The gunman heard her approach and turned his head, likely saving his life.

The ax's stone head just clipped the man's scalp as its wooden handle collided with his crown. At the same time, he pulled the trigger. The shot fired high over the heads of Dirk and Norsang, echoing off the mountainside. The gunman then sank to the ground and grabbed his bloodied skull.

As Summer staggered forward from the momentum of her swing, she kicked down a tent pole, which collapsed the fabric over the man. She regained her footing and started running. "Let's get out of here," she said as she burst past Dirk and Norsang and headed uphill.

The two men needed no encouragement. Dirk grabbed Norsang's backpack, and they proceeded to follow Summer. But Norsang took only a step or two before he crumpled to the ground.

Dirk grabbed him by the arm and pulled him up. "No time to linger."

"It's my legs. They're numb. Please . . . go on without me."

Dirk ignored the request and pulled the big Tibetan up the incline. Norsang gave his best, half crawling and half running, as blood now tingled through his legs.

Behind them, they heard cursing from the other tent. A flashlight turned on, and its rays scanned the hillside. The beam caught Dirk and Norsang as they reached the crest. A second later, automatic gunfire split the night air.

The two men dived to the ground as a seam of

bullets struck the dirt at their feet. They slithered forward, crossed the top of the ridge, and tumbled down the opposite side. They slid to a stop on a flat berm, which Dirk recognized as the location of their earlier campsite.

Summer rushed to their side and helped pull both men to their feet. "Come on. We need to get down the mountainside and into the tree line."

"I will never make it in time," Norsang said as they started to move off. Feeling was slowly and painfully returning to his legs, but he would need another few minutes to regain his mobility.

Summer tugged at his arm, enticing him to move. "We'll help you."

Dirk stood at Norsang's other side. He was looking neither downhill nor at the ridge above, where the armed Chinese would soon appear. Instead, his focus was west, along the lower ridge leading to the peak named Whisky.

"No, he's right," Dirk said. "None of us will make it to the trees on foot. But I think I know a quicker way down."

53

The two uninjured operatives reached the crest of the ridge a minute later and peered down the southern slope. Mao stood with a pistol and a flashlight, working the beam across the rocky mountainside. His partner held an assault rifle and struggled to slip on a pair of night vision goggles.

The goggles were unnecessary, as Dirk, Summer, and Norsang were signaling their location. Not by sight, but by sound.

From the upper ridgeline, by the glacier's edge, they heard a metallic noise. Mao turned his light in that direction.

Fifty yards distant, the flashlight's beam weakly illuminated the figure of Norsang. The Tibetan lay facedown on the ground. On either side, Dirk and Summer were hunched over, dragging him laterally across the rocks.

It took Mao a second to realize they were pulling him on a large metal plate, which was generating the loud scraping sound. Mao stepped in their direction and fired two undisciplined shots from his pistol. He turned to his comrade. "Come, we have them."

The C-47's wingtip was constructed mostly of lightweight aluminum. The bottom surface had remained intact, and it slid without protest over the rocks, even with the added weight of Norsang atop it. But Dirk and Summer had little wind left, and they struggled to keep moving. They were picking up their pace when a pair of bullets whizzed overhead.

"I think . . . they want us . . . to stop," Summer said between breaths.

Dirk glanced along the slope. "Only twenty feet to the glacier. We can make it."

The wingtip in their hands suddenly grew lighter. Norsang had slid off it and climbed to his feet. "Keep going," he said. "My legs are better."

Dirk began pulling the wing at a near run as Summer fought to keep up on the opposite side. The metal screeched over the rocky surface like fingernails on a blackboard as they approached the ice. Only a narrow ravine separated them from the glacier. Both Dirk and Summer lost their footing on the steep-sided gulch and tumbled into it, the wingtip landing on top of them.

Staggering in obvious pain, Tenzin Norsang reached them a second later. He stepped into the trough, grabbed under the root end of the wing, and shoved it up the opposite incline. Dirk and Summer scrambled to their feet and helped push the wingtip all the way out and onto the glacier's ice.

Summer scampered onto the ice and helped Norsang climb out. Dirk pulled himself up a second later, burdened by the heavy Idol he carried in the man's backpack. He glanced toward the ridge and spotted the dancing beam of the flashlight and the shadowy figures of the two gunmen. They were close enough for Dirk to see the one with the rifle stop and raise his weapon.

"Everybody down." He pushed Summer and Norsang to the ground.

The Chinese rifle barked a second later, sending a burst of gunfire in their direction. A seam of bullets ripped across the wingtip.

When the firing stopped, Dirk rushed to the leading edge of the wing and began pushing it down the ice-covered slope. "Get aboard," he said as it picked up speed.

Norsang took a hurried step and collapsed onto the outside. Summer raced forward and helped push the aluminum sled, then jumped aboard when it began to outpace her. Dirk followed a second later, sandwiching Summer between himself and Norsang.

Gunfire erupted again from the top of the ridge, this time from both the pistol and the assault rifle. But the escapees were now a fast-moving target, sliding out of range of the flashlight as a blur on the slick landscape. Both gunmen emptied their magazines, but to no effect.

The mountain's upper terrain was extremely steep, and the makeshift sled accelerated to a harrowing speed. Summer felt her stomach drop, as if taking a plunge on a roller coaster. Lying in the middle, she could only grasp the wing's curved leading edge in front of her for security. Riding headfirst only inches from the ground magnified the sensation of speed. Summer closed her eyes, more out of fear than to avoid the spray of icy particles pricking her face.

As the speed increased, the ruts and hollows in the glacier's surface began to rock and jostle the wingtip. A shallow dip briefly sent it airborne at one point. When it slammed back to earth, all three riders nearly bounced off. Summer lost her grip entirely, but Norsang grabbed her coat and pulled her back down.

They slid along the glacier's edge, dangerously close to the exposed rocks on the left. Dirk dropped back a few inches until his feet dangled over the rear edge, then tried digging his toes into the ice to slow things down. The mountainside was too steep for that move to generate much success, but, like a rudder, his dragging feet provided a bit of guidance. He extended his right leg to the side and dug in his toe, which swung the wing slightly to the right. Holding steady, Dirk eventually coaxed it toward the center of the glacier, steering clear of a potential lethal plunge into the rocks on either side.

The glacier narrowed as they descended, the gradient lessening as they went. Though their speed was less terrifying, they still were racing over the ice and quickly putting the ridge far behind them. They soon reached timberline, where scrub trees, then tall pines, whirred past.

The glacier narrowed again, and they found themselves sliding down the middle of a ravine. They rattled back and forth as if on a bobsled until the gorge melded with an uneven slope. The ice beneath them dropped steeply again, allowing a brief glimpse of the glacier ahead. The nighttime visibility was only a hundred yards, which rushed by in a heartbeat.

But it was enough to show the riders their luck had run out when a thicket of dark trees appeared directly in front of them.

54

Air Force Two landed at Kaohsiung International Airport in southern Taiwan shortly after dusk. The Boeing C-32 jet rolled to a stop in front of a private hangar, where a small motorcade awaited. There was no fanfare, no throng of officials to greet the visitors, only the director of the American Institute in Taiwan, who was the United States' de facto ambassador, and a few of his aides. It was exactly the kind of arrival that Vice President James Sandecker had requested.

The defense pact Sandecker carried with him, already signed by the President, was sure to inflame relations with the People's Republic of China. For that reason, Sandecker had requested a low-key affair. A private signing ceremony with Taiwan's President would take place on a U.S. Navy ship at ten in the morning, far away from the prying eyes of the media.

"Welcome to the Republic of China, Mr. Vice

President," the AIT director said as Sandecker stepped from the jet's boarding stairs.

"Good to see you again, Hank." Sandecker shook hands. "I'm glad to see you kept the press away."

"They think you're flying in to Taoyuan Airport in the morning," Henry Buchanon replied with a wink. "We'll have the ceremony completed before anyone is the wiser." He pointed across the tarmac. "It's just a short ride from here to the dock, where a tender is waiting to take you aboard the USS **Johnson**."

"We'd like to take a detour along the way, if you don't mind." Sandecker turned and introduced Loren Smith and Rudi Gunn, who had followed him down the stairs.

"Certainly," Buchanon said. "Would you like to stop at a restaurant? A hotel?"

"No." Sandecker smiled. "A dry dock."

The small motorcade pulled into a gritty shipyard in the commercial port and stopped at a large dry dock. The **Caledonia** sat inside it like a toy boat in an empty bathtub, elevated above the bay waters and brightly illuminated by dozens of overhead lights. Sparks flew from a welder as a flurry of workers toiled about the ship's damaged hull.

Gunn took the lead, turning up the collar of his coat against the brisk wind as he located a gangway and led Sandecker and Smith aboard the ship. The bridge appeared deserted, so he made his way to the subsea operations center.

The bay was a beehive of activity. A large video board, normally displaying data from the seafloor, was covered with satellite images and radar weather profiles. Every workstation was occupied, while several people, including Captain Stenseth, stood talking next to the screen. The murmur of voices fell silent as people gradually realized the Vice President of the United States had entered.

Stenseth stepped over to greet them. "Good to see you, Loren, Mr. Vice President. I wasn't expecting to see you here with Rudi."

"We'd like an update on the search status," Sandecker said.

Bill Stenseth saw the concern in all their eyes, especially Loren's. She appeared as if she hadn't slept at all on the flight from Washington.

"The weather has been a real challenge," Stenseth said. "As you know, we've had a typhoon rolling through here, which grounded all regional surveillance aircraft and obscured most of our satellite data. We finally got a P-3 Orion from Okinawa off the ground late this afternoon, along with another from the Taiwan Air Force. Unfortunately, they didn't have much daylight operations time over the dive site."

"Any trace of the tender?" Gunn asked.

Stenseth shook his head.

Loren looked him in the eye. "And the submersible?"

"Nothing either, I'm afraid. We'll have a fresh

start in the morning, with improved weather conditions. Both vessels could have been blown far off-site by the storm," he said, trying to offer encouragement. "We'll keep expanding our search areas to be sure. The Navy has three ships en route, which will add some key resources."

"What of the other vessel that was nearby?" Gunn asked.

"The **Melbourne**? She apparently left the area as well, though we're not sure where she is now. She disabled her commercial tracking system, which is unusual."

"Could she have sunk in the typhoon?"

"No, I don't think so. In fact, we think Hiram Yaeger may have just found her." Stenseth stepped to a workstation. "Pull up that last satellite image that Yaeger sent," he said to the operator.

A fuzzy image of the ocean's surface obscured by clouds appeared on the screen. A dark linear object was visible at the very top, running off the edge of the photo.

"We're not positive, but we think that could be her," Stenseth said. "If so, she appears to be sailing northwest to Taiwan . . . at least, as of a few hours ago."

"Is it possible," Sandecker asked, "that Pitt and Giordino are aboard her?"

"There's always a chance, although they seemed more adversarial when the **Caledonia** was in danger of sinking."

"Send a ship to find out, once the weather allows," Sandecker said. He had been as close to Dirk Pitt and Al Giordino as anyone and was shaken by their disappearance, though he tried not to show it. "Do you have all the resources you need?"

"Yes, sir. We're coordinating with the Navy and the Taiwan military. Everyone is doing all they can."

"I'll be staying here on the ship to lend a hand," Gunn said. "We'll let you know the instant we discover anything."

"Very well." Sandecker turned and took Loren's hand. "Shall we head to our Navy accommodations? You look like you could use some rest."

Loren nodded and followed Sandecker to the door, then hesitated. "Don't stop looking," she told Gunn and Stenseth. "He's there somewhere. I know it."

The two men nodded. After Loren departed, Rudi turned to the captain. "Is there any real hope?"

Stenseth gave a slow shake of his head. "Not much, I'm afraid."

"Well, then let's follow Sandecker's hunch," Gunn said, "and start by locating the **Melbourne**."

55

The glacier made a sharp dogleg turn to the left before extending down the mountainside. There was no way the wingtip could be maneuvered through the bend, and Dirk knew it. He again dug the toes of both boots in, in a futile effort to slow the craft while warning the others. "Get ready to jump off," he shouted. "Trees ahead."

Under the starlight, the river of ice ahead was a silvery blue, bordered by the black spires of tall pines. Icy crystals and wind battered Dirk's face, sending tears down his cheeks, as he scrutinized their route. A curtain of black arose in front of them as the glacier swung left.

"Now," he shouted.

Realizing Summer was trapped in the middle, he grabbed her coat and rolled her onto him as he tumbled off the wing. The glacial surface was hard, and he continued sliding at a high speed with Summer sprawled atop him.

He'd landed on his side, and ice blew inside the neck of his jacket as they rushed downhill. He planted his feet in the ice as best he could, but he had no real leverage, and the compacted surface refused to yield.

The wingtip accelerated ahead of them, scraping across the surface. It kicked up a cloud of icy particles that obscured whether Norsang had jumped. Dirk had little time to consider the Tibetan's fate, as a wall of trees loomed dead ahead. He dug his boots in harder, and could hear Summer do the same, as they desperately fought to scrub speed.

Just ahead, the scraping of the wingtip fell silent, followed by a thunderous crash as it sailed into the thicket. The noise prompted Dirk to dig an elbow into the glacier, in a further attempt to slow their momentum. It was not enough.

Dirk and Summer slid into a raised bank at the edge of the glacier and up its side. For several seconds, they flew through the darkness. When they plunged to the ground, they tumbled through low shrubs and over small saplings, then smacked to a halt against a thick birch. Their reduced speed had saved them from the fate of the wingtip, which had been carried much farther into a guardian stand of tall pines.

Dirk lay still a moment, taking inventory of his aches and pains while catching his breath. "You okay?" he finally asked.

"Yeah." Summer slowly got to her feet. "You

made for a pretty good cushion, except for that Idol. I think it cracked my spine." She rubbed her back, then lent Dirk a hand as he staggered to his feet.

"I could have done without the ice down my pants." Dirk shook his legs. "Where's our friend?"

Summer turned to the east and surveyed the bushes. "Norsang?" she called out. "Help me find him," she said to Dirk, and they both set off through the brush.

They made their way to the remains of the wing-tip, which lay at the foot of two thick-trunked pines. The crushed, twisted aluminum validated the wisdom of Dirk's bailing out. But Norsang was nowhere to be seen. They spread out and back-tracked to the glacier.

Summer spotted him sprawled in a low thicket. She rushed to his side as he raised his head. "Tenzin, are you hurt?" She searched in the darkness for obvious signs of injury.

"Yes," he said as he raised himself onto his elbows. "My head met with a rock when I slid off the glacier." He sat fully upright and rubbed a knot on the side of his skull. "You and Dirk are uninjured?"

"We're okay." Dirk stepped over to join them.

"Do you have the Nechung Idol?"

Dirk twisted around to show that he still carried the backpack on his shoulders. As he turned back, he noticed a dark stain on Norsang's left arm.

"Are you cut?" Dirk asked.

"I think I reopened my old wound."

"Let's have a look." Summer helped him remove his jacket and sweater. She found a trickle of blood from the earlier gunshot to his triceps. She held her palm over the gauze covering. "You could use a new bandage."

"There should be a medical kit in the outer pocket of my backpack," Norsang said.

Dirk unzipped the pack and located the small kit. Summer took over, applying an antiseptic cream, then wrapping his arm tightly with a new bandage.

"Thank you." Norsang admired her handiwork. "Looks very professional."

"I've had a lifetime of practice on my thrill-seeking brother."

"Can you walk?" Dirk asked.

"Yes, my legs are operating strongly now." He looked shaky when he first stood, then stomped his feet to prove his recovery.

Dirk looked up the glacier. A small light wavered near the summit. "We've got a nice separation from our friends. How about we keep it that way?"

"They will not be happy." Norsang led the way back to the glacier. "They must have tracked us here from Dambung . . . or Gangtok."

"I thought it odd," Summer said, "that they didn't seem to know what the Idol was before we recovered it."

"I am also troubled by the gunman's words," Norsang said. "He stated the Nechung Idol has value to his government as something other than a religious relic."

"We have heard speculation," Dirk said, "that the material it is carved from, **thokcha**, may be what the Chinese are actually pursuing. It apparently has extraordinarily high thermal properties that give it potential military applications."

Norsang gazed up at the distant light. "If they regard its value as a weapon, there is no limit to what extremes they will pursue to obtain it."

The proud Tibetan turned and began down the glacier, Dirk and Summer following close behind. They hiked for an hour before splitting a trail bar three ways and half a bottle of water rummaged from the bottom of the backpack. They were exhausted, but gave no thought to stopping to rest. They marched at a steady and deliberate pace.

As the light of dawn began to paint the sky, they reached the point where the glacier ended at the headwaters of the valley stream. They crossed to its western bank and followed its frigid waters, retracing the steps of their trek in.

Summer was thankful an hour later when the warm rays of the sun crept over the mountaintops. The familiar ground seemed to pass more quickly, and soon they crossed a high thicket to find themselves back at their van.

"I hope someone remembered to bring the keys." Summer plopped down on a rock to rest.

Norsang dug into his pants pockets and produced

the keys. He jangled them in front of him, then tossed them to Summer. "You better drive. I only have one good arm."

During their exchange, Dirk eyed a four-wheel-drive vehicle parked behind their Tata van. Norsang followed as he stepped over to inspect it.

It was a Toyota Fortuner SUV, built in India and painted beige. Though well used, it had fresh off-road tires. Through the driver's-side window, Dirk noticed a modern two-way radio mounted beneath the dash and, on the center console, an empty pack of Chinese-brand cigarettes.

Dirk nodded. "I think this belongs to our pursuers."

Norsang pulled on the rear door handle and was surprised when it opened. He poked his head inside, then looked at Dirk. "I think you're right. Come take a look at this."

Dirk peered inside. A large white drone lay on the backseat.

"Summer said she heard a buzzing when we started out. They must have been tracking our route." He nodded at Norsang. "This has to be their car."

He pulled out his folding knife and wedged it into the sidewall of the rear tire, letting out a hiss of air.

Norsang smiled as he repeated the drill on the front tire. "I certainly hope they enjoy hiking," Norsang said, then made his way to the van.

Summer had already started the Tata and turned it around. Dirk had begun to follow when he hesitated and returned to the Toyota. Opening the back door, he plucked up the drone and its control box and took them with him.

Summer pulled up alongside and gave him a bewildered gaze as he climbed into the backseat. "Stealing toys, are we?"

"No," Dirk said. "I'm just tired of people following us."

56

Leaving the disabled SUV behind in her rearview mirror, Summer drove through the settlement of Dambung and headed west. The unpaved road was empty as she recrossed the small bridge over the Lachung River and turned toward the town of the same name. As she followed the road south through a clearing, a loud thumping sounded from behind.

"Helicopter," Dirk said after peering out the back window. "Coming in low."

The van was buffeted by the wash of rotor blades as a sleek, green-camouflaged helicopter buzzed low over them at high speed. The chopper zoomed a hundred yards past the van, then slowed and turned in a lazy arc.

As the aircraft's full profile was revealed, Norsang spotted a red decal on the fuselage with a five-point star and bar outlined in yellow. "It's Chinese," he said.

The CAIC Z-10 was a modern attack helicopter designed for anti-tank warfare. The narrow-bodied aircraft, known as the Fierce Thunderbolt, was operated by two pilots seated in tandem. Its firepower was evident as it banked in the sky. The barrel of a thirty-millimeter machine gun protruded from its chin, while anti-tank missiles hung beneath squat wings that extended amidships. As the helicopter aligned with the road and faced down the van, there was no question of its intent.

Summer stood on the brakes, then spun the wheel, raising a thick cloud of dust. As the Tata slid and started to pivot, she turned harder and let off the brakes. The front end bounced off the shoulder and carried back onto the gravel road, facing the opposite direction. She floored it.

"We need cover," she said.

"Stay with it," Dirk said from the backseat. "There's trees ahead."

The van reached a descending, serpentine section of road as the helicopter's copilot lined up a laser sight and fired a missile. The slim projectile roared off the helicopter's fuselage and just missed contact, striking a rise behind the van's flank. The booming explosion rattled the van and showered it with gravel and dirt, but caused no mechanical damage. The billowing cloud gave Summer a precious few seconds of cover as she willed the vehicle to go faster.

The white Tata bounced along the uneven road as

if on springs. With no seatbelt in the backseat, Dirk smacked his head on the ceiling with every rut. Behind him, a tire iron broke loose from its mounting and began clanging around. Dirk reached back and grabbed it, pulling it to the seat beside him. Summer didn't need any more distractions.

The road wound through an open meadow for another fifty yards, then dropped into a narrow chute flanked by stands of pines.

"Shoot for those trees," Dirk said. "We can't outrun them, but we can hide in the trees. Stop at the first offer of cover."

Summer nodded, all her energies focused on keeping the van on all four wheels. Her knuckles gleamed white as she squeezed the steering wheel while wrestling through turns at speeds she had no right attempting. Dirk and Norsang gazed at the tall pines and held their breath so that they could reach them before the helicopter fired again.

Norsang saw the stress on Summer Pitt's face and patted her knee. "Your spirit is strong."

It seemed an odd thing to hear at such a moment, but it had the desired effect. Summer felt herself relax slightly, while her focus sharpened. While she saw the road before her, she visualized something more. As if she could see through the trees, she pictured the van in a safe place amid the forest.

Behind her, the helicopter pilots saw the smoke clear and realized the van was still on the move, speeding down the road, trailing dust behind it.

"Off-target." The pilot cursed over his headset.

"Re-sighting for another shot," the copilot said.

The pilot adjusted the collective while engaging the throttle and sped forward, bursting through the cloud of smoke. He could see the van clearly now, careening through the road below. He, too, saw the patch of pine forest, but it would offer no hindrance to destroying the vehicle. But he also knew that after stopping it, they would have to land and quickly recover the Nechung Idol. It would be best to halt the van out in the open, so they would have to act quickly.

He approached within a hundred yards and commanded the copilot to activate another anti-tank missile.

"Target acquired," the copilot said.

The pilot watched as the Tata reached the tree line, then gave the command.

"Fire."

57

The instant the van passed the first line of trees, Summer stomped on the brakes, then jammed the automatic transmission into park. The vehicle skidded across the gravel road as she yelled, "Everybody out."

Dirk already had the side door open. The drone and tire iron were in his way, so he shoved them out, then leaped out the door. By the luck of his stride and quick reflexes, he somehow stayed on his feet, running alongside the vehicle until he caught his balance and peeled off into the trees.

Norsang was close behind, having waited an extra second for the Tata to slow before jumping. He tumbled to the ground, rolled twice, then bounced to his feet and followed Dirk. He was almost to the trees when the missile struck.

They likely would all have been killed had it not been for Summer's sudden braking, which threw up a thick wall of dust. The helicopter copilot hesitated as the cloud obscured the van. Not wishing to disobey a superior officer, he had launched the missile at the pilot's command into the dust without having a clear line of sight.

His aim was slightly low. The missile blasted away from the helicopter, struck the ground, and detonated just behind the van's rear wheels.

The boom was deafening to Dirk and Norsang as they dived to the ground amid a rain of debris. The explosion upended the van, sending it tumbling forward in a rising fireball.

Dirk tried to look past the smoke and flames to find Summer. He gazed at the trees on the opposite side of the road, but she wasn't there. With a sick feeling, he spotted her prone on the road some twenty feet behind the smoldering vehicle. She had jettisoned safely, but wrenched her knee as she tumbled to the ground. Unable to walk, she was trying to crawl to the trees.

Dirk started to get up when he felt someone clasp his arm.

"I'll get her." Norsang yanked Dirk back down as he jumped up and ran toward Summer.

They weren't the only ones to spot her. The Z-10 had moved in to investigate, and both the pilot and copilot saw her creeping toward the trees.

"Take her out with the thirty-millimeter," the pilot ordered.

The copilot activated the nose-mounted machine gun that pivoted with the movement of his headset.

As he tried to take aim, Summer stood and tried to run. Her right knee collapsed, but Norsang appeared out of nowhere to grab her. Together, they hopped to the cover of the nearby trees.

"Get him, too," the pilot ordered.

He rotated the hovering craft to better face the fleeing pair, but that offset the copilot's aim just as he fired. A hail of bullets tore into the ground, striking at their heels. The copilot held fire and readjusted his aim just as Summer and Norsang found cover behind a thick pine.

The machine gun rattled off several long bursts, sending up a shower of bark and wood chunks. Then the gun fell silent, the copilot having exhausted his ammunition.

"Do you see them?" The pilot peered over the copilot's shoulder into the trees. He flew over the forested section, but didn't spot anyone.

"Let's put two missiles on their position to be sure," he said, "and then we'll land. Arm the HJ-9s."

He banked the helicopter until it again hovered over the road, a short distance from the burning van.

On the ground, Dirk ducked behind a pine as the helicopter briefly came toward him before looping around. Summer and Norsang crouched behind a thick stand a few yards from the road. They might not be visible from the helicopter, but that wouldn't stop the Chinese from continuing to fire there.

He scrambled a few yards through the trees until

he was directly behind the helicopter. A few feet away, the drone lay on the side of the road where he had knocked it from the van. Dirk crept over and grabbed it and the control panel, along with the tire iron.

He moved back to the road's shoulder, astern of the helicopter, and set down the drone. It was a large, heavy-duty unit, almost two feet across, and powered by four rotors. Dirk wedged the tire iron between the drone's bottom-mounted camera and its landing skids. Then he crawled back into the trees and powered it on.

Even with the weight of the iron, the drone rose quickly into the air. Dirk had flown one before and had a sense of how it operated, but he took a second or two manipulating the joystick to get a feel for its sensitivity.

A loud whoosh came from above as another missile launched from the helicopter's left wing pod.

It slammed into the ground twenty yards from where Summer and Norsang were hiding. The detonation shook the ground and sent a spray of tree limbs and splinters flying high. Dirk could see the couple were unscathed, but only for the moment. The pilot walked the helicopter twenty yards down the road and hovered again, this time directly in front of Summer and Norsang.

Dirk elevated the drone and guided it in parallel to the helicopter, keeping it below and behind the larger craft's rotor wash. When the helicopter stopped and hovered, Dirk sent the drone shooting skyward, above the tail of the Z-10.

The pilot stared at his target. "Arm and fire one more."

From his slightly elevated perch behind the co-pilot, he glimpsed something out of the corner of his eye. He looked back and saw a dark object flying overhead. Focusing a second, he was surprised to see it was a drone. He cranked his neck as he watched the device rise high over the tail assembly, then suddenly drop like a stone.

He jammed his feet on the anti-torque pedals to swing the tail clear, but his reaction was too late. Although beyond his field of vision, he heard the results when Dirk guided the drone directly into the assembly.

The Chinese helicopter's tail rotor was made of composite materials designed to withstand the impact from light debris and even small-arms fire. It easily devoured the plastic frame of the drone, but then it met the tire iron. The thick metal rod tore away two of the four rotor blades at their mountings, while chipping the other two. The spinning debris sliced through the helicopter's tail assembly, severing the right stabilizer.

Without its horizontal-stabilizing force, the Z-10 began spinning on its axis. The pilot fought to counter the force, but hovering so low, he had no chance. The craft lost altitude as it spiraled forward. Then its main rotors clipped the trees. The

Z-10 lurched forward and crashed into the ground nose first.

Any chance of survival for its occupants vanished when the copilot fell against the firing button of the armed missile, sending it erupting into the ground upon impact.

The resulting fireball was more than double that of the Tata van's, the helicopter's fuel and other armaments adding to the explosion. Multiple shock waves rippled through the woods as a black mushroom cloud rose overhead.

Once the fragments of the shattered main rotor had spun into the ground, Dirk picked himself up from the grove of trees opposite. He wiped at a cut on his leg from some flying debris and then stepped across the road. Summer and Norsang hobbled from the trees a minute later.

"Ankle?" Dirk asked.

"Knee," Summer said. "Jammed it when I jumped out of the van. Better than the alternative."

She motioned toward the vehicle's still-smoldering remains. The three of them turned and examined the helicopter from a safe distance. There was little left to see. The nose and forward fuselage had been obliterated by the crash and missile detonation. The main engine assembly burned in a ditch, while the remains of the tail assembly lay mostly unscathed in the middle of the road.

"Your toy proved both valuable and deadly," Norsang said.

"The same device they used to track us up the valley and ultimately kill your comrades," Dirk said.

Summer pointed at the red Chinese star outlined in yellow on a panel at their feet. "Do you think they'll send another one?"

Her query was answered a few seconds later when a pair of gray fighter jets roared by at low altitude. When they circled for a second pass, Dirk spotted a green-, white-, and orange-striped fin flash on the vertical stabilizers. He raised an arm and waved. "They're Indian."

The Russian-made Su-30s circled for several minutes until a military truck, followed by a light utility vehicle, thundered down the road from Lachung and pulled to a stop. A half dozen armed troops piled from the truck and took up a position around the helicopter. The unit's commander, a slim lieutenant with deep-set eyes, climbed out of the smaller vehicle and approached the three foreigners.

"Who are you?" he asked in a wary tone. "And what are you doing here?"

"We were returning from a hiking trip in the mountains when we stopped for lunch," Dirk said. "The helicopter appeared out of nowhere, flying very low over the road, and collided with our vehicle. Is it one of yours?"

The Indian officer stared at Dirk without blinking. "I will need to see your identification."

"I'm afraid our passports and visas were in the van."

The lieutenant looked at Norsang. "Who are you?"

"Tenzin Norsang, sir. I am with the Central Tibetan Administration in Dharamsala."

"You are a long way from home." He studied Norsang more closely. "I have served with men from the Administration. Did you serve in the Army?"

"The National Security Guard."

The Indian's brow raised as he turned away, knowing the Guard was an elite unit of special forces. He examined the smoldering helicopter for several minutes, then viewed the van. He stepped back to the trio with a measured gait.

"It appears your van was traveling north, into the mountains, when it was damaged."

"It was struck very hard," Dirk said with a thin smile.

"Have any of you been across the border to China?" He looked to each to respond. When they all replied in the negative, he nodded. "I can give you a ride to Gangtok. You will need to manage your affairs from there. Follow me."

As he started toward his truck, Norsang stopped him. "Wait. We had something of importance with us." He looked to Dirk for assurance.

Dirk shook his head and kicked at the ground. "I'm afraid I left it in the van."

Norsang walked to the van, the others following. It was a mangled, smoking mess, its white exterior singed black, while its charred interior was still smoldering. The passenger's side showed slightly less damage, and the Tibetan approached the rear door, which had slammed shut after Dirk's exit.

He tried to slide it open, but the door moved only a foot or so before it ground to a stop against twisted metal. Inside, there was little to be seen. The cushions of the front seat had burned away, leaving a skeleton frame and blackened springs. Its seatback had broken free and was wedged in front of the backseat, which was otherwise empty.

Norsang pulled out the remains of a singed blue strap, which he recognized from his backpack. He held it up to the others. "It is no more."

Dirk shook his head, then nudged past Norsang and leaned inside to see for himself. While the backseat was empty, the floor in front of it was not. He reached for the edge of the seatback. It was still hot to the touch, but he grabbed it with a quick yank and tossed it aside.

Norsang and Summer moved to the open door and peered inside. When they froze and said nothing, the Indian Army officer leaned over their shoulder.

"What is it?" he asked.

Sitting upright on the floor, fully intact and gleaming as if polished by its fiery ordeal, the Nechung Idol answered for itself.

58

Two armed commandos marched Pitt and Giordino to the rear of the **Melbourne**. They stopped in front of a pair of steel doors along the side of the aft blockhouse. The first door, made of solid steel, had a dogleg handle that was fastened by a length of chain wrapped to a bulkhead hook. To the right, the second door featured a tinted glass porthole and was secured by a padlock that still held its key.

The two commandos talked between themselves before selecting the door on the right. One removed the lock and opened the door, the other nudged Pitt and Giordino inside with the muzzle of his rifle.

The door clanged shut behind them, followed by the sound of the lock snapping closed. Pitt waited a moment for the men to walk away before he tested the interior handle and confirmed they were indeed locked inside.

Giordino groped along the doorframe, found a light switch, and flicked it on. Even before the overhead fluorescent bulb buzzed dimly to life, he could tell where they were by the odor. A dozen five-gallon drums of paint were stacked against the compartment's back wall, along with an assortment of brushes and smaller cans.

"The paint locker." Giordino slid over one of the drums and took a seat. Even that minor movement made him wince from the blows he'd suffered at the hands of Ning. "Could we have done any worse?"

"The lower bilge, I suppose," Pitt said. "At least we can change the color of the walls if we get bored."

"Dying from paint fumes might be more desirable than what our Chinese pals have in mind for us."

"How are the ribs?" Pitt asked as he walked around the room and took stock. He noticed a thick roll of duct tape atop a paint can and tossed it onto Giordino's lap.

"Bruised, but not broken, I'd say." Giordino rejected the thought of taping his ribs. "It only hurts when I breathe."

Pitt took inventory of the locker. "A dozen buckets of paint, a can of kerosene, and some more tape."

"Not much help in escaping a steel box." Giordino tossed his tape back to Pitt.

"Nothing's impossible with a little duct tape," Pitt said.

He eyed the door, turned off the light, then pressed his face against the porthole and looked at the deck outside. No one was within view. Turning the light back on, he tore off several strips of tape and placed them over the porthole, covering the glass.

"Not enough privacy for you?" Giordino asked.

Pitt shook his head. "The sound of shattering glass grates on my nerves." He picked up one of the metal paint buckets and swung it in a wide arc. Stepping toward the door, he drove the base of the container into the center of the covered porthole. The glass audibly cracked under the blow. Pitt carefully peeled away the edges of the tape until he could remove the entire shattered porthole in one section.

As he set the glass off to the side, Giordino grinned. "You'd make a good cat burglar. You think he left the key in the lock again?"

"We can always hope." Pitt wiped the port's ring of any remaining glass with a wad of tape, then poked his head through the opening.

The porthole was large enough for him to extend his head or his arm and shoulder through, but not both at the same time. It had grown dark outside, and he couldn't quite see the bottom of the padlock. He pulled his head in and extended his arm, groping around the door handle and running his fingers to the lock. The key was gone, and a tug on the lock confirmed it was engaged.

He retreated back into the bay. "No dice, I'm afraid."

"It was worth a shot." Giordino felt a gust of wind through the opening. "At least we get a reprieve from the paint and kerosene fumes."

"Kerosene . . ." Pitt repeated.

He stuck his head through the porthole again and looked down at their door's hinges. There were two of them, and they both appeared within arm's reach. The steel door had two downward-facing bolts attaching it to its frame, which slid into a pair of thick hinge pads welded to the bulkhead. A heavy nut secured each bolt at the bottom of the pad.

Pitt ducked inside the locker, picked up the can of kerosene, and held it up to the porthole for size. Seeing it would fit through lengthwise, he removed the cap and extended it through the opening. Using the back of his hand for guidance, he slid the can along the door to the top hinge, then poured the liquid over its bolt, pad, and nut. He repeated the baptism with the lower hinge.

Pitt knew that the kerosene, as a petroleum distillate, would act as both a solvent and a lubricant on the weathered assemblies. He waited a half hour, noting a sentry passing by without noticing the missing porthole glass, then applied another dose. He sealed up the can, wrapped it in a rag, then used it in place of a hammer, pounding it against each of the nuts. He stopped and listened for any approaching commando, but heard only a faint tapping from elsewhere on the ship.

"Think you can get it to budge?" Giordino asked when Pitt set down the kerosene can.

"Ship's not that old, so there's a chance."

"I haven't seen any wrenches around here . . . or any other tools, for that matter."

Pitt grinned. "You forgot about our trusty duct tape."

He pulled off an arm's-length strip of tape and carefully folded it over three times, matching the width of the hinge nuts. At one end he added a short tab of the same width, dangling off with an open, sticky side.

Pitt wiped the hinge nuts clean with a rag, then extended the tape through the door. Feeling for the upper hinge, he wrapped the sticky end around the side of the nut. He continued winding the layered tape clockwise several times around it, then pulled the tape snug. He reached both hands through the porthole, grabbed the loose end of the tape, and pulled.

The tape held, but the nut didn't budge. Pitt made several attempts, then retrieved the kerosene can and pounded it against the nut. Again, he gripped the tape and gave it another pull. This time, he felt a slight give. Unsure if the tape was simply stretching, he wrapped another loop around the hinge nut and pulled. He could clearly feel it twist.

The steel fastener fought him the entire way, but with continued effort he eventually worked it to the end of the bolt and finished unscrewing it with his fingers. He brought it inside the locker and tossed it to Giordino. "One down, one to go."

"All those hours tinkering with your old cars," Giordino said, "was worth something after all."

Pitt attacked the lower hinge, but this time without success. It was a longer reach, which made for an awkward pull. He tugged and strained against it for several minutes until the tape began to rip. He then retreated to the locker and constructed a new wrench from tape while shaking off the muscle fatigue in his arms.

"Let me give it a shot," Giordino said when Pitt held up a new strip of tape.

"Not sure you can reach it. I'm having a tough time."

The porthole was barely head height for Giordino, so he slid a five-gallon paint bucket against the door and climbed on it. He took the tape from Pitt, reached out, and just barely managed to wrap it around the lower hinge nut. He took a deep breath, wincing from the pain in his side, and, with a grunt, gave the tape a sharp pull.

He jumped off the can and rubbed his hand, which was raw from the tape, and slowly pulled himself upright. "I think you'll find it ready to depart from its mate."

Sure enough, Giordino had broken it loose. Pitt continued the effort and eventually worked the nut off the lower bolt.

Pitt ducked back inside with the second nut. "Glad you've been eating your spinach."

Giordino stepped to the door and prepared to lift it from its hinges when Pitt waved him off.

"I think the sentry's due by shortly." Pitt glanced at his watch. "They seem to make a pass every half hour."

Giordino nodded and turned off the light. Both men stood near the door, looking out the porthole. Just as Pitt predicted, a dark-clad commando passed by a few minutes later. As before, the man focused his attention on the roiling sea as he made his way aft.

Pitt and Giordino gave him five minutes before they jointly muscled the heavy steel door off its hinges and pushed it aside. They stepped quietly onto the deck. With no one in sight, they put the door back in place. As the bolts clanged into the hinges, Pitt again heard a tapping sound. It was coming from the bay next door.

He stopped Giordino, who was already moving forward. "Al, let's see what's behind door number two."

Pitt unwrapped the chain tie-down, turned the latch, and opened the door. He was met by a fetid stench. A gaunt man with a three-day growth of beard stood by the doorway and stared at Pitt with vacant eyes. In his hand was a shard of wood from a crate that he had used to tap against the bulkhead.

His eyes widened when he saw that Pitt and Giordino were not dressed in fatigues and carrying weapons. "Who . . . who are you?" he asked in a raspy voice.

"Fellow captives," Pitt said. "How many are you?"

The man stepped aside so Pitt could see for himself. Close to twenty crewmen lay on the floor of the bay in weakened states. Many appeared near death.

"How long have you been in here?" he asked.

The man tried to count, his mind in a haze. "It's been about three days, I think. We are all rather dehydrated."

Giordino pulled Pitt back onto the deck and spoke in a low tone. "I don't think they'll be much help in launching a coup."

"No. They need medical attention. And soon."

Giordino pointed toward the stern. "They're towing their boarding vessel behind the ship. Might be the best ticket out of here."

Pitt squinted at the silhouette of the boat on the dark seas and nodded. "See if you can bring it alongside. I'll get them moving to the stern."

As Giordino vanished across the deck, Pitt stepped back into the bay. The man in the doorway appeared invigorated by the fresh air, his brown eyes looking more lucid.

"What's your name?" Pitt asked.

"Chuck Sonntag. Ship's navigator. Are the terrorists still aboard?"

Pitt nodded. "We need to get everyone to the stern as quickly as possible. Can you help?"

"You bet."

Sonntag looked around the bay, which served as a storage area for batteries, chargers, and test equipment.

"Every man who can get to your feet, do so," Sonntag said. "We're moving out, lads, but no talking. Help those who need it."

Sonntag paired off the stronger men with those who could barely stand. A young, debilitated Filipino steward was left unsupported. Pitt helped the man up and hoisted his arm over his shoulder.

Pitt led the sickly group toward the stern, keeping the men tight along the bulkhead to avoid detection. Sonntag took up the rear, closing the door and helping the stragglers. Pitt reached the back of the stern blockhouse and led the men across an open stretch of deck to the **Stingray**, where they huddled in its shadow. The NUMA submersible sat a few yards from the stern rail, still attached to the lift crane and covered in a large tarp.

A short distance away on the port quarter, Giordino was operating an electric capstan, reeling in the crew boat by its towline. Pitt joined him as the boat was brought alongside, its flank banging against the ship's hull due to the wave action. Pitt jumped aboard and located a stern line, which he tossed to Giordino to secure the boat.

The **Melbourne**'s crewmen were waved over in small groups. Giordino helped lower each man to Pitt on the heaving boat below. A long, covered salon with bench seating on either side sat astern of the wheelhouse and offered room for all the crewmen. When the last man was lowered onto the boat, Pitt climbed onto the roof and pulled himself over the **Melbourne**'s rail, where Giordino and Sonntag stood in the shadows.

"Are you fit enough to sail her to shore?" Pitt asked the Australian navigator.

"Yes, I think so. You're not coming with us?"

Pitt shook his head. "We'll try to free Margot and her father."

"I'll hold the boat for you."

"No, that will be too dangerous. Some of your men are almost dead. Try to get them to shore as soon as possible. We'll make a grab for the helicopter if we can free the Thorntons."

"It would probably be best," Giordino advised, "if you drift back a good distance before starting the engine."

"I'll take a wide berth around the ship," Sonntag said. "Don't worry."

"They might catch you on radar, but land doesn't look too far away." Pitt pointed to a cottony glow on the northeast horizon.

Sonntag shook hands with each man. "Thanks for getting us out. Good luck."

Pitt helped lower him onto the boat as Giordino tossed over the stern line. Sonntag staggered onto the boat's bow with another crewman, untied the towline, and tossed it into the sea. He gave Pitt and Giordino a thumbs-up as he made his way into the wheelhouse.

Pitt was watching the boat drift back from the **Melbourne** and fade into darkness when Giordino tapped him on the shoulder. Pitt looked up to see an armed sentry making his way down the port deck, a few minutes ahead of his scheduled rounds.

59

Pitt and Giordino stood completely exposed at the corner rail, but froze where they were. Ahead on the deck, the sentry moved at an unhurried pace near the stern blockhouse. When he stopped at the rail and gazed out to sea, they scurried across the open deck to the **Stingray** and tucked themselves in the shadows beneath its hull.

The sentry resumed his rounds and made his way to the fantail, where he stopped at the port rail. He turned and began to step across the stern, but paused at the capstan. Loose coils of towline dangled from its drum and spread across the deck to the port rail, where it hung limply over the side.

The man pulled a radio from his belt and spoke into it as he stepped again to the rail and peered at the empty ocean behind the ship. He barely got his first words out when he heard footfalls on the deck and turned to see a tall, dark-haired man lunge at him.

Pitt launched himself at the sentry just as he turned. His shoulder drove into the commando's midsection and knocked the breath out of him. He was driven hard against the side rail with Pitt wrapped around him, then both men collapsed to the deck.

The gunman was momentarily stunned, but had somehow fallen on top of Pitt. He sat up and tried to bring his rifle to bear when a dark shadow loomed over him. He looked up to be greeted by a roundhouse punch from Giordino that struck him on the chin like a sledgehammer. The gunman crumpled to the ground as Pitt got to his feet.

"Thanks for the assist," Pitt said as Giordino caught himself on the rail. "You okay?"

Giordino straightened and rubbed his right side. "Methinks I should have thrown a left."

The rumble of the ship's engines fell away beneath their feet, and they detected new lights and activity on the forward part of the ship.

"We better get him out of here." Pitt grabbed the back of the sentry's collar as Giordino scooped up the man's rifle.

Pitt dragged the unconscious man across the deck to the submersible, where he paused to rest a moment. With the immediate portside deck still quiet, he dragged the man forward to the storage bay where the ship's crew had been held captive. Giordino opened the door and gave way as Pitt pulled the man inside. He closed the door, turned on the light, and examined the young commando's unmarked uniform.

"Looks more your height," Pitt said to Giordino. "Care to join the dark side?"

"Only if I can quit by dinner." He passed Pitt the rifle, stripped the sentry of his uniform, and put it on over his own clothes. The sleeve and leg seams just about tore apart accommodating his contours, but after he rolled up the cuffs a bit, it was deemed a close enough fit.

Giordino completed the impersonation by pulling on the black ball cap the sentry had worn. "The bridge or the wardroom?"

"Their commander said Thornton was in the wardroom," Pitt said. "Let's start there."

Pitt killed the light and opened the door. As they stepped onto the deck and chained the door closed, they heard the sound of the Z-10 warming up on the starboard pad.

"So much for a scenic flight home," Giordino said.

"They must be going after the crew boat," Pitt said. "We need to stop them."

They took off at a run and backtracked to a narrow crossover deck that put them on the starboard rail. The ship seemed to be coming alive around them, with generators firing to life and cranes repositioning their booms over the side. Yet no crew was visible orchestrating the actions.

The two men made their way forward, weaving through the assortment of heavy equipment, until they came within sight of the helipad. Two armed commandos stood on the pad, and one turned in their direction. Pitt and Giordino ducked behind a spool of cable.

"They're not making it easy to get off a clear shot," Giordino said.

"Better if we could get forward of the pad and catch her as she takes off into the wind."

They didn't get the chance. As they looked around the spool, anticipating their move, the helicopter rose off the helipad and bolted forward, vanishing ahead of the ship.

60

The sentry had radioed Ning, who rushed up to the bridge. "I have a report that we lost the crew boat," he said to Zheng and Yan. "My man on watch is not responding, but I have sent two others to investigate."

"An escape?" Yan asked.

"I don't know, sir. It's possible the rope detached, due to the rough seas. Shall we turn back?"

Zheng stepped to the radarscope and scanned the surrounding area. A small white smudge appeared nearby. He watched it a moment, then looked up at Ning in anger. "It's not adrift, it's angling east under its own power. Off our port bow."

Ning turned pale. "I will launch an inflatable and pursue them myself."

Zheng shook his head. "You would have trouble catching them swiftly in these seas. Send the helicopter. It will be quicker."

"The helicopter is unarmed." Yan stared at Zheng. "You can't sink it from the air."

"We don't need to sink it," he said, "just disable it. And a gunner can do that."

Zheng stepped to the front of the bridge and pointed out the window. The first gray streaks of dawn were appearing, but not enough to extinguish the glow on the horizon far in front of them.

"That is Kaohsiung, Taiwan," he said. "We are at the target defense site of Project Waterfall." He tapped the radar screen. "We just need to slow the crew boat until we can initiate the system. Then we will sink them, along with the American destroyer, on the way to striking the coastal plain of Taiwan."

Ning's radio crackled, and he took the call with a distressed look. "Our man on watch has been located in the locked bay where the crew was secured. They all are missing, as are the two men from the submersible."

"Get the helicopter airborne," Zheng said. "Now."

As Ning fled the bridge, Yan stepped to the helm and gazed at the flickering lights along the coastline. "How long will it take to deploy and activate the system?"

"Less than an hour," Zheng said. "Most of the deployment is handled automatically by computers."

"I would have preferred to wait until the scheduled

diplomatic meeting, but perhaps an earlier assault would be better." He turned and faced his nephew. "Launch the tsunami as soon as possible. Let's destroy Taiwan and the American warship before they can sign their precious defense pact."

61

Sonntag had the crew boat's throttles pushed to their stops. It meant a rougher ride through the high swells, but he didn't care. Once they had drifted well back of the **Melbourne** and started the engine, he had only one objective. To get his crew to shore as quickly as possible.

He periodically glanced at the lights of the big mining ship as he sped past it a half mile to the north. The ship was not in pursuit, and in fact appeared to have stopped. Probably to deploy a small boat to give chase, he thought. But the crew boat was fast in the heavy seas, and he had a healthy head start.

It was a chef from the galley staff, standing with him in the wheelhouse, who saw their pursuers. "Sir, it's a chopper. From the ship."

Sonntag turned and saw the flashing navigation lights of the Chinese Z-10 as it flew ahead of the

Melbourne, then turned in a wide arc and approached the crew boat from the bow.

"Tell the men to take cover." Sonntag kept his eyes glued on the aircraft.

The helicopter came in low and to the starboard side of the boat. Its side door was open, and a commando with an assault rifle raked the boat as it flew by. The bullets tore through the wheelhouse and salon roof, angling out the opposite bulkhead, but sparing the crewmen huddled on the floor.

The Z-10 circled around the stern, then pulled even with the wheelhouse.

Sonntag couldn't hear the chatter of the weapon over the roar of the boat's engine and the thumping of the helicopter's blades, but he saw its muzzle flash and dived to the floor. The pilothouse exploded in a shower of glass and debris as the gunman concentrated his fire. Sonntag reached over and spun the wheel from the floor as a series of short bursts shattered the helm console, navigation screen, and radio.

The fury ceased when Sonntag's action turned the boat hard over, running directly beneath the helicopter.

"Cookie, you okay?" he called to the galley chef, who had pulled himself to a sitting position against the bulkhead. His right sleeve was soaked with blood, and he clasped his elbow with his left hand.

"Just dinged, sir. I'm all right."

Sonntag crouched at the helm, whipping the ship's wheel one way and then another to throw off the gunman's aim.

The Z-10 took a new approach, circling around and tailing the boat. Sonntag hoped they were out of ammunition, but he wasn't that lucky.

The chopper eased over the boat's stern, trying to match its zigzag movements. Sonntag glanced out the shattered rear window to see the helicopter's passenger lean out the open door and drop a small object.

It was a grenade, which bounced off the deck near the transom, then detonated. Sonntag saw the flash and heard the bang, but that was nothing compared to what happened a second later. Grenade fragments pierced the thin rear deck and penetrated the boat's fuel tanks just below. Vapor inside the tanks ignited, generating a spectacular fireball.

Barely avoiding the eruption, the helicopter fell back and hovered a few yards behind the stricken vessel. From their vantage point, its occupants casually watched as the crew boat's stern burned in a blazing inferno.

62

The **Melbourne** had taken on a new life. Though its massive turbine engines had fallen silent, the vessel's dynamic positioning system had been activated, with computer-controlled thrusters locking the ship in position over the Taiwanese defense site. Automated cranes swung outboard on either side of the ship, deploying floating booms that extended for more than twenty yards. Networks of cables were spooled out to three large yellow buoys spaced across the booms, which in turn allowed acoustic streamers attached to the cables to be lowered into the depths. Project Waterfall was gearing up for its biggest test yet.

Pitt and Giordino ducked into a cross passageway and watched as several of the commandos helped launch the equipment, directed by an elderly Asian man in a white lab coat. He looked unsteady, grasping a side rail for support as Ning stood beside him holding a pistol to his back.

Pitt led Giordino across to the port deck, where a similar scene was unfolding. In the distance, over the rumble of the Z-10, faint gunfire sounded across the water. An angry bitterness struck both men when they observed a bright orange fireball rise into the sky from the crew boat.

The two men snaked their way forward through cranes, cable drums, and assorted deck equipment while avoiding contact with any of the commandos. The handful of gunmen handling the acoustic system were too preoccupied to notice the two men slithering along the bulkhead shadows. Reaching the forward blockhouse, Pitt found the door to the wardroom, and they quietly entered.

Margot and Alistair Thornton were sitting at a table on the far side of the room, their arms bound behind them. An armed guard sat across the table from them, studying a chart while casually smoking a cigarette.

"I see only one, on the far side," Pitt whispered to Giordino, then tucked his hands behind his back and staggered into the room. Giordino pulled his black cap lower over his eyes and followed Pitt in. He made like he was poking the assault rifle in Pitt's back, while staying in the taller man's shadow.

The guard jumped to his feet and turned his rifle on Pitt. He stood back from the table, but relaxed when he saw the black-clad gunman at Pitt's back.

Ignoring Margot and her father, Pitt walked

straight to the guard, stopped at his empty chair and looked down at it, as if asking permission to sit. The guard took the bait. He nodded and swung the muzzle of his rifle toward the chair.

Pitt sprang forward, throwing his free hands against the muzzle and jamming it against the wall. The guard struggled to free the weapon, ignoring Pitt's ostensible captor. Giordino stepped forward and slammed the stock of his rifle into the side of the guard's head. The gunman dropped his weapon and melted to the floor, unconscious. Pitt grabbed the rifle and slung it over his shoulder.

Margot had stifled a scream when she realized it was Giordino dressed as one of the commandos. Now she sagged in relief.

"Are you two all right?" Pitt began untying their bindings. He could see that Alistair Thornton had been beaten badly.

"Very glad to see you two." Margot immediately checked her father.

"I'm fine, dear," Thornton said in a tired voice as he rubbed his wrists. He reached over and swallowed some of the remaining coffee the guard had been drinking.

He paused when he heard some external clunks as cables being fed into the sea scraped against the side of the ship. "They're going to do it." He shook his head. "The bloody buggers are really going to do it."

"Do what?" Giordino asked after making sure the guard was still out cold.

"Smash Taiwan with a tsunami." Thornton poked the chart on the table with an angry jab.

Pitt looked at Margot, who nodded. "It's true," she said. "They've put the ship in position to activate Project Waterfall with a strike against Taiwan. Can't you hear the racket? They're deploying it now."

"You sure they know how to use the system?" Giordino asked.

Thornton looked down and slowly nodded. "Dr. Yee, an engineering director from the Taiwan Ministry of National Defense . . . he and I tried to deceive them as best we could, but they found all the plans and operating documents. They then threatened and coerced their way in to obtain an understanding." He gazed at his daughter. "Yee was barely alive the last I saw him."

"Are you sure it will work here?" Pitt asked.

"Yes. They have apparently brought the ship here, to one of the Waterfall defensive positions." He pointed to some red marks on the chart. Pitt could see the designated spot was about twenty miles southwest of Kaohsiung.

"This is one of the sites where the Taiwanese hoped to establish a permanent system," he said. "They'd surveyed the waters here and found it was a prime location to deploy the system. Deepwater canyons, sharp elevation changes, rapid seafloor currents."

"So the ship can really generate a tsunami here," Giordino asked, "and direct it toward Taiwan?"

"Without question," Thornton said. "And from Taiwan's standpoint, you couldn't pick a worse spot."

He dragged a finger along the island's southwest coast. "This whole part of Taiwan is a low, flat plain. A large tsunami would create damage far inland. Two of the country's largest cities, Tainan and Kaohsiung, will be devastated."

As Pitt and Giordino tried to comprehend the impact, Margot cleared her throat. "There's one other thing you should know. The timing of their attack is not random. The officer who arrived on the helicopter said the American Vice President just arrived to sign a defense pact with Taiwan. He's on a Navy ship off Kaohsiung—directly in the path of the wave."

"Sandecker is here?" Giordino asked.

Margot nodded. "Chinese intelligence informed him the Vice President was seen arriving last night with a Congresswoman. They are aboard a destroyer for the pact signing, which will take place this morning."

The words struck Pitt like a punch to the gut. His wife, Loren, sat on the House Foreign Affairs Committee and was good friends with the Vice

President. It could be no coincidence. The Congresswoman traveling with James Sandecker had to be Loren Smith.

"Why would the Chinese attack Taiwan with the Vice President there?" Giordino asked. "They're risking outright war with the United States."

"I don't know," Margot said. "I sense it's a rogue operation."

"They'll do it because they can blame us," Alistair said. "It's easy. They just kill us, then sink the **Melbourne** after the event. It will make for great propaganda for the Chinese, blaming the hawks in Taiwan for a defense system that backfired."

He swallowed the last of the guard's coffee. "Who knows, maybe they intend to use the disaster as a step toward unification. China could come in as a savior by providing medical aid and assistance. Or perhaps they'd use the resulting chaos to launch a military takeover. Either way, they're sitting pretty, bringing Taiwan into the fold and upsetting the balance of power in the entire region."

As he spoke, a high-pitched whining came from the bowels of the ship, and the wardroom lights flickered. The whine continued for a minute or two, then died away.

"That was a first pulse," Thornton said with alarm in his eyes. "They've got it deployed and activated."

"Will that create a wave?" Giordino asked.

"Not yet. The system builds on a series of pulses

that gradually generate something akin to a Venturi effect. Each cycle takes about ten minutes. The resulting surface wave usually occurs on the third or fourth cycle."

"How can we stop it?" Pitt asked.

Thornton grimly shook his head. "The system is highly automated and activated by the operations bay. But it's built like a vault, at the center of the ship. When I was last there, they had three or four armed men stationed inside and one outside. There's no way you're going to bust in there and take command."

"What about its power?" Giordino asked. "Can we kill the electrical source?"

"That might be possible." He rubbed his fingers across his chin. "The system is powered by a dedicated turbine beneath the operations center, but that's its only access. We could try to disable the output through the power cables, or try to short the acoustic strands themselves. Either would take time and risk being seen on the deck."

A ship's alarm suddenly blared in the wardroom, joined by the wail of a dozen other sirens simultaneously activated throughout the ship.

Pitt glanced at the alarm near the corner of the ceiling and saw a video camera mounted next to it. "We don't have the time now," he said. "Someone's seen us here. Let's move."

Pitt led the group onto the port deck, where

they overheard commands being issued from the forward part of the ship. Armed men at the bow began moving in their direction.

Giordino pointed offshore toward the burning crew boat and the helicopter hovering over it. "Guess our copter's not rendering itself available."

Pitt calmly took in the scene, his mind calculating their best means of escape. But foremost in his thoughts were Loren and Sandecker being in the path of the coming cataclysm. "Let's leave the way we came," he said.

Giordino nodded. "I'll hold them up and meet you on the stern." He took up a defensive position behind a generator and aimed his assault rifle. A moment later, two black shapes came into view, and he opened fire, taking one man down and sending the other ducking for cover.

Pitt grabbed Margot's hand and dragged her aft, with Thornton on their heels. Her ankle was still too sore to run, but she hobbled quickly, with Pitt giving her support. They reached the stern block-house as a gun battle erupted behind them.

When they reached the storeroom where the crew had been held captive, Pitt stopped and yanked open the door. "Thornton, are you up to hoisting a battery or two?"

The rugged old engineer followed Pitt into the bay and emerged a second later carrying two large twelve-volt batteries as if they were loaves of bread. Pitt followed with two of his own and led the way to the **Stingray** on the stern deck. He set down the batteries, unslung the rifle from his shoulder, and handed it to Thornton.

"I need a few minutes here. Shoot anything that moves, except Al."

"Gladly." Thornton helped Margot to the corner stern rail, which she leaned against for support. From there, he had a clear view up the port rail, as well as across the fantail deck. He watched as Pitt climbed inside the submersible and returned a moment later with a fistful of tools.

Pitt opened a panel on the base of the **Stingray** and pulled out four subsea batteries. He replaced them with the batteries from the storeroom, reattached their connectors, and secured the panel.

The gunfire had ceased, but the rotor thump from the Z-10 grew loud as the Chinese craft returned to the ship. Alerted by Zheng on the bridge, the pilot had turned on its landing lights and slowly skimmed the chopper along the **Melbourne**'s port deck. The bright lights soon picked up the shadow of Giordino sprinting along the port rail.

Giordino ducked beneath a winch and turned to fire on the helicopter, but his borrowed rifle clicked empty. He tossed the weapon over the side and took off at a run. Gunfire opened anew as the chopper swooped close to the ship, bathing Giordino in its spotlight.

"Shoot out the lights," Pitt called to Thornton.

Pitt yanked away the tarp covering the **Stingray**

and scampered into the operator's cab of the large fixed crane behind the submersible. He identified the power controls and started the motor that activated its hydraulic system.

Thornton stood at the rail and calmly took aim at the Z-10, firing several rounds. Having served in the Australian Army, and being an avid dove hunter, he was no stranger to guns. Two of the helicopter's three landing lights shattered, and the pilot veered away.

Thornton turned the weapon up the port rail, waiting until a panting Giordino ran into view and darted to his side before he fired again in the darkness. A weapon clattered to the deck as he put down a pursuing commando.

"Thanks," Giordino said as he caught his breath.

He barely got the words out when a section of the ship's rail beside him disintegrated in a burst of gunfire. "Drop the weapon."

Giordino and Thornton turned to see Ning standing at the transom, having approached unseen from the starboard deck. He had an expectant grin on his face, and an assault rifle held to his shoulder that was leveled at Margot's heart.

63

Thornton gripped his rifle tightly.

"Down," Ning yelled over the din of the Z-10, "or she dies now."

Staring at the commando with loathing, Thornton held the weapon in front of him and dropped it to the deck. Then he sidestepped along the rail to join his daughter. Margot gripped his hand and huddled next to him at the rear corner of the deck.

Ning took a quick look around. He trained his rifle at Giordino and motioned for him to join the others.

Pitt had ducked when Ning looked his way, but now sat upright in the cab and reviewed the crane's controls. As he did, the helicopter hovered off the ship's quarter, pointing aft to aim its remaining landing light on the three captives. Its rotor easily drowned out the crane's hydraulic motor. As Pitt glanced at Giordino stalling for time, he knew exactly what to do.

"What?" Giordino yelled. He raised his arms high, yet pretended not to understand Ning's instruction.

Ning just about shot him on the spot, but decided he would curry more favor by letting Zheng exact his own revenge. "Move," he yelled, directing with his rifle.

Giordino nodded and began to move at a turtle's pace toward Margot and Thornton, limping as if injured.

As he did so, Pitt feathered the crane's lift control, watching in front of him as the slack cable drew taut above the **Stingray**. He held the control at the slowest setting as the cable spool took up the weight of the submersible and slowly lifted it off the deck. Pitt eased the vessel up another five feet, then paused.

Ning had his back to the submersible and was oblivious to its movement as he herded Giordino to the others. But the gunman in the helicopter had seen Pitt's actions, and he waved to Ning. Unable to get his attention, he opened the side door and fired at the crane's cab.

The window in front of Pitt shattered, but he didn't flinch. He had one chance to do it right and no time to wait. He grasped the controls and swung the boom to his right toward the port rail.

He quickly stopped and extended the boom forward, forcing the submersible to swing toward the stern. With his left hand he simultaneously released the lifting cable, then held his breath.

At the sound of the gunfire, Ning had first turned to the Z-10. The airborne gunman was firing at a target behind him, so when the glass shattered, Ning spun around. He was instantly met by the free-falling submersible, which plowed into and on top of him, burying him under its ten-ton mass. Only the roar of the helicopter masked the sounds of his bones being crushed beneath the massive weight.

The helicopter gunman watched in disbelief. He aimed again at Pitt, but his rifle clicked empty. Out of ammunition, he ordered the pilot to the helipad and radioed the **Melbourne**'s bridge.

Giordino retrieved Ning's fallen rifle, observing the commando's legs protruding from beneath the submersible like the Wicked Witch of the East's under Dorothy's house. He raised the weapon, but the helicopter was already skirting around the bow to land on the ship's opposite side.

"Inside." From the crane, Pitt pointed to the **Stingray**.

Giordino called Margot and Thornton over and gave each a boost up to a half ladder, which allowed them to climb atop the submersible. As they slid through the hatch, Giordino followed them up the exterior ladder. His feet no sooner left the deck than Pitt raised the **Stingray** into the air and extended it over the stern rail with the telescopic boom.

As it cleared the ship, Giordino saw two more commandos sprint down the port deck. He raised and fired the assault rifle while clinging to the hatch with one hand. His aim was thrown off by the submersible's swaying, but it was enough to slow the commandos and warn Pitt. Giordino glanced at the crane's cab and saw Pitt point to the ship's starboard side. Giordino nodded as the **Stingray** dropped beneath the transom and splashed into the sea.

Giordino stood and unhooked the lift line as the cable fell slack, then squirmed into the open hatch. A gunman appeared at the rail and fired at the now floating vessel just as he closed the hatch and dropped into the interior.

"Coming through." Giordino squeezed past Margot and took the empty pilot's seat. Thornton sat in the copilot's seat with his hands on a toggle control, already steering the submersible away from the **Melbourne**.

"I took the liberty of activating the thrusters," he said, "but the ballast controls don't seem to be working."

Above them, they could hear tinging bullets striking the exposed hull.

"It's a hot-wire job." Giordino activated a remote switch he had jury-rigged at North Island, which flooded the one good ballast tank. He held the pump on for a minute until the submersible had dropped ten feet below the surface. "I'll drive from here, if you don't mind," he said as he grabbed the joystick.

"What about Dirk?" Margot asked.

Giordino didn't respond, taking his bearings and turning the **Stingray** around.

"You're not going back to the ship?" Thornton said. "You'll get us killed."

Giordino nodded as he reached over and turned on the lone functioning exterior light.

"Sorry, but the man is going to need a lift."

64

Giordino's stray burst of gunfire had saved Pitt. The two commandos attacking the submersible were too focused on Giordino to consider Pitt in the crane's cab. By the time the **Stingray** vanished under the waves and they turned to the crane's shattered control booth, Pitt was gone.

Pitt snaked his way across the stern deck, hugging the bulkhead where he could. The sound of the Chinese helicopter landing on the forward helipad greeted him as he reached the far side. Moving quickly, he ran past the corner of the blockhouse . . . and collided with a gunman sprinting down the starboard deck.

The two men bounced off each other like rubber. The commando, a shorter man, fell backward onto his rear end by the rail. Pitt stumbled back, yet stayed on his feet. He quickly reversed momentum and stepped toward the supine man. The startled commando remained on the ground, but swung his rifle forward as Pitt launched himself toward him.

The man fired before he realized Pitt wasn't lunging at him, but was diving past him. The commando's aim was low, but he raised the rifle as he fired, shredding the heel of Pitt's shoe as he disappeared over the rail above him.

Pitt struck the water in a clean forward dive and kicked a few strokes for added depth. He opened his eyes and performed a quick scan around him. The water was murky from the storm, but he spotted what he was looking for. It was a dull light that shone green underwater, somewhere off the **Melbourne**'s starboard beam. Pitt took off in that direction, swimming twenty yards, before turning toward the surface.

He broke from the water just long enough to gasp a breath of fresh air and dive back under. The commando on the ship who was scouring the waters for him opened fire, but only after Pitt was safely beneath the surface.

The light of the **Stingray** was close now, Giordino lingering at a safe distance until he spotted Pitt. They met at an eight-foot depth. Pitt grasped the steel handle on the hatch and rapped three times. Giordino responded by killing the floodlight and hitting all thrusters while turning away from the **Melbourne**. Pitt had only to hang on as he was whisked through the waters, holding his breath without exertion.

Giordino checked his watch, keeping the throttles down for nearly two minutes before he heard another rap on the hatch. He quickly surfaced and cut power. Margot opened the hatch at Giordino's direction and stuck out her head.

Pitt grinned at her, clinging to the side of the hatch. "Got room . . . for a drowned rat?" he asked between deep breaths.

"Guess it's my turn to pull you in from the sea," she said. "Al says to make it fast."

Pitt crawled through the opening and sealed the hatch behind him. He dropped into the crowded interior as Giordino guided the submersible to deeper water. Thornton stood and offered Pitt the copilot's seat.

"Nice work getting us off, lad." He squeezed together with Margot at the rear. "Take a seat and have a rest."

Pitt squished onto the seat in his wet clothes.

Giordino gave him a grin. "You meet the strangest hitchhikers in these waters."

"Thanks for pulling over," Pitt said. "How are we for power?"

"The new batteries are winners. We've got better than seventy percent power reserves. Maybe even enough to get us to Taiwan."

"We can't move ahead of the **Melbourne**," Thornton said. "They'll be generating a destructive wave in no time."

"We need to stop it somehow," Giordino said.

"There's no way to stop it now," Thornton said. "Not us, in a tiny submarine."

"We don't need to stop it," Pitt said, "only change its path." He pointed out the viewport. "The acoustic strands are lowered by cables from the outward booms. What if we grab hold of the cables and reposition them? Will that dissipate or redirect the wave?"

Thornton thought for a moment. "Yes, it would." His face brightened. "The sensors and transponders are computer controlled to act on the water dynamics, but it's all based on a leading wall ahead of the ship. If we relocate the acoustic curtain, it will certainly change the path of the wave, and maybe its size."

"I recall some lab tests that looked at varying deployment angles," Margot said. "If the starboard curtain was shifted ninety degrees, it would definitely influence the angle of the wave formation. Based on the current positioning, the flow of the wave would redirect to the north, although that would place the **Melbourne** in a dangerous position near the vortex."

"The starboard boom assembly shouldn't be too far in front of us," Giordino said. He turned on the exterior spotlight, then added thrust and guided the submersible forward. As the **Stingray** cut through the water, a high-pitched whine vibrated through the craft, gradually increasing in intensity.

"It's the second activation," Thornton said. "They'll generate some current movement with this one."

"We went through that brain-scrambling game before," Giordino said, "when we were on the seafloor. Sent us rolling across the bottom like a tin can."

"It will be nothing like that close to the surface," Margot said. "At least not yet."

The submersible continued moving forward, all eyes in search of the acoustic mechanism. Giordino began to feel a vibration through the controls, and the whole vessel began to be buffeted.

"We may have gone too far and missed it," Pitt said.

"Yes. Turn us around quickly," Thornton said, an edge in his voice. "We must be in the cavitation zone."

Giordino turned the **Stingray** in a half circle, but it began moving in a lateral direction. The craft shook as Giordino fought to keep it on an even keel.

"Depth increasing," Pitt said. "We're getting pulled down."

He activated Giordino's ballast pump control to counter the effect. Giordino angled the thrusters with the same goal in mind, but it was a losing effort. The submersible seemed to be falling away on a jarring ride to the depths.

Suddenly, it all reversed and the submersible accelerated upward. Margot felt her stomach rise up in her throat as if she were on a carnival ride. The water around them seemed to boil, then they broke the surface. The heavy craft lifted several feet above the swells, then settled back into the sea.

As the waters around them calmed, Giordino turned the **Stingray** to face northeast and cut its power. Through the viewport, they saw a large wave rolling eastward under the dawn-streaked sky.

"We were on the tail end of it," Thornton said. "Lucky thing, or we would have been carried with it."

"That makes two activations," Pitt said.

"The next one," Thornton said, "will be a monster."

Giordino turned the **Stingray** toward the **Melbourne**, which lay with its bow facing them a hundred yards away.

Pitt looked to the Aussie engineer. "How much time to the next wave?"

"Eight, maybe nine minutes," Thornton said. He raked his fingers through his hair and shook his head.

"It's nowhere near enough time to stop it."

65

No one aboard the crew boat saw the **Stingray** arise from the depths. But when one of the hands on the burning vessel raised the alert that a large wave was bearing down on them, Chuck Sonntag had no doubt about its source. Just minutes before, they had been rocked by a smaller rogue wave. Sonntag knew that it was only a precursor to much worse.

He emptied yet another bucket of seawater onto the blazing aft deck. He was on the verge of exhaustion, having almost single-handedly fought the fire after dragging some of the crewmen to safety.

When the Z-10 helicopter had stopped shooting and flown away, he thought they might still have a chance. After the initial flames settled down, he had been able to douse the worst of the fire. The boat would eventually sink, he knew, but drowning seemed a better way for the men to go than burning alive. He still maintained hope that a passing ship might have noticed the inferno and come to investigate.

He dropped his empty fire bucket and looked over the stern rail. Across the sea, a fast-moving ripple on the surface was moving toward them.

"Hang on," he yelled to the emaciated men inside the salon. "There's a wave coming."

He grabbed hold of the doorway and watched it approach.

They were close enough to the **Melbourne** that the wave had little time to build or break, something it would do as it traversed the shallows along the coastline. The watery mass looked smooth and symmetrical, almost serene, as it moved quietly across the sea.

It struck the crew boat with equal silence, rolling into the stern dead center and lifting it high into the dark sky. The action drove the boat forward until the wave passed beneath and beyond it, kicking the bow upward as the stern sank. Debris crashed through the boat as it righted itself, but the vessel remained intact. Sonntag clung to the doorway as the vessel bucked beneath his feet, and he watched as a low wall of seawater washed forward across the deck, then fell aft and gurgled out the rear scuppers. To his amazement, the brief flooding seemed to douse the remaining flames.

The **Melbourne**'s navigator checked on the crewmen in the salon, then returned to inspect the damage. White smoke rose in a hiss from the charred motor and fuel tanks, but the fire was definitely extinguished. Unfortunately, more damage remained unseen. The hull had been breached by the explosion and fire, and the vessel was taking on water.

Borrowed time was all it was, he thought. Perhaps he was just fooling himself. He had done everything physically possible to keep the boat afloat, but the time was nigh. He was too spent to raise another finger anyway. His exhaustion brought a calm sense of defeat. As Sonntag stood and appraised the severity of the damage, the **Melbourne**'s galley chef hobbled beside him, his bloodied arm in a makeshift sling. "Put the fire out, did it?" he asked with a crooked grin.

"Yes, but the next one won't be so kind." Sonntag started to dismiss their chance of survival, then hesitated when he took a look at the wiry man. His white smock was stained black from smoke, the right side coated with blood. With his face bruised and his hair singed, he looked even more exhausted than Sonntag felt. Yet the man grinned with a contagious optimism.

Sonntag put his arm around the chef's shoulders. "Cookie, let's go find us a bilge pump. I could use some exercise."

66

"Rudi, are you still awake?" From half a world away, Hiram Yaeger's voice came over the screen in the **Caledonia**'s video conference room.

"I'm here." Gunn took a seat in front of the screen. But he didn't see Yaeger, only a photo of swirling gray clouds that he had posted.

Gunn had never gone to bed after he'd arrived on the dry-docked ship. Instead, he'd engaged in an hours-long conference with Yaeger in Washington to try to locate Pitt and Giordino. That it was five a.m., local time, meant little to him, as his body hadn't yet absorbed the twelve-hour time difference.

"I was just on the phone with the Taiwan Coast Guard," Gunn said. "The weather has cleared enough to enable a search and rescue helicopter to get off the ground at first light."

"Glad to hear," Yaeger said. "I just received a new

download of satellite imagery for south-central Taiwan. It appears to be time-stamped about two hours ago."

"I hope it looks better," Gunn said, "than the mass of cotton balls we've been staring at all night."

The two men had been scouring all available satellite imagery for signs of the **Stingray**, the **Caledonia**'s tender, and the Australian mining ship. Due to the severity of the typhoon, most of the images were of no value.

"Before I get to that," Yaeger said, "one thing just came up."

The cloud-covered image vanished from the screen, replaced with the live image of a long-haired man in a T-shirt and **Blind Faith** ball cap, seated at a conference table. "One of our DART buoys just triggered a minor warning about a minute ago."

DART, or Deep-ocean Assessment and Reporting of Tsunamis, is a buoy system deployed throughout the Pacific that detects large water pressure changes near the seafloor, symptomatic of a passing tsunami.

"Whereabouts?" Gunn asked.

"Just nineteen and a half miles south-southwest of Kaohsiung. Only reason I saw it is because I have that region of the world pulled up right now."

"Hold on."

Gunn stepped out of the conference room to an adjoining deck. He peered across the dry dock toward Kaohsiung Harbor, which was still and lifeless in the early hour except for water rippling against the shoreline. He returned to the conference room. "It's quiet here. No alarms are sounding. Was there an earthquake nearby?"

"We've picked up no seismic readings, so perhaps it was only a minor landslide. The pressure swing wasn't big enough to trigger an outright warning, but I'll monitor the area all the same."

"As if we don't have enough to worry about," Gunn said. "Thanks anyway. Now let's see what you have from up high."

Yaeger's image was replaced by a fuzzy, high-altitude view of the ocean.

"That's a bit better," Gunn said.

"This satellite uses synthetic aperture radar imaging, so it is not quite photographic quality, but they can see through most cloud cover. This image should encompass the site where the submersible was launched from the **Caledonia**."

The scene revealed no objects on the surface, so they proceeded to scan several dozen more images of the region. They stopped at one that showed a vessel steaming to the northwest.

"Can you zoom in on that?" Gunn asked.

As the image was enlarged, Gunn nodded. "That looks like a match to the photos you found of the **Melbourne**. Appears she's still headed to Taiwan."

"Let me see if I can find more recent images closer to land," Yaeger said.

The screen went blank for a moment, then

another array of satellite images appeared. They located the vessel in two of them, progressing toward Taiwan's southwest coast.

"Looks like she's making for Kaohsiung," Yaeger said. "Maybe there's a chance Pitt and Giordino are aboard."

"We can hope."

Gunn studied the image. "Hiram, based on the time and location of the photos, can you determine where the **Melbourne** would be right now?"

"Hang on."

Yaeger posed the question to Max, the supercomputer he managed in the NUMA headquarters building. In the blink of an eye, it captured the time and location of the images, the ship's heading, computed speed, and the area weather conditions. Yaeger's face turned pale when he saw the results. "You're not going to believe this."

"Tell me," Gunn said.

"She should be nineteen-point-six miles south-southwest of the Port of Kaohsiung."

67

Zheng stepped onto the **Melbourne**'s bridge after speaking with the helicopter's crew on the deck below. After learning of Ning's death, he began to panic about losing control of the situation. But he wasn't prepared to show further weakness in front of his uncle. He took a deep breath and stepped toward Yan Xiaoming.

The Colonel stood at the rear of the bridge, peering over the shoulder of Dr. Yee.

The Taiwanese engineer, after so many beatings the past few days, struggled to sit upright in a console chair. His white lab coat was flaked with dried blood, which had pooled beneath his chair from an especially vicious blow to his head administered by Ning. The life was slowly ebbing from Yee's eyes, and he knew it.

Yee sat before a workstation that displayed a

three-dimensional image of the water column in front of the ship, which swirled up from the seabed like an inverted tornado.

Yan stood upright and looked out the port window to where the crew boat had been burning a few minutes earlier. The flames had vanished, and he saw no sign of the boat in the early morning darkness. Yan turned to his nephew. "Was the helicopter successful in sinking her?"

"No, but she was left disabled," Zheng said. "If she didn't sink with that wave, she will with the next one." A glance at the radarscope told him it was still afloat, but he said nothing.

"What was all the trouble about on the aft deck?" Yan asked.

"The two men on the submersible. They helped the crew escape on the boat. Apparently, they stayed aboard and freed Thornton and his daughter."

"They escaped, too?" Yan gave his nephew a withering look.

"Yes, but they are as good as dead," Zheng said. "They fled off the stern in their submersible, but the vessel is useless. It was damaged and had no power when we brought it aboard. They surely have sunk to the bottom by now."

A bridge wing door opened, and the gunman who had encountered Pitt entered. "Sir, one of the submersible operators has escaped. He had lowered the submersible over the side, then remained aboard. We fired at him in the water, but he got away."

"Got away to where?" Zheng asked, his frustration mounting. "There is nothing but open water around us."

"The submersible. We think it may have picked him up."

"The submersible has no power," Zheng said, his voice rising.

The commando hesitated. "We . . . saw it. It had a light on and was moving in the water."

The vein on Zheng's temple bulged, but he contained his anger. "That's impossible," he muttered.

"Where did it go?" Yan asked.

"It was off the starboard beam, then traveled forward. We lost sight of it when the wave emerged, but it was in front of the ship."

"A lucky break for you, Lieutenant," Yan said to Zheng. "They should also be finished with the next wave, at any rate. Isn't that right, Professor?"

Yee nodded meekly. He kept his eyes on the computer monitor, refusing to look at his captors.

"Has the next activation begun?" Zheng asked.

"Yes," Yee said softly. "Your men in the ops room are spooling up for a third pulse in five or six minutes."

"And this will be it?" Yan said. "This will be the tsunami?"

Yee didn't respond right away, for something

caught his eye. It was a movement in the starboard acoustic curtain, which was upsetting the expected water column currents. He casually looked away from the data and stared at his captors with a faint smile.

"Yes, this will be it."

68

The acoustic curtain materialized in front of the **Stingray** like shimmering strands of pearls dangling in the deep. Dozens of the long, thin cables stretched toward the seafloor, dotted with metallic sensors and transponders every few feet. Closer to the surface, they merged into a single framework of heavier cables, supported by a floating boom and buoy. Three booms supported a separate curtain of sensors on either side of the **Melbourne**.

"Approach from the far end," Pitt said, "and we'll try to gather them up."

It had been his idea to dive and alter the position of the acoustic strands. The surface booms would be too rigid for the submersible to move, and would make them visible to the commandos on the ship. The upper cables would also be heavy, so they had to go deeper.

The water depth was relatively shallow, at five hundred feet, and Pitt had recalled that some of the strands contained tiny tracking lights readily visible underwater. Pitt flooded the ballast tank while Giordino drove the **Stingray** in a sharp dive, and at two hundred feet the acoustic strands appeared.

Giordino guided the submersible as if it were an attacking dive bomber. He descended in a graceful arc at the **Stingray**'s maximum power and aimed for the line of dangling cables at the far end. As he did, Pitt activated the manipulator arm, extending it to its full length off the submersible's right side. He curled the articulated hand toward the vessel to create something of a hook. Giordino saw the deployment and adjusted his path to approach just to the left of the strands. He was nearly upon the first line when he detected the first stirrings of the high-pitched whine.

Giordino ignored the sound and steered the submersible to the curtain. The first strand tinged against the mechanical arm. The submersible continued forward, collecting the next strand a few yards away. The extended arm held the cables in place as they were harvested one by one.

As they reached the last of the strands extending from the first boom, Giordino began feeling resistance in the controls from their accumulated weight dangling far below.

"Mr. Thornton," Pitt asked, "is there a preferred angle we should draw them toward?"

Thornton grabbed a clipboard and began drawing arcs and angles while jotting down a few mathematical equations. Giordino was already gathering up the second block of strands when Thornton leaned forward with an answer.

"Everything's a guess, but if the Chinese don't override the system, we have a chance. If you can make it through the third curtain assembly, I'd steer a heading of ten degrees north."

"Sweep across the **Melbourne**'s bow?" Pitt said.

Thornton gave a sullen nod. "Best we can do, under the circumstances, to counter the portside deployment. We'll be right in the thick of things, but it will disrupt the planned wave formation. It should keep the surface action well clear of Taiwan."

He raised his hands to his ears as the high-frequency transmissions grew stronger. The submersible charged ahead, collecting the second curtain of transducers. The **Stingray**'s progress slowed to a crawl with the collection of the long strands, then the vessel lurched ahead. Unseen to its occupants, the topsides end boom had given way, allowing the entire section to swing forward.

The collected cables pulled the submersible to the right as Giordino approached the last group. He fought the controls to keep the vessel steady as some of them began flashing brightly, illuminating the fear on Margot's and her father's faces. She noticed the two men in the pilots' seats seemed oblivious to the stress of the moment.

"Coming up on the last one," Pitt said in a loud voice.

Giordino nodded. "Turning zero-one-zero degrees." As he snatched the last strand and made the course adjustment, the submersible began to jostle. The acoustic barrage grew in intensity until everyone covered their ears.

Pitt again felt the ringing headache and sense of nausea, but knew that was the least of their worries. To their left, the faint curtain of lights from the **Melbourne**'s port boom flashed in the distance. But then, an entirely different scene erupted.

From the unseen depths rose a dark, funnel-shaped mass. It grew exponentially by the second, rising directly in front of them.

"Hold on," Pitt said. "It's going to be a rough ride."

Thornton stared in amazement, seeing the power of his invention from an underwater perspective. As the phenomenon drew closer, they could see it was a swirling mass of current, its dark color from sand and sediment drawn from the seafloor.

It was like sailing into a black hole. Giordino held the controls firm as the portside curtain lights vanished from view and the buffeting slowly increased. Then they were engulfed by the maelstrom.

The current rocketed the vessel sideways at high speed, battering the occupants. Most of the acoustic strands broke free of the manipulator, but those that didn't began whipping the submersible in a frenzy. The **Stingray**'s lone exterior light was the first thing pummeled into submission, followed by the thrusters' blades and rotor housings.

Margot clasped the entry ladder with one hand, her father with the other, and shut her eyes. But she couldn't block the acoustic whine, nor the thrashing strands that beat against the hull like a thousand steel bullwhips. Yet all that was secondary to the agitation of the submersible as it careened through the darkness at an unforgiving speed.

Amid the gyrations, Pitt managed to retract the mechanical arm and purge the ballast tank, but that had no effect on their wild ride. Like the others, he could only hang on and wait for the end.

The tempest somehow grew worse, the shaking even more teeth-jarring. The **Stingray** seemed to be flying through the water at hypersonic speed, but absent any guidance. Margot opened her eyes to see a black image appear out the viewport. It seemed to be a corrugated wall of darkness. Seconds later, they collided with a savage impact. Her head banged into the ladder, and she collapsed into her father's arms, certain their journey to Hades was over at last.

69

Zheng stood at the forward bridge window, observing a roiling in the water ahead of the ship. His anger at allowing the captives to escape the **Melbourne** had quickly passed, as had any sorrow over the death of Ning. He paced with a proud smile, knowing it was he, not Colonel Yan, who had inspired the coming assault. He would soon be a hero to the Communist Party, but perhaps his uncle's stature would be restored as well.

"It is building," he said to no one in particular. "I can see it."

A new commando entered the bridge and saluted the Colonel and Zheng. "Sir, the explosives have been planted in the lower hold. They are timed to detonate in two hours."

"Very good," Zheng said. "Once the next surface wave has been set in motion, assemble the team and depart on one of the ship's tenders. Once you are beyond sight of the ship, I shall issue a mayday call to the Taiwanese. The Colonel and I will then leave on the helicopter."

Zheng turned his back on the man, who saluted anyway and left the bridge.

"Time?" Zheng called to Dr. Yee. "Shouldn't it have surfaced by now?"

Through the deck, they could feel the vibration of the acoustic system's turbine generating power to the cable strands.

"Another minute or two," Yee said.

The bridge phone rang, and Zheng picked it up. He listened for a moment, then slammed down the receiver. He pulled out his pistol and took a step toward Yee.

"They say something doesn't look right in the operations room. The signals from the right-side deployment are garbled."

Yee shrugged and placed a finger on his computer screen, drawing out his response. "Yes . . . there is something slightly amiss . . . It appears the starboard booms are out of alignment."

Zheng stepped to the starboard window, Yan joining him. Under the morning light, he could see the three fixed-boom sections floating on the water, only they weren't perpendicular to the ship as deployed. All three booms were pulled forward, angling across the ship's bow.

"What does this mean?" Yan asked.

"The water disturbance will be unpredictable," Yee said matter-of-factly.

Zheng raised his pistol and fired twice. A pair of red blots appeared on the chest of Yee's white lab coat, and he slumped to the deck.

"What is happening, Yijong?" the Colonel yelled. "I demand to know—"

Zheng never answered, as the ship began a violent tremble. The deck seesawed beneath their feet, and both men struggled to maintain their footing.

Zheng looked to the ocean and saw an unnerving sight. A band of water rose from the depths, crossing beneath the vessel nearly amidships. The water column shot upward in an explosive mass, lifting the vessel as if on a pedestal. The bow and stern, no longer supported by the water, simultaneously sagged at an unnatural angle. The ship's entire weight was briefly balanced on just a narrow central portion of its keel.

A thunderous shriek sounded beneath them, but not the cry of any human. It was the sound of the ship's steel plates shearing under a stress they were never designed to bear. Seconds later, the keel snapped like a twig. Without its rigid spine, the **Melbourne**, from the lower hull to the topside decks, began to fracture with a deafening roar. The rising mass of water held just long enough for it to break the ship completely in two.

As the ship separated in the middle, the decks fell victim to a tempest of flying debris as cranes, winches, and generators tumbled into the waves.

Zheng stared as the Z-10 flipped off its helipad like a child's toy and vanished in the sea.

Zheng clung to a window frame as Yan was flung forward, his body slamming into the helm. Yan managed to grab the ship's wheel for support as blood flowed from a blow to his head. He looked to Zheng with a pained resignation, then squeezed his eyes closed in defeat.

He would never reopen them.

The boom assembly from a high crane on the port deck broke free and collapsed onto the bridge. Yan was killed instantly as the boom crushed the center of the roof nearly flat to the deck. Standing to the side, Zheng avoided the falling boom, but was knocked to the floor by the impact.

The watery uprising that had lifted the ship became a rolling mound that moved off in a northwesterly direction, but not before capsizing the **Melbourne**'s stern section. It sank immediately.

The bow section fell back to the sea upright, momentarily stabilizing before an inflow of seawater set her foundering. Zheng tried to stand up in the collapsed bridge, but his legs were pinned beneath the caved-in ceiling. A shooting pain from his left leg told him it was broken. He reached for the side door as leverage to pull himself free, but he couldn't quite grasp it. "Colonel? Are you there?" he called through the wreckage.

He heard only silence on the bridge, but the rest

of the ship spoke to him loudly. Groans from the strained metal structure in the flooded compartments competed with rushing water and hissing air pockets. When Zheng realized his fate would be of a slow drowning, he sought to kill himself. But his pistol had been knocked from his hand when the ceiling collapsed and lost somewhere amid the debris.

Zheng had nearly ten minutes to contemplate his life before the floodwaters flowed into the bridge, the bow eased under the waves, and he was carried to the depths below.

70

Rudi held Loren's hand as the Taiwan Coast Guard search and rescue helicopter lifted off from Kaohsiung Airport and skimmed over the commercial harbor. The **Caledonia** was visible out Gunn's passenger's window, and he looked down on the turquoise research ship. Perched upright in the dry dock, it reminded him of a swan, appearing much less elegant out of the water.

The morning's events had come fast and furious since he and Yaeger had discovered the **Melbourne** less than twenty miles away. An initial plea to the Coast Guard to send a cutter to investigate had gone unheeded until Gunn woke the Vice President aboard the Navy destroyer **Lyndon B. Johnson**. He could only smile at picturing Sandecker in his bathrobe on the destroyer's bridge, phoning the Taiwanese President at five-thirty in the morning to request assistance.

The news since had been grim. A fishing boat was

the first to report seeing the **Melbourne** break apart and sink. When it sailed closer to investigate, it discovered the foundering crew boat and rendered aid until the Coast Guard cutter arrived. Miraculously, all the crewmen had survived, thanks to the heroic efforts of Sonntag and the ship's cook.

It was Sonntag who reported the disheartening news that Pitt and Giordino were indeed aboard the Australian ship and had remained there to rescue Thornton and his daughter. Their planned means of escape had not materialized. Sonntag confirmed seeing the destruction of the Z-10 helicopter shortly before the **Melbourne** sank. But the Taiwan authorities were reluctant to believe his claim that the ship, under Chinese command, had tried to assault the country with a tsunami.

Gunn, however, knew that to be true. Oceanographic data collected by Yaeger showed three large waves originating from the location of the stricken ship, the last one a behemoth that roared off to the northwest. Damage reports had yet to surface from China's west coast province of Fujian, but the impact was expected to be severe.

No one, including Sonntag, had any idea why things had apparently backfired. After two waves perfectly directed at Kaohsiung, the final, devastating tsunami traveled in another direction, sparing not only Taiwan, but also Smith and Sandecker aboard the USS **Johnson**.

But Gunn knew. Without any evidence, he knew Pitt and Giordino were behind it, in perhaps a final act of self-sacrifice. It was simply their hallmark.

As the helicopter passed the harbor entrance and skimmed over open water, Rudi glanced at Loren. She had insisted on accompanying him on the flight, and had even beaten him to the airport. She remained stoic when Gunn relayed the latest news, maintaining her composure even when his voice cracked in the telling. She knew Pitt and his indomitable spirit better than anyone, and she wasn't ready to give up hope.

The helicopter passed the angular-shaped **Lyndon B. Johnson** just offshore, a row of pennants flying from its peak mast to the bow. Sandecker was still aboard. The signing of the defense pact with the President of Taiwan was scheduled to begin soon, the significance suddenly growing.

They flew southeast for a few minutes before arriving over two more vessels. One was the crew boat, under tow by the Coast Guard patrol craft. Even though the boat was riding low in the water, Gunn could see several sailors on deck manning emergency pumps. He couldn't miss the fire damage blackening the stern that had nearly sunk her.

The helicopter circled once, then continued east. A mile farther, they approached two more vessels. One was large, a sleek white Taiwan Coast Guard cutter named **Yilan**. The other was a small aged fishing boat, which had been the first to arrive on the scene. Both were combing the area for survivors.

Gunn could tell they were at the site of the sinking by the large oil slick that marked the choppy seas. The fact was confirmed when the **Yilan** released a small inflatable boat to retrieve a body. The helicopter inched close enough for Rudi and Loren to see that the victim wore black fatigues and appeared to be Asian.

There was little else on the surface to indicate a massive mining ship had sunk there. Some broken pallets, a wooden desk chair, and some random bits of flotsam were all that appeared. The chopper took up its own aerial survey, sweeping back and forth in broad swaths.

"There, what's that?" Loren pointed to a round yellow object barely visible amid the waves. They zoomed in for a close inspection, revealing only a buoy affixed to a semi-submerged boom that was trailing a mass of cables.

The helicopter hovered over the debris for a short while, then resumed searching. They spent another two hours in the air, expanding their range far beyond the oil slick, before the pilot told Gunn that they needed to return to base.

They flew low over the site once more, then slowly proceeded toward Kaohsiung. Rudi reached over and squeezed Loren's hand. "The Taiwan Navy is sending a salvage ship with an ROV to the site in a few hours. We'll check every inch of the bottom, but we have to accept the reality. They might be lost to the sea."

Loren stared off at the gray ocean, then shook her head slightly. "They may be lost in the sea," she said with a tear in her eye, "but I don't think they are lost to the sea."

71

W e're caught on a snag."

Jiang Ji peered back from the cramped wheelhouse to see his hired mate waving his arms like a desperate hitchhiker. A second later, the boat shuddered and lost all forward momentum. Jiang threw the motor into neutral and stepped onto the rear deck.

His boat was small, less than twenty-five feet in length, but like most private Taiwan fishing boats, it was colorful and appeared sleek in its functionality. It had a high bow, capped by a sharply pointed prow that tapered gracefully to a blunt stern. Bright blues and golds trimmed the white hull and topsides, adding a festive flair to the hardworking vessel.

Jiang glanced toward shore before considering the snagged net that trailed behind his boat. They were less than a quarter mile from the southern tip of Qimei, a hilly, green dot in the Penghu Islands. Once controlled by the French and then the Japanese, the island chain some forty miles west of Taiwan had remained part of the Republic of China since World War II.

Jiang estimated their position by triangulating some landmarks on the island, then shook his head. He had fished this area for years and had never caught a snag. Like all frugal fishermen, he avoided known snags, as the cost of a damaged net could easily exceed a day's catch.

He looked over the stern as his mate, a barefoot youth in a T-shirt and cutoffs, tugged on the net behind the boat. The net trailed taut across the surface twenty feet before disappearing into the depths.

"I think it's coming free," the boy said.

The net began to pool at their feet as he drew it in by hand.

"Wait," Jiang yelled as he raised a hand. The net was coiled around something. A boil of bubbles disturbed the water, followed by the emergence of a large yellow object.

Jiang rubbed his eyes as a submersible ascended to the surface, draped in netting. The undersea vessel looked ready for the junkyard. It was battered and dented, with a wide streak of black across the top from an encounter with another vessel. The forward light fixtures were smashed, matching the appearance of its stern thrusters. More surprising, a seam of bullet holes were stitched across the turret and upper hull.

Jiang and his mate stared in wonder as the submersible bobbed behind them. Through a hazy viewport, they spotted three men and a woman inside. After a moment, the upper hatch opened. A weathered man with dark hair poked his head out the top and gave the two fishermen a jaunty wave.

"Excuse me," Pitt said with a tired smile. "Do you know the way to San Jose?"

EPILOGUE

Altar of the Nechung Idol

72

The rich aroma of cedar trees filled the air as a crisp breeze blew down from the Himalayas, offering an early bite of winter. Walking down the main street of McLeod Ganj with her brother, Summer felt the chill and shivered. She zipped her down jacket and stuffed her hands in her pockets. "The mountains are certainly beautiful, but I'll be happy if we beat the first snowfall out of here."

"It might arrive sooner than later." Dirk looked toward the mass of clouds that grazed the peaks west of the town.

They approached the entrance to the Tsuglagkhang complex, which saw only a scattering of tourists with the turning of seasons. Tenzin Norsang waited for them inside the gate and waved them through security.

"Thank you for coming before you departed India," he said. "It delights me to see you one more time." Although he spoke to both of them, his eyes were glued to Summer.

She returned his gaze. "We wouldn't have left without saying good-bye."

"Come this way, there is someone I would like you to meet."

Norsang led them across the complex. As they approached the temple, they passed a row of large bronze prayer wheels covered with ornate carvings. Dirk took a second to spin one, careful to turn it clockwise.

"Each one offers an individual prayer, which is inscribed on the outside," Norsang explained.

"What did I get?" Dirk asked.

Norsang waited for the wheel to stop spinning, then read the inscription. "'An unexpected wealth awaits you,'" he said, followed with a laugh.

They continued past the Tsuglagkhang Temple, where a group of red-robed monks sat on the patio ground in prayer. Norsang led them into an adjacent building, a part of the Namgyal Monastery that was closed to the public.

Past a large open hall, they entered an office in the rear corner. An elderly man in a red robe sat at a desk stacked high with papers. Norsang bowed as he entered. "I have brought my friends who assisted me in Sikkim." He turned to the pair. "Dirk, Summer, this is Khyentse Rinpoche."

The elder lama smiled when they bowed toward him.

"I am very pleased to meet you." He rose to greet them. "Tenzin told me of your adventures in recovering the Nechung Idol. It means a great deal to the monastery, and to all of Tibet."

"We were glad to be of help in returning it to the rightful owners," Dirk said. "I trust it will remain safe?"

"Indeed. Would you like to see it?"

Dirk and Summer both nodded.

"Due to its importance, we have taken extra precautions to protect its location in the complex," the lama said. "For that reason, I must ask that you both be led blindfolded to the location."

He reached into a desk drawer and retrieved two white silk scarves, known as **khata**, normally used as ceremonial offerings. He handed them to Norsang, who wrapped them around each of their heads.

"If you offer me a cigarette next," Dirk joked, "I may have to reconsider."

"I must ask you not to smoke at this time," the lama replied, not understanding the quip. "Now please turn around. Summer, you may place a hand on Tenzin's shoulder, and Dirk, place a hand on your sister's. Tenzin will lead the way."

The security man led them out of the monastery in single file, with Rinpoche taking up the rear. The scarf was loose around Summer's lower face, enabling her to see the ground. They crossed another large open patio and moved away from the main structures. Norsang guided them down a flight of stone steps, then stopped in front of a small wooden structure built up against the hillside.

A wheelbarrow filled with cement bags was parked next to a small door, which Norsang opened and entered. Summer detected the business ends of some rakes and shovels, in what seemed a small garden shed. She also noted the polished black dress shoes and neatly pressed slacks of two men standing against the rear wall.

The lama spoke to the men in the local Kangri dialect, and they stood aside. One of them slid open a false wood-paneled wall, revealing a narrow flight of circular stairs. Norsang guided Summer to the stairs, placed her hand on the rail, and gave directions, until she and Dirk descended with him to a lower level. They heard the sliding panel close behind them as the lama followed down the stairs.

They stood for a moment at the landing, where Summer inhaled the exotic aroma of juniper and incense.

"You may take the scarves off now," the lama said in a hushed tone.

They pulled off their blindfolds, and Summer couldn't help but gasp at the sight. They stood in a small cavern that rose just inches over their heads. Summer couldn't tell if it was a natural formation or had been excavated, as the walls were completely covered in bright burgundy and gold tapestries.

While corner lamps illuminated the space, dozens of candles gave it a warm, cozy glow.

It took her a moment to recognize the Nechung Idol, which stood as the centerpiece of an elaborate altar at the cavern's far end. The **thokcha** carving had been placed on a high pedestal and draped with a gold brocade cloth. Smaller gold statues, tiered candelabras, and carved wooden panels in red and gold hues surrounded the treasured piece.

At the base of the Nechung Idol lay a bounty of offerings, including swords, mirrors, gold and silver cups, and many more candles. Next to the altar, Dirk spotted a massive gold helmet, crowned with peacock feathers and perched on a wooden stand. He knew, from Norsang's telling, that it was the headdress of the Nechung Oracle, worn when he entered a trance to communicate with the deity Pehar.

On the opposite side of the altar, Summer noticed a pair of conch shells adjacent to a platter of fresh fruit. While the whole scene was dizzying, it wasn't the sight of the ornate altar that had taken her breath away. It was the presence of the Dalai Lama himself.

The exiled leader of Tibet and Tibetan Buddhism had been seated on the ground before the altar. At hearing the others enter, he stood and padded over to greet them. Dirk and Summer joined Norsang and the lama in bowing as he approached.

"Who are these towering firs you have brought here?" he asked with a jovial smile. "We will have to raise the ceiling."

"Dirk and Summer Pitt, Your Holiness," Norsang said. "We would not have recovered the Nechung Idol without their assistance."

"Yes, of course. I owe you a debt of gratitude," he said with a nod. "The Oracle, in fact, attributed my recovery from recent illness to the arrival of the Idol. He was very unhappy at my presumed impending departure without its presence, but now he can rest peacefully."

Summer beamed at the man's warmth and humor, which she had not expected in such a revered figure.

But the Dalai Lama turned solemn for a moment. "Because of this," he said, waving a hand toward the altar, "you may have given me another life, and a greater hope for the next generation of Tibetans."

"May your spirit live forever," Dirk said.

"And also that of your creator," the Dalai Lama said, now with a sad smile.

Khyentse Rinpoche, behind the group, cleared his throat, signaling that the visit was over. The Dalai Lama lingered to shake their hands. "It was very nice of you to visit. Thank you again for helping young Tenzin."

Summer felt an unknown awe, but also a

strange yearning. As Norsang raised the scarf to wrap around her eyes, she raised her hand. "Your Holiness. One question, if I may?"

The Dalai Lama's eyes turned bright. "You already know the answer," he said before she could ask.

Summer hesitated. "A happy life filled with adventure?" she asked.

The Dalai Lama laughed. "You are a wise one, for your years." He turned and stepped back to the altar.

Norsang retied the blindfolds and led Dirk and Summer from the sanctuary. Back in the monastery, they returned the white scarves to Rinpoche and bid farewell to the elder lama. Summer's mind was in a whirl after the encounter with the Dalai Lama as they made their way across the compound.

"I wanted to tell you I have notified Ramapurah Chodron about our trip and our successful recovery of the Nechung Idol," Norsang said. "He was very pleased at the news."

"We couldn't have done it without him," Dirk said.

"He will be visiting next week. The monastery is performing a ceremony in remembrance of Thupten Gungtsen, the monk who rescued the Idol from the Nechung Monastery."

"I hope you allow Ram a peek at it, like you let us," Summer said.

"I believe that will be permitted."

As they approached the complex's exit, Norsang led them aside. "There is one more thing I must show you."

He guided them to a garage close by the gate. Inside was the old International Harvester that Dirk had nearly destroyed. The damage to the front fenders had been hammered out, and a new coat of green paint applied.

"She lives," Dirk said.

Norsang pulled keys from his pocket and handed them to Dirk. "The Dalai Lama wishes to give the vehicle to you in gratitude. He gave the order to begin the repair work even before we traveled to India."

Dirk reluctantly took the keys. "Thank you."

"It's your own 'holy roller,'" Summer said, trying not to laugh.

"Well, I guess I can have it shipped to Washington," Dirk said. "There's plenty of room to store it in Dad's hangar with his car collection."

He started to climb into the driver's seat, but noticed a large wooden crate in the truck bed. "What's that?" he asked.

Norsang climbed in back and pried open the lid. Inside was a large collection of shiny black stones of varying shapes and sizes. Some had been carved into idols, while others were raw. Tenzin picked up a fist-sized example and tossed it to Dirk.

"These are **thokcha**," he said. "Meteorites. Of the same variety as the Nechung Idol. They come from the Tibetan Plateau, and I am told they are quite rare."

"I don't understand," Dirk said. "Why would the Dalai Lama give us a whole crateful?"

"It was the Oracle's doing," he said. "It was the result of his first medium ceremony in the presence of the Nechung Idol."

Dirk looked at Summer and shrugged.

"Why would the Oracle suggest that?" Summer asked.

"I don't know," Norsang said. "The Oracle said it was a necessary gift that your country would know what to do with."

The Tibetan walked to the front of the building and opened a garage door, which led to the street. Dirk climbed in and started the truck, then leaned out and shook hands with Norsang.

"Give our thanks to the Dalai Lama," Dirk said.

"May all your journeys be safe, my friend."

Norsang turned and approached Summer, who stood on the other side of the truck. They stared at each other for a moment, then he embraced and kissed her. "I hope we will meet again soon. If not, my spirit will await yours in the next life."

Summer could only mutter a weak good-bye, then slid into the passenger's seat.

Dirk put the truck in gear and drove out of the garage, waving at Norsang as he turned up the street into central McLeod Ganj. As he drove, he glanced at his sister.

Summer had a dazed look on her face and seemed to be in another world.

"You okay?" he asked.

"Yes," she replied. "I just came to the realization that the afterlife might not be so bad after all."

73

TEN MONTHS LATER

The B-2 Spirit streaked high across a bright, cloudless sky. An empty expanse of placid blue water spread beneath the bomber's delta wings like an endless carpet. Flying slightly north of the equator, the stealth bomber found itself positioned dead center over the Pacific Ocean.

The plane's bomb bay doors glided open. At a touch from the mission commander, seated next to the pilot, a single cruise missile dropped from the compartment.

The bomber immediately banked to the south as the white missile fell for a moment until its motor ignited. A solid booster burned for a few seconds before a prototype scramjet engine engaged, thrusting the missile ahead with an acceleration that would shame a top fuel dragster.

A sonic boom rocked the vacant sky as the

missile quickly surpassed the speed of sound. But there was no letup to the acceleration as the missile passed Mach 25. The satellite navigation system nudged it in tiny increments on a path to a dead spot of ocean within the Ronald Reagan Ballistic Missile Defense Test Site in the Marshall Islands.

It never got there.

Shortly after the cruise missile took flight, another missile launched. This one, a ground-based interceptor, was fired a thousand miles to the north from the Pacific Missile Range Facility on the Hawaiian island of Kauai.

Like a lightning-footed bloodhound, the interceptor locked onto the cruise missile with the aid of a complex network of satellite and ground radar inputs. It contained a similar scramjet motor, but was built to exceed Mach 30. The missile streaked across the morning sky, too fast to be seen by the naked eye as it traveled at ten times the speed of a bullet. Only a faint vapor trail gave any indication of its passage.

Flying at a lesser, though still blistering, speed, the cruise missile altered course at random intervals to throw off the pursuer. It would be for naught, as the interceptor closed ranks and zeroed in on its flight path. High above the blue Pacific, the pursuing missile made a perfect intercept, colliding with the cruise missile midflight and obliterating it with the sheer force of kinetic energy.

At the Pacific Missile Range Facility back on

Kauai, the monitoring engineers and military officials stood and cheered when the data results were streamed back.

It was the first successful test of the new hypersonic interceptor missile, code-named Lama Defender 1.

CLIVE CUSSLER was the author of more than seventy books in five bestselling series, including Dirk Pitt®, NUMA Files®, **Oregon** Files®, Isaac Bell®, and Sam and Remi Fargo®. His life nearly paralleled that of his hero Dirk Pitt. Whether searching for lost aircraft or leading expeditions to find famous shipwrecks, he and his NUMA crew of volunteers discovered and surveyed more than seventy-five lost ships of historic significance including the long-lost Civil War submarine **Hunley**, which was raised in 2000 with much publicity. Like Pitt, Cussler collected classic automobiles. His collection featured more than one hundred examples of custom coachwork. Cussler passed away in February 2020.

DIRK CUSSLER is the coauthor with Clive Cussler of eight previous Dirk Pitt adventures: **Black Wind**, **Treasure of Khan**, **Arctic Drift**, **Crescent Dawn**, **Poseidon's Arrow**, **Havana Storm**, **Odessa Sea**, and **Celtic Empire**. For the past several years, he has been an active participant and partner in his father's NUMA expeditions and has served as president of the NUMA advisory board of trustees. He lives in Connecticut.